DEMONS!

EDITED BY
JACK DANN & GARDNER DOZOIS

ACE BOOKS, NEW YORK

DEMONS!

An Ace Fantasy Book/published by arrangement with
the editors

PRINTING HISTORY
Ace Fantasy edition / July 1987

ISBN: 0-441-14264-8

Ace Fantasy Books are published by
The Berkley Publishing Group,
200 Madison Avenue, New York, New York 10016.

PRINTED IN THE UNITED STATES OF AMERICA

"That's a hell of a spell you're using," said the demon, "if I'm the best you can call up."

He wasn't much, Bill Hitchens had to admit. He looked lost in the center of that pentacle. His basic design was impressive enough—snakes for hair, curling tusks, a sharp-tipped tail, all the works—but he was something under an inch tall.

"Nobody's wasted time and power on a misfit like me for years," the demon went on. "Where'd you get the spell?"

"Just a little something I whipped up," said Bill modestly.

The demon grunted and muttered something about people that thought they were magicians.

"But I'm not a magician," Bill explained. "I'm a biochemist."

The demon shuddered. "I land the damnedest cases," he mourned. "Working for that psychiatrist wasn't bad enough, I should draw a biochemist. Whatever that is."

Bill couldn't check his curiosity. "And what did you do for a psychiatrist?"

"He showed me to people who were followed by little men and told them I'd chase the little men away . . ."

—from "Snulbug" by Anthony Boucher

Magic Tales Anthology Series From Ace Fantasy Books

UNICORNS! edited by Jack Dann and Gardner Dozois
MAGICATS! edited by Jack Dann and Gardner Dozois
FAERY! edited by Terri Windling
BESTIARY! edited by Jack Dann and Gardner Dozois
MERMAIDS! edited by Jack Dann and Gardner Dozois
SORCERERS! edited by Jack Dann and Gardner Dozois
DEMONS! edited by Jack Dann and Gardner Dozois

Acknowledgment is made for permission to print the following material:

"Grail" by Harlan Ellison originally appeared in *The Twilight Zone* magazine; copyright © 1981 by The Kilimanjaro Corporation. Reprinted with permission of, and by arrangement with, the Author and the Author's agent, Richard Curtis Associates, Inc., New York. All rights reserved.

"The Willow Platform" by Joseph Payne Brennan. Copyright © 1973 by Stuart David Schiff for *Whispers #1*. Reprinted by permission of the author.

"The Night of White Bhairab" by Lucius Shepard. Copyright © 1984 by Mercury Press, Inc. Originally appeared in *The Magazine of Fantasy & Science Fiction,* October 1984. Reprinted by permission of the author.

"The Mangler" by Stephen King. Copyright © 1976, 1977, 1978 by Stephen King. First appeared in *Cavalier,* December 1972. Reprinted by permission of Doubleday & Co., the author, and the author's agent, Kirby McCauley, Ltd.

"The Last Demon" by Isaac Bashevis Singer. Reprinted with permission of Farrar, Straus & Giroux, Inc. From *Short Friday* by Isaac Bashevis Singer, copyright © 1961, 1962, 1963, 1964 by Isaac Bashevis Singer.

"The Golden Rope" by Tanith Lee. Copyright © 1983 by Tanith Lee. First appeared in *Red as Blood,* DAW Books, 1983. Reprinted by permission of the author.

"Basileus" by Robert Silverberg. Copyright © 1983 by Ogberg, Ltd. First appeared in *The Best of Omni Science Fiction No. 5* (Omni Publications International Ltd., 1983). Reprinted by permission of the author.

"Twilla" by Tom Reamy. Copyright © 1974 by Mercury Press, Inc. First appeared in *The Magazine of Fantasy & Science Fiction,* September 1974. Reprinted by permission of the Estate of Tom Reamy.

"The Purple Pterodactyls" by L. Sprague de Camp. Copyright © 1976 by Mercury Press, Inc. First appeared in *The Magazine of Fantasy & Science Fiction,* August 1976. Reprinted by permission of the author.

The editors would like to thank the following people for their help and support:

Susan Casper, Jeanne Van Buren Dann, Patrick Delahunt, Edward Ferman, Virginia Kidd, Trina King, Shawna McCarthy, Brian Perry and Tawna Lewis of Fat Cat Books (263 Main St., Johnson City, New York 13790), Stuart Schiff, Bernie Sheredy, the staff of the Vestal Public Library, Michael Swanwick, Bob Walters, Tom Whitehead of the Special Collections Department of the Paley Library at Temple University (and his staff, especially John Betencourt and Connie King), and special thanks to our editors, Susan Allison and Ginjer Buchanan.

For Lucius Shepard

CONTENTS

But woudst thou bid the demons fly
Like mist before the dawning sky.

—*Sir Walter Scott*

DEMON

1. In ancient Greek mythology: A supernatural being of a nature intermediate between that of gods and men; an inferior divinity, spirit, genius (including the souls or ghosts of deceased persons, esp. deified heroes).

b. Sometimes, particularly, an attendant, ministering, or indwelling spirit; a genius.

2. An evil spirit.

a. Applied to the idols or gods of the heathen, and to the "evil" or "unclean spirits" by which demoniacs were possessed or actuated.

b. In general current use: An evil spirit; a malignant being of superhuman nature; a devil.

c. Applied to a person (animal or agency personified), of malignant, cruel, terrible, or destructive nature, or of hideous appearance. (*Cf.* devil)

d. An evil passion or agency personified.

—Excerpted from *The Oxford English Dictionary*

Grail

by

Harlan Ellison

One of the most acclaimed and controversial figures in modern letters, Harlan Ellison has produced thirty-seven books and over nine hundred stories, articles, essays, film and television scripts. He is the editor of Dangerous Visions; Again, Dangerous Visions; Medea: Harlan's World; *and the forthcoming* The Last Dangerous Visions. *His short story collections include* Partners in Wonder, Alone Against Tomorrow, The Beast that Shouted Love at the Heart of the World, Approaching Oblivion, Deathbird Stories, Strange Wine, *and* Shatterday. *A multiple award winner, he has won Nebula, Hugo, and Edgar Awards, and three Writers Guild of America Awards for Most Outstanding Television Script.*

In the story that follows, he gives us a harrowing study of a man who is willing to literally search through Hell and back—for love.

* * *

YEARS LATER, WHEN HE WAS WELL INTO YOUNG ADULTHOOD, Christopher Caperton wrote about it in the journal he had begun to keep when he turned twenty-one. The entry had everything to do with the incident, though he had totally forgotten it.

What he wrote was this: *The great tragedy of my life is that in my search for the Holy Grail everyone calls True Love, I see myself as Zorro, a romantic and mysterious highwayman—and the women I desire see me as Porky Pig.*

The incident lost to memory that informed his observation had taken place fourteen years earlier, in 1953 when he was thirteen years old.

During a Halloween party from which chaperoning adults had been banished, it was suggested that the boys and girls play a kissing game called "flashlight." All the lights were turned off, everyone paired up, and one couple held a flashlight. If you were caught kissing when the flashlight was turned on you, then it became your turn to hold the flash while the others had free rein to neck and fondle in the dark.

Because he was shy, Christopher volunteered to be the first holder of the light. Because he was shy, and because he had, as usual, been paired with Jean Kettner who adored him but whom he could not find it within himself even to like. Across the room the most beautiful girl he had ever seen, the improbably named Briony Catling, sat on the lap of Danny Shipley, who played baseball and had blond, wavy hair.

Chris Caperton ached for Briony Catling with an intensity that gave him cramps.

Another rule of the game was that if the wielder of the flashlight caught another couple "doing it," he or she could demand a switch in partners.

Because he was shy, because he was paired with Jean Kettner, and because he knew exactly where he would shine the flashlight after allowing several minutes to pass in which the couples would become too interested in kissing to prepare themselves.

He caught Briony and Danny Shipley, and demanded a switch. Of the four involved in the transaction, only Christopher felt elation. Briony Catling had no interest in Christopher Caperton. She ached for Danny Shipley with an intensity that gave her cramps.

But they switched, and when the lights went on Christopher hugged Briony frantically and shoved his face toward hers. The kiss splatted somewhere between her nose and mouth.

She blew out air, made a yuchhing sound, swiped at the slaver on her upper lip, and jumped off his lap.

Fourteen years later the shame and the pain still lurked in his unconscious like pariahs.

Briony Catling had not been his first great love. That had been Miss O'Hara in the third grade, who had shone down on him at the age of eight like the field lights at a night baseball game. He had loved her purely and with all his heart; and the present he gave her at the Christmas party held by his home room had cost him all the money he'd made raking leaves through that Autumn. She had been embarrassed and had kissed his cheek lightly, never knowing it caused his first erection.

After Miss O'Hara, it had been the actress Helen Gahagan in

the 1935 version of *She*, which he saw at the Utopia Theater on a re-release double-bill. When he belatedly went to see *Snow White and the Seven Dwarfs* on one of its periodic reissues, he recognized at once that Disney had appropriated the garb and look of Helen Gahagan as She-Who-Must-Be-Obeyed for the character of the wicked Queen Grimhilde; and when he learned of the foul campaign Richard Nixon had waged against her in the 1950 Senatorial race, when she had become Helen Gahagan Douglas, he vowed a revenge that only manifested itself when he twice voted for Nixon's presidential opponents.

The year before Briony Catling filled him with self-loathing, he fell desperately in love with the Swedish actress Marta Toren. He watched her vamping Dick Powell in *Rogue's Regiment* on the *Late Late Show* and made a point of being in the audience the night *Paris Express* with Claude Rains opened. Miss O'Hara, Helen Gahagan and even Briony Catling paled by comparison. She was precisely and exactly the embodiment of True Love in his eyes. Four years later, six months after Christopher had lost his virginity to a young woman who bore only a passing resemblance to Marta Toren, he read in the newspaper that she had died from a rare brain trauma called a subarachnoidal hemorrhage that struck like Jack the Ripper and killed her within forty-eight hours.

He closed himself in his room and tore at his clothes.

In February of 1968, attached to General William Westmoreland's headquarters in Saigon, Capt. Christopher Caperton, age 28, stumbled upon the astonishing fact that True Love, in a physical form, existed. The *Tet* offensive had begun and Saigon was burning. Had he not had his own assigned jeep and driver, he would not have been able to get around; there was virtually no public transportation and the cyclos and taxis had been commandeered for the wealthy trying to flee. The hospitals were so crowded that only emergency cases were being accepted; patients were sleeping on the floors, jamming the corridors. Coffins lay unburied for days; the gravediggers had gone south. Chris's business was good.

Chris was in the business of helping GI's cope with the anguish of serving in a war they had come to despise.

In business with, and in love with, his lover and business partner, a thirty-nine year old Eurasian of French and Thai parentage, Capt. Chris was the main conduit for "Js," "OJs," Binoctal, and a luscious black opium from the Laotian poppy fields to

America's fighting men in Indochina.

Because their goods—marijuana joints; joints dipped in liquid opium; the French headache killer, and the most potent smoking opium—were superlative goods. Christopher Caperton and Sirilabh Doumic had established a flourishing trade in I and II Corps. And from this enterprise they had managed to bank over a million and a half dollars (converted to Swiss francs) in an unnumbered Zurich account, despite the crushing overhead and the payoffs to officials of Thieu's provincial government.

And because he was in love in a terrible place, and because he and his love wanted nothing more than to survive, to win release from that terrible place, he felt no guilt about the traffic. There was no self-delusion that he was engaged in humanitarian activities, neither the war nor the drug traffic; what he *did* feel was a sense of keeping busy, of working at something that held light and hope at its conclusion, that without the dope some of his clients would either go mad or turn their rifles on the nearest 1st Lieutenant. But mostly he was in love.

Siri was small and light. He could lift her with one arm to carry her to the bed. Her features were fine and delicate, yet they changed dramatically with each noticeable variation in the light. Monet would have had to do her portrait eighteen times, as he did the Rouen Cathedral, from dawn to sunset, to capture even one expression. She was the daughter of a French attaché in the Bangkok consulate and a young temple dancer Doumic first saw at the Kathin ceremony marking the end of the Buddhist Lent. From her father she inherited a wiliness that kept her alive in street society, from her mother—who had come from Chumphon to the south—a speech filled with musical inflection. How she had come to Saigon ten years before was not something she cared to talk about. But Chris winced every time they made love and his hands brushed the thick scars on her inner thighs.

On that night in February of 1968, they were just sitting down to a dinner of beef satay Siri had made in their apartment on Nguyen Cong Tru Street when a 122mm shell came across the Saigon River and hit the face of the building opposite Caperton's. The rocket round ripped the building out of the ground like a rotten tooth and threw shrapnel in every direction.

Not the biggest chunk, but big enough, it came straight through the window and tore into Siri's back, taking off most of her left shoulder.

There was no use trying to move her; it was obvious she would never make it down the stairs, much less across the city to the

American hospital that had been opened at Tan Son Nhut.

He tried to stanch the flow with a bedspread and all the white tennis socks in his drawer, and miraculously, she lived for almost an hour. In that hour they talked, and in that hour of farewell she gave him the only gift in the world he wanted, the only thing he could not get for himself. She told him how he could find True Love.

"We have talked of it so many times, and I always knew."

He tried to smile. "In a business partnership like ours there shouldn't be any secrets. How else can I trust you?"

Pain convulsed her and she gripped his hand till the bones ground. "We've no time for foolishness, my love. Very soon now you'll be alone again, as you have been so often. I have this one thing I can give you in return for the love you gave me . . . and it will take some believing on your part."

"Whatever you tell me I'll believe."

Then she instructed him to go to the kitchen and get an empty condiment bottle from the spice rack. When he brought back the bottle labeled chopped coriander leaves, which was empty because they had been unable to get fresh coriander since a Claymore mine had gone off in the central market, she told him he must not argue with her, that he must fill it with her blood. He argued, wasting precious minutes; but finally, filled with a vaguely familiar self-loathing, he did it.

"I have always sought perfection," she said. "Always knowing that one must die to reach perfection, for life is imperfect."

He tried to argue, but she stopped him. Sternly.

"Chris! You *must* listen to me."

He nodded and was silent.

"For each woman there *is* a perfect man; and for each man there *is* a perfect woman. You were not perfect for me, but you were as close to what I sought as I ever found. But I never stopped searching . . . though my movement was very slow since we met. I should have been content. It's easy to be smart, later.

"But knowing what I knew, that True Love is a real thing, that it can be picked up and turned in the hands, that it can be looked at and understood . . . that kept me always dissatisfied. As you have been.

"Because somehow, without possessing the knowledge I chanced upon ten years ago, you knew it was real. And now I will tell you how to go about finding it. And that, my dearest, is the best way I can apologize to you for not giving up the search when we met."

Then with her voice fading off and coming back a little less strong each time, she told him of an artifact that had never been described, that had first been unearthed during Evans's excavations of the Palace of Minos at Knossos in 1900.

It was taken from a walled-up niche behind an elaborate fresco painted on a wall of the Corridor of the Procession, and had been hidden there since 2000 BC. Where it had come from before that time, not even the archeologist who discovered it and smuggled it away from Crete could begin to guess.

He recognized it for what it was the instant the light of his torch fell on it. He disappeared that night and was presumed to have returned to England; but was never seen again. Record of his find was revealed in 1912 during the dying reminiscences of Bessie Chapman, one of 711 survivors of the sinking of the *Titanic* picked up by the *Carpathia.*

Suffering from extreme exposure and seemingly delirious, the immigrant passenger babbled a story heard only by those few *Carpathia* deckhands and ministering survivors who tried to make her last hours easier. Apparently she had been a London doxy who, after an evening of sport with "a real elegant nob, a brick 'e was," actually saw the artifact. She spoke of it with such wonder that when she died it seemed she had passed over having known all there was to know of joy in this life.

One of the deckhands, an Irish stoker named Haggerty, it was later reported, hung about the dying woman and seemed to be paying close attention to her story.

Haggerty jumped ship on the return of the Cunard liner to New York.

Sgt. Michael James Haggerty was killed during the Battle of Ypres, November 9th, 1914. His kit bag, scavenged by a German soldier when the French and British trenches were overrun (it was reported by a survivor who had played possum and had been overlooked in the random bayoneting of corpses), disappeared. Others in Haggerty's company said he slept with the kit bag under his pillow, that it seemed quite heavy, and that he once broke the arm of a messmate who playfully tried to see what the Irishman was carrying in it.

Between 1914 and 1932 the object—while never described—turned up three times: once in the possession of a White Russian nobleman in Sevastopol, twice in the possession of a Dutch aircraft designer, and finally in the possession of a Chicago mobster reputed to have been the man who gunned down Dion O'Banion in his flower shop at 738 North State Street.

In 1932 a man visiting New York for the opening of the Radio City Music Hall just after Christmas, reported to the police who found him lying in an alley on West 51st Street just below Fifth Avenue, that he had been mugged and robbed of "the most important and beautiful thing in the world." He was taken to Bellevue Hospital but no matter how diligently he was interrogated, he would not describe the stolen article.

In 1934 it was reputed to be in the private collection of the German architect Walter Gropius; after Gropius's self-imposed exile from Nazi Germany it was reputed to have passed into the personal collection of Hermann Goering, 1937; in 1941 it was said to be housed with Schweitzer in French Equatorial Africa; in 1946 it was found to be one of the few items not left by Henry Ford at his death to the Ford Foundation.

Its whereabouts were unknown between 1946 and February of 1968. But Siri told Chris, her final love, that there was one sure, dangerous way of finding it. The way she had used originally to learn the hand-to-hand passage of the artifact that was True Love from the Palace of Minos to its present unknown resting place.

Then she released his hand, realizing she had squeezed it so hard while telling her story that it was as white as unsmoked meerschaum; and she asked him very softly if he would bring her the little cloisonné minaudiére he had bought her in Hong Kong.

He gave it to her and she clutched it far more tightly than she had his hand. Because it was a minute later, and the pain was much worse.

"Do you remember the flea market?"

"Yes," she said, closing her eyes. "And we were holding hands in the crowd; and then you let go and I was swept along; and I thought I'd lost you; and you were gone for fifteen minutes . . ."

"And you panicked."

"And when I got back to the car there you were."

"You should have seen your face. What relief."

"What love. That was the moment I slowed the never-ending search. And you smiled and held out this to me." And she opened her hand where the exquisite blue and gold minaudiére lay in her palm, now filmed with moisture.

But her story had worked its magic. He knelt beside her on the floor, lifted her head and the pillows, and cradled them in his lap. "What is the True Love? What does it look like?"

"I don't know. I've never seen it. It cost too much the first time, just to get the information. The actual search has to be done without . . ." and she hesitated as if picking the exact words, the words that would not frighten him, because he was beginning to look more frightened than anguished, ". . . without special assistance."

"But how could you have learned all this?"

"I had an informant. You must seek him out. But go very carefully. It's dangerous, it costs a great deal; care has to be taken . . . once I didn't care . . ." She paused. "You'll need my blood."

"An informant . . . your blood . . .? I don't . . ."

"Adrammelech, Supreme Ruler of the Third Hour."

He could not help her. She was dying, he felt the stiffness in his throat, he loved her so much, and she was raving.

"An Angel of the Night, Chris."

Bewildered and suffering, nonetheless he went to the bedroom and fetched the brass-and-silver bound chest she called a bahut. He brought it back to her and she said, "Look at it. Do you see how it opens?"

He studied it but could find no lock or clasp that would open the coffer. "It is made of agalloch, lign aloes, the wood of the aloe, according to the directions of Abramelin. The cross-spines are of almond-tree wood. Are you beginning to understand, do you believe me?"

"Siri . . ."

"You'll need Surgat to open it. Look."

And she touched a symbol, a character cut into the rounded top of the chest:

"He won't harm you. He serves only one purpose: he opens all locks. Take a hair from my head . . . don't argue with me, Chris, do it . . . please . . ." And because her voice was now barely a whisper, he did it. And she said, "He'll demand a hair of your head. Don't give it to him. Make him take mine. And this is what you say to invoke his presence."

In her last minutes she went over it with him till he realized she was serious, that she was not delirious, that he ought to write it down. So he transcribed her words exactly.

"Once you get the bahut opened, all the rest will be clear. Just be careful, Chris. It's all I have to give you, so make the best of it." Her eyes were half-closed and now she opened them completely, with effort, and looked at him. "Why are you angry with me?"

He looked away.

"I can't help it that I'm dying, dear. I'm sorry, but that's what's happening. You'll just have to forgive me and do the best you can."

Then she closed her eyes and her hand opened and the cloisonné herb container fell to the carpet; and he was alone.

He spoke to her, though he was alone. "I didn't love you enough. If I'd loved you more it wouldn't have happened."

It's easy to be smart, later.

By the time he was twenty-five, Chris had read everything he could find on the arcane subject of love. He had read Virgil and Rabelais, Ovid and Liu Hsiao-Wei, Plato's *Symposium* and all the Neoplatonists, Montaigne and Johannes Secundus; he had read everything by the English poets from the anonymous lyrics of the 13th and 15th centuries through Rolle, Lydgate, Wyatt, Sidney, Campion, Shakespeare, Jonson, Donne, Marvell, Herrick, Suckling, Lovelace, Blake, Burns, Lord Byron, Percy Shelley, Keats, Tennyson, Robert Browning and Emily Brontë, he had read as many translations as existed on the Sanskrit *Kama Sutra* and the *Anangaranga*, which led him to the Persians; he read *The Perfumed Garden* of the Sheik Nefzawi, the *Beharistan* of Jami and the *Gulistan* of Sa-Di, the anonymously-written *Ta'dib ul-Niszvan* and the *Zenan-Nahmeh* of Fazil Bey, which led him to seven Arabic handbooks of sex, which he quickly put aside: sex was not the issue, he understood that as well as anyone need to. Understood it well enough to write in his journal:

I was making love to Connie Halban when her husband Paul came back unexpectedly from a business trip. When he saw us he began crying. It was the most awful thing I'd ever stood witness to. I was reminded of Ixion, tied to a turning wheel in Hades as punishment for making love to Zeus's wife, Hera. I'll never touch another married woman. It simply isn't worth the torture and guilt.

And so he was able to avoid all the texts that dealt solely with physical love in its seemingly endless permutations. He made no value judgments; he understood early on that everyone sought True Love in often inarticulate ways they often did not, themselves, understand; but his was an idealized, traditional concept of what True Love was, and his search for the grail need not be sidetracked or slowed by excursions into those special places.

He read Waley's translation of *The Chin P-ing Mei* and everything even remotely pertinent by Freud; he sought out *La Fleur Lascivie Orientale* and the even rarer English translation of *Contes Licencieux de Constantinople et de l'Asie Mineure*; he dipped into the memoirs of Clara Bow, Charles II, Charlie Chaplin, Isadora Duncan, Marie Duplessis, Lola Montez and George Sand; he read novelists—Moravia, Gorky, Maupassant, Roth, Cheever and Brossard—but found they knew even less than he.

He absorbed the thoughts of the aphorists, and believed every utterance; Balzac: "True love is eternal, infinite, and always like itself. It is equal and pure, without violent demonstrations; it is seen with white hairs and is always young in the heart."; Moliére: "Reason is not what directs love"; Terence: "It is possible that a man can be so-changed by love as hardly to be recognized as the same person."; Voltaire: "Love is a canvas furnished by Nature and embroidered by imagination."; La Rochefoucauld: "When we are in love, we often doubt what we most believe."

Yet even nodding his agreement with every contradictory image and representation of love—seen as Nature, God, a bird on the wing, sex, vanity—he knew they had perceived only the barest edge of what True Love was. Not Kierkegaard or Bacon or Goethe or Nietzsche, for all their insight, for all their wisdom, had any better idea of what True Love looked like than the commonest day-laborer.

The *Song of Solomon* spurred him on, but did not indicate the proper route to discovery.

He found the main path on that night in February of 1968. But once found, he was too frightened to set foot upon it.

Surgat, a subordinate spirit to Sargatanas who, in the Descending Hierarchy from Lucifer to Lucifuge Rofacale, opens all locks, came when Chris Caperton summoned him. He was too insignificant a demon to refuse, no matter how ineptly couched the invocation. But he was less than cooperative.

Chris used Siri's blood to draw the pentagram of Solomon on the floor. He didn't think about what he was doing . . . that he was dipping his finger in the blood of the woman who lay covered with a sheet on the sofa . . . that he had to do it repeatedly because it was getting thick . . . that he had been warned all ten sides of the five-pointed star enclosed in a circle must be without break . . . he just did it. He did not cry. He just did it.

Then he set candles at the five points and lighted them. Every apartment in Saigon in those days had a supply of candles.

Then he stood in the exact center of the runes and lines and read from the dictation he had taken. Siri had assured him if he stayed within the pentagram he would be safe, that Surgat only opened locks and was not really powerful enough to cause him trouble . . . if he kept his wits about him.

The words were contained in the *Grimorium Verum* and Siri had said they need not be spoken precisely, nor need Chris worry about having done the special cleansing necessary when summoning the more powerful Field Marshals of Lucifer's Infernal Legions.

He read the words. "I conjure thee, Surgat, by the great living God, the Sovereign Creator of all things, to appear under a comely human form, without noise and without terror, to answer truly unto all questions that I shall ask thee. Hereunto I conjure thee by the virtue of these Holy and Sacred Names. O Surmy ✠ Delmusan ✠ Atalsolym ✠ Chrusihoa ✠ Melany ✠ Liamintho ✠ Colehon ✠ Paron ✠ Madoin ✠ Merloy ✠ Bulerator ✠ Donmeo ✠ Hone ✠ Peloym ✠ Ibasil ✠ Meon." And on and on, eighteen more names, concluding with, "Come, therefore, quickly and peaceably, by the Names Adonai, Elohim, Tetragrammaton! *Come!*"

From across the Saigon River he could hear the sound of the city's rockets, flattening Charlie's supposed emplacements. But in the little apartment on Nguyen Cong Tru Street everything began to shimmer and wash down like the aurora borealis.

It was an apartment no longer. He stood on the polished wood floor, inside the pentagram of Solomon, but the polished wood floor came to an end at the edges of Siri's dried blood. Beyond lay a fallen temple. Great gray stones, enormous and bearing the marks of claws that had ripped them loose from mountains, tumbled and thrown carelessly, rose up around Chris. And out of the shadows something came toward him.

It slouched and dragged its arms behind as it came out of the darkness. When the flickering illumination from the candles struck it, Chris felt sick to his stomach. He clutched the paper with Siri's words as if it would save him.

Surgat came and stood with the point of one goat-hoof almost touching Siri's blood. Chris could smell where it had been and what it had been doing when he had interrupted its dining. He felt faint and could not breathe deeply because of the smell Surgat had carried from its mess hall.

The head of the demon changed. Toad to goat to worm to spider to dog to ape to man to a thing that had no name.

"Open the lock of the casket," Chris yelled. He had to yell: the sound of wind was overpowering, deafening, insane.

Surgat kicked the bahut. Chris had left it, as Siri had instructed, outside the pentagram. Surgat kicked it again. No mark was put on the coffer, but where the demon's foot had rested in the dust of the fallen temple's floor, a cloven footprint burned and smoked.

"Open the lock!"

Surgat leaned forward and shrieked. Words poured forth. They made no sense to Chris. They were from a throat that was not human. If a hyena had been given the ability to speak with the tongue of a man, it would have sounded less guttural, less deranged, less terrifying.

Siri had said the demon would be troublesome, but would finally do as bidden. It had no choice. It was not that important or powerful a spirit. When Chris remembered that assurance, and perceived just how staggering was the sight before him, he trembled at the thought of one of Surgat's masters. "Open it, you goddam ugly sonofabitch! Open it right now!"

Surgat vomited maggots that hit an invisible plane at the edge of the pentagram. And babbled more words. And reached out a lobster-claw that stopped just outside the invisible plane. It wanted something.

Then Chris remembered the hair from Siri's head. It will want the hair of a fox, she had said. Forget that. It will try to get a hair from *your* head. Whatever you do, don't let it have one. All of you is contained in each hair; you can be reconstructed from a hair; then it has you. Give it mine.

He extended her long, thick strand of hair.

Surgat screamed, would not take it. Chris extended it through the invisible plane. Surgat pointed to Chris's head and pulled long strips of bleeding flesh from its body and threw them against the fallen stones where they plopped with the sickening sound of meat against concrete. Chris did not move. The hair hung down outside the invisible plane.

Surgat screamed and capered and tore at itself.

"Take it, you disgusting sonofabitch!" Chris yelled. "Take it and be damned, she *died* to give it to you, puking garbage dump! Take it or get nothing! Nothing's worth this, not even that thing she looked for all her life! So *take it*, you crummy piece of shit! *Take it* or go back where you came from and let me alone!"

The words Surgat spoke became very clear, then. The voice modulated, became almost refined. It spoke in a language Chris had never heard. He could not have known that it was a tongue unspoken for a thousand years before the birth of Christ: Surgat spoke in Chaldean.

And having spoken, having acknowledged obedience at the threat of being dismissed without the proper license to depart, the threat of being trapped here in this halfway place of fallen stones, and the wrath of Asmoday or Beelzebuth, the lock-picking demon ran its tentacle forward and took Siri's hair. The hair burst into flame, the smale shot up toward the shadowed ceiling of the fallen temple, Surgat turned the flame on the casket . . . and the flame washed over the wood . . . and the casket opened.

Quickly, Chris read the final words on the paper he held. "O Spirit Surgat, because thou has diligently answered my demands, I do hereby license thee to depart, without injury to man or beast. Depart, I say, and be thou willing and ready to come, whensoever duly exorcised and conjured by the Sacred Rites of Magic. I conjure thee to withdraw peaceably and quietly, and may the peace of God continue forever between me and thee. Amen."

And Surgat looked across the pentagram's protective plane and said, in perfectly understandable English, "I do not go empty-handed."

Then the demon slouched away into the shadows, the aurora borealis effect began again, rippling and sliding and flowing down till he was in his own apartment again. Even then he waited an hour before leaving the charmed circle.

To discover that as Siri had promised, everything had its price. Surgat had not gone empty-handed.

The body of his lover was gone. He could not look at what had been left in its place.

He began to cry, hoping it *had* been an exchange; hoping that what lay on the sofa was not Siri.

The bahut contained more items than its outside dimensions would have indicated. It held grimoires and many notebooks filled with Siri's handwriting. It held talismans and runic symbols in stone and silver and wood. It held vials of powders and hair and bird-claws and bits of matter, each vial labeled clearly. It held conjurations and phials and philtres and maps and directions and exorcising spells. It held the key to finding True Love.

But it also held Siri's observations of what had happened to her when she had summoned the entity she called "the supreme hideousness, the most evil of the ten Sephiroths, the vile Adrammelech." He read the ledgers until his eyes burned, and when his fingers left the pages, the paper was smudged with his sweat. He began to tremble, there in the room where the smell of Surgat's dining table lingered, and knew he could not summon the strength to summon this most powerful of dark beings.

He read every word on every page Siri had written; and he vowed silently that he would pick up her quest where she had fallen. But he could not go to her informant. His assistance had cost her too much, and she had been unable to go on. The price was too high.

But there were clues to the trail of the artifact that was True Love. And he took the bahut and left the apartment on Nguyen Cong Tru Street, and never returned. He had money to continue the search, and he would do it without help from things that dragged long, rubbery arms through the dust of fallen temples.

All he had to do was wait for the end of the war.

By 1975 Christopher Caperton had traced it to New Orleans. He was thirty-five years old; he had been married and divorced because in a moment of weariness he had thought *she* might suffice in place of True Love; and he wrote this in his journal: *It is the vanity of searching for embodiments.* Flèches d'amour. *Incarnations which are never satisfactory, which never answer* all *longings and questions.*

Once, when he had thought he might die of a jungle fever contracted while running down a false clue in Paramaribo, he heard himself cursing Siri's memory. If she had not told him it actually existed, he might have settled for something less, never knowing for certain that there was more. But he *did* know, and in his tantrum of fever he cursed her to Hell.

When he recovered, he was more than ashamed of himself. Considering who she had been, where she had gone, and the owners of her spirit, he might have called down a sentence on her that she did not deserve. One never knew the total cost, nor at what point the obligation was considered voided.

After he had been rotated home in 1970 he spent a few months tying up all previous relationships—family, friends, business associates, acquaintances—and set out on the trail that had grown cold since 1946.

Without dipping into capital he was able to underwrite his expenses handsomely. Even though the gnomes of Zurich had done away with unnumbered, secret accounts, he had made his money in a way that caused no concern among the assessors, custom-house officials, tithe-seekers and running-dogs of the IRS desiring duty, levy, tribute, tallage, liver and lights. He moved freely under a variety of passports and a number of names. He came to think of himself as a nameless, stateless person, someone out of a Graham Greene suspense novel.

There were clues, beginning with one of the appraisers who had worked on the Ford bequests. He was quite old by the time Chris located him in a retirement trailer camp in Sun City, but he remembered the item clearly. No, he had never seen it; it was crated with specific instructions that it should not, under even the most extreme circumstances, be opened. If he was lying, he did it well. Chris was paying a high enough premium for the information that it didn't matter either way. But the trail picked up with the old appraiser's recollection that whatever the crate had contained, it had been bequeathed to a contemporary of Henry Ford's, a man with whom he had been friends and then fallen out, fifty years before.

Chris managed to locate the bills of lading and traced the crate to Madison, Indiana. The recipient of the crate had been deceased for fifteen years. The contents of the crate had been sold at auction . . .

And so it went. From place to place. From clue to clue. And each clue indicated that having been in touch with the artifact, the owner had known great joy or great sorrow; but all were dead. The Holy Grail always lay just ahead, always just out of Chris's reach. Yet he could never bring himself to take the easy way out: to summon up the horror Siri had called Adrammelech. He knew if he finally gave in, that even if he found True Love he would never be able to savor it.

In January of 1975 Christopher Caperton followed a clue from Trinidad to New Orleans. His source had assured him that the artifact had passed into the hands of a *houngan*, a priest of the *conjur*, a disciple of the voodoo of Doctor Cat, a pioneer of mail order Voodoo in 1914.

On Perdido Street, in a back room lit only by votive candles in rubyglass jars, Chris met "Prince Basile Thibodeux," whose title at birth had been merely Willie Link Dunbar. Prince Basile swore he had known and loved the real and true Marie Laveau. As the old black man looked no more than sixty—though he claimed to be ninety-two—such a claim was, either way, highly dubious. Absolute proof exists that Marie Laveau, the first of many Marie Laveau's, died on June 24th, 1881, at the approximate age of eighty-five. Two years before Willie Link "Thibodeux" had been born, if he was ninety-two; and thirty-four, if he was lying.

Christopher Caperton did not care what lies Prince Basile told to sell his worthless hoodoo goods in the drugstore of Love Oils, Goofer Dust, Devil's Shoe Strings and War Water, as long as he told him a straight story about the artifact.

When he walked into the little back room, washed in bloody shadows from the candles, he was prepared to pay a premium price for the information he sought, or to assure Prince Basile that there were two men living on Prytania Street who would, for only a fraction of that premium price, inflict great bodily sorrow on a sixty or ninety-two year old black man, and he would worry about the black goat dancing on his grave at a later time. But Prince Basile took one look at him and fear filled the withered face. "Doan put dat *gris-gris* on me, mistuh," he pleaded. "Jus' whatever you want, that's be what you gone get. Ah'm at y'service."

And Chris walked out of the little back room on Perdido Street with the information—that he knew to be absolutely reliable because no one that terrified could lie without dying in the act—that Willie Link Dunbar had worked on a smuggling operation from the Islands to the Keys in 1971 and he had seen the artifact. He swore before Damballa that he could not remember what it looked like . . . but it had been as lovely as anything he knew. His face, when he said it, was a strange mix of terror at the sight of Chris and joy at the last scintilla of memory of what he had seen.

And he told Chris the name of the smuggler who had taken the item from the boat.

And when Chris asked him why he was so frightened of just another white man, Prince Basile said, "You been kissin' the Old Ones. I kilt a hunnerd crows and cocks I couldn't save mah soul if you was t'touch me, mistuh. I be jus' playin' at whut I does, but *you* . . . you knows the fire."

Chris shuddered. And that was only from a minor, weak servant of Adrammelech. He left hurriedly.

He stood in the darkness of the alley off Perdido Street and thought about it, about True Love, whatever it was. He had wanted it for so long, had sought it in so many women, had glimpsed hints of its totality so many times, that he only now paused to examine what he had become. Even if he got it, would he be worthy of it? Wasn't the one who found the Holy Grail supposed to be pure in every way, perfect in every way, without flaw or blemish or self-doubt? Knights on white chargers, saints, defenders of the faith; those were the candidates for the honor. Prince Charming always won Snow White, not Porky Pig.

Without flaw. No, not without flaw. He had come too far for perfection. He had had to experience too much.

Yet he knew he was closer to True Love than anyone had ever been. Not even those who had possessed it had known what to do with it. He knew he had it within himself to become one with True Love, as no one before him ever could. No one. Not one of the perhaps thousand owners of it before and since it found its way to the Palace of Minos, no matter how fine or great or deserving they had been.

Christopher Caperton knew his destiny was to hold True Love in his hands. Known to demons, casting no shadow, he walked away from the fear in Perdido Street.

The final clue was so mundane he could not even breathe a sigh of relief. True Love had been sold in blind bid auction at Sotheby's in April of 1979. It now belonged to a man who lived high above the rest of the human race, in a tower overlooking New York, where almost eight million people gave a portion of each day to wondering where True Love resided.

From Siri's notebooks Chris recognized the name of the man. In 1932 he had visited New York City for the opening of the Radio City Music Hall. The artifact had been stolen from him. He had spent forty-seven years trying to regain his lost property. In the process, somehow, he had become enormously powerful, enormously wealthy, enormously secretive.

Home again, home again, jiggedy jig.

Christopher Caperton took one final look at the cover of the December 1980 issue of *Esquire*. It showed a woman in a seductive bridal gown. The cover illustrated an article called *Looking for a Wife* and the slug-line read "With all the beautiful, intelligent women out there, why is she so hard to find?"

He smiled thinking they might have done the reverse on *Ms.* magazine, with a photograph of an equally unreachable male.

The model they had selected for the shot was achingly innocent, yet seductive; poised in a timeless moment of utter perfection. Had he been anyone else, this might well have been the physical manifestation of True Love for him.

But it was only the most recent in a congeries of photos, motion pictures, billboards and women glimpsed in cars going past on city streets who were idealized manifestations of what he sought.

Tonight he would hold the real thing. Tonight he would obtain True Love.

He put the last of the vials from Siri's bahut he might need in the capacious pockets of his London Fog topcoat, and left the hotel. It was thirty degrees in the Manhattan streets, and the wind was blowing in off the East River. By tomorrow, perhaps before two AM, there would be snow. It was the sort of evening he had always imagined for this final leg of the journey.

Christopher Caperton was forty years old.

Every bribe had been well-placed. The boiler room door was unlocked. The key to the private service elevator had been properly copied. No one stopped him.

He walked through the palatial tower suite in darkness. He heard a door closing away off in the rear of the apartment. The floor-plan he had been given was precise and he touched nothing as he walked quickly to the door of the master bedroom.

The old man was lying in the exact center of the huge bed. As reported, he was dying.

Chris closed the door behind him. Only one light near the bed illuminated the room. The old man opened his eyes and looked at Chris. His eyes were very blue.

"There's never enough money to buy silence, boy. You can buy entrance, but not silence. There's always some mouth that's hungrier."

Chris smiled and walked to the bed. "I would have tried to bargain with you if I'd thought it would do any good. I'm not a thief by profession.

The old man snorted softly. He didn't seem to be in pain. "No price."

"Yes, I rather thought that might be the case. But look on the bright side: you can't take it with you, it won't do you any good on the other side; and I've been looking for it for a long time."

The old man laughed gently, no more strenuously than he had snorted. "What the hell do I care how long you looked for it, boy? Not as long as I looked for it."

"Since Christmas, 1932."

"Well, well. You did your homework, did you?"

"I've paid as much as you, in all kinds of coin."

"Not my concern, boy. You'll never find it."

"It's here. In this room. In the safe."

The old man's eyes widened. "Smarter than I thought. Didn't stop any of that cash you were doling out; got good people working for me; didn't see any reason why they shouldn't pick up a few extra dollars; they've got families to take care of. Didn't expect you'd know about the safe."

"I know about it."

"Doesn't matter. You'll look forever and never find it. Even if you do, you'll never get it open." He coughed shallowly, smiled at the ceiling and recited: "Hidden where you can't find it; but if you do you'll be looking at six foot thick walls of concrete reinforced with molybdenum-steel alloy cords, backed by a foot of tempered high-carbon high-chromium steel, another foot of unseamed silico-manganese shock-resisting steel and six inches of eighteen-tungsten, four-chrome, one-vanadium high-speed industrial tool steel. The vault door is stainless steel faced, an inch and a half of cast steel, another twelve inches of burn-resisting steel, another inch and a half of open-hearth steel, and the pneumatic hinges are inside the sandwich. The vault door has twenty bolts, each an inch in diameter: eight on one side, eight on the other, two top and two bottom. This holds the door into a sixteen inch jamb of moly-tungsten high speed steel, set into eighteen inches of concrete crosshatched by burn-resisting steel bars running horizontally and vertically." He coughed once more, pleased with himself, and added as a fillip, "The door's precision-made so you can't pour nitro in between the seam of the door and the vault."

Chris let a beaten look cross his face. "And I suppose that isn't even all of it. I suppose there are thermostats that trip some kind of trap if the temperature rises . . . if I used a torch."

"You got some smarts, boy. Tear gas. And the floor gets electrified." He was grinning widely now, but what little color had been in his face was gone. His eyes were closing.

"You beat me," Chris said. "I guess it's yours to keep."

But the old man only heard the first part. By the end, Chris was talking to himself. The old man was gone.

"On the other hand," Chris said softly, "there's no lock that can't be opened."

He stood by the bed for a while, staring down at the previous owner of True Love. He didn't seem to have died happier or sadder for having passed on with it in his possession.

Then Christopher Caperton got down on his knees in the center of the great bedroom and took out the vial Siri had labeled *Blood of Helomi* and he unstoppered the vial and began sprinkling out the dusty contents in lines that formed the pentagram of Solomon. He placed the candles and lit them; and he stood in the center of the design. And he read from a smudged piece of paper twelve years old.

And Surgat came again.

This time it came to the tower suite; this time it did not take Chris to the fallen temple. And this time it spoke in the soft refined voice it had used when taking Siri's body.

"So soon?" Surgat said. "You need me again so soon?"

Chris felt nausea rising in his throat. The demon had not been dining this time. It had been indulging in whatever passed for fornication among demons. Its love-partner was still attached. Whatever it was, it wasn't human. (A momentary thought shrieked through Chris's skull. Might it ever have *been* human; and might it have been . . .? He slammed the lid on the thought.)

"Twelve years . . . it's been twelve years . . ." Chris said, with difficulty.

Surgat let a human face appear in its stomach and the human face smiled offhandedly. "How time flies when one is enjoying oneself." The love-partner moaned and gave a spastic twitch.

Chris would not think of it.

"Open the safe," he ordered the demon.

"I'll need you out here to assist me. In one of my very difficult rituals." The voice was a snake's hiss, from the moth's head.

"Go fuck yourself. Open the safe."

"But I *need* you," the demon said, wheedling disingenuously.

Chris fished in his topcoat pocket for a scrap of parchment from the bahut. He began to read. "By the powerful Principality of the infernal abysses, I conjure thee with power and with exorcism; I warn thee hearken forthwith and immediately to my words; observe them inviolably, as sentences of the last dreadful day of judgment, which thou must obey inviolably . . ."

As he began to speak, a sweat of pus and blood began to break out on the demon's armored flesh. Soft purple bruises appeared, as if Surgat were being struck from within.

"I hear. I obey!"

And it reached for the hair. Chris took the vial of fox hairs from his pocket, withdrew one and handed it across the invisible plane. The hair burst into flame as before, and Surgat turned, aiming the flame at the ceiling. The fire washed the ceiling of the tower suite bedroom and the ceiling opened and the central section of the floor on which Chris stood rose up on hydraulic lifts into a chamber above the penthouse.

Then Surgat turned the flame on the stainless steel door of the vault that formed the wall of the chamber above, and the door swung open ponderously. And the vault within was revealed.

Then Chris intoned the license to depart, but before Surgat vanished it said, "Master, powerful Master, may I leave you with a gift?"

"No. I don't want anything more from you, not ever again."

"But Master, you will need this gift. I swear by my Lord Adrammelech."

Chris felt terror swirl through him. "What is it?"

"Then you willingly accept my gift without condition or let?"

Chris heard Siri's voice in his memory: *He won't harm you. He serves only one purpose: he opens all locks. Just be careful.* "Yes, I accept the gift."

Surgat caused a pool of stagnant water to appear just beyond the protective design. Then the human face appeared again in the thorax of the insect Surgat had become, and the human face smiled invitingly and said, "Look," and Surgat sucked in within itself and grew smaller and smaller and then vanished.

Leaving the pool of foul water in which Chris saw—

A scene from a motion picture. He recognized it. A scene from *Citizen Kane*. A day in 1940. The interior of the skyscraper office of the old man, Bernstein. He is being interviewed by the newsreel researcher, Thompson, who asks him what Charles Foster Kane's dying word, "Rosebud," meant.

Bernstein thinks, then says, "Maybe some girl? There were a lot of them back in the early days and—"

Thompson is amused. He says, "It's hardly likely, Mr. Bernstein, that Mr. Kane could have met some girl casually and then, fifty years later, on his deathbed—"

Bernstein cuts in, "You're pretty young, Mr.—" he remembers the name, "—Mr. Thompson. A fellow will remember things you wouldn't think he'd remember. You take me. One day, back in 1896, I was crossing over to Jersey on a ferry and as we pulled out there was another ferry pulling in." Everett Sloane, as the aged Bernstein, looks wistful, speaks slowly. "And on it there was a girl waiting to get off. A white dress she had on . . . and she was carrying a white parasol . . . and I only saw her for one second and she didn't see me at all . . . but I'll bet a month hasn't gone by since that I haven't thought of that girl." He smiled triumphantly. "See what I mean?"

And the scene faded, and the water boiled away, and Chris was alone in the dimly-lit vault room above the tower suite. Alone with the dawning fear that he had learned too much.

He saw himself suddenly as a human puppet, controlled from above by a nameless force that had held every man and woman on the end of strings, making them dance the dance, manipulating them to seek the unobtainable, denying them peace or contentment because of the promise of a Holy Grail out there somewhere.

Even if the strings were broken, and puny mortals wandered the blasted landscape of their lives on their own, they would finally, inevitably, tragically return to the great puppeteer, to try and retie the strings. Better to dance the hopeless dance that lied about True Love than to admit they were all alone, that they might never, never find that perfect image to become one with. He stood in the center of the pentagram of Solomon and thought of the achingly beautiful girl on the cover of *Esquire*. The girl who was not real. True Love. Snare and delusion? He felt tears on his cheeks, and shook his head. No, it was here. It was just inside the threshold of the vault. It existed. It had a form and a reality. The truth was only a few footsteps from him. Siri could not have died for it if it weren't real.

He stepped out of the magic design and walked to the door of the vault. He kept his eyes down. He stepped over the raised jamb and heard his footsteps on the steel floor.

The vault was lit by hidden tubing at the juncture of walls and ceiling. A soft off-white glow that filled the vault.

He looked up slowly.

It sat on a pedestal of silver and lucite.

He looked at True Love.

It was an enormous loving cup. It was as gaudy as a bowling trophy. Exactly a foot and a half high, with handles. Engraved on the face were the words *True Love* in flowing script, embellished with curlicues. It shone with a light of its own, and the glow was the brassy color of an intramural award.

Christopher Caperton stood with his arms hanging at his sides. It was in him, at that moment, to laugh. But he had the certain knowledge that if he laughed, he would never stop; and they would come in to get the old man's body this morning and find him still standing there, crying piteously and laughing.

He had come through a time and a distance to get this real artifact, and he would take it. He stepped to the pedestal and reached for it. Remembering at the last moment the demon's gift.

Surgat could not touch him; but Surgat could reach him.

He looked down into the loving cup that was True Love and in the silver liquid swirling there he saw the face of True Love. For an instant it was his mother, then it was Miss O'Hara, then it was poor Jean Kettner, then it was Briony Catling, then it was Helen Gahagan, then it was Marta Toren, then it was the girl to whom he had lost his virginity, then it was one woman after another he had known, then it was Siri—but was Siri no longer than any of the others—then it was his wife, then it was the face of the achingly beautiful bride on the cover of *Esquire*, and then it resolved finally into the most unforgettable face he had ever seen. And it stayed.

It was no face he recognized.

Years later, when he was near death, Christopher Caperton wrote the answer to the search for True Love in his journal. He wrote it simply, as a quotation from the Japanese poet Tanaka Katsumi.

What he wrote was this:

"I know that my true friend will appear after my death, and my sweetheart died before I was born."

In that instant when he saw the face of True Love, Christopher Caperton knew the awful gift the demon had given him. To reach the finest moment of one's life, and to *know* it was the finest moment, that there would never be a more golden, more perfect, nobler or loftier or thrilling moment . . . and to continue to have to live a life that was all on the downhill side.

That was the curse and the blessing.

He knew, at last, that he *was* worthy of such a thing. In torment and sadness he knew he was *just* that worthy, and no more.

But it's easy to be smart . . . later.

The Willow Platform

by

Joseph Payne Brennan

A grimoire is literally a black magic textbook, a compendium of ancient spells, potions, ceremonies, and incantations to induce the various dark lords, devils, demons, shades, and elementals to manifest themselves and serve the sorcerer in his pursuit of power, wealth, or knowledge. The earliest and most legendary grimoire is the Emerald Table of Hermes Trismegistus, *which is still shrouded in mystery. The original tablet, carved out of pure emerald, has never been found, although a variant Latin version surfaced in the thirteenth century. There are other texts:* The Key of Solomon; The Lemegeton, or Lesser Key of Solomon; The Grimorium Verum; The Red Dragon; The Heptameron; *the German grimoire known as* Doctor Faust's Great and Powerful Sea-Spirit; *and others. The great grimoires concentrate on the most important of the dark dignitaries, cataloging and describing them, for it's all important to know the true name and form of a summoned demon or lord. But lesser spirits are also cataloged: those demons that are slightly easier to summon and command, such as the malignant and implacable elementals born of fire, water, air, or earth; and their cold and sinister cousins, the fly-the-lights that can be brought to life only in darkness. The mature and experienced sorcerer tries to control these nightmarish beings and force them to his will, but this can be an even more shocking and dangerous enterprise for a neophyte.*

In fact, a little knowledge can be . . . deadly, as veteran horror writer Joseph Payne Brennan shows us in this disquieting tale of summoning and sacrifice set in rural New England.

Joseph Payne Brennan's short stories and poems have been included in over a hundred anthologies, and his fiction and poetry has appeared in Commonweal, Esquire, Alfred Hitchcock's Mystery Magazine, American Scholar, New York Times, Magazine of Horror, *and* Georgia Review. *His short fiction can be found in his own collections* Nine Horrors and a Dream, The Dark Returner, Scream at Midnight, The Casebook of Lucius Leffing, *and* The Shapes of Midnight, *among others. His poetry collections include* Webs of Time, As Evening Advances, Death Poems, *and* Edges of Night. *Two of his stories have been adapted for NBC's* Thriller *television series, and another story, "The Calamander Chest," was recorded by Vincent Price. He has been awarded the Leonara Speyer Memorial Award of the Poetry Society of America, and the Clark Ashton Smith Poetry Award for life work.*

* * *

THIRTY YEARS AGO JUNIPER HILL WAS AN ISOLATED TOWNship, with a small village, dirt roads and high hilly tracts of evergreen forest—pine, hemlock, tamarack and spruce. Scattered along the fringes of wood were boulder-strewn pastures, hay fields and glacially formed, lichen-covered knolls.

Ordinarily I stayed in Juniper Hill from early June until late September. As I returned year after year, I came to be accepted almost as a native—many notches above the few transient "summer people" who stayed for a month or so and then hurried back to the world of traffic, tension and tedium.

I wrote when I felt like it. The rest of the time I walked the dirt roads, explored the woods and chatted with the natives.

Within a few years I got to know everyone in town, with the exception of a hermit or two and one irascible landowner who refused to converse even with his own neighbors.

To me, however, a certain Henry Crotell was the most intriguing person in Juniper Hill. He was sometimes referred to as "the village idiot," "that loafer," "that good-for-nothing," etc., but I came to believe that these epithets arose more from envy than from conviction.

Somehow, Henry managed to subsist and enjoy life without doing any work—or at least hardly any. At a time when this has become a permanent way of life for several million persons, I must quickly add that Henry did not receive one dime from the township of Juniper Hill, either in cash or goods.

He lived in a one-room shack on stony land which nobody claimed and he fed himself. He fished, hunted, picked berries and raised a few potatoes among the rocks behind his shack. If his hunting included a bit of poaching, nobody seemed to mind.

Since Henry used neither alcohol nor tobacco, his needs were minimal. Occasionally, if he needed a new shirt, or shoes, he would split wood, dig potatoes or fill in as an extra hay-field hand for a few days. He established a standard charge which never varied; one dollar a day plus meals. He would never accept any more cash. You might prevail upon him to take along a sack of turnips, but if you handed him a dollar and a quarter for the day, he'd smilingly return the quarter.

Henry was in his early thirties, slab-sided, snuff-brown, with a quick loose grin and rather inscrutable, faded-looking blue eyes. His ginger colored hair was getting a trifle thin. When he smiled, strangers assumed he was wearing false teeth because his own were so white and even. I once asked him how often he brushed his teeth. He doubled up with silent laughter. "Nary brush! Nary toothpaste!" I didn't press the point, but I often wondered what his secret was—if he had one.

Henry should have lived out his quiet days at Juniper Hill and died at ninety on the cot in his shack. But it was not to be.

Henry found the book.

Four or five miles from Henry's shack lay the crumbling ruins of the old Trobish house. It was little more than a cellar hole filled with rotten boards and fallen beams. Lilac bushes had forced their roots between the old foundation stones; maple saplings filled the dooryard. Old Hannibal Trobish, dead for fifty years, had been an eccentric hermit who drove off intruders with a shotgun. When he died, leaving no heirs and owing ten years' taxes, the town had taken over the property. But the town had no need of it, nor use for it, and so the house had been allowed to decay until finally the whole structure, board by board, had dropped away into the cellar hole. There were hundreds of such collapsed and neglected houses throughout New England. Nobody paid much attention to them.

Henry Crotell, however, seemed fascinated by the moldering remains of the Trobish house. He prowled the area, poked about in the cellar hole and even lifted out some of the mildewed beams. Once, reaching in among the sagging foundation stones, he was nearly bitten by a copperhead.

Old Dave Baines admonished Henry when he heard about it. "That's an omen, Henry! You'd better stay away from that cellar hole!"

Henry pushed out his upper lip and looked at his shoes. "Ain't 'fraid of no old snake! Seen bigger. Last summer I rec'lect. Big tom rattler twice as big!"

Not long after the copperhead incident, Henry found the book. It was contained in a small battered tin box which was jammed far in between two of the foundation stones in the Trobish cellar.

It was a small, vellum-bound book, measuring about four by six inches. The title page and table of contents page had either disintegrated or been removed, and mold was working on the rest of the pages, but it was still possible to read most of the print—that is, if you knew Latin.

Henry didn't, of course, but, no matter, he was entranced by his find. He carried the book everywhere. Sometimes you'd see him sitting in the spruce woods, frowning over the volume, baffled but still intrigued.

We underestimated Henry. He was determined to read the book. Eventually he prevailed upon Miss Winnie, the local teacher, to lend him a second-hand Latin grammar and vocabulary.

Since Henry's formal schooling had been limited to two or three years, and since his knowledge of English was, at best, rudimentary, it must have been a fearful task for him to tackle Latin.

But he persisted. Whenever he wasn't prowling the woods, fishing, or filling in for an ailing hired hand, he'd sit puzzling over his find. He'd trace out the Latin words with one finger, frown, shake his head and pick up the textbooks. Then, stubbornly, he'd go back to the vellum-bound volume again.

He ran into many snags. Finally he returned to Miss Winnie with a formidable list of words and names which he couldn't find in the grammar.

Miss Winnie did the best she could with the list. Shortly afterwards she went to see Dave Baines. Although, in his later years, Baines held no official position, he was the patriarch of the town. Nearly everyone went to him for counsel and advice.

Not long after Miss Winnie's visit, he stopped in to see me. After sipping a little wine, he came to the point.

"I wish," he said abruptly, "you'd try to get that damned book away from Henry."

I looked up with surprise. "Why should I, Dave? It keeps him amused apparently."

Baines removed his steel-rimmed spectacles and rubbed his eyes. "That list Henry brought Miss Winnie contains some very strange words—including the names of at least four different devils. And several names which must refer to—entities—maybe worse than devils."

I poured more wine. "I'll see what I can do. But I really can't imagine what harm could come of it. That book is just a new toy to Henry. He'll tire of it eventually."

Dave replaced his spectacles. "Well, maybe. But the other day Giles Cowdry heard this funny high-pitched voice coming out of the woods. Said it gave him the creeps. He slipped in to investigate and there was Henry standing in a clearing among the pines reading out of that moldy book. I suppose his Latin pronunciation was pretty terrible, but Giles said a strange feeling came over him as Henry went on reading. He backed away and I guess he was glad enough to get out of earshot."

I promised Dave I'd see what I could do. About a week later while I was taking a walk through the woods in the vicinity of Henry's shack, I heard a kind of chant emanating from nearby.

Pushing through a stand of pines, I spotted Henry standing in a small open area among the trees. He held a book in one hand and mouthed a kind of gibberish which, to me at least, only faintly resembled Latin.

Unobtrusively, I edged into sight. A fallen branch cracked as I stepped on it and Henry looked up.

He stopped reading immediately.

I nodded. "Mornin', Henry. Just taking a stroll and I couldn't help hearing you. Must be a might interesting little book you've got there. Can I take a look at it?"

Ordinarily, Henry would greet me with an easy grin. This time he scowled, "Ain't givin' my book to nobody!" he exclaimed, stuffing the volume into a pocket.

I was annoyed and I suppose I showed it. "I didn't ask to *keep* the book, Henry. I merely wanted to look at it." Actually this wasn't entirely true; I had hoped to persuade him to give me the book.

He shrugged, hesitated and then, turning, started off through the woods. "I got chores. No time for talk," he muttered over his shoulder.

The next day I reported my failure to Dave Baines.

"Too bad," he commented, "but I suppose we'd better just forget about it. If he won't give that infernal book to you, he won't give it to anybody. Let's just hope he loses interest in it after a time."

But Henry didn't lose interest in the vellum-bound book. On the contrary, he developed an obsession about it. He went hunting or fishing only when driven by acute hunger. He neglected his potato patch. His shack, never very sturdy, began to disintegrate.

Less often during the day now, but more often at night, his high-pitched voice would be heard arising from one of the dense groves of pines or hemlocks which bordered the dusty country roads. Scarcely anyone in Juniper Hill knew Latin, but everyone who heard Henry's chant drifting from the dark woods agreed that it was an eerie and disturbing experience. One farmer's wife averred that Henry's nocturnal readings had given her nightmares.

Somebody asked how Henry could see to read in the dark, since nobody ever had seen a light in the woods from whence the sounds emanated.

It was, as is said, "a good question." We never found out for sure. It was possible that Henry had finally memorized the contents of the book, or part of it. This, however, I personally found difficult to believe.

Henry's explanation, when it came, was even more difficult to accept.

One hot summer morning he turned up at the village general store. He looked emaciated and his clothes were in tatters, but he seemed imbued with a kind of supressed animation. Perhaps exhilaration might be a better word.

He bought a two-dollar work shirt and three tins of corned beef. He did not appear chagrined that these purchases very obviously emptied his tattered wallet.

Loungers at the store noticed that he was wearing a ring. Some commented on it.

Surprisingly, Henry held it out for inspection. He was visibly proud of it. Everyone agreed later that they had never seen a ring like it before. The band might have been shaped out of silver, but worked into it were tiny veins of blue which appeared to glow faintly. The stone was disappointing; black, flat-cut and dull in luster.

Unusually voluble, Henry volunteered some information on the stone. "Ain't no good in daylight. Nighttime it comes alive. Throws out light, it do!"

He gathered up his purchases and started for the door. He paused at the threshold, chuckling, and turned his head. "Light a-plenty," he said, " 'nuff light to read by!"

Still chuckling to himself, he walked out into the hot sunlight and off down the road.

The only other information we received about the ring came

from Walter Frawley, the town constable, who met Henry in the woods one day. Frawley reported that he had asked Henry where he had acquired the ring.

Henry insisted that he found it, purely by chance, tangled up among the roots of a huge pine tree which formerly grew near the ruins of the old Trobish house. The great pine had toppled in a severe windstorm several years before. Natives estimated the tree was at least one hundred years old.

Nobody could satisfactorily explain how the ring had become entangled in the roots of a century-old pine. It was possible, of course, that old Hannibal Trobish had buried it there many decades ago—either to hide it, or to get rid of it.

As the hot summer advanced, Henry went on chanting in the woods at night, giving late travelers "a case of the nerves" and causing some of the farm watch dogs to howl dismally.

One day I met Miss Winnie in the village and asked for her opinion of Henry's book, based on the list of words and names which he had brought to her for translation or clarification.

"The book is medieval in origin," she told me. "And I think it was written by someone who pretended to be a wizard or sorcerer. Poor Henry is out there in the woods at night chanting invocations to nonexistent devils dreamed up by some medieval charlatan who was quite possibly burned at the stake!"

I frowned. "Why do you say 'nonexistent devils,' Miss Winnie?"

"I don't *believe* in such things," she replied a bit stiffly. "I went to Dave Baines about the book because I thought it was having a bad effect on Henry. Heaven knows I'd be delighted if he learned Latin, but I don't think he's going about it properly. And he's neglecting everything. People tell me his little hut is falling apart and that he doesn't eat properly anymore."

I thanked her and went my way, even more concerned than I had been before, but totally unable to see how I could help. I felt that Henry still liked me, but I knew his stubbornness was monumental.

Not long after my talk with Miss Winnie, I heard rumors that Henry was building some kind of stage or platform on a small knoll adjacent to one of the deeper stands of hemlock. The knoll was about a mile from one of the less-traveled country roads. It was quite high, almost level with the tops of the hemlocks. I had been on it a few times and recalled that on a clear day it overlooked a huge expanse of forest and field.

One afternoon when the summer heat had subsided somewhat,

I went to have a look at Henry's platform. After nearly becoming lost in the dark hemlock woods, I slipped into the sunlight and climbed the side of the knoll, a small hill made up of glacial stones and gravel.

It was barren except for a few stunted shrubs, ground creepers and dried lichen patches. Centered on the exact top was a twenty-foot structure built primarily out of willow saplings. A few stakes of heavier wood had been driven in around the base to strengthen the whole. The top of the bizarre lookout tapered to a tiny wooden platform, just large enough for one person. A crude hand-ladder had been attached to one side and a kind of rail ran around the perimeter of the platform.

It was, altogether, shaky and perilous-looking. Henry was no heavyweight, and he would probably survive a twenty-foot drop onto the slippery side of a knoll, but I felt, nevertheless, that he was risking serious injury.

I circled the little structure and sat down nearby for a time, but Henry did not appear. At length, as the afternoon sun beat down on the knoll, I got up and made my way uneventfully through the hemlocks and back to the road.

Dave Baines shook his head when he learned of the willow platform. "That Latin book is drivin' Henry loco. I expect he'll fall off that thing, break a leg, or maybe his spine, and end up in the county hospital."

I suggested condemning the willow tower since it was obviously hazardous and was, moreover, built on land to which Henry had no title.

Dave shrugged. "What good would it do? He'd be madder than a hundred wet hens, and he'd likely just go out and rig up another somewhere else."

I let it go at that. I wasn't a native of the town and I certainly wasn't going to spearhead any "movement" to demolish Henry's willow platform.

Not long after my talk with Dave, the stories started circulating. At night, it was rumored, Henry's chanting could be heard all over town. It was becoming louder all the time.

Frank Kenmore came in with a story about Henry screeching from the top of the willow-tower while it swayed wildly in the wind and "tongues of fire" floated over the hemlock trees.

John Pendle complained that his old mare had bolted and thrown him from his buggy into the ditch one night when Henry started his "crazy yellin'. "

Young Charlie Foxmire swore that he had crept through the

woods at midnight and seen Henry on his tower "laughin' like a madman and talkin' to somebody in the trees."

I determined to find out for myself what actually was taking place. Late one evening I went out to the front veranda and listened. Sure enough, when the wind was right, I could hear Henry's steady chanting.

I turned off my lights and started out for the willow tower.

It was tough going through the hemlocks, but Henry's high-pitched chant kept me on my course. When I reached the knoll, I circled around until I was directly at Henry's back. I advanced only a few feet up the side of the knoll, crouched down and then very cautiously lifted my head.

Henry, book in hand, was standing on the tiny platform. The flimsy structure was swaying slightly in the wind. A bluish glow, whose source I could not at first locate, illuminated the book and part of Henry's face. His chant rose and fell eerily. He kept glancing from the book out over the top of the black hemlock forest, almost as if he were addressing a huge unseen audience which listened among the trees. In spite of the relative warmth of the summer night, I found myself shuddering.

His chant seemed to go on endlessly, as he turned the pages of the book. His voice became stronger as he continued. The wind rose and the platform swayed a little more.

I crouched motionless until my muscles ached, but there was no response from the depths of the hemlock woods. I was shocked when I realized that I had been *waiting* for a response!

I saw clearly at last that the strange blue glow emanated from the ring on Henry's finger. I experienced the weird conviction that the glow strengthened as Henry's chant grew stronger.

At length, the tension, plus the uncomfortable position in which I remained crouched, began to tire me. I had intended to stay until Henry finished his nocturnal incantations, but on second thought I decided to leave before he descended. I was convinced that he would be furious if he found me spying on him when he came down.

Moving carefully, I slipped backwards into the trees. A carpet of hemlock needles, inches deep, effectively muffled my footsteps. I groped my way to the road and walked home. I was too exhausted to assess the full implications of what I had seen. In spite of my fatigue, I did not sleep well. Unpleasant dreams, bordering on nightmare, harried me until morning.

I reported to Dave Baines. He appeared deeply concerned.

"Henry's going to destroy himself—or be destroyed by something if we don't get him away from there."

I nodded. "That's the way I feel—but what can we do?"

Dave began polishing his spectacles. "I'll think of something."

Three days later as I was returning from the village store early one morning, I met Henry. He was shuffling along dispiritedly. I inquired, casually, where he was heading.

He stopped, eyes on the ground, and began kicking at the dirt road with one foot.

"Dave Baines," he told me, "got me on over ta Miller's place. Extra hay hand. Says they be hard up for help. Wants me to go—sort of a favor to *him!*"

He shook his head and scowled. "Wouldn't go fer nobody else. Nobody! But Dave done me favors. Lots of favors. So I got to go."

"That's fine, Henry!" I said. "You'll be well fed and earn a few dollars! The almanac's predicting a long winter!"

He looked at me scornfully. "Ain't worried about winter. You know what I think?"

"What's that, Henry?"

He hesitated. "Well, I trust Dave, I reckon. But it could be somebody put him to it—so's they could get in my shack and take my book!"

His faded blue eyes took on an unfamiliar glint. He continued before I could comment.

"It won't do nobody no good! Because I got my book right here!" He tapped his overall pocket. "Right here!" he repeated triumphantly.

I assured him that Dave was undoubtedly acting in good faith and that nobody I knew in Juniper Hill would trespass in his absence.

Somewhat mollified, but still dispirited, he shuffled off. I noticed that he was still wearing his unusual ring with the flat black stone.

Kent Miller's place was at the far northern end of Juniper Hill. And Miller possessed several huge hay fields. If I judged correctly, Henry would not be back for several days.

That evening I decided to pay another visit to Henry's willow platform. As I started through the hemlock woods toward the knoll, I felt a bit like an intruder. But then I reminded myself that the knoll did not belong to Henry. And perhaps I might stumble on some clue which would be the key to Henry's obsession.

The thick hemlock woods were like a dark and aromatic tomb. I reached the knoll with a feeling of relief. At least I was in the open; I could see sky and feel a breeze on my face.

As I glanced up at the willow tower, I almost laughed aloud. How absurd it looked! Poorly constructed, fragile, swaying in the slight wind—how foolish I was to have been so impressed by a country loafer's childish obsession!

I scrambled up the shaky ladder nailed to one side of the tower and cautiously edged out onto the flimsy platform. The moon had not yet risen and there was not much to see—the dark continuing mass of hemlocks, a few fireflies and, far off, the twinkling light in a farmhouse window.

I was both relieved and disappointed. I told myself that I was a fool. What *had* I expected to see?

As I was about to start down the ladder, I thought I heard a faint chant somewhere in the deep distance. It was like an echo, almost inaudible—yet I paused with my hand on the platform railing and listened.

As I waited, it grew stronger, but only by a small degree. I looked out over the hemlocks and frowned. The contour of the woods seemed to have changed; the outlines of the trees seemed different.

I strained my eyes into the darkness, unable to comprehend what I thought I was witnessing. The wind rose, and the chant grew louder.

Henry was returning, I told myself, and I must hurry away before he reached the knoll with his infernal book and the ring that glowed in the dark.

Two things happened then almost simultaneously. As I started to let myself over the side to go down the ladder, I glanced once more toward the black mass of hemlocks. Only they weren't hemlocks. They were immense, towering trees, tropical in outline, which resembled giant ferns against the sky.

And as I stared in amazement and disbelief, a figure faced me on the platform—a figure with distorted features and glittering eyes which looked like an evil caricature of Henry Crotell!

With a rush of horror, I realized that I could see *through* the figure to the night sky beyond.

After a frozen moment of immobility, I went over the side of the platform. I slid partway down the apology for a ladder and fell the rest of the way.

As soon as my feet touched earth, they were racing for the trees. And when I entered them, they were the dark sweet hemlocks which I knew.

I rushed through them, gouging and scratching myself on projecting branches. Henry's chant, somewhat weak but still persistent, followed me.

I could hear it, far off in the night, when I stumbled onto my porch and opened the door.

I sat up for hours drinking coffee and at last fell asleep in my chair. I was slumped there, red-eyed and unshaven, when someone knocked.

I got up with a start, noticing that sunlight was pouring through a nearby window, and opened the door.

Dave Baines looked at me keenly, both abashed and a bit amused. "Sorry I woke you up. I'll come back—"

I shook my head. "No, no! Sit down. You're the very person I want to see!"

He heard me out in silence. After he had polished his glasses for five minutes, he spoke.

"I'm not sure, but I'd be willing to venture the opinion that the figure you saw on that platform was what some folks call an 'astral projection.' Henry's still at the Miller place; I called this morning to find out. One of the field hands came in after midnight and saw him fast asleep—he never would have had time to come down here, rant on that crazy tower of his and walk back again. Henry, consciously or unconsciously, projected part of himself back here to the knoll. A kind of intense wish fulfillment, I guess. Chances are he doesn't even remember it this morning."

I shook my head in disbelief. "But what did I *hear?*"

Dave replaced his spectacles. "You heard his chanting all right, but not with your ears. You heard it inside your head, with your mind only. No reason telepathy, or projection, can't be audible as well as visual. It's all the result of a mind's—or a psyche's—fierce desire to be in another place. The desire is so strong that part of that person—call it 'ectoplasm' or what you will—actually does return."

"But what about the trees?" I interjected. "What made the wood and the hemlocks change? Why did I seem to be looking out over a great forest of tropical fern trees—or whatever they were?"

Dave got up, rather wearily. "That I can't explain, at least not now." He sighed. "I wish the whole business was over with. I just have a feelin' Henry's going to come a cropper."

Henry did "come a cropper" the very next night. Just before dusk, as we learned later, when the haying crews at Miller's were leaving the fields for supper, Henry, scorning both a meal and the pay due him, slipped over a fence and set out on the main road for Juniper Hill.

It was after eleven, and I was about to get ready for bed, when Henry's familiar chant, clear and strong, came to me on the night breeze.

I told myself that he had "projected" himself again and that only an ectoplasmic caricature of him was chanting on the willow platform.

But I could not convince myself that such was the case. His voice was too high-pitched and powerful. There was none of the weak, tentative quality of the night before.

I set out for the knoll with many misgivings. I suppose I felt a kind of obligation to see the business through. Perhaps a sense of responsibility moved me. In addition, I will admit to a degree of curiosity.

As I started through the hemlock woods, however, I experienced a feeling of acute apprehension. Henry's garbled chant, this night, was louder than I had ever heard it before. It flooded the wood. And I detected in his voice an edge of excitement bordering on hysteria.

I reached the knoll without incident and paused within the shadows cast by the surrounding hemlocks. Something seemed to warn me to keep well out of sight.

Henry, book in hand, stood on the willow platform, chanting rapidly in a shrill voice. His ring glowed more brightly than ever, bathing the book and his own face in an eerie blue light. There was a moderate wind; the tower swayed gently from side to side.

I studied the figure on the platform carefully; there was no doubt in my mind that it was Henry in the flesh. What I saw was not the projection, or apparition, of the previous night.

As he moved his head to read from the book, or to look out over the black expanse of the hemlock woods, I noticed that his expression mirrored intense agitation and expectancy.

His chant rose and fell in the night, and again I sensed a frightening transformation in the contour and general appearance of the surrounding forest. Massive trees which did not resemble hemlocks seemed to loom against the darkened sky.

Once again I felt that a vast unseen audience waited among these alien trees—and that Henry was aware of their presence.

His chant swiftly became an incoherent shriek. His eyes appeared to protrude from his head; his face became so contorted it was scarcely recognizable.

I quickly became convinced that while formerly he was chanting to invoke someone or something—he was suddenly chanting frantically in an attempt to forestall the advent of whatever he had been trying to conjure.

Too late. The thing came slowly prancing and gliding over the tops of the huge fern-like trees. It was black even against the darkness of the night sky, but it seemed to contain within itself a kind of lambent flame. An aura of cold blue fire flickered about it.

If it had a definite shape, that shape was not easily apparent, because it continually flowed in upon itself, contorting and writhing in a manner which I found intensely repellent.

In size, it was enormous. If you can imagine a team of six or eight black horses, somehow joined together and all attempting to gallop off in different directions at once, you might have some faint conception of the appalling thing's appearance.

Henry saw it. His shrill chanting ceased and his mouth fell open. He was frozen into immobility. His face became wooden. Only his eyes remained alive—two bulging points of blue light which glazed with ultimate horror even before the monstrous entity came over the knoll.

I wanted desperately to intervene, but I was nearly as terrified as poor Henry. And I sensed that, in any case, I would be completely helpless if I did attempt to interfere.

Deliberately and inexorably, the prancing nightmare made for the knoll. Once overhead, it paused. The blue fires which animated it intensified.

It descended slowly, straight for Henry. It seemed to tread on air, very carefully, as it came down above him. I could detect neither eyes nor mouth in the fearful creature, but I knew that it must be equipped with a sensory apparatus—quite probably superior to my own.

Its convulsions almost ceased as it dropped toward the willow platform. When it was within a few feet of that upward-staring white face, its legs—or whatever kind of appendages they were—snaked down and wrapped themselves tightly around the doomed man.

At last he was able to scream. His shriek of agony transfixed me. It was heard all over the township of Juniper Hill—and beyond. It would be useless for me to attempt to convey the torment and terror which that cry contained. I cannot. The writhing thing ascended slowly. As it rose, Henry almost disappeared within the hideous seething tangle of the creature. But as it glided off, away from the knoll, out over the tops of those enormous trees, that terrible shriek rang on and on.

The fearful intruder, flickering with fire, finally vanished in the night, its progress marked by a tiny bit of blue flame.

I have no recollection of how I groped my way out of the woods and reached home. When Dave Baines stopped in the next morning, I was still sitting in the chair, staring at the wall. He told me later that he feared I was in shock.

At length, however, I was able to relate the events I had witnessed just a few hours before.

Dave listened without comment, interrupting only once to tell me that Henry's final scream had awakened people all over the town.

I finished weakly, grateful for the flask of whiskey which Dave had produced.

He removed his glasses and polished them very carefully. "We'll never see Henry alive again—and maybe not dead either!"

I set down my glass. "But, Dave, what *was* it? I was sober and in my right mind—and yet my brain refuses to accept what it tells me I saw."

Dave helped himself to the whiskey. "Henry was tampering with malign forces, entities which probably existed when the earth was young. Nature, you know, was an experimenter with many life forms—and not all of those life forms were necessarily on the physical plane, or at least not as we know it. Some of them probably existed and passed away, and the tenuous elements of which they were composed left no traces—certainly nothing like heavy skulls and body bones which could survive physically for millions of years.

"I think Henry summoned up, as it were, an early form which we now vaguely refer to as an 'elemental.' In a sense, it still exists—but in another time, you might say another dimension. From what you've described, it was quite probably looked on as a god to be worshipped by earlier inhabitants of this planet. What those inhabitants were—or who they were—I can't say. Perhaps the present location of the knoll and the hemlock wood was the place of worship. And quite possibly those early worshippers offered up sacrifices to the thing which they venerated and feared."

Dave shook his head. "I don't know—it's speculation. But that's all that I can offer. I believe that old Hannibal Trobish was somehow involved in the business. I think both that Latin book and Henry's ring belonged to him. He may have invoked that damnable entity and survived. Probably he knew how to keep out of its clutches once it appeared. Poor Henry learned just enough Latin to chant those incantations and summon up the thing, but, obviously, he had no idea how to escape it, or dismiss it, once it was evoked.

"That ring *may* have been a protective talisman. But chances are the ring itself was of no help unless the intruder was placated or its powers nullified by various sacrifices and/or specific formulas. I imagine these formulas were contained somewhere in the book, but that Henry had not learned enough Latin to avail himself of them.

"The great fern-tree forest you thought you saw—well, I don't know. It may have been a sort of telepathic image projected from the past—possibly, even, from the organ which served that creature as a brain. Even if the thing existed in another plane or time continuum, Henry's chants undoubtedly enabled it to slip through—temporarily at least—to the present."

Old Dave got up and moved toward the door. "If you'd ever lived in the far north—as I did at one time—you'd know the legend of the wendigo. A lot of people today think it is sheer nonsense. But they haven't sat around a campfire at midnight and heard the best guide in Canada swear by all the saints that he had glimpsed such a thing! I don't say that Henry's nightmare, necessarily, was just that—but it appears to have been a related entity."

A week later, in a cornfield more than twenty miles from the northern edge of the township of Juniper Hill, a farmer found a bundle of bones which appeared to have passed through a blast furnace. The bones were burned to the marrow. The ghastly skeleton might have remained forever unidentifiable save for one thing—on the brittle finger bone of one hand a peculiar-looking ring was found. In spite of the condition of the skeleton, the ring was undamaged by the fire. The shining band was shaped out of a metal which resembled silver, fretted with tiny veins of blue which glowed faintly. The ring's stone was black, flat-cut and dull in luster.

The burned remains of Henry Crotell were borne back to Juniper Hill and buried. The ring was left on the finger bone.

A few weeks later, on orders of Dave Baines, the cellar hole of the old Trobish house was filled in and leveled off.

The willow tower went down under high winds during the

winter. In the spring, as improved highways were planned in Juniper Hill, a track was cut through the hemlock woods and the entire knoll which held the willow platform was bulldozed away in order to secure its stone and gravel for the new roadbeds.

The Latin book which led Henry to his doom was never located. I think it safe to assume that it was reduced to ashes by the same terrible fires which consumed him.

The Night of White Bhairab

by

Lucius Shepard

The exotic, richly textured story that follows takes place in Katmandu, the capital of Nepal and a city that author Lucius Shepard has lived in. As he says "In Katmandu everything is spirit. The place is about *religion. Spirits are everywhere. People get possessed by gods and demons; it's not out of the ordinary to see an incarnation of some god or another walking slackjawed down the street." It's a place where young girls are chosen to be worshiped as goddesses . . . a place where carved images of Shiva or Vishnu or Shakti can come alive.*

In Nepal, as in India, demons and gods seem to merge into one another, and can assume terrible shapes—that of various animals, or thousand-armed giants, or monsters with the heads and limbs of beasts. Nepal is a place of shifting shape-changers, a place where the face of the god Bhairab stares down into the festival-crowded streets of Durbar Square, and mischievous local spirits called kaa *flow and pool like dark shadows . . . .*

Lucius Shepard began publishing in 1983, and in a very short time has become one of the most popular and prolific new writers in science fiction. In 1985 Shepard won the John W. Campbell award as the year's Best New Writer, as well as being on the Nebula Award final ballot an unprecedented three times in three separate categories; he also showed up on the final Hugo ballot twice, as well as being a finalist for the British Fantasy Award, the John W. Campbell Memorial Award, the Philip K. Dick Award, and the World Fantasy Award. His short fiction has appeared in Playboy, Isaac Asimov's Science Fiction Magazine, The Magazine of Fantasy & Science Fiction, Universe, *and elsewhere.*

His acclaimed first novel, Green Eyes, *was an Ace Special. Upcoming is a new novel called* Life in Wartime, *and a collection,* The Jaguar Hunter.

* * *

WHENEVER MR. CHATTERJI WENT TO DELHI ON BUSINESS, twice yearly, he would leave Eliot Blackford in charge of his Katmandu home, and prior to each trip, the transfer of keys and instructions would be made at the Hotel Anapurna. Eliot—an angular, sharp-featured man in his mid-thirties, with thinning blond hair and a perpetually ardent expression—knew Mr. Chatterji for a subtle soul, and he suspected that this subtlety had dictated the choice of meeting place. The Anapurna was the Nepalese equivalent of a Hilton, its bar equipped in vinyl and plastic, with a choirlike arrangement of bottles fronting the mirror. Lights were muted, napkins monogrammed. Mr. Chatterji, plump and prosperous in a business suit, would consider it an elegant refutation of Kipling's famous couplet ("East is East," etc.) that he was at home here, whereas Eliot, wearing a scruffy robe and sandals, was not; he would argue that not only the twain met, they had actually exchanged places. It was Eliot's own measure of subtlety that restrained him from pointing out what Mr. Chatterji could not perceive: that the Anapurna was a skewed version of the American Dream. The carpeting was indoor-outdoor runner; the menu was rife with ludicrous misprints *(Skotch Miss, Screwdiver),* and the lounge act—two turbaned, tuxedoed Indians on electric guitar and traps—was managing to turn "Evergreen" into a doleful raga.

"There will be one important delivery." Mr. Chatterji hailed the waiter and nudged Eliot's shot glass forward. "It should have been here days ago, but you know these custom people." He gave an effeminate shudder to express his distaste for the bureaucracy, and cast an expectant eye on Eliot, who did not disappoint.

"What is it?" he asked, certain that it would be an addition to Mr. Chatterji's collection: he enjoyed discussing the collection with Americans; it proved that he had an overview of their culture.

"Something delicious!" said Mr. Chatterji. He took the tequila bottle from the waiter and—with a fond look—passed it to Eliot. "Are you familiar with the Carversville Terror?"

"Yeah, sure." Eliot knocked back another shot. "There was a book about it."

"Indeed," said Mr. Chatterji. "A best seller. The Cousineau mansion was once the most notorious haunted house of your New England. It was torn down several months ago, and I've succeeded in acquiring the fireplace, which"—he sipped his drink—"which was the locus of power. I'm very fortunate to have obtained it." He fitted his glass into the circle of moisture on the bar and waxed scholarly. "Aimée Cousineau was a most unusual spirit, capable of a variety of . . ."

Eliot concentrated on his tequila. These recitals never failed to annoy him, as did—for different reasons—the sleek Western disguise. When Eliot had arrived in Katmandu as a member of the Peace Corps, Mr. Chatterji had presented a far less pompous image: a scrawny kid dressed in Levi's that he had wheedled from a tourist. He'd been one of the hangers-on—mostly young Tibetans—who frequented the grubby tea rooms on Freak Street, watching the American hippies giggle over their hash yogurt, lusting after their clothes, their women, their entire culture. The hippies had respected the Tibetans: they were a people of legend, symbols of the occultism then in vogue, and the fact that they liked James Bond movies, fast cars, and Jimi Hendrix had increased the hippies' self-esteem. But they had found laughable the fact that Ranjeesh Chatterji—another Westernized Indian—had liked these same things, and they had treated him with mean condescension. Now, thirteen years later, the roles had been reversed; it was Eliot who had become the hanger-on.

He had settled in Katmandu after his tour was up, his idea being to practice meditation, to achieve enlightenment. But it had not gone well. There was an impediment in his mind—he pictured it as a dark stone, a stone compounded of worldly attachments—that no amount of practice could wear down, and his life had fallen into a futile pattern. He would spend ten months of the year living in a small room near the temple of Swayambhunath, meditating, rubbing away at the stone; and then, during March and September, he would occupy Mr. Chatterji's house and debauch himself with liquor and sex and drugs. He was aware that Mr. Chatterji considered him a burnout, that the position of caretaker was in effect a form of revenge, a means by which his employer could exercise his own brand of condescension; but Eliot minded neither the label nor the attitude. There were worse things to be than a burnout in Nepal. It was beautiful country, it was inexpensive, it was far from Minnesota (Eliot's home). And the concept of personal failure was meaningless here. You lived, died, and were reborn over and over until at last you attained the ultimate success of nonbeing: a terrific consolation for failure.

". . . yet in your country," Mr. Chatterji was saying, "evil has a sultry character. Sexy! It's as if the spirits were adopting vibrant personalities in order to contend with pop groups and movie stars."

Eliot thought of a comment, but the tequila backed up on him and he belched instead. Everything about Mr. Chatterji—teeth, eyes, hair, gold rings—seemed to be gleaming with extraordinary brilliance. He looked as unstable as a soap bubble, a fat little Hindu illusion.

Mr. Chatterji clapped a hand to his forehead. "I nearly forgot. There will be another American staying at the house. A girl. Very shapely!" He shaped an hourglass in the air. "I'm quite mad for her, but I don't know if she's trustworthy. Please see she doesn't bring in any strays."

"Right," said Eliot. "No problem."

"I believe I will gamble now," said Mr. Chatterji, standing and gazing toward the lobby. "Will you join me?"

"No, I think I'll get drunk. I guess I'll see you in October."

"You're drunk already, Eliot." Mr. Chatterji patted him on the shoulder. "Hadn't you noticed?"

Early the next morning, hung over, tongue cleaving to the roof of his mouth, Eliot sat himself down for a final bout of trying to visualize the Avalokitesvara Buddha. All the sounds outside—the buzzing of a motor scooter, birdsong, a girl's laughter—seemed to be repeating the mantra, and the gray stone walls of his room looked at once intensely real and yet incredibly fragile, papery, a painted backdrop he could rip with his hands. He began to feel the same fragility, as if he were being immersed in a liquid that was turning him opaque, filling him with clarity. A breath of wind could float him out the window, drift him across the fields, and he would pass through the trees and mountains, all the phantoms of the material world . . . but then a trickle of panic welled up from the bottom of his soul, from that dark stone. It was beginning to smolder, to give off poison fumes: a little briquette of anger and lust and fear. Cracks were spreading across the clear substance he had become, and if he didn't move soon, if he didn't break off the meditation, he would shatter.

He toppled out of the lotus position and lay propped on his elbows. His heart raced, his chest heaved, and he felt very much like screaming his frustration. Yeah, that was a temptation. To just say the hell with it and scream, to achieve through chaos what he could not through clarity: to empty himself into the scream. He was trembling, his emotions flowing between self-hate and self-pity. Finally, he struggled up and put on jeans and a cotton shirt. He knew he was close to a breakdown, and he realized that he usually reached this point just before taking up residence at Mr. Chatterji's. His life was a frayed thread stretched tight between those two poles of debauchery. One day it would snap.

"The hell with it," he said. He stuffed the remainder of his clothes into a duffel bag and headed into town.

Walking through Durbar Square—which wasn't really a square but a huge temple complex interspersed with open areas and wound through by cobbled paths—always put Eliot in mind of his brief stint as a tour guide, a career cut short when the agency received complaints about his eccentricity. (". . . As you pick your way among the piles of human waste and fruit rinds, I caution you not to breathe too deeply of the divine afflatus; otherwise, it may forever numb you to the scent of Prairie Cove or Petitpoint Gulch or whatever citadel of gracious living it is that you call home. . . .") It had irked him to have to lecture on the carvings and history of the square, especially to the just-plain-folks who only wanted a Polaroid of Edna or Uncle Jimmy standing next to that weird monkey god on the pedestal. The square was a unique place, and in Eliot's opinion, such unenlightened tourism demeaned it.

Pagoda-style temples of red brick and dark wood towered on all sides, their finials rising into brass lightning bolts. They were alien-looking—you half expected the sky above them to be of an otherworldly color, and figured by several moons. Their eaves and window screens were ornately carved into the images of gods and demons, and behind a large window screen on the temple of White Bhairab lay the mask of that god. It was almost ten feet high, brass, with a fanciful headdress and long-lobed ears and a mouth full of white fangs; its eyebrows were enameled red, fiercely arched, but the eyes had the goofy quality common to Newari gods—no matter how wrathful they were, there was something essentially friendly about them, and they reminded Eliot of cartoon germs. Once a year—in fact, a little more than a week from now—the screens would be opened, a pipe would be inserted into the god's mouth, and rice beer would jet out into the mouths of the milling crowds; at some point a fish would be slipped into the pipe, and whoever caught it would be deemed the luckiest soul in the Katmandu Valley for the next year. It was one of Eliot's traditions to make a try for the fish, though he knew that it wasn't luck he needed.

Beyond the square, the streets were narrow, running between long brick buildings three and four stories tall, each divided into dozens of separate dwellings. The strip of sky between the roofs was bright, burning blue—a void color—and in the shade the bricks looked purplish. People hung out the windows of the upper stories, talking back and forth: an exotic tenement life. Small shrines—wooden enclosures containing statuary of stucco or brass—were tucked into wall niches and the mouths of alleys. The gods were everywhere in Katmandu, and there was hardly a corner to which their gaze did not penetrate.

On reaching Mr. Chatterji's, which occupied half a block-long building, Eliot made for the first of the interior courtyards; a stair led up from it to Mr. Chatterji's apartment, and he thought he would check on what had been left to drink. But as he entered the courtyard—a phalanx of jungly plants arranged around a lozenge of cement—he saw the girl and stopped short. She was sitting in a lawn chair, reading, and she was indeed very shapely. She wore loose cotton trousers, a T-shirt, and a long white scarf shot through with golden threads. The scarf and the trousers were the uniform of the young travelers who generally stayed in the expatriate enclave of Temal: it seemed that they all bought them immediately upon arrival in order to identify themselves to each other. Edging closer, peering between the leaves of a rubber plant, Eliot saw that the girl was doe-eyed, with honey-colored skin and shoulder-length brown hair interwoven by lighter strands. Her wide mouth had relaxed into a glum expression. Sensing him, she glanced up, startled; then she waved and set down her book.

"I'm Eliot," he said, walking over.

"I know. Ranjeesh told me." She stared at him incuriously.

"And you?" He squatted beside her.

"Michaela." She fingered the book, as if she were eager to get back to it.

"I can see you're new in town."

"How's that?"

He told her about the clothes, and she shrugged. "That's what I am," she said. "I'll probably always wear them." She folded her hands on her stomach; it was a nicely rounded stomach, and Eliot—a connoisseur of women's stomachs—felt the beginnings of arousal.

"Always?" he said. "You plan on being here that long?"

"I don't know." She ran a finger along the spine of the book. "Ranjeesh asked me to marry him, and I said maybe."

Eliot's infant plan of seduction collapsed beneath this wrecking ball of a statement, and he failed to hide his incredulity. "You're in love with Ranjeesh?"

"What's that got to do with it?" A wrinkle creased her brow; it was the perfect symptom of her mood, the line a cartoonist might have chosen to express petulant anger.

"Nothing. Not if it doesn't have anything to do with it." He tried a grin, but to no effect. "Well," he said after a pause. "How do you like Katmandu?"

"I don't get out much," she said flatly.

She obviously did not want conversation, but Eliot wasn't ready to give up. "You ought to," he said. "The festival of Indra Jatra's about to start. It's pretty wild. Especially on the night of White Bhairab. Buffalo sacrifices, torchlight . . ."

"I don't like crowds," she said.

Strike two.

Eliot strained to think of an enticing topic, but he had the idea it was a lost cause. There was something inert about her, a veneer of listlessness redolent of Thorazine, of hospital routine. "Have you seen the Khaa?" he asked.

"The what?"

"The Khaa. It's a spirit . . . though some people will tell you it's partly animal, because over here the animal and spirit worlds overlap. But whatever it is, all the old houses have one, and those that don't are considered unlucky. There's one here."

"What's it look like?"

"Vaguely anthropomorphic. Black, featureless. Kind of a living shadow. They can stand upright, but they roll instead of walk."

She laughed. "No, I haven't seen it. Have you?"

"Maybe," said Eliot. "I thought I saw it a couple of times, but I was pretty stoned."

She sat up straighter and crossed her legs; her breasts jiggled and Eliot fought to keep his eyes centered on her face. "Ranjeesh tells me you're a little cracked," she said.

Good ol' Ranjeesh! He might have known that the son of a bitch would have sandbagged him with his new lady. "I guess I am," he said, preparing for the brush-off. "I do a lot of meditation, and sometimes I teeter on the edge."

But she appeared more intrigued by this admission than by

anything else he had told her; a smile melted up from her carefully composed features. "Tell me some more about the Khaa," she said.

Eliot congratulated himself. "They're quirky sorts," he said. "Neither good nor evil. They hide in dark corners, though now and then they're seen in the streets or in the fields out near Jyapu. And the oldest ones, the most powerful ones, live in the temples in Durbar Square. There's a story about the one here that's descriptive of how they operate . . . if you're interested."

"Sure." Another smile.

"Before Ranjeesh bought this place, it was a guesthouse, and one night a woman with three goiters on her neck came to spend the night. She had two loaves of bread that she was taking home to her family, and she stuck them under her pillow before going to sleep. Around midnight the Khaa rolled into her room and was struck by the sight of her goiters rising and falling as she breathed. He thought they'd make a beautiful necklace, so he took them and put them on his own neck. Then he spotted the loaves sticking out from her pillow. They looked good, so he took them as well and replaced them with two loaves of gold. When the woman woke, she was delighted. She hurried back to her village to tell her family, and on the way, she met a friend, a woman, who was going to market. This woman had four goiters. The first woman told her what had happened, and that night the second woman went to the guesthouse and did exactly the same things. Around midnight the Khaa rolled into her room. He'd grown bored with the necklace, and he gave it to the woman. He'd also decided that bread didn't taste very good, but he still had a loaf and he figured he'd give it another chance. So in exchange for the necklace, he took the woman's appetite for bread. When she woke, she had seven goiters, no gold, and she could never eat bread again the rest of her life."

Eliot had expected a response of mild amusement, and had hoped that the story would be the opening gambit in a game with a foregone and pleasurable conclusion; but he had not expected her to stand, to become walled off from him again.

"I've got to go," she said, and with a distracted wave, she made for the front door. She walked with her head down, hands thrust into her pockets, as if counting the steps.

"Where are you going?" called Eliot, taken back.

"I don't know. Freak Street, maybe."

"Want some company?"

She turned back at the door. "It's not your fault," she said, "but I don't really enjoy your company."

Shot down!

Trailing smoke, spinning, smacking into the hillside, and blowing up into a fireball.

Eliot didn't understand why it had hit him so hard. It had happened before, and it would again. Ordinarily he would have headed for Temal and found himself another long white scarf and pair of cotton trousers, one less morbidly self-involved (that, in retrospect, was how he characterized Michaela), one who would help him refuel for another bout of trying to visualize Avalokitesvara Buddha. He did, in fact, go to Temal; but he merely sat and drank tea and smoked hashish in a restaurant, and watched the young travelers pairing up for the night. Once he caught the bus to Patan and visited a friend, an old hippie pal named Sam Chipley who ran a medical clinic; once he walked out to Swayambhunath, close enough to see the white dome of the stupa, and atop it, the gilt structure on which the all-seeing eyes of Buddha were painted: they seemed squinty and mean-looking, as if taking unfavorable notice of his approach. But mostly over the next week he wandered through Mr. Chatterji's house, carrying a bottle, maintaining a buzz, and keeping an eye on Michaela.

The majority of the rooms were unfurnished, but many bore signs of recent habitation: broken hash pipes, ripped sleeping bags, empty packets of incense. Mr. Chatterji let travelers—those he fancied sexually, male and female—use the rooms for up to months at a time, and to walk through them was to take a historical tour of the American counterculture. The graffiti spoke of concerns as various as Vietnam, the Sex Pistols, women's lib, and the housing shortage in Great Britain, and also conveyed personal messages: "Ken Finkel please get in touch with me at Am. Ex. in Bangkok . . . love Ruth." In one of the rooms was a complicated mural depicting Farah Fawcett sitting on the lap of a Tibetan demon, throttling his barbed phallus with her fingers. It all conjured up the image of a moldering, deranged milieu. Eliot's milieu. At first the tour amused him, but eventually it began to sour him on himself, and he took to spending more and more time on a balcony overlooking the courtyard that was shared with the connecting house, listening to the Newari women sing at their chores and reading books from Mr. Chatterji's library. One of the books was titled *The Carversville Terror.*

". . . bloodcurdling, chilling . . ." said the *New York Times* on the front flap. ". . . the Terror is unrelenting. . . ." commented

Stephen King. ". . . riveting, gut-wrenching, mind-bending horror. . . ." gushed *People* magazine. In neat letters, Eliot appended his own blurb: ". . . piece of crap. . . ." The text—written to be read by the marginally literate—was a fictionalized treatment of purportedly real events, dealing with the experiences of the Whitcomb family, who had attempted to renovate the Cousineau mansion during the sixties. Following the usual build-up of apparitions, cold spots, and noisome odors, the family—Papa David, Mama Elaine, young sons Tim and Randy, and teenage Ginny—had met to discuss the situation.

. . . even the kids, thought David, had been aged by the house. Gathered around the dining room table, they looked like a company of the damned—haggard, shadows under their eyes, grim-faced. Even with the windows open and the light streaming in, it seemed there was a pall in the air that no light could dispel. Thank God the damned thing was dormant during the day!

"Well," he said, "I guess the floor's open for arguments."

"I wanna go home!" Tears sprang from Randy's eyes, and on cue, Tim started crying, too.

"It's not that simple," said David. "This *is* home, and I don't know how we'll make it if we do leave. The savings account is just about flat."

"I suppose I could get a job," said Elaine unethusiastically.

"I'm not leaving!" Ginny jumped to her feet, knocking over her chair. "Every time I start to make friends, we have to move!"

"But Ginny!" Elaine reached out a hand to calm her. "You were the one . . ."

"I've changed my mind!" She backed away, as if she had just recognized them all to be mortal enemies. "You can do what you want, but I'm staying!" And she ran from the room.

"Oh, God," said Elaine wearily. "What's gotten into her?"

What had gotten into Ginny, what was in the process of getting into her and was the only interesting part of the book, was the spirit of Aimée Cousineau. Concerned with his daughter's behavior, David Whitcomb had researched the house and learned a great deal about the spirit. Aimée Cousineau, née Vuillemont, had been a native of St. Berenice, a Swiss village at the foot of the mountain known as the Eiger (its photograph, as well as one of Aimée—a coldly beautiful woman with black hair and cameo features—was included in the central section of the book). Until the age of fifteen, she had been a sweet, unexceptional child;

however, in the summer of 1889, while hiking on the slopes of the Eiger, she had become lost in a cave.

The family had all but given up hope, when, to their delight—three weeks later—she had turned up on the steps of her father's store. Their delight was short-lived. This Aimée was far different from the one who had entered the cave. Violent, calculating, slatternly.

Over the next two years, she succeeded in seducing half the men of the village, including the local priest. According to his testimony, he had been admonishing her that sin was not the path to happiness, when she began to undress. "I'm wed to Happiness," she told him. "I've entwined my limbs with the God of Bliss and kissed the scaly thighs of Joy." Throughout the ensuing affair, she made cryptic comments concerning "the God below the mountain," whose soul was now forever joined to hers.

At this point the book reverted to the gruesome adventures of the Whitcomb family, and Eliot, bored, realizing it was noon and that Michaela would be sunbathing, climbed to Mr. Chatterji's apartment on the fourth floor. He tossed the book onto a shelf and went out onto the balcony. His continued interest in Michaela puzzled him. It occurred to him that he might be falling in love, and he thought that would be nice. Though it would probably lead nowhere, love would be a good kind of energy to have. But he doubted this was the case. Most likely his interest was founded on some fuming product of the dark stone inside him. Simple lust. He looked over the edge of the balcony. She was lying on a blanket—her bikini top beside her—at the bottom of a well of sunlight: thin, pure sunlight like a refinement of honey spreading down and congealing into the mold of a little gold woman. It seemed her heat that was in the air.

That night Eliot broke one of Mr. Chatterji's rules and slept in the master bedroom. It was roofed by a large skylight mounted in a ceiling painted midnight blue. The normal display of stars had not been sufficient for Mr. Chatterji, and so he'd had the skylight constructed of faceted glass that multiplied the stars, making it appear that you were at the heart of a galaxy, gazing out between the interstices of its blazing core. The walls consisted of a photomural of the Khumbu Glacier and Chomolungma; and, bathed in the starlight, the mural had acquired the illusion of depth and chill mountain silence. Lying there, Eliot could hear the faith sounds of Indra Jatra: shouts and cymbals, oboes and drums. He was drawn to the sounds; he wanted to run out into the streets, become an element of the drunken crowds, be whirled through torchlight and delirium to the feet of an idol stained with sacrificial blood. But he felt bound to the house, to Michaela. Marooned in the glow of Mr. Chatterji's starlight, floating above Chomolungma and listening to the din of the world below, he could almost believe he was a bodhisattva awaiting a call to action, that his watchfulness had some purpose.

The shipment arrived late in the afternoon of the eighth day. Five enormous crates, each requiring the combined energies of Eliot and three Newari workmen to wrangle up to the third-floor room that housed Mr. Chatterji's collection. After tipping the men, Eliot—sweaty, panting—sat down against the wall to catch his breath. The room was about twenty-five feet by fifteen, but looked smaller because of the dozens of curious objects standing around the floor and mounted one above the other on the walls. A brass doorknob, a shattered door, a straight-backed chair whose arms were bound with a velvet rope to prevent anyone from sitting, a discolored sink, a mirror streaked by a brown stain, a slashed lampshade. They were all relics of some haunting or possession, some grotesque violence, and there were cards affixed to them testifying to the details and referring those who were interested to materials in Mr. Chatterji's library. Sitting surrounded by these relics, the crates looked innocuous. Bolted shut, chest-high, branded with customs stamps.

When he had recovered, Eliot strolled around the room, amused by the care that Mr. Chatterji had squandered on his hobby; the most amusing thing was that no one except Mr. Chatterji was impressed by it: it provided travelers with a footnote for their journals. Nothing more.

A wave of dizziness swept over him—he had stood too soon—and he leaned against one of the crates for support. Jesus, he was in lousy shape! And then, as he blinked away the tangles of opaque cells drifting across his field of vision, the crate shifted. Just a little shift, as if something inside had twitched in its sleep. But palpable, real. He flung himself toward the door, backing away. A chill mapped every knob and articulation of his spine, and his sweat had evaporated, leaving clammy patches on his skin. The crate was motionless. But he was afraid to take his eyes off it, certain that if he did, it would release its pent-up fury.

"Hi," said Michaela from the doorway.

Her voice electrified Eliot. He let out a squawk and wheeled around, his hands outheld to ward off attack.

"I didn't mean to startle you," she said. "I'm sorry."

"Goddamn!" he said. "Don't sneak up like that!" He remembered the crate and glanced back at it. "Listen, I was just locking . . ."

"I'm sorry," she repeated, and walked past him into the room. "Ranjeesh is such an idiot about all this," she said, running her hand over the top of the crate. "Don't you think?"

Her familiarity with the crate eased Eliot's apprehension. Maybe he had been the one who had twitched: a spasm of over-strained muscles. "Yeah, I guess."

She walked over to the straightbacked chair, slipped off the velvet rope, and sat down. She was wearing a pale brown skirt and a plaid blouse that made her look schoolgirlish. "I want to apologize about the other day," she said; she bowed her head, and the fall of her hair swung forward to obscure her face. "I've been having a bad time lately. I have trouble relating to people. To anything. But since we're living here together, I'd like to be friends." She stood and spread the folds of her skirt. "See? I even put on different clothes. I could tell the others offended you."

The innocent sexuality of the pose caused Eliot to have a rush of desire. "Looks nice," he said with forced casualness. "Why've you been having a bad time?"

She wandered to the door and gazed out. "Do you really want to hear about it?"

"Not if it's painful for you."

"It doesn't matter," she said, leaning against the doorframe. "I was in a band back in the States, and we were doing O.K. Cutting an album, talking to record labels. I was living with the guitarist, in love with him. But then I had an affair. Not even an affair. It was stupid. Meaningless. I still don't know why I did it. The heat of the moment, I guess. That's what rock 'n' roll's all about, and maybe I was just acting out the myth. One of the other musicians told my boyfriend. That's the way bands are—you're friends with everyone, but at the same time. See, I told this guy about the affair. We'd always confided. But one day he got mad at me over something. Something else stupid and meaningless." Her chin was struggling to stay firm; the breeze from the courtyard drifted fine strands of hair across her face. "My boyfriend went crazy and beat up my . . ." She gave a dismal laugh. "I don't know what to call him. My lover. Whatever. My boyfriend killed him. It was an accident, but he tried to run, and the police shot him."

Eliot wanted to stop her; she was obviously seeing it all again, seeing blood and police flashers and cold white morgue lights. But she was riding a wave of memory, borne along by its energy, and he knew that she had to crest with it, crash with it.

"I was out of it for a while. Dreamy. Nothing touched me. Not the funerals, the angry parents. I went away for months, to the mountains, and I started to feel better. But when I came home, I found that the musician who'd told my boyfriend had written a song about it. The affair, the killings. He'd cut a record. People were buying it, singing the hook when they walked down the street or took a shower. Dancing to it! They were dancing on blood and bones, humming grief, shelling out $5.98 for a jingle about suffering. Looking back, I realize I was crazy, but at the time everything I did seemed normal. More than normal. Directed, inspired. I bought a gun. A ladies' model, the salesman said. I remember thinking how strange it was that there were male and female guns, just like with electric razors. I felt enormous carrying it. I had to be meek and polite or else I was sure people would notice how large and purposeful I was. It wasn't hard to track down Ronnie—that's the guy who wrote the song. He was in Germany, cutting a second album. I couldn't believe it, I wasn't going to be able to kill him! I was so frustrated that one night I went down to a park and started shooting. I missed everything. Out of all the bums and joggers and squirrels, I hit leaves and air. They locked me up after that. A hospital. I think it helped, but . . ." She blinked, waking from a trance. "But I still feel so disconnected, you know?"

Eliot carefully lifted away the strands of hair that had blown across her face and laid them back in place. Her smile flickered. "I know," he said. "I feel that way sometimes."

She nodded thoughtfully, as if to verify that she had recognized this quality in him.

They ate dinner in a Tibetan place in Temal; it had no name and was a dump with flyspecked tables and rickety chairs, specializing in water buffalo and barley soup. But it was away from the city center, which meant they could avoid the worst of the festival crowds. The waiter was a young Tibetan wearing jeans and a T-shirt that bore the legend *Magic Is The Answer*; the earphones of personal stereo dangled about his neck. The walls—visible through a haze of smoke—were covered with snapshots, most featuring the waiter in the company of various tourists, but a few showing an older Tibetan in blue robes and turquoise jewelry, carrying an automatic rifle; this was the owner, one of the Khampa tribesmen who had fought a guerrilla war against the Chinese. He rarely put in an appearance at the restaurant, and when he did, his glowering presence tended to dampen conversation.

Over dinner, Eliot tried to steer clear of topics that might unsettle Michaela. He told her about Sam Chipley's clinic, the time the Dalai Lama had come to Katmandu, the musicians at Swayambhunath. Cheerful, exotic topics. Her listlessness was such an inessential part of her that Eliot was led to chip away at it, curious to learn what lay beneath; and the more he chipped away, the more animated her gestures, the more luminous her smile became. This was a different sort of smile than she had displayed on their first meeting. It came so suddenly over her face, it seemed an autonomic reaction, like the opening of a sunflower, as if she were facing not you but the principle of light upon which you were grounded. It was aware of you, of course, but it chose to see past the imperfections of the flesh and know the perfected thing you truly were. It boosted your sense of worth to realize that you were its target, and Eliot—whose sense of worth was at low ebb—would have done pratfalls to sustain it. Even when he told his own story, he told it as a joke, a metaphor for American misconceptions of oriental pursuits.

"Why don't you quit it?" she asked. "The meditation, I mean. If it's not working out, why keep on with it?"

"My life's in perfect suspension," he said. "I'm afraid that if I quit practicing, if I change anything, I'll either sink to the bottom or fly off." He tapped his spoon against his cup, signaling for more tea. "You're not really going to marry Ranjeesh, are you?" he asked, and was surprised at the concern he felt that she actually might.

"Probably not." The waiter poured their tea, whispery drumbeats issuing from his earphones. "I was just feeling lost. You see, my parents sued Ronnie over the song, and I ended up with a lot of money—which made me feel even worse. . . ."

"Let's not talk about it," he said.

"It's all right." She touched his wrist, reassuring, and the skin remained warm after her fingers had withdrawn. "Anyway," she went on, "I decided to travel, and all the strangeness . . . I don't know. I was starting to slip away. Ranjeesh was a kind of sanctuary."

Eliot was vastly relieved.

Outside, the streets were thronged with festivalgoers, and Michaela took Eliot's arm and let him guide her through the crowds. Newar wearing Nehru hats and white trousers that bagged at the hips and wrapped tightly around the calves; groups of tourists, shouting and waving bottles of rice beer; Indians in white robes and saris. The air was spiced with incense, and the strip of empurpled sky above was so regularly patterned with stars that it looked like a banner draped between the roofs. Near the house, a wild-eyed man in a blue satin robe rushed past, bumping into them, and he was followed by two boys dragging a goat, its forehead smeared with crimson powder: a sacrifice.

"This is crazy!" Michaela laughed.

"It's nothing. Wait'll tomorrow night."

"What happens then?"

"The night of White Bhairab." Eliot put on a grimace. "You'll have to watch yourself. Bhairab's a lusty, wrathful sort."

She laughed again and gave his arm an affectionate squeeze.

Inside the house, the moon—past full, blank and golden—floated dead center of the square of night sky admitted by the roof. They stood close together in the courtyard, silent, suddenly awkward.

"I enjoyed tonight," said Michaela; she leaned forward and brushed his cheek with her lips. "Thank you," she whispered.

Eliot caught her as she drew back, tipped her chin and kissed her mouth. Her lips parted, her tongue darted out. Then she pushed him away. "I'm tired," she said, her face tightened with anxiety. She walked off a few steps, but stopped and turned back. "If you want to . . . to be with me, maybe it'll be all right. We could try."

Eliot went to her and took her hands. "I want to make love with you," he said, no longer trying to hide his urgency. And that *was* what he wanted: to make love. Not to ball or bang or screw or any other inelegant version of the act.

But it was not love they made.

Under the starlit blaze of Mr. Chatterji's ceiling, she was very beautiful, and at first she was very loving, moving with a genuine involvement; then abruptly, she quit moving altogether and turned her face to the pillow. Her eyes were glistening. Left alone atop her, listening to the animal sound of his breathing, the impact of his flesh against hers, Eliot knew he should stop and comfort her. But the months of abstinence, the eight days of wanting her, all this fused into a bright flare in the small of his back, a reactor core of lust that irradiated his conscience, and he continued to plunge into her, hurrying to completion. She let out a gasp when he withdrew, and curled up, facing away from him.

"God, I'm so sorry," she said, her voice cracked.

Eliot shut his eyes. He felt sickened, reduced to the bestial. It had been like two mental patients doing nasty on the sly, two fragments of people who together didn't form a whole. He understood now why Mr. Chatterji wanted to marry her: he planned to add her to his collection, to enshrine her with the other splinters of violence. And each night he would complete his revenge, substantiate his cultural overview, by making something less than love with this sad, inert girl, this American ghost. Her shoulders shook with muffled sobs. She needed someone to console her, to help her find her own strength and capacity for love. Eliot reached out to her, willing to do his best. But he knew it shouldn't be him.

Several hours later, after she had fallen asleep, unconsolable, Eliot sat in the courtyard, thoughtless, dejected, staring at a rubber plant. It was mired in shadow, its leaves hanging limp. He had been staring for a couple of minutes when he noticed that a shadow in back of the plant was swaying ever so slightly; he tried to make it out, and the swaying subsided. He stood. The chair scraped on the concrete, sounding unnaturally loud. His neck prickled, and he glanced behind him. Nothing. Ye Olde Mental Fatigue, he thought. Ye Olde Emotional Strain. He laughed, and the clarity of the laugh—echoing up through the empty well—alarmed him; it seemed to stir little flickers of motion everywhere in the darkness. What he needed was a drink! The problem was how to get into the bedroom without waking Michaela. Hell, maybe he should wake her. Maybe they should talk more before what had happened hardened into a set of unbreakable attitudes.

He turned toward the stairs . . . and then, yelling out in panic, entangling his feet with the lawn chairs as he leaped backward midstep, he fell onto his side. A shadow—roughly man-shaped and man-sized—was standing a yard away; it was undulating the way a strand of kelp undulates in a gentle tide. The patch of air around it was rippling, as if the entire image had been badly edited into reality. Eliot scrambled away, coming to his knees. The shadow melted downward, puddling on the cement; it bunched in the middle like a caterpillar, folded over itself, and flowed after him: a rolling sort of motion. Then it reared up, again assuming its manlike shape, looming over him.

Eliot got to his feet, still frightened, but less so. If he had previously been asked to testify as to the existence of the Khaa, he would have rejected the evidence of his bleared senses and come down on the side of hallucination, folktale. But now, though he was tempted to draw that same conclusion, there was too much evidence to the contrary. Staring at the featureless black cowl of the Khaa's head, he had a sense of something staring back. More than a sense. A distinct impression of personality. It was as if the Khaa's undulations were producing a breeze that bore its psychic odor through the air. Eliot began to picture it as a loony, shy old uncle who liked to sit under the basement steps and eat flies and cackle to himself, but who could tell when the first frost was due and knew how to fix the tail on your kite. Weird, yet harmless. The Khaa stretched out an arm: the arm just peeled away from its torso, its hand a thumbless black mitten. Eliot edged back. He wasn't quite prepared to believe it was harmless. But the arm stretched farther than he had thought possible and enveloped his wrist. It was soft, ticklish, a river of furry moths crawling over his skin.

In the instant before he jumped away, Eliot heard a whining note inside his skull, and that whining—seeming to flow through his brain with the same suppleness that the Khaa's arm had displayed—was translated into a wordless plea. From it he understood that the Khaa was afraid. Terribly afraid. Suddenly it melted downward and went rolling, bunching, flowing up the stairs; it stopped on the first landing, rolled halfway down, then up again, repeating the process over and over. It came clear to Eliot (*Oh, Jesus! This is nuts!*) that it was trying to convince him to follow. Just like Lassie or some other ridiculous TV animal, it was trying to tell him something, to lead him to where the wounded forest ranger had fallen, where the nest of baby ducks was being threatened by the brush fire. He should walk over, rumple its head, and say, "What's the matter, girl? Those squirrels been teasing you?" This time his laughter had a sobering effect, acting to settle his thoughts. One likelihood was that his experience with Michaela had been sufficient to snap his frayed connection with consensus reality; but there was no point in buying that. Even if that were the case, he might as well go with it. He crossed to the stairs and climbed toward the rippling shadow on the landing.

"O.K., Bongo," he said. "Let's see what's got you so excited."

On the third floor, the Khaa turned down a hallway, moving fast, and Eliot didn't see it again until he was approaching the room that housed Mr. Chatterji's collection. It was standing beside the door, flapping its arms, apparently indicating that he should enter. Eliot remembered the crate.

"No, thanks," he said. A drop of sweat slid down his rib cage, and he realized that it was unusually warm next to the door.

The Khaa's hand flowed over the doorknob, enveloping it, and when the hand pulled back, it was bulging, oddly deformed, and there was a hole through the wood where the lock mechanism had been. The door swung open a couple of inches. Darkness leaked out of the room, adding an oily essence to the air. Eliot took a backward step. The Khaa dropped the lock mechanism—it materialized from beneath the black, formless hand and clattered to the floor—and latched onto Eliot's arm. Once again he heard the whining, the plea for help, and since he did not jump away, he had a clearer understanding of the process of translation. He could feel the whining as a cold fluid coursing through his brain, and as the whining died, the message simply appeared—the way an image might appear in a crystal ball. There was an undertone of reassurance to the Khaa's fear, and though Eliot knew this was the mistake people in horror movies were always making, he reached inside the room and fumbled for the wall switch, half expecting to be snatched up and savaged. He flicked on the light and pushed the door open with his foot.

And wished that he hadn't.

The crates had exploded. Splinters and shards of wood were scattered everywhere, and the bricks had been heaped at the center of the room. They were dark red, friable bricks like crumbling cakes of dried blood, and each was marked with black letters and numbers that signified its original position in the fireplace. But none were in their proper position now, though they were quite artfully arranged. They had been piled into the shape of a mountain, one that—despite the crudity of its building blocks—duplicated the sheer faces and chimneys and gentle slopes of a real mountain. Eliot recognized it from its photograph. The Eiger. It towered to the ceiling, and under the glare of the lights, it gave off a radiation of ugliness and barbarity. It seemed alive, a fang of dark red meat, and the charred smell of the bricks was like a hum in Eliot's nostrils.

Ignoring the Khaa, who was again flapping its arms, Eliot broke for the landing; there he paused, and after a brief struggle between fear and conscience, he sprinted up the stairs to the bedroom, taking them three at a time. Michaela was gone! He stared at the starlit billows of the sheets. Where the hell . . . her room! He hurtled down the stairs and fell sprawling on the second-floor landing. Pain lanced through his kneecap, but he came to his feet running, certain that something was behind him.

A seam of reddish-orange light—not lamplight—edged the bottom of Michaela's door, and he heard a crispy, chuckling in a hearth. The wood was warm to the touch. Eliot's hand hovered over the doorknob. His heart seemed to have swelled to the size of a basketball and was doing a fancy dribble against his chest wall. The sensible thing to do would be to get out quick, because whatever lay beyond the door was bound to be too much for him to handle. But instead he did the stupid thing and burst into the room.

His first impression was that the room was burning, but then he saw that though the fire looked real, it did not spread; the flames clung to the outlines of things that were themselves unreal, that had no substance of their own and were made of the ghostly fire: belted drapes, an overstuffed chair and sofa, a carved mantelpiece, all of antique design. The actual furniture—production-line junk—was undamaged. Intense reddish-orange light glowed around the bed, and at its heart lay Michaela. Naked, her back arched. Lengths of her hair lifted into the air and tangled, floating in an invisible current; the muscles of her legs and abdomen were coiling, bunching, as if she were shedding her skin. The crackling grew louder, and the light began to rise from the bed, to form into a column of even brighter light; it narrowed at the midpoint, bulged in an approximation of hips and breasts, gradually assuming the shape of a burning woman. She was faceless, a fiery silhouette. Her flickering gown shifted as with the movements of walking, and flames leaped out behind her head like windblown hair.

Eliot was pumped full of terror, too afraid to scream or run. Her aura of heat and power wrapped around him. Though she was within arm's length, she seemed a long way off, inset into a great distance and walking toward him down a tunnel that conformed exactly to her shape. She stretched out a hand, brushing his cheek with a finger. The touch brought more pain than he had ever known. It was luminous, lighting every circuit of his body. He could feel his skin crisping, cracking, fluids leaking forth and sizzling. He heard himself moan: a gush of rotten sound like something trapped in a drain.

Then she jerked back her hand, as if *he* had burned *her*.

Dazed, his nerves screaming, Eliot slumped to the floor and—through blurred eyes—caught sight of a blackness rippling by the door. The Khaa. The burning woman stood facing it a few feet away. It was such an uncanny scene, this confrontation of fire and darkness, of two supernatural systems, that Eliot was shocked to alertness. He had the idea that neither of them knew what to do. Surrounded by its patch of disturbed air, the Khaa undulated; the burning woman crackled and flickered, embedded in her eerie distance. Tentatively, she lifted her hand; but before she could complete the gesture, the Khaa reached with blinding swiftness and its hand enveloped hers.

A shriek like tortured metal issued from them, as if some ironclad principle had been breached. Dark tendrils wound through the burning woman's arms, seams of fire striped the Khaa, and there was a high-pitched humming, a vibration that jarred Eliot's teeth. For a moment he was afraid that spiritual versions of antimatter and matter had been brought into conjunction, that the room would explode. But the hum was sheared off as the Khaa snatched back its hand: a scrap of reddish orange flame glimmered within it. The Khaa melted downward and went rolling out the door. The burning woman—and every bit of flame in the room—shrank to an incandescent point and vanished.

Still dazed, Eliot touched his face. It felt burned, but there was no apparent damage. He hauled himself to his feet, staggered to bed, and collapsed next to Michaela. She was breathing deeply, unconscious, "Michaela!" He shook her. She moaned, her head rolled from side to side. He heaved her over his shoulder in a fireman's lift and crept out into the hall. Moving stealthily, he eased along the hall to the balcony overlooking the courtyard and peered over the edge . . . and bit his lip to stifle a cry. Clearly visible in the electric blue air of the predawn darkness, standing in the middle of the courtyard, was a tall, pale woman wearing a white nightgown. Her black hair fanned across her back. She snapped her head around to stare at him, her cameo features twisted by a gloating smile, and that smile told Eliot everything he had wanted to know about the possibility of escape. Just try to leave, Aimée Cousineau was saying. Go ahead and try. I'd like that. A shadow sprang erect about a dozen feet away from her, and she turned to it. Suddenly there was a wind in the courtyard: a violent, whirling wind of which she was the calm center. Plants went flapping up into the well like leathery birds; pots shattered, and the shards flew toward the Khaa. Slowed by Michaela's weight, wanting to get as far as he could from the battle, Eliot headed up the stairs toward Mr. Chatterji's bedroom.

It was an hour later, an hour of peeking down into the courtyard, watching the game of hide-and-seek that the Khaa was playing with Aimée Cousineau, realizing that the Khaa was protecting them by keeping her busy . . . it was then that Eliot remembered the book. He retrieved it from the shelf and began to skim through it, hoping to learn something helpful. There was nothing else to do. He picked up at the point of Aimée's rap about her marriage to Happiness, passed over the transformation of Ginny Whitcomb into a teenage monster, and found a second section dealing with Aimée.

In 1895 a wealthy Swiss-American named Armand Cousineau had returned to St. Berenice—his birthplace—for a visit. He was smitten with Aimée Vuillemont, and her family, seizing the opportunity to be rid of her, allowed Cousineau to marry Aimée and sail her off to his home in Carversville, New Hampshire. Aimée's taste for seduction had not been curbed by the move. Lawyers, deacons, merchants, farmers: they were all grist for her mill. But in the winter of 1905, she fell in love—obsessively, passionately in love—with a young schoolmaster. She believed that the schoolmaster had saved her from her unholy marriage, and her gratitude knew no bounds. Unfortunately, when the schoolmaster fell in love with another woman, neither did her fury. One night while passing the Cousineau mansion, the town doctor spotted a woman walking the grounds. ". . . a woman of flame, not burning but composed of flame, her every particular a fiery construct . . ." Smoke was curling from a window; the doctor rushed inside and discovered the schoolmaster wrapped in chains, burning like a log in the vast fireplace. He put out the small blaze spreading from the hearth, and on going back onto the grounds, he stumbled over Aimée's charred corpse.

It was not clear whether Aimée's death had been accidental, a stray spark catching on her nightgown, or the result of suicide; but it *was* clear that thereafter the mansion had been haunted by a spirit who delighted in possessing women and driving them to kill their men.The spirit's supernatural powers were limited by the flesh, but were augmented by immense physical strength. Ginny Whitcomb, for example, had killed her brother Tim by twisting off his arm, and then had gone after her other brother and her father, a harrowing chase that had lasted a day and a night: while in possession of a body the spirit was not limited to nocturnal activity . . .

Christ!

The light coming through the skylight was gray.

They were safe!

Eliot went to the bed and began shaking Michaela. She

moaned, her eyes blinked open. "Wake up!" he said. "We've got to get out!"

"What?" She batted at his hands. "What are you talking about?"

"Don't you remember?"

"Remember what?" She swung her legs onto the floor, sitting with her head down, stunned by wakefulness; she stood, swayed, and said, "God, what did you do to me? I feel . . ." A dull, suspicious expression washed over her face.

"We have to leave," He walked around the bed to her. "Ranjeesh hit the jackpot. Those crates of his had an honest-to-God spirit packed in with the bricks. Last night it tried to possess you." He saw her disbelief. "You must have blanked out. Here." He offered the book. "This'll explain . . ."

"Oh, God!" she shouted. "What did you do? I'm all raw inside!" She backed away, eyes wide with fright.

"I didn't do anything." He held out his palms as if to prove he had no weapons.

"You raped me! While I was asleep!" She looked left, right, in a panic.

"That's ridiculous!"

"You must have drugged me or something! Oh, God! Go away!"

"I won't argue," he said. "We have to get out. After that you can turn me in for rape or whatever. But we're leaving, even if I have to drag you."

Some of her desperation evaporated, her shoulders sagged.

"Look," he said, moving closer. "I didn't rape you. What you're feeling is something that goddamn spirit did to you. It was . . ."

She brought her knee up into his groin.

As he writhed on the floor, curled up around the pain, Eliot heard the door open and her footsteps receding. He caught at the edge of the bed, hauled himself to his knees, and vomited all over the sheets. He fell back and lay there for several minutes, until the pain had dwindled to a powerful throbbing, a throbbing that jolted his heart into the same rhythm; then, gingerly, he stood and shuffled out into the hall. Leaning on the railing, he eased down the stairs to Michaela's room and lowered himself into a sitting position. He let out a shuddering sigh. Actinic flashes burst in front of his eyes.

"Michaela," he said. "Listen to me." His voice sounded feeble: the voice of an old, old man.

"I've got a knife," she said from just behind the door. "I'll use it if you try to break in."

"I wouldn't worry about that," he said. "And I sure as hell wouldn't worry about being raped. Now will you listen?"

No response.

He told her everything, and when he was done, she said, "You're insane. You raped me."

"I wouldn't hurt you. I . . ." He had been on the verge of telling her he loved her, but decided it probably wasn't true. He probably just wished that he had a good, clean, truth like love. The pain was making him nauseated again, as if the blackish, purple stain of his bruises were seeping up into his stomach and filling him with bad gases. He struggled to his feet and leaned against the wall. There was no point in arguing, and there was not much hope that she would leave the house on her own, not if she reacted to Aimée like Ginny Whitcomb. The only solution was to go to the police, accuse her of some crime. Assault. She would accuse him of rape, but with luck they would both be held overnight. And he would have time to wire Mr. Chatterji . . . who would believe him. Mr. Chatterji was by nature a believer; it simply hadn't fit his notion of sophistication to give credence to his native spirits. He'd be on the first flight from Delhi, eager to document the Terror.

Himself eager to get it over, Eliot negotiated the stairs and hobbled across the courtyard; but the Khaa was waiting, flapping its arms in the shadowed alcove that led to the street. Whether it was an effect of the light or of its battle with Aimée, or, specifically, of the pale scrap of fire visible within its hand, the Khaa looked less substantial. Its blackness was somewhat opaque, and the air around it was blurred, smeary, like waves over a lens; it was as if the Khaa were being submerged more deeply in its own medium. Eliot felt no compunction about allowing it to touch him; he was grateful to it, and his relaxed attitude seemed to intensify the communication. He began to see images in his mind's eye: Michaela's face, Aimée's, and then the two faces were superimposed. He was shown this over and over, and he understood from it that the Khaa wanted the possession to take place. But he didn't understand why. More images. Himself running, Michaela running. Durbar Square, the mask of White Bhairab, the Khaa. Lots of Khaa. Little black hieroglyphs. These images were repeated, too, and after each sequence the Khaa would hold its hand up to his face and display the glimmering scrap of Aimée's fire. Eliot thought he understood, but whenever he tried to convey that he wasn't sure, the Khaa merely repeated the images.

At last, realizing that the Khaa had reached the limits of its ability to communicate, Eliot headed for the street. The Khaa melted down, reared up in the doorway to block his path, and flapped its arms desperately. Once again Eliot had a sense of its weird-old-man-ness. It went against logic to put his trust in such an erratic creature, especially in such a dangerous plan; but logic had little hold on him, and this was a permanent solution. If it worked. If he hadn't misread it. He laughed. The hell with it!

"Take it easy, Bongo," he said. "I'll be back as soon as I get my shootin' iron fixed."

The waiting room of Sam Chipley's clinic was crowded with Newari mothers and children, who giggled as Eliot did a bow-legged shuffle through their midst. Sam's wife led him into the examination room, where Sam—a burly, bearded man, his long hair tied in a ponytail—helped him onto a surgical table.

"Holy shit!" he said after inspecting the injury. "What you been into, man?" He began rubbing ointment into the bruises.

"Accident," gritted Eliot, trying not to cry out.

"Yeah, I bet," said Sam. "Maybe a sexy little accident who had a change of heart when it come down to strokes. You know, not gettin' it steady might tend to make you a tad intense for some ladies, man. Ever think about that?"

"That's not how it was. Am I all right?"

"Yeah, but you ain't gonna be superstud for a while." Sam went to the sink and washed his hands. "Don't gimme that innocent bullshit. You were tryin' to slip it to Chatterji's new squeeze, right?"

"You know her?"

"He brought her over one day, showin' her off. She's a head case, man. You should know better."

"Will I be able to run?"

Sam laughed. "Not hardly."

"Listen, Sam." Eliot sat up, winced. "Chatterji's lady. She's in bad trouble, and I'm the only one who can help her. I have to be able to run, and I need something to keep me awake. I haven't slept for a couple of days."

"I ain't givin' you pills, Eliot. You can stagger through your doper phase without my help." Sam finished drying his hands and went to sit on a stool beside the window; beyond the window was a brick wall, and atop it a string of prayer flags snapped in the breeze.

"I'm not after a supply, damn it! Just enough to keep me going tonight. This is important, Sam!"

Sam scratched his neck. "What kind of trouble she in?"

"I can't tell you now," said Eliot, knowing that Sam would laugh at the idea of something as metaphysically suspect as the Khaa. "But I will tomorrow. It's not illegal. Come on, man! There's got to be something you can give me."

"Oh, I can fix you up. I can make you feel like King Shit on Coronation Day." Sam mulled it over. "O.K., Eliot. But you get your ass back here tomorrow and tell me what's happenin'." He gave a snort of amusement. "All I can say is it must be some strange damn trouble for you to be the only one who can save her."

After wiring Mr. Chatterji, urging him to come home at once, Eliot returned to the house and unscrewed the hinges of the front door. He was not certain that Aimée would be able to control the house, to slam doors and make windows stick as she had with her house in New Hampshire, but he didn't want to take any chances. As he lifted the door and set it against the wall of the alcove, he was amazed by its lightness; he felt possessed of a giddy strength, capable of heaving the door up through the well of the courtyard and over the roofs. The cocktail of painkillers and speed was working wonders. His groin ached, but the ache was distant, far removed from the center of his consciousness, which was a fount of well-being. When he had finished with the door, he grabbed some fruit juice from the kitchen and went back to the alcove to wait.

In midafternoon Michaela came downstairs. Eliot tried to talk to her, to convince her to leave, but she warned him to keep away and scuttled back to her room. Then, around five o'clock, the burning woman appeared, floating a few feet above the courtyard floor. The sun had withdrawn to the upper third of the well, and her fiery silhouette was inset into slate-blue shadow, the flames of her hair dancing about her head. Eliot, who had been hitting the painkillers heavily, was dazzled by her: had she been a hallucination, she would have made his All-Time Top Ten. But even realizing that she was not, he was too drugged to relate to her as a threat. He snickered and shied a piece of broken pot at her. She shrank to an incandescent point, vanished, and that brought home to him his foolhardiness. He took more speed to counteract his euphoria, and did stretching exercises to loosen the kinks and to rid himself of the cramped sensation in his chest.

Twilight blended the shadows in the courtyard, celebrants passed in the street, and he could hear distant drums and cymbals. He felt cut off from the city, the festival. Afraid. Not even the presence of the Khaa, half merged with the shadows along the wall, served to comfort him. Near dusk, Aimée Cousineau walked into the courtyard and stopped about twenty feet away, staring at him. He had no desire to laugh or throw things. At this distance he could see that her eyes had no whites or pupils or irises. They were dead black. One moment they seemed to be the bulging head of black screws threaded into her skull; the next they seemed to recede into blackness, into a cave beneath a mountain where something waited to teach the joys of hell to whoever wandered in. Eliot sidled closer to the door. But she turned, climbed the stairs to the second landing, and walked down Michaela's hallway.

Eliot's waiting began in earnest.

An hour passed. He paced between the door and the courtyard. His mouth was cottony; his joints felt brittle, held together by frail wires of speed and adrenaline. This was insane! All he had done was to put them in worse danger. Finally, he heard a door close upstairs. He backed into the street, bumping into two Newari girls who giggled and skipped away. Crowds of people were moving toward Durbar Square.

"Eliot!"

Michaela's voice. He'd expected a hoarse, demon voice, and when she walked into the alcove, her white scarf glowing palely against the dark air, he was surprised to see that she was unchanged. Her features held no trace of anything other than her usual listlessness.

"I'm sorry I hurt you," she said, walking toward him. "I know you didn't do anything. I was just upset about last night."

Eliot continued to back away.

"What's wrong?" She stopped in the doorway.

It might have been his imagination, the drugs, but Eliot could have sworn that her eyes were much darker than normal. He trotted off a dozen yards or so and stood looking at her.

"Eliot!"

It was a scream of rage and frustration, and he could scarcely believe the speed with which she darted toward him. He ran full tilt at first, leaping sideways to avoid collisions, veering past alarmed, dark-skinned faces; but after a couple of blocks, he found a more efficient rhythm and began to anticipate obstacles, to glide in and out of the crowd. Angry shouts were raised behind him. He glanced back. Michaela was closing the distance, beelining for him, knocking people sprawling with what seemed effortless blows. He ran harder. The crowd grew thicker, and he kept near the walls of the houses, where it was thinnest; but even there it was hard to maintain a good pace. Torches were waved in his face; young men—singing, their arms linked—posed barriers that slowed him further. He could no longer see Michaela, but he could see the wake of her passage. Fists shaking, heads jerking. The entire scene was starting to lose cohesiveness to Eliot. There were screams of torchlight, bright shards of deranged shouts, jostling waves of incense and ordure. He felt like the only solid chunk in a glittering soup that was being poured through a stone trough.

At the edge of Durbar Square, he had a brief glimpse of a shadow standing by the massive gilt doors of Degutale Temple. It was larger and a more anthracitic black than Mr. Chatterji's Khaa: one of the old ones, the powerful ones. The sight buoyed his confidence and restored his equilibrium. He had not misread the plan. But he knew that this was the most dangerous part. He had lost track of Michaela, and the crowd was sweeping him along; if she caught up to him now, he would not be able to run. Fighting for elbow room, struggling to keep his feet, he was borne into the temple complex. The pagoda roofs sloped up into darkness like strangely carved mountains, their peaks hidden by a moonless night; the cobbled paths were narrow, barely ten feet across, and the crowd was being squeezed along them, a lava flow of humanity. Torches bobbed everywhere, sending wild licks up the walls, revealing scowling faces on the eaves. Atop its pedestal, the gilt statue of Hanuman—the monkey god—looked to be swaying. Clashing cymbals and arrhythmic drumming scattered Eliot's heartbeat; the sinewy wail of oboes seemed to be graphing the fluctuations of his nerves.

As he swept past Hanuman Dhoka Temple, he caught sight of the brass mask of White Bhairab shining over the heads of the crowd like the face of an evil clown. It was less than a hundred feet away, set in a huge niche in a temple wall and illuminated by light bulbs that hung down among strings of prayer flags. The crowd surged faster, knocking him this way and that; but he managed to spot two more Khaa in the doorway of Hanuman Dhoka. Both melted downward, vanishing, and Eliot's hopes soared. They must have located Michaela, they must be attacking! By the time he had been carried to within a few yards of the mask, he was sure that he was safe. They must have finished her exorcism by now. The only problem left was to find her. That, he realized, had been the weak link in the plan. He'd been an idiot not to have foreseen it. Who knows what might happen if she were to fall in the midst of the crowd. Suddenly he was beneath the pipe that stuck out of the god's mouth; the stream of rice beer arching from it looked translucent under the lights, and as it splashed his face (no fish), its coldness acted to wash away his veneer of chemical strength. He was dizzy, his groin throbbed. The great face, with its fierce fangs and goofy, startled eyes, appeared to be swelling and rocking back and forth. He took a deep breath. The thing to do would be to find a place next to a wall where he could wedge himself against the flow of the crowd, wait until it had thinned, and then search for her. He was about to do that very thing when two powerful hands gripped his elbows from behind.

Unable to turn, he craned his neck and peered over his shoulder. Michaela smiled at him: a gloating "got-cha!" smile. Her eyes were dead-black ovals. She shaped his name with her mouth, her voice inaudible above the music and shouting, and she began to push him ahead of her, using him as a battering ram to forge a path through the crowd. To anyone watching, it might have appeared that he was running interference for her, but his feet were dangling just off the ground. Angry Newar yelled at him as he knocked them aside. He yelled, too. No one noticed. Within seconds they had got clear into a side street, threading between groups of drunkards. People laughed at Eliot's cries for help, and one guy imitated the funny loose-limbed way he was running.

Michaela turned into a doorway, carrying him down a dirt-floored corridor whose walls were carved into ornate screens; the dusky orange lamplight shining through the screens cast a lacework of shadow on the dirt. The corridor widened to a small courtyard, the age-darkened wood of its walls and doors inlaid with intricate mosaics of ivory. Michaela stopped and slammed him against a wall. He was stunned, but he recognized the place to be one of the old Buddhist temples that surrounded the square. Except for a life-sized statue of a golden cow, the courtyard was empty.

"Eliot." The way she said it, it was more of a curse than a name.

He opened his mouth to scream, but she drew him into an embrace; her grip on his right elbow tightened, and her other hand squeezed the back of his neck, pinching off the scream.

"Don't be afraid," she said. "I only want to kiss you."

Her breasts crushed into his chest, her pelvis ground against him in a mockery of passion, and inch by inch she forced his face down to hers. Her lips parted, and—*oh, Christ Jesus!*—Eliot writhed in her grasp, enlivened by a new horror. The inside of her mouth was as black as her eyes. She wanted him to kiss that blackness, the same she had kissed beneath the Eiger. He kicked and clawed with his free hand, but she was irresistible, her hands like iron. His elbow cracked, and brilliant pain shot through his arm. Something else was cracking in his neck. Yet none of that compared to what he felt as her tongue—a burning black poker—pushed between his lips. His chest was bursting with the need to scream, and everything was going dark. Thinking this was death, he experienced a peevish resentment that death was not—as he'd been led to believe—an end to pain, that it merely added a tickling sensation to all his other pain. Then the searing heat in his mouth diminished, and he thought that death must just have been a bit slower than usual.

Several seconds passed before he realized that he was lying on the ground, several more before he noticed Michaela lying beside him, and—because darkness was tattering the edges of his vision—it was considerably longer before he distinguished the six undulating darknesses that had ringed Aimée Cousineau. They towered over her; their blackness gleamed like thick fur, and the air around them was awash with vibration. In her fluted white nightgown, her cameo face composed in an expression of calm, Aimée looked the antithesis of the vaguely male giants that were menacing her, delicate and finely worked in contrast to their crudity. Her eyes appeared to mirror their negative color. After a moment, a little wind kicked up, swirling about her. The undulations of the Khaa increased, becoming rhythmic, the movements of boneless dancers, and the wind subsided. Puzzled, she darted between two of them and took a defensive stance next to the golden cow; she lowered her head and stared up through her brows at the Khaa. They melted downward, rolled forward, sprang erect and hemmed her in against the statue. But the stare was doing its damage. Pieces of ivory and wood were splintering, flying off the walls toward the Khaa, and one of them was fading, a mist of black particles accumulating around its body; then, with a shrill noise that reminded Eliot of a jet passing overhead, it misted away.

Five Khaa remained in the courtyard. Aimée smiled and turned her stare on another. Before the stare could take effect, however, the Khaa moved close, blocking Eliot's view of her; and when they pulled back, it was Aimée who showed signs of damage. Rills of blackness were leading from her eyes, webbing her cheeks, making it look as if her face were cracking. Her night-gown caught fire, her hair began to leap. Flames danced on her fingertips, spread to her arms, her breast, and she assumed the form of the burning woman.

As soon as the transformation was complete, she tried to shrink, to dwindle to her vanishing point; but acting in unison, the Khaa extended their hands and touched her. There was that shriek of tortured metal, lapsing to a high-pitched hum, and to Eliot's amazement, the Khaa were sucked inside her. It was a rapid process. The Khaa faded to a haze, to nothing, and veins of black marbled the burning woman's fire; the blackness coalesced, forming into five tiny stick figures, a hieroglyphic design patterning her gown. With a fuming sound, she expanded again, regaining her normal dimensions, and the Khaa flowed back out, surrounding her. For an instant she stood motionless, dwarfed: a schoolgirl helpless amidst a circle of bullies. Then she clawed at the nearest of them. Though she had no features with which to express emotion, it seemed to Eliot there was desperation in gesture, in the agitated leaping of her fiery hair. Unperturbed, the Khaa stretched out their enormous mitten hands, hands that spread like oil and enveloped her.

The destruction of the burning woman, of Aimée Cousineau, lasted only a matter of seconds; but to Eliot it occurred within a bubble of slow time, a time during which he achieved a speculative distance. He wondered if—as the Khaa stole portions of her fire and secreted it within their bodies—they were removing disparate elements of her soul, if she consisted of psychologically distinct fragments: the girl who had wandered into the cave, the girl who had returned from it, the betrayed lover. Did she embody gradations of innocence and sinfulness, or was she a contaminated essence, an unfractionated evil? While still involved in this speculation—half a reaction to pain, half to the metallic shriek of her losing battle—he lost consciousness, and when he reopened his eyes, the courtyard was deserted. He could hear music and shouting from Durbar Square. The golden cow stared contentedly into nowhere.

He had the idea that if he moved, he would further break all the broken things inside him; but he inched his left hand across the dirt and rested it on Michaela's breast. It was rising and falling with a steady rhythm. That made him happy, and he kept his hand there, exulting in the hits of her life against his palm. Something shadowy above him. He strained to see it. One of the Khaa . . . No! It was Mr. Chatterji's Khaa. Opaquely black, scrap of fire glimmering in its hand. Compared to its big brothers, it had the look of a skinny, sorry mutt. Eliot felt camaraderie toward it.

"Hey, Bongo," he said weakly. "We won."

A tickling at the top of his head, a whining note, and he had an impression not of gratitude—as he might have expected—but of intense curiosity. The tickling stopped, and Eliot suddenly felt clear in his mind. Strange. He was passing out once again, his consciousness whirling, darkening, and yet he was calm and unafraid. A roar came from the direction of the square. Somebody—the luckiest somebody in the Katmandu Valley—had caught the fish. But as Eliot's eyelids fluttered shut, as he had a last glimpse of the Khaa looming above them and felt the warm measure of Michaela's heartbeat, he thought maybe that the crowd was cheering the wrong man.

Three weeks after the night of White Bhairab, Ranjeesh Chatterji divested himself of all worldly possessions (including the gift of a year's free rent at his house to Eliot) and took up residence at Swayambhunath, where—according to Sam Chipley, who visited Eliot in the hospital—he was attempting to visualize the Avalokitesvara Buddha. It was then that Eliot understood the nature of his newfound clarity. Just as it had done long ago with the woman's goiters, the Khaa had tried his habituation to meditation on for size, had not cared for it, and had sloughed it off in a handy repository: Ranjeesh Chatterji.

It was such a delicious irony that Eliot had to restrain himself from telling Michaela when she visited that same afternoon; she had no memory of the Khaa, and news of it tended to unsettle her. But otherwise she had been healing right along with Eliot. All her listlessness had eroded over the weeks, her capacity for love was returning and was focused solely on Eliot. "I guess I needed someone to show me that I was worth an effort," she told him. "I'll never stop trying to repay you." She kissed him. "I can hardly wait till you come home." She brought him books and candy and flowers; she sat with him each day until the nurses shooed her away. Yet being the center of her devotion disturbed him. He was still uncertain whether or not he loved her. Clarity, it seemed, made a man dangerously versatile, his conscience flexible, and instituted a cautious approach to commitment. At least this was the substance of Eliot's clarity. He didn't want to rush into anything.

When at last he did come home, he and Michaela made love beneath the starlight glory of Mr. Chatterji's skylight. Because of Eliot's neck brace and cast, they had to manage the act with extreme care, but despite that, despite the ambivalence of his feelings, this time it *was* love they made. Afterward, lying with his good arm around her, he edged nearer to commitment. Whether or not he loved her, there was no way this part of things could be improved by any increment of emotion. Maybe he'd give it a try with her. If it didn't work out, well, he was not going to be responsible for her mental health. She would have to learn to live without him.

"Happy?" he asked, caressing her shoulder.

She nodded and cuddled closer and whispered something that was partially drowned out by the crinkling of the pillow. He was sure he had misheard her, but the mere thought that he hadn't was enough to lodge a nugget of chill between his shoulder blades.

"What did you say?" he asked.

She turned to him and propped herself on an elbow, silhouetted by the starlight, her features obscured. But when she spoke, he realized that Mr. Chatterji's Khaa had been true to its erratic traditions on the night of White Bhairab; and he knew that if she were to tip back her head ever so slightly and let the light shine into her eyes, he would be able to resolve all his speculations about the composition of Aimée Cousineau's soul.

"I'm wed to Happiness," she said.

The Mangler

by

Stephen King

In the Middle Ages the ancient custom of naming inanimate objects reached its peak. Medieval people had proper names for their houses, jewels, swords, ships, bells, and war machines, as if these objects were imbued with their own special life. Some of this has trickled down to our own "modern" times. We still have names for particularly precious (and cursed) jewels such as the Hope Diamond. During World War Two we had a name for our big guns, and we still name our ships, and even small boats. We even name our hurricanes.

Perhaps some ancient instinct tells us that anything "created" is in some sense alive. Perhaps we name the things around us to help us maintain the illusion that we can control *them. Or perhaps it is the primitive understanding that the spiritual—the sublime or the demonic—can adhere in* anything. *The demons that modern, enlightened psychology has supposedly exorcised might be* real. *Even now they might be taking up residence in our cars, our houses . . . or our factories.*

And even the most neutral of objects might be suddenly turned into a thing as sinister and malignant as the mangler. . . .

It hardly seems necessary to introduce Stephen King, since he is one of the most famous writers alive and one of the best-selling authors of all time. King is without doubt the foremost contemporary practitioner of the modern horror story, a subgenre that he is almost single-handedly responsible for bringing to a widespread public in the 1970's. He has dominated the best-seller lists for almost a decade with books such as Salem's Lot, The Shining, The Stand, Firestarter, Christine, The Dead Zone, *and* Cujo, *most of which have been made into films as well. Recently, he was revealed as the author of the "Richard Bachman" thrillers, and they promptly topped the best-seller lists as well. His most recent books are* Pet Semetary, *a novel, and* Skeleton Crew, *a collection.*

* * *

OFFICER HUNTON GOT TO THE LAUNDRY JUST AS THE AMBULANCE was leaving—slowly, with no siren or flashing lights. Ominous. Inside, the office was stuffed with milling, silent people, some of them weeping. The plant itself was empty; the big automatic washers at the far end had not even been shut down. It made Hunton very wary. The crowd should be at the scene of the accident, not in the office. It was the way things worked—the human animal had a built-in urge to view the remains. A very bad one, then. Hunton felt his stomach tighten as it always did when the accident was very bad. Fourteen years of cleaning human litter from highways and streets and the sidewalks at the bases of very tall buildings had not been able to erase that little hitch in the belly, as if something evil had clotted there.

A man in a white shirt saw Hunton and walked toward him reluctantly. He was a buffalo of a man with head thrust forward between shoulders, nose and cheeks vein-broken either from high blood pressure or too many conversations with the brown bottle. He was trying to frame words, but after two tries Hunton cut him off briskly:

"Are you the owner? Mr. Gartley?"

"No . . . no. I'm Stanner. The foreman. God, this—"

Hunton got out his notebook. "Please show me the scene of the accident, Mr. Stanner, and tell me what happened."

Stanner seemed to grow even more white; the blotches on his nose and cheeks stood out like birthmarks. "D-do I have to?"

Hunton raised his eyebrows. "I'm afraid you do. The call I got said it was serious."

"Serious—" Stanner seemed to be battling with his gorge; for a moment his Adam's apple went up and down like a monkey on a stick. "Mrs. Frawley is dead. Jesus, I wish Bill Gartley *was* here."

"What happened?"

Stanner said, "You better come over here."

He led Hunton past a row of hand presses, a shirt-folding unit, and then stopped by a laundry-marking machine. He passed a shaky hand across his forehead. "You'll have to go over by yourself, Officer. I can't look at it again. It makes me . . . I can't. I'm sorry."

Hunton walked around the marking machine with a mild feeling of contempt for the man. They run a loose shop, cut corners, run live steam through home-welded pipes, they work with dangerous cleaning chemicals without the proper protection, and finally, someone gets hurt. Or gets dead. Then they can't look. They can't—

Hunton saw it.

The machine was still running. No one had shut it off. The machine he later came to know intimately: the Hadley-Watson Model-6 Speed Ironer and Folder. A long and clumsy name. The people who worked here in the steam and the wet had a better name for it. The mangler.

Hunton took a long, frozen look, and then he performed a first in his fourteen years as a law-enforcement officer: he turned around, put a convulsive hand to his mouth, and threw up.

"You didn't eat much," Jackson said.

The women were inside, doing dishes and talking babies while John Hunton and Mark Jackson sat in lawn chairs near the aromatic barbecue. Hunton smiled slightly at the understatement. He had eaten nothing.

"There was a bad one today," he said. "The worst."

"Car crash?"

"No. Industrial."

"Messy?"

Hunton did not reply immediately, but his face made an involuntary, writhing grimace. He got a beer out of the cooler between them, opened it, and emptied half of it. "I suppose you college profs don't know anything about industrial laundries?"

Jackson chuckled. "This one does. I spent a summer working in one as an undergraduate."

"Then you know the machine they call the speed ironer?"

Jackson nodded. "Sure. They run damp flatwork through them, mostly sheets and linen. A big, long machine."

"That's it," Hunton said. "A woman named Adelle Frawley got caught in it at the Blue Ribbon Laundry crosstown. It sucked her right in."

Jackson looked suddenly ill. "But . . . that can't happen, Johnny. There's a safety bar. If one of the women feeding the machine accidentally gets a hand under it, the bar snaps up and stops the machine. At least that's how I remember it."

Hunton nodded. "It's a state law. But it happened."

Hunton closed his eyes and in the darkness he could see the

Hadley-Watson speed ironer again, as it had been that afternoon. It formed a long, rectangular box in shape, thirty feet by six. At the feeder end, a moving canvas belt moved under the safety bar, up at a slight angle, and then down. The belt carried the damp-dried, wrinkled sheets in continuous cycle over and under sixteen huge revolving cylinders that made up the main body of the machine. Over eight and under eight, pressed between them like thin ham between layers of superheated bread. Steam heat in the cylinders could be adjusted up to 300 degrees for maximum drying. The pressure on the sheets that rode the moving canvas belt was set at 800 pounds per square foot to get out every wrinkle.

And Mrs. Frawley, somehow, had been caught and dragged in. The steel, asbestos-jacketed pressing cylinders had been as red as barn paint, and the rising steam from the machine had carried the sickening stench of hot blood. Bits of her white blouse and blue slacks, even ripped segments of her bra and panties, had been torn free and ejected from the machine's far end thirty feet down, the bigger sections of cloth folded with grotesque and blood-stained neatness by the automatic folder. But not even that was the worst.

"It tried to fold everything," he said to Jackson, tasting bile in his throat. "But a person isn't a sheet, Mark. What I saw . . . what was left of her . . ." Like Stanner, the hapless foreman, he could not finish. "They took her out in a basket," he said softly.

Jackson whistled. "Who's going to get it in the neck? The laundry or the state inspectors?"

"Don't know yet," Hunton said. The malign image still hung behind his eyes, the image of the mangler wheezing and thumping and hissing, blood dripping down the green sides of the long cabinet in runnels, the burning *stink* of her . . . "It depends on who okayed that goddamn safety bar and under what circumstances."

"If it's the management, can they wiggle out of it?"

Hunton smiled without humor. "The woman died, Mark. If Gartley and Stanner were cutting corners on the speed ironer's maintenance, they'll go to jail. No matter who they know on the City Council."

"Do you think they were cutting corners?"

Hunton thought of the Blue Ribbon Laundry, badly lighted, floors wet and slippery, some of the machines incredibly ancient and creaking. "I think it's likely," he said quietly.

They got up to go in the house together. "Tell me how it comes out, Johnny," Jackson said. "I'm interested."

* * *

Hunton was wrong about the mangler; it was clean as a whistle. Six state inspectors went over it before the inquest, piece by piece. The net result was absolutely nothing. The inquest verdict was death by misadventure.

Hunton, dumbfounded, cornered Roger Martin, one of the inspectors, after the hearing. Martin was a tall drink of water with glasses as thick as the bottoms of shot glasses. He fidgeted with a ball-point pen under Hunton's questions.

"Nothing? Absolutely nothing doing with the machine?"

"Nothing," Martin said. "Of course, the safety bar was the guts of the matter. It's in perfect working order. You heard that Mrs. Gillian testify. Mrs. Frawley must have pushed her hand too far. No one saw that; they were watching their own work. She started screaming. Her hand was gone already, and the machine was taking her arm. They tried to pull her out instead of shutting it down—pure panic. Another woman, Mrs. Keene, said she *did* try to shut it off, but it's a fair assumption that she hit the start button rather the stop in the confusion. By then it was too late."

"Then the safety bar malfunctioned," Hunton said flatly. "Unless she put her hand over it rather than under?"

"You can't. There's a stainless-steel facing above the safety bar. And the bar itself didn't malfunction. It's circuited into the machine itself. If the safety bar goes on the blink, the machine shuts down."

"Then how did it happen, for Christ's sake?"

"We don't know. My colleagues and I are of the opinion that the only way the speed ironer could have killed Mrs. Frawley was for her to have fallen into it from above. And she had both feet on the floor when it happened. A dozen witnesses can testify to that."

"You're describing an impossible accident," Hunton said.

"No. Only one we don't understand." He paused, hesitated, and then said: "I will tell you one thing, Hunton, since you seem to have taken this case to heart. If you mention it to anyone else, I'll deny I said it. But I didn't like that machine. It seemed . . . almost to be mocking us. I've inspected over a dozen speed ironers in the last five years on a regular basis. Some of them are in such bad shape that I wouldn't leave a dog unleashed around them—the state law is lamentably lax. But they were only machines for all that. But this one . . . it's a spook. I don't know why, but it is. I think if I'd found one thing, even a technicality, that was off whack, I would have ordered it shut down. Crazy, huh?"

"I felt the same way," Hunton said.

"Let me tell you about something that happened two years ago in Milton," the inspector said. He took off his glasses and began to polish them slowly on his vest. "Fella had parked an old icebox out in his backyard. The woman who called us said her dog had been caught in it and suffocated. We got the state policeman in the area to inform him it had to go to the town dump. Nice enough fella, sorry about the dog. He loaded it into his pickup and took it to the dump the next morning. That afternoon a woman in the neighborhood reported her son missing."

"God," Hunton said.

"The icebox was at the dump and the kid was in it, dead. A smart kid, according to his mother. She said he'd no more play in an empty icebox than he would take a ride with a strange man. Well, he did. We wrote it off. Case closed?"

"I guess," Hunton said.

"No. The dump caretaker went out next day to take the door off the thing. City Ordinance No. 58 on the maintenance of public dumping places." Martin looked at him expressionlessly. "He found six dead birds inside. Gulls, sparrows, a robin. And he said the door closed on his arm while he was brushing them out. Gave him a hell of a jump. That mangler at the Blue Ribbon strikes me like that, Hunton. I don't like it."

They looked at each other wordlessly in the empty inquest chamber, some six city blocks from where the Hadley-Watson Model-6 Speed Ironer and Folder sat in the busy laundry, steaming and fuming over its sheets.

The case was driven out of his mind in the space of a week by the press of more prosaic police work. It was only brought back when he and his wife dropped over to Mark Jackson's house for an evening of bid whist and beer.

Jackson greeted him with: "Have you ever wondered if that laundry machine you told me about is haunted, Johnny?"

Hunton blinked, at a loss. "What?"

"The speed ironer at the Blue Ribbon Laundry, I guess you didn't catch the squeal this time."

"What squeal?" Hunton asked, interested.

Jackson passed him the evening paper and pointed to an item at the bottom of page two. The story said that a steam line had let go on the large speed ironer at the Blue Ribbon Laundry, burning three of the six women working at the feeder end. The accident had occurred at 3:45 P.M. and was attributed to a rise in steam pressure from the laundry's boiler. One of the women,

Mrs. Annette Gillian, had been held at City Receiving Hospital with second-degree burns.

"Funny coincidence," he said, but the memory of Inspector Martin's words in the empty inquest chamber suddenly recurred: *It's a spook* . . . And the story about the dog and the boy and the birds caught in the discarded refrigerator.

He played cards very badly that night.

Mrs. Gillian was propped up in bed reading *Screen Secrets* when Hunton came into the four-bed hospital room. A large bandage blanketed one arm and the side of her neck. The room's other occupant, a young woman with a pallid face, was sleeping.

Mrs. Gillian blinked at the blue uniform and then smiled tentatively. "If it was for Mrs. Cherinikov, you'll have to come back later. They just gave her medication."

"No, it's for you, Mrs. Gillian." Her smile faded a little. "I'm here unofficially—which means I'm curious about the accident at the laundry. John Hunton." He held out his hand.

It was the right move. Mrs. Gillian's smile became brilliant and she took his grip awkwardly with her unburnt hand. "Anything I can tell you, Mr. Hunton. God, I thought my Andy was in trouble at school again."

"What happened?"

"We was running sheets and the ironer just blew up—or it seemed that way. I was thinking about going home an' getting off my dogs when there's this great big bang, like a bomb. Steam is everywhere and this hissing noise . . . awful." Her smile trembled on the verge of extinction. "It was like the ironer was breathing. Like a dragon, it was. And Alberta—that's Alberta Keene—shouted that something was exploding and everyone was running and screaming and Ginny Jason started yelling she was burnt. I started to run away and I fell down. I didn't know I got it worst until then. God forbid it was no worse than it was. That live steam is three hundred degrees."

"The paper said a steam line let go. What does that mean?"

"The overhead pipe comes down into this kinda flexible line that feeds the machine. George—Mr. Stanner—said there must have been a surge from the boiler or something. The line split wide open."

Hunton could think of nothing else to ask. He was making ready to leave when she said reflectively:

"We never used to have these things on that machine. Only lately. The steam line breaking. That awful, awful accident with

Mrs. Frawley, God rest her. And little things. Like the day Essie got her dress caught in one of the drive chains. That could have been dangerous if she hadn't ripped it right out. Bolts and things fall off. Oh, Herb Diment—he's the laundry repairman—has had an awful time with it. Sheets get caught in the folder. George says that's because they're using too much bleach in the washers, but it never used to happen. Now the girls hate to work on it. Essie even says there are still little bits of Adelle Frawley caught in it and it's sacrilege or something. Like it had a curse. It's been that way ever since Sherry cut her hand on one of the clamps."

"Sherry?" Hunton asked.

"Sherry Ouelette. Pretty little thing, just out of high school. Good worker. But clumsy sometimes. You know how young girls are."

"She cut her hand on something?"

"Nothing strange about *that*. There are clamps to tighten down the feeder belt, see. Sherry was adjusting them so we could do a heavier load and probably dreaming about some boy. She cut her finger and bled all over everything." Mrs. Gillian looked puzzled. "It wasn't until after that the bolts started falling off. Adelle was . . . you know . . . about a week later. As if the machine had tasted blood and found it liked it. Don't women get funny ideas sometimes, Officer Hinton?"

"Hunton," he said absently, looking over her head and into space.

Ironically, he had met Mark Jackson in a washateria in the block that separated their houses, and it was there that the cop and the English professor still had their most interesting conversations.

Now they sat side by side in bland plastic chairs, their clothes going round and round behind the glass portholes of the coin-op washers. Jackson's paperback copy of Milton's collected works lay neglected beside him while he listened to Hunton tell Mrs. Gillian's story.

When Hunton had finished, Jackson said, "I asked you once if you thought the mangler might be haunted. I was only half joking. I'll ask you again now."

"No," Hunton said uneasily. "Don't be stupid."

Jackson watched the turning clothes reflectively. "Haunted is a bad word. Let's say possessed. There are almost as many spells for casting demons in as there are for casting them out. Frazier's *Golden Bough* is replete with them. Druidic and Aztec lore contain others. Even older ones, back to Egypt. Almost all of them can be reduced to startlingly common denominators. The most common, of course, is the blood of a virgin." He looked at Hunton. "Mrs. Gillian said the trouble started after this Sherry Ouelette accidentally cut herself."

"Oh, come on," Hunton said.

"You have to admit she sounds just the type," Jackson said.

"I'll run right over to her house," Hunton said with a small smile. "I can see it. 'Miss Ouelette, I'm Officer John Hunton. I'm investigating an ironer with a bad case of demon possession and would like to know if you're a virgin.' Do you think I'd get a chance to say goodbye to Sandra and the kids before they carted me off to the booby hatch?"

"I'd be willing to bet you'll end up saying something just like that," Jackson said without smiling. "I'm serious, Johnny. That machine scares the hell out of me, and I've never seen it."

"For the sake of conversation," Hunton said, "what are some of the other so-called common denominators?"

Jackson shrugged. "Hard to say without study. Most Anglo-Saxon hex formulas specify graveyard dirt or the eye of a toad. European spells often mention the hand of glory, which can be interpreted as the actual hand of a dead man or one of the hallucinogenics used in connection with the Witches' Sabbath—usually belladonna or a psilocybin derivative. There could be others."

"And you think all those things got into the Blue Ribbon ironer? Christ, Mark, I'll bet there isn't any belladonna within a five-hundred-mile radius. Or do you think someone whacked off their Uncle Fred's hand and dropped it in the folder?"

"If seven hundred monkeys typed for seven hundred years—"

"One of them would turn out the works of Shakespeare," Hunton finished sourly. "Go to hell. Your turn to go across to the drugstore and get some dimes for the dryers."

It was very funny how George Stanner lost his arm in the mangler.

Seven o'clock Monday morning the laundry was deserted except for Stanner and Herb Diment, the maintenance man. They were performing the twice-yearly function of greasing the mangler's bearings before the laundry's regular day began at seven-thirty. Diment was at the far end, greasing the four secondaries and thinking of how unpleasant this machine made him feel lately, when the mangler suddenly roared into life.

He had been holding up four of the canvas exit belts to get at the motor beneath and suddenly the belts were running in his hands, ripping the flesh off his palms, dragging him along.

He pulled free with a convulsive jerk seconds before the belts would have carried his hands into the folder.

"What the Christ, George!" he yelled. "Shut the frigging thing *off*!"

George Stanner began to scream.

It was a high, wailing, blood-maddened sound that filled the laundry, echoing off the steel faces of the washers, the grinning mouths of the steam presses, the vacant eyes of the industrial dryers. Stanner drew in a great, whooping gasp of air and screamed again: *"Oh God of Christ I'm caught I'M CAUGHT—"*

The rollers began to produce rising steam. The folder gnashed and thumped. Bearings and motors seemed to cry out with a hidden life of their own.

Diment raced to the other end of the machine.

The first roller was already going a sinister red. Diment made a moaning, gobbling noise in his throat. The mangler howled and thumped and hissed.

A deaf observer might have thought at first that Stanner was merely bent over the machine at an odd angle. Then even a deaf man would have seen the pallid, eye-bulging rictus of his face, mouth twisted open in a continuous scream. The arm was disappearing under the safety bar and beneath the first roller; the fabric of his shirt had torn away at the shoulder seam and his upper arm bulged grotesquely as the blood was pushed steadily backward.

"Turn it off!" Stanner screamed. There was a snap as his elbow broke.

Diment thumbed the off button.

The mangler continued to hum and growl and turn.

Unbelieving, he slammed the button again and again—nothing. The skin of Stanner's arm had grown shiny and taut. Soon it would split with the pressure the roll was putting on it; and still he was conscious and screaming. Diment had a nightmare cartoon image of man flattened by a steamroller, leaving only a shadow.

"Fuses—" Stanner screeched. His head was being pulled down, down, as he was dragged forward.

Diment whirled and ran to the boiler room, Stanner's screams chasing him like lunatic ghosts. The mixed stench of blood and steam rose in the air.

On the left wall were three heavy gray boxes containing all the fuses for the laundry's electricity. Diment yanked them open and began to pull the long, cylindrical fuses like a crazy man, throwing them back over his shoulders. The overhead lights went out; then the air compressor; then the boiler itself, with a huge dying whine.

And still the mangler turned. Stanner's screams had been reduced to bubbly moans.

Diment's eye happened on the fire ax in its glassed-in box. He grabbed it with a small, gagging whimper and ran back. Stanner's arm was gone almost to the shoulder. Within seconds his bent and straining neck would be snapped against the safety bar.

"I can't," Diment blubbered, holding the ax. "Jesus, George, I can't, I can't, I—"

The machine was an abattoir now. The folder spat out pieces of shirt sleeve, scraps of flesh, a finger. Stanner gave a huge, whooping scream and Diment swung the ax up and brought it down in the laundry's shadowy lightlessness. Twice. Again.

Stanner fell away, unconscious and blue, blood jetting from the stump just below the shoulder. The mangler sucked what was left into itself . . . and shut down.

Weeping, Diment pulled his belt out of its loops and began to make a tourniquet.

Hunton was talking on the phone with Roger Martin, the inspector. Jackson watched him while he patiently rolled a ball back and forth for three-year-old Patty Hunton to chase.

"He pulled *all* the fuses?" Hunton was asking. "And the off button just didn't function, huh? . . . Has the ironer been shut down? . . . Good. Great. Huh? . . . No, not official." Hunton frowned, then looked sideways at Jackson. "Are you still reminded of that refrigerator, Roger? . . . Yes. Me too. Good-bye."

He hung up and looked at Jackson. "Let's go see the girl, Mark."

She had her own apartment (the hesitant yet proprietary way she showed them in after Hunton had flashed his buzzer made him suspect that she hadn't had it long), and she sat uncomfortably across from them in the carefully decorated, postage-stamp living room.

"I'm Officer Hunton and this is my associate, Mr. Jackson. It's about the accident at the laundry." He felt hugely uncomfortable with this dark, shyly pretty girl.

"Awful," Sherry Ouelette murmured. "It's the only place I've ever worked. Mr. Gartley is my uncle. I liked it because it let me have this place and my own friends. But now . . . it's so *spooky*."

"The State Board of Safety has shut the ironer down pending a full investigation," Hunton said. "Did you know that?"

"Sure." She sighed restlessly. "I don't know what I'm going to do—"

"Miss Ouelette," Jackson interrupted, "you had an accident with the ironer, didn't you? Cut your hand on a clamp, I believe?"

"Yes, I cut my finger." Suddenly her face clouded. "That was the first thing." She looked at them woefully. "Sometimes I feel like the girls don't like me so much anymore . . . as if I were to blame."

"I have to ask you a hard question," Jackson said slowly. "A question you won't like. It seems absurdly personal and off the subject, but I can only tell you it is not. Your answers won't ever be marked down in a file or record."

She looked frightened. "D-did I do something?"

Jackson smiled and shook his head; she melted. *Thank God for Mark,* Hunton thought.

"I'll add this, though: the answer may help you keep your nice little flat here, get your job back, and make things at the laundry the way they were before."

"I'd answer anything to have that," she said.

"Sherry, are you a virgin?"

She looked utterly flabbergasted, utterly shocked, as if a priest had given communion and then slapped her. Then she lifted her head, made a gesture at her neat efficiency apartment, as if asking them how they could believe it might be a place of assignation.

"I'm saving myself for my husband," she said simply.

Hunton and Jackson looked calmly at each other, and in that tick of a second, Hunton knew that it was all true: a devil had taken over the inanimate steel and cogs and gears of the mangler and had turned it into something with its own life.

"Thank you," Jackson said quietly.

"What now?" Hunton asked bleakly as they rode back. "Find a priest to exorcise it?"

Jackson snorted. "You'd go a far piece to find one that wouldn't hand you a few tracts to read while he phoned the booby hatch. It has to be our play, Johnny."

"Can we do it?"

"Maybe. The problem is this: We know something is in the mangler. We don't know *what*." Hunton felt cold, as if touched by a fleshless finger. "There are a great many demons. Is the one we're dealing with in the circle of Bubastis or Pan? Baal? Or the Christian deity we call Satan? We don't know. If the demon had been deliberately cast, we would have a better chance. But this seems to be a case of random possession."

Jackson ran his fingers through his hair. "The blood of a virgin, yes. But that narrows it down hardly at all. We have to be sure, very sure."

"Why?" Hunton asked bluntly. "Why not just get a bunch of exorcism formulas together and try them out?"

Jackson's face went cold. "This isn't cops 'n' robbers, Johnny. For Christ's sake, don't think it is. The rite of exorcism is horribly dangerous. It's like controlled nuclear fission, in a way. We could make a mistake and destroy ourselves. The demon is caught in that piece of machinery. But give it a chance and—"

"It could get out?"

"It would love to get out," Jackson said grimly. "And it likes to kill."

When Jackson came over the following evening, Hunton had sent his wife and daughter to a movie. They had the living room to themselves, and for this Hunton was relieved. He could still barely believe what he had become involved in.

"I canceled my classes," Jackson said, "and spent the day with some of the most god-awful books you can imagine. This afternoon I fed over thirty recipes for calling demons into the tech computer. I've got a number of common elements. Surprisingly few."

He showed Hunton the list: blood of a virgin, graveyard dirt, hand of glory, bat's blood, night moss, horse's hoof, eye of toad.

There were others, all marked secondary.

"Horse's hoof," Hunton said thoughtfully. "Funny—"

"Very common. In fact—"

"Could these things—any of them—be interpreted loosely?" Hunton interrupted.

"If lichens picked at night could be substituted for night moss, for instance?"

"Yes."

"It's very likely," Jackson said. "Magical formulas are often ambiguous and elastic. The black arts have always allowed plenty of room for creativity."

"Substitute Jell-O for horse's hoof," Hunton said. "Very popular in bag lunches. I noticed a little container of it sitting under the ironer's sheet platform on the day the Frawley woman died. Gelatin is made from horses' hooves."

Jackson nodded. "Anything else?"

"Bat's blood . . . well, it's a big place. Lots of unlighted nooks and crannies. Bats seem likely, although I doubt if the management would admit to it. One could conceivably have been trapped in the mangler."

Jackson tipped his head back and knuckled bloodshot eyes. "It fits . . . it all fits."

"It does?"

"Yes. We can safely rule out the hand of glory, I think. Certainly no one dropped a hand into the ironer *before* Mrs. Frawley's death, and belladonna is definitely not indigenous to the area."

"Graveyard dirt?"

"What do you think?"

"It would have to be a hell of a coincidence," Hunton said. "Nearest cemetery is Pleasant Hill, and that's five miles from the Blue Ribbon."

"Okay," Jackson said. "I got the computer operator—who thought I was getting ready for Halloween—to run a positive breakdown of all the primary and secondary elements on the list. Every possible combination. I threw out some two dozen which were completely meaningless. The others fall into fairly clear-cut categories. The elements we've isolated are in one of those."

"What is it?"

Jackson grinned. "An easy one. The mythos centers in South America with branches in the Caribbean. Related to voodoo. The literature I've got looks on the deities as strictly bush league, compared to some of the real heavies, like Saddath or He-Who-Cannot-Be-Named. The thing in that machine is going to slink away like the neighborhood bully."

"How do we do it?"

"Holy water and a smidgen of the Holy Eucharist ought to do it. And we can read some of the Leviticus to it. Strictly Christian white magic."

"You're sure it's not worse?"

"Don't see how it can be," Jackson said pensively. "I don't mind telling you I was worried about that hand of glory. That's very black juju. Strong magic."

"Holy water wouldn't stop it?"

"A demon called up in conjunction with the hand of glory could eat a stack of Bibles for breakfast. We would be in bad trouble messing with something like that at all. Better to pull the goddamn thing apart."

"Well, are you completely sure—"

"No, but fairly sure. It all fits too well."

"When?"

"The sooner, the better," Jackson said. "How do we get in? Break a window?"

Hunton smiled, reached into his pocket, and dangled a key in front of Jackson's nose.

"Where'd you get that? Gartley?"

"No," Hunton said. "From a state inspector named Martin."

"He know what we're doing?"

"I think he suspects. He told me a funny story a couple of weeks ago."

"About the mangler?"

"No," Hunton said. "About a refrigerator. Come on."

Adelle Frawley was dead; sewed together by a patient undertaker, she lay in her coffin. Yet something of her spirit perhaps remained in the machine, and if it did, it cried out. She would have known, could have warned them. She had been prone to indigestion, and for this common ailment she had taken a common stomach tablet call E-Z Gel, purchasable over the counter of any drugstore for seventy-nine cents. The side panel holds a printed warning: People with glaucoma must not take E-Z Gel, because the active ingredients causes an aggravation of that condition. Unfortunately, Adelle Frawley did not have that condition. She might have remembered the day, shortly before Sherry Ouelette cut her hand, that she had dropped a full box of E-Z Gel tablets into the mangler by accident. But she was dead, unaware that the active ingredient which soothed her heartburn was a chemical derivative of belladonna, known quaintly in some European countries as the hand of glory.

There was a sudden ghastly burping noise in the spectral silence of the Blue Ribbon Laundry—a bat fluttered madly for its hole in the insulation above the dryers where it had roosted, wrapping wings around its blind face.

It was a noise almost like a chuckle.

The mangler began to run with a sudden, lurching grind—belts hurrying through the darkness, cogs meeting and meshing and grinding, heavy pulverizing rollers rotating on and on.

It was ready for them.

* * *

When Hunton pulled into the parking lot it was shortly after midnight and the moon was hidden behind a raft of moving clouds. He jammed on the brakes and switched off the lights in the same motion; Jackson's forehead almost slammed against the padded dash.

He switched off the ignition and the steady thump-hiss thump became louder. "It's the mangler," he said slowly. "It's the mangler. Running by itself. In the middle of the night."

They sat for a moment in silence, feeling the fear crawl up their legs.

Hunton said, "All right. Let's do it."

They got out and walked to the building, the sound of the mangler growing louder. As Hunton put the key into the lock of the service door, he thought that the machine *did* sound alive—as if it were breathing in great hot gasps and speaking to itself in hissing, sardonic whispers.

"All of a sudden I'm glad I'm with a cop," Jackson said. He shifted the brown bag he held from one arm to the other. Inside was a small jelly jar filled with holy water wrapped in waxed paper, and a Gideon Bible.

They stepped inside and Hunton snapped up the light switches by the door. The fluorescents flickered into cold life. At the same instant the mangler shut off.

A membrane of steam hung over its rollers. It waited for them in its new ominous silence.

"God, it's an ugly thing," Jackson whispered.

"Come on," Hunton said. "Before we lose our nerve."

They walked over to it. The safety bar was in its down position over the belt which fed the machine.

Hunton put out a hand. "Close enough, Mark. Give me the stuff and tell me what to do."

"But—"

"No argument."

Jackson handed him the bag and Hunton put it on the sheet table in front of the machine. He gave Jackson the Bible.

"I'm going to read," Jackson said. "When I point at you, sprinkle the holy water on the machine with your fingers. You say: In the name of the Father, and of the Son, and of the Holy Ghost, get thee from this place, thou unclean. Got it?"

"Yes."

"The second time I point, break the wafer and repeat the incantation again."

"How will we know if it's working?"

"You'll know. The thing is apt to break every window in the place getting out. If it doesn't work the first time, we keep doing it until it does."

"I'm scared green," Hunton said.

"As a matter of fact, so am I."

"If we're wrong about the hand of glory—"

"We're not," Jackson said. "Here we go."

He began. His voice filled the empty laundry with spectral echoes. "Turnest not thou aside to idols, nor make molten gods of yourself. I am the Lord thy God . . ." The words fell like stones into a silence that had suddenly become filled with a creeping, tomblike cold. The mangler remained still and silent under the fluorescents, and to Hunton it still seemed to grin.

". . . and the land will vomit you out for having defiled it, as it vomited out nations before you." Jackson looked up, his face strained, and pointed.

Hunton sprinkled holy water across the feeder belt.

There was a sudden, gnashing scream of tortured metal. Smoke rose from the canvas belts where the holy water had touched and took on writhing, red-tinged shapes. The mangler suddenly jerked into life.

"We've got it!" Jackson cried above the rising clamor. "It's on the run!"

He began to read again, his voice rising over the sound of the machinery. He pointed to Hunton again, and Hunton sprinkled some of the host. As he did so he was suddenly swept with a bone-freezing terror, a sudden vivid feeling that it had gone wrong, that the machine had called their bluff—and was the stronger.

Jackson's voice was still rising, approaching climax.

Sparks began to jump across the arc between the main motor and the secondary; the smell of ozone filled the air, like the copper smell of hot blood. Now the main motor was smoking; the mangler was running at an insane, blurred speed: a finger touched to the central belt would have caused the whole body to be hauled in and turned to a bloody rag in the space of five seconds. The concrete beneath their feet trembled and thrummed.

A main bearing blew with a searing flash of purple light, filling the chill air with the smell of thunderstorms, and still the mangler ran, faster and faster, belts and rollers and cogs moving at a speed that made them seem to blend and merge, change, melt, transmute—

Hunton, who had been standing almost hypnotized, suddenly

took a step backward. "Get away!" he screamed over the blaring racket.

"We've almost got it!" Jackson yelled back. "Why—"

There was a sudden indescribable ripping noise and a fissure in the concrete floor suddenly raced toward them and past, widening. Chips of ancient cement flew up in a star burst.

Jackson looked at the mangler and screamed.

It was trying to pull itself out of the concrete, like a dinosaur trying to escape a tar pit. And it wasn't precisely an ironer anymore. It was still changing, melting. The 550-volt cable fell, spitting blue fire into the rollers, and was chewed away. For a moment two fireballs glared at them like lambent eyes, eyes filled with a great and cold hunger.

Another fault line tore open. The mangler leaned toward them, within an ace of being free of the concrete moorings that held it. It leered at them; the safety bar had slammed up and what Hunton saw was a gaping, hungry mouth filled with steam.

They turned to run and another fissure opened at their feet. Behind them, a great screaming roar as the thing came free. Hunton leaped over, but Jackson stumbled and fell sprawling.

Hunton turned to help and a huge, amorphous shadow fell over him, blocking the fluorescents.

It stood over Jackson, who lay on his back, staring up in a silent rictus of terror—the perfect sacrifice. Hunton had only a confused impression of something black and moving that bulked to a tremendous height above them both, something with glaring electric eyes the size of footballs, an open mouth with a moving canvas tongue.

He ran; Jackson's dying scream followed him.

When Roger Martin finally got out of bed to answer the doorbell, he was still only a third awake; but when Hunton reeled in, shock slapped him fully into the world with a rough hand.

Hunton's eyes bulged madly from his head, and his hands were claws as he scratched at the front of Martin's robe. There was a small oozing cut on his cheek and his face was splashed with dirty gray specks of powdered cement.

His hair had gone dead white.

"Help me . . . for Jesus' sake, help me. Mark is dead. Jackson is dead."

"Slow down," Martin said. "Come in the living room."

Hunton followed him, making a thick whining noise in his throat, like a dog.

Martin poured him a two-ounce knock of Jim Beam and Hunton held the glass in both hands, downing the raw liquor in a choked gulp. The glass fell unheeded to the carpet, and his hands, like wandering ghosts, sought Martin's lapels again.

"The mangler killed Mark Jackson. It . . . it . . . oh God, it might get out! We can't let it out! We can't . . . we . . . oh—" He began to scream, a crazy, whooping sound that rose and fell in jagged cycles.

Martin tried to hand him another drink but Hunton knocked it aside. "We have to burn it," he said. "Burn it before it can get out. Oh, what if it gets out? Oh Jesus, what if—" His eyes suddenly flickered, glazed, rolled up to show the whites, and he fell to the carpet in a stonelike faint.

Mrs. Martin was in the doorway, clutching her robe to her throat. "Who is he, Rog? Is he crazy? I thought—" She shuddered.

"I don't think he's crazy." She was suddenly frightened by the sick shadow of fear on her husband's face. "God, I hope he came quick enough."

He turned to the telephone, picked up the receiver, froze.

There was a faint, swelling noise from the east of the house, the way that Hunton had come. A steady, grinding clatter, growing louder. The living-room window stood half open and now Martin caught a dark smell on the breeze. An odor of ozone . . . or blood.

He stood with his hand on the useless telephone as it grew louder, louder, gnashing and fuming, something in the streets that was hot and steaming. The blood stench filled the room.

His hand dropped from the telephone.

It was already out.

The Last Demon

by

Isaac Bashevis Singer

The next story, by Nobel Prize winner Isaac Bashevis Singer, is about the very last demon in the world. We'll let the demon explain to you himself—he's quite a complainer—how he came to such a terrible fate . . . and how we writers have appropriated his trade.

Isaac Bashevis Singer grew up in Warsaw, Poland, and emigrated to the United States in 1935. He has written the autobiographical memoir In My Father's Court, *and the novels* The Family Moskat, The Magician of Lublin, The Manor, Shosha, *and* Enemies, a Love Story, *among others. He has several short story collections, including* Gimple the Fool, Short Friday, A Crown of Feathers, and Other Stories, An Isaac Bashevis Singer Reader, *and* The Spinoza of Market Street. *Many of these stories have been collected in* The Collected Stories of Isaac Bashevis Singer.

* * *

I, A DEMON, BEAR WITNESS THAT THERE ARE NO MORE DEmons left. Why demons, when man himself is a demon? Why persuade to evil someone who is already convinced? I am the last of the persuaders. I board in an attic in Tishevitz and draw my sustenance from a Yiddish storybook, a leftover from the days before the great catastrophe. The stories in the book are pablum and duck milk, but the Hebrew letters have a weight of their own. I don't have to tell you that I am a Jew. What else, a Gentile? I've heard that there are Gentile demons, but I don't know any, nor do I wish to know them. Jacob and Esau don't become in-laws.

I came here from Lublin. Tishevitz is a God-forsaken village;

Adam didn't even stop to pee there. It's so small that a wagon goes through town and the horse is in the market place just as the rear wheels reach the toll gate. There is mud in Tishevitz from Succoth until Tishe b'Ov. The goats of the town don't need to lift their beards to chew at the thatched roofs of the cottages. Hens roost in the middle of the streets. Birds build nests in the women's bonnets. In the tailor's synagogue a billy goat is the tenth in the quorum.

Don't ask me how I managed to get to this smallest letter in the smallest of all prayer books. But when Asmodeus bids you go, you go. After Lublin the road is familiar as far as Zamosc. From there on you are on your own. I was told to look for an iron weathercock with a crow perched upon its comb on the roof of the study house. Once upon a time the cock turned in the wind, but for years now it hasn't moved, not even in thunder and lightning. In Tishevitz even iron weathercocks die.

I speak in the present tense as for me time stands still. I arrive. I look around. For the life of me I can't find a single one of our men. The cemetery is empty. There is no outhouse. I go to the ritual bathhouse, but I don't hear a sound. I sit down on the highest bench, look down on the stone on which the buckets of water are poured each Friday, and wonder. Why am I needed here? If a little demon is wanted, is it necessary to import one all the way from Lublin? Aren't there enough devils in Zamosc? Outside the sun is shining—it's close to the summer solstice—but inside the bathhouse it's gloomy and cold. Above me is a spider web, and within the web a spider wiggling its legs, seeming to spin but drawing no thread. There's no sign of a fly, not even the shell of a fly. "What does the creature eat?" I ask myself, "its own insides?" Suddenly I hear it chanting in a Talmudic singsong: "A lion isn't satisfied by a morsel and a ditch isn't filled up with dirt from its own walls."

I burst out laughing.

"Is that so? Why have you disguised yourself as a spider?"

"I've already been a worm, a flea, a frog. I've been sitting here for two hundred years without a stitch of work to do. But you need a permit to leave."

"They don't sin here?"

"Petty men, petty sins. Today someone covets another man's broom; tomorrow he fasts and puts peas in his shoes. Ever since Abraham Zalman was under the illusion that he was the Messiah, the son of Joseph, the blood of the people has congealed in their veins. If I were Satan, I wouldn't even send one of our first-graders here."

"How much does it cost him?"

"What's new in the world?" he asks me.

"It's not been so good for our crowd."

"What's happened? The Holy Spirit grows stronger?"

"Stronger? Only in Tishevitz is he powerful. No one's heard of him in the large cities. Even in Lublin he's out of style."

"Well, that should be fun."

"But it isn't," I say. " 'All Guilty is worse for us than All Innocent.' It has reached a point where people want to sin beyond their capacities. They martyr themselves for the most trivial of sins. If that's the way it is, what are we needed for? A short while ago I was flying over Levertov Street, and I saw a man dressed in a skunk's coat. He had a black beard and wavy sidelocks; an amber cigar holder was clamped between his lips. Across the street from him an official's wife was walking, so it occurs to me to say, 'That's quite a bargain, don't you think, Uncle?' All I expected from him was a thought. I had my handkerchief ready if he should spit on me. So what does the man do? 'Why waste your breath on me?' he calls out angrily. 'I'm willing. Start working on her.' "

"What sort of a misfortune is this?"

"Enlightenment! In the two hundred years you've been sitting on your tail here, Satan has cooked up a new dish of kasha. The Jews have now developed writers. Yiddish ones, Hebrew ones, and they have taken over our trade. We grow hoarse talking to every adolescent, but they print their *kitsch* by the thousands and distribute it to Jews everywhere. They know all our tricks—mockery, piety. They have a hundred reasons why a rat must be kosher. All that they want to do is to redeem the world. Why, if you could corrupt nothing, have you been left here for two hundred years? And if you could do nothing in two hundred years, what do they expect from me in two weeks?"

"You know the proverb, 'A guest for a while sees a mile.' "

"What's there to see?"

"A young rabbi has moved here from Modly Bozyc. He's not yet thirty, but he's absolutely stuffed with knowledge, knows the thirty-six tractates of the Talmud by heart. He's the greatest Cabalist in Poland, fasts every Monday and Thursday, and bathes in the ritual bath when the water is ice cold. He won't permit any of us to talk to him. What's more he has a handsome wife, and that's bread in the basket. What do we have to tempt him with? You might as well try to break through an iron wall. If I were asked my opinion, I'd say that Tishevitz should be removed from our files. All I ask is that you get me out of here before I go mad."

"No, first I must have a talk with this rabbi. How do you think I should start?"

"You tell me. He'll start pouring salt on your tail before you open your mouth."

"I'm from Lublin. I'm not so easily frightened."

2

On the way to the rabbi, I ask the imp, "What have you tried so far?"

"What haven't I tried?" he answers.

"A woman?"

"Won't look at one."

"Heresy?"

"He knows all the answers."

"Money?"

"Doesn't know what a coin looks like."

"Reputation?"

"He runs from it."

"Doesn't he look backwards?"

"Doesn't even move his head."

"He's got to have some angle."

"Where's it hidden?"

The window of the rabbi's study is open, and in we fly. There's the usual paraphernalia around: an ark with the Holy Scroll, bookshelves, a mezuzah in a wooden case. The rabbi, a young man with a blond beard, blue eyes, yellow sidelocks, a high forehead, and a deep widow's peak sits on the rabbinical chair peering in the Gemara. He's fully equipped: *yarmulka*, sash, and fringed garment with each of the fringes braided eight times. I listen to his skull: pure thoughts! He sways and chants in Hebrew, *"Rachel t'unah v'gazezah,"* and then translates, "a wooly sheep fleeced."

"In Hebrew Rachel is both a sheep and a girl's name," I say.

"So?"

"A sheep has wool and a girl has hair."

"Therefore?"

"If she's not androgynous, a girl has pubic hair."

"Stop babbling and let me study," the rabbi says in anger.

"Wait a second," I say, "Torah won't get cold. It's true that Jacob loved Rachel, but when he was given Leah instead, she wasn't poison. And when Rachel gave him Bilhah as a concubine, what did Leah do to spite her sister? She put Zilpah into his bed."

"That was before the giving of Torah."

"What about King David?"

"That happened before the excommunication by Rabbi Gershom."

"Before or after Rabbi Gershom, a male is a male."

"Rascal. *Shaddai kra Satan,*" the rabbi exclaims. Grabbing both of his sidelocks, he begins to tremble as if assaulted by a bad dream. "What nonsense am I thinking?" He takes his ear lobes and closes his ears. I keep on talking but he doesn't listen; he becomes absorbed in a difficult passage and there's no longer anyone to speak to. The little imp from Tishevitz says, "He's a hard one to hook, isn't he? Tomorrow he'll fast and roll in a bed of thistles. He'll give away his last penny to charity."

"Such a believer nowadays?"

"Strong as a rock."

"And his wife?"

"A sacrificial lamb."

"What of the children?"

"Still infants."

"Perhaps he has a mother-in-law?"

"She's already in the other world."

"Any quarrels?"

"Not even half an enemy."

"Where do you find such a jewel?"

"Once in a while something like that turns up among the Jews."

"This one I've got to get. This is my first job around here. I've been promised that if I succeed, I'll be transferred to Odessa."

"What's so good about that?"

"It's as near paradise as our kind gets. You can sleep twenty-four hours a day. The population sins and you don't lift a finger."

"So what do you do all day?"

"We play with our women."

"Here there's not a single one of our girls." The imp sighs. "There was one old bitch but she expired."

"So what's left?"

"What Onan did."

"That doesn't lead anywhere. Help me and I swear by Asmodeus' beard that I'll get you out of here. We have an opening for a mixer of bitter herbs. You only work Passovers."

"I hope it works out, but don't count your chickens."

"We've taken care of tougher than he."

3

A week goes by and our business has not moved forward; I find myself in a dirty mood. A week in Tishevitz is equal to a year in Lublin. The Tishevitz imp is all right, but when you sit two hundred years in such a hole, you become a yokel. He cracks jokes that didn't amuse Enoch and convulses with laughter; he drops names from the Haggadah. Every one of his stories wears a long beard. I'd like to get the hell out of here, but it doesn't take a magician to return home with nothing. I have enemies among my colleagues and I must beware of intrigue. Perhaps I was sent here just to break my neck. When devils stop warring with people, they start tripping each other.

Experience has taught that of all the snares we use, there are three that work unfailingly—lust, pride, and avarice. No one can evade all three, not even Rabbi Tsots himself. Of the three, pride has the strongest meshes. According to the Talmud a scholar is permitted the eighth part of an eighth part of vanity. But a learned man generally exceeds his quota. When I see that the days are passing and that the rabbi of Tishevitz remains stubborn, I concentrate on vanity.

"Rabbi of Tishevitz," I say. "I wasn't born yesterday. I come from Lublin where the streets are paved with exegeses of the Talmud. We use manuscripts to heat our ovens. The floors of our attics sag under the weight of Cabala. But not even in Lublin have I met a man of your eminence. How does it happen," I ask, "that no one's heard of you? True saints should hide themselves, perhaps, but silence will not bring redemption. You should be the leader of this generation, and not merely the rabbi of this community, holy though it is. The time has come for you to reveal yourself. Heaven and earth are waiting for you. Messiah himself sits in the Bird Nest looking down in search of an unblemished saint like you. But what are you doing about it? You sit on your rabbinical chair laying down the law on which pots and which pans are kosher. Forgive me the comparison, but it is as if an elephant were put to work hauling a straw."

"Who are you and what do you want?" the rabbi asks in terror. "Why don't you let me study?"

"There is a time when the service of God requires the neglect of Torah," I scream. "Any student can study the Gemara."

"Who sent you here?"

"I was sent; I am here. Do you think they don't know about you up there? The higher-ups are annoyed with you. Broad shoulders must bear their share of the load. To put it in rhyme: the humble can stumble. Hearken to this: Abraham Zalman was Messiah, son of Joseph, and you are ordained to prepare the way for Messiah, son of David, but stop sleeping. Get ready for battle. The world sinks to the forty-ninth gate of uncleanliness, but you have broken through to the seventh firmament. Only one cry is heard in the mansions, the man from Tishevitz. The angel in charge of Edom has marshalled a clan of demons against you. Satan lies in wait also. Asmodeus is undermining you. Lilith and Namah hover at your bedside. You don't see them, but Shabriri and Briri are treading at your heels. If the Angels were not defending you, that unholy crowd would pound you to dust and ashes. But you do not stand alone, Rabbi of Tishevitz. Lord Sandalphon guards your every step. Metratron watches over you from his luminescent sphere. Everything hangs in the balance, man of Tishevitz; you can tip the scales."

"What should I do?"

"Mark well all that I tell you. Even if I command you to break the law, do as I bid."

"Who are you? What is your name?"

"Elijah the Tishbite. I have the ram's horn of the Messiah ready. Whether the redemption comes, or we wander in the darkness of Egypt another 2,689 years is up to you."

The rabbi of Tishevitz remains silent for a long time. His face becomes as white as the slips of paper on which he writes his commentaries.

"How do I know you're speaking the truth?" he asks in a trembling voice. "Forgive me, Holy Angel, but I require a sign."

"You are right. I will give you a sign."

And I raise such a wind in the rabbi's study that the slip of paper on which he is writing rises from the table and starts flying like a pigeon. The pages of the Gemara turn by themselves. The curtain of the Holy Scroll billows. The rabbi's *yarmulka* jumps from his head, soars to the ceiling, and drops back onto his skull.

"Is that how Nature behaves?" I ask.

"No."

"Do you believe me now?"

The rabbi of Tishevitz hesitates.

"What do you want me to do?"

"The leader of this generation must be famous."

"How do you become famous?"

"Go and travel in the world."

"What do I do in the world?"

"Preach and collect money."

"For what do I collect?"

"First of all collect. Later on I'll tell you what to do with the money."

"Who will contribute?"

"When I order, Jews give."

"How will I support myself?"

"A rabbinical emissary is entitled to a part of what he collects."

"And my family?"

"You will get enough for all."

"What am I supposed to do right now?"

"Shut the Gemara."

"Ah, but my soul yearns for Torah," the rabbi of Tishevitz groans. Nevertheless he lifts the cover of the book, ready to shut it. If he had done that, he would have been through. What did Joseph de la Rinah do? Just hand Samael a pinch of snuff. I am already laughing to myself, "Rabbi of Tishevitz, I have you all wrapped up." The little bathhouse imp, standing in a corner, cocks an ear and turns green with envy. True, I have promised to do him a favor, but the jealousy of our kind is stronger than anything. Suddenly the rabbi says, "Forgive me, my Lord, but I require another sign."

"What do you want me to do? Stop the sun?"

"Just show me your feet."

The moment the rabbi of Tishevitz speaks these words, I know everything is lost. We can disguise all the parts of our body but the feet. From the smallest imp right up to Ketev Meriri we all have the claws of geese. The little imp in the corner bursts out laughing. For the first time in a thousand years I, the master of speech, lose my tongue.

"I don't show my feet," I call out in rage.

"That means you're a devil. *Pik,* get out of here," the rabbi cries. He races to his bookcase, pulls out the *Book of Creation* and waves it menacingly over me. What devil can withstand the *Book of Creation?* I run from the rabbi's study with my spirit in pieces.

To make a long story short, I remain stuck in Tishevitz. No more Lublin, no more Odessa. In one second all my stratagems turn to ashes. An order comes from Asmodeus himself, "Stay in Tishevitz and fry. Don't go farther than a man is allowed to walk on the Sabbath."

How long am I here? Eternity plus a Wednesday. I've seen it all, the destruction of Tishevitz, the destruction of Poland. There are no more Jews, no more demons. The women don't pour out water any longer on the night of the winter solstice. They don't avoid giving things in even numbers. They no longer knock at dawn at the antechamber of the synagogue. They don't warn us before emptying the slops. The rabbi was martyred on a Friday in the month of Nisan. The community was slaughtered, the holy books burned, the cemetery desecrated. The *Book of Creation* has been returned to the Creator. Gentiles wash themselves in the ritual bath. Abraham Zalman's chapel has been turned into a pig sty. There is no longer an Angel of Good nor an Angel of Evil. No more sins, no more temptations! The generation is already guilty seven times over, but Messiah does not come. To whom should he come? Messiah did not come for the Jews, so the Jews went to Messiah. There is no further need for demons. We have also been annihilated. I am the last, a refugee. I can go anywhere I please, but where should a demon like me go? To the murderers?

I found a Yiddish storybook between two broken barrels in the house which once belonged to Velvel the Barrelmaker. I sit there, the last of the demons. I eat dust. I sleep on a feather duster. I keep on reading gibberish. The style of the book is in our manner: Sabbath pudding cooked in pig's fat: blasphemy rolled in piety. The moral of the book is: neither judge, nor judgment. But nevertheless the letters are Jewish. The alphabet they could not squander. I suck on the letters and feed myself. I count the words, make rhymes, and tortuously interpret and reinterpret each dot.

Aleph, the abyss, what else waited?
Bet, the blow, long since fated.
Geemel, God, pretending he knew,
Dalet, death, its shadow grew.

Hey, the hangman, he stood prepared;

Wov, wisdom, ignorance bared.
Zayeen, the zodiac, signs distantly loomed;
Chet, the child, prenatally doomed.
Tet, the thinker, an imprisoned lord;
Jod, the judge, the verdict a fraud.

Yes, as long as a single volume remains, I have something to sustain me. As long as the moths have not destroyed the last page, there is something to play with. What will happen when the last letter is no more, I'd rather not bring to my lips.

When the last letter is gone,
The last of the demons is done.

Translated by MARTHA GLICKLICH AND CECIL HEMLEY

The Golden Rope

by

Tanith Lee

One of the best-known and most prolific of modern fantasists, Tanith Lee has well over a dozen books to her credit, including (among many others) The Birthgrave, Drinking Sapphire Wine, Don't Bite The Sun, Night's Master, The Storm Lord, Sung In Shadow, Volkhavaar, *and* Anackire. *Her short story "Elle Est Trois (La Mort)" won a World Fantasy Award in 1984; her sly and brilliant collection of retold folktales,* Red As Blood, *was also a finalist for the World Fantasy Award that year, in the Best Collection Category. Her most recent books are* Tamastara, or the Indian Nights, *a collection, and a novel.*

In the timeless and mythic tale that follows, Lee tells a tale of witchcraft and ritual, of scarlet butterflies and silver maidens, and gives us a very different perspective on the nature of faith, love, obedience . . . and sacrifice.

* * *

1

IN THE STONE HOUSE AMID THE WHITE WOOD, THE WOMAN sat and brooded on a power that only one might give her. She had wooed him long and diligently, and she had given her life over to learning and study that she might commune with him. But, like an unrequited love, so far she had been ignored.

All around the house the dead trees, a palisade, outstared the moon. They were a constant reminder of her youth which she had given up, her vitality which had been drained. And yet, tonight, it seemed to her there was a strange stirring in the trees, and in her blood.

When loud knocking came on her gates, she was not amazed, nor quite calm. Very seldom did any seek admittance here. Those who knew of her—and she had not courted fame—understood her scholarship and disliked it. Others guessed her ambition, and feared her. Presently, her servant entered the room, a tall, dark-skinned man from the East, dressed in silken clothes, and tongueless. He bowed low, then indicated to her, in a gesture language she had taught him, and which none but she and he could comprehend, that a city fellow had sought her door. He was of the lowest urban class, a rogue requiring her aid for his wife, who, it seemed, was sick to the death.

Her normal practice, in such a case, was to dismiss the petitioner without seeing him. Now she instructed her servant to bring the man in. She gave the order with a curious excitement, and took care to compose herself that nothing of her mood should be detectable.

The man appeared a moment later. By her trained instincts and intelligence the woman told instantly much about him. He was a thief, one of the dregs of the world. That he cared so for his wife's health that he came seeking a witch implied no love, merely that his wife was some use to him. The woman noted, too, that her visitor was afraid of her. And that, under its filth, his hair was like new gold.

"So," she said. "What do you want?"

"My wife is with child. The condition does not suit her. I dread she may die."

The woman nodded coldly. He would never have known how her pulse had quickened.

"I understand. Your wife sells her body and brings you a fair wage from the enterprise. You suppose that when she grows big and cumbersome, her customers will dwindle."

The man faltered, then smiled at her ingratiatingly.

"I see I was a fool to try hiding anything from you, my lady. As you say. I find it hard to come by honest work. If we starve, it will do none of us any good. But if you could give me some of your clever herbs, so the trouble goes away—"

"And this child is yours, you think, that you will be rid of it so freely."

"I do not, alas, know."

"*I* know. It is. You are aware," she said. "I ask a price for any service."

He grinned and panted like an eager dog.

"When she is well, her first month's wages shall all be yours." The woman watched him. He grew uneasy. "We would never cheat you."

"Tell me, then, what that month's wage would be."

He shuffled, and named a sum.

The woman waited, concentrating until she read from him the aura of thought which showed his wife. Though he had made a whore of her, this girl was beautiful.

The woman nodded again.

"I think you have halved the amount. No arguments, if you please. I shall be generous to you. I myself will double the coins, and you shall be given such a figure every twenty days. Providing your wife carries to term, and bears."

The cutpurse gaped.

"A wonderful bargain for you," she said. "You will benefit outrageously by it."

"But why—"

"Once the child is fit to travel, you will bring it here to me."

"But—"

"I will then settle upon you one last payment, to compensate your doleful loss."

"But—"

"Do not dare," she said, "to question me."

He balked. Clearly he was unsure if he was in luck, or if she was simply a lunatic who might renege, then harm him.

"Or," she said, "to doubt me."

"Ah no, *no*, my lady."

She rose, he cowered.

"Wait here, and touch nothing. There are safeguards on my property which prove injurious to meddlers. Do you believe me?" His pallor showed he did. "When I return, I will have for you your first payment. Also herbs and powders you must give your wife to strengthen her, so the child is robust."

She went from the room and along a passageway. She unlocked, in an unusual manner, a black lacquer door, and passed down a long flight of steps to the vast underground chamber that was her study and her insularium. As her fingers busied themselves in the preparation of those medicines she had prescribed, they trembled slightly.

Infallibly, she knew a golden rope had been placed in her hands. She had only, with patience and wisdom, to draw it in.

* * *

The child was born, and opened its unfocused eyes on dirt and squalor. Then, if it was even properly aware of such things, came an upheaval, a cessation of warmth, the dim wailing of a woman —someone was sorry to see it go after all. The child cried, then slept. Bundled in its covers it was taken to high gates, and given over to a pair of dark, lean hands. Money rang inside a leather bag. As thin snow began to fall, a door thudded shut.

"A girl," said the woman. "That is very well. This wisp of hair is dark now, but will change inside a year. She is whole and will be lovely."

The world was altered.

The earliest memory, the first impression, did not linger, was wiped away. Life was this: A beautiful apartment which opened on a large garden. The walls about the garden were very tall; on three sides the stone piles of the house leaned over it. On the fourth a few dead branches, like a handful of white bones, were all that might be glimpsed of any other place. The ceilings of the beautiful apartment were themselves extremely lofty, but they sank a little closer as the years passed, just as the childish bed and chairs and desk were taken away, and adult furniture replaced them. There came to be an exquisite harpsichord, two guitars of dark and blond wood, with ivory frets. Tapestries and paintings came, and hand-painted books, sweeping pleated dresses of pale lemon silk and cream satin and blanched-almond brocade where there had hung little-girl dresses of similar materials and tints. In a box lined in velvet lay some pieces of priceless flawless jewelry, several of an Eastern cast.

The child, too, had changed, was no longer a child. She was thirteen, the age at which many a damsel of good house might already be contracted if not married. The girl had, however, never seen a man, save in a painting, never heard of one save in a book. She knew they existed, just as lions, wolves, unicorns existed, far beyond the walls, another species in another country. Yet from this same outer wonderland her toys, her furnishings, her books somehow transpired. Everything was delivered as she slept, or taken away as she slept—like magic. Sometimes shocking, and sometimes delightful, yet she was used to it. Magic, as with the apartment, the garden, was an everyday matter.

And beyond the walls of the house and the garden which divided her from the far-off mythology of the earth? The bones of the trees gave evidence of a waste. No other evidence was awarded her.

The woman, whom she did not call "Mother" but "my lady," was the only live thing the young girl saw, or had ever seen. It was a fact, as the ceilings drew lower, the woman became smaller, until she and the girl were almost of the same height. Otherwise, the woman seemed not to change at all. She wore plain clothes, dark and without ornament. Her face was colorless, expressionless. She offered neither love nor friendship, not even the shelter of another personality. Yet it was this woman who, without passion, without enthusiasm of any kind, taught the girl all she had come to know, and brought in to her, by those mysterious nocturnal means, the literature, the musical instruments, that were the accessories and gilding of knowledge; the elegant garments, and the jewels.

The young girl knew her origins, also. My lady had told her from the first. "You are not the child of my body. You are the child of a man and woman who did not want you. I wanted you, and so you were brought to me. You are named Jaspre, since I sent to your mother powders of jaspre to strengthen her while she carried you. Do not feel any regret or any betrayal. Your natural parents are nothing to you." And the girl named Jaspre felt nothing. The ideas of parentage, of love, even, were unconvincing, alien to her. In her world, such things did not exist.

Sometimes, Jaspre would wander through the large garden, among its avenues, of which there were many, between its uncannily manicured box hedges, in and out of its grottoes where nymphs of mossy stone played statically with each other but never with her. Occasionally birds flew over the garden. In some naive manner, she understood they represented freedom, but freedom held no particular allure. Jaspre's world was of the intellect and the spirit. Even her daydreams were contained within the garden. She had never seen a lion or a man or a forest or a mountain. She had never seen beyond the door of her apartment.

Nor, when she looked into her long mirrors, did she realize what looked back at her was the most beautiful thing in the beautiful room.

But the woman realized. She had nurtured Jaspre like a rare plant, its white stem, its bright petals. The woman, who had no lust for human flesh, who lusted only for one thing, had caught her breath, seeing the glowing creature drift toward her from the sunset shade of an ilex tree in the walled garden. The skin like pearl melting in the dress of pearl silk, scarcely any difference observable. The loosely plaited hair like a golden rope . . .

"Do you recall how old you are, Jaspre?"

"Yes, my lady. I am thirteen years of age."

"You have never," said the woman, "asked me anything concerning the rest of the house."

"It is," said Jaspre, "the house." To this non-questioning the woman had molded her in subtle, gentle ways. It was not apathy. It was an intelligent disinterest in those things that could have no bearing on one's existence.

And yet now, "I will show you, today, a door. It has remained hidden, Jaspre, but now we shall use it, you and I."

Jaspre nodded calmly.

"Yes, my lady."

The door was concealed behind a section of the wall which moved. It gave on a stair. It was the stair to the insularium.

To the world of the apartment and the garden, then, was added this new continent of marvels. In ranks, the tall stoppered vials, from which a pinch of powder dropped into air might burn, another produce sweet perfume. Slim flattened statues of bronze stood in the shadows, a bronze bull with wings. While on a platform reached by several narrow steps, was a great instrument which, when tilted up at an extravagant angle, pierced some opening in the side of the house, and by means of mirrors and lenses captured the stars and planets in the green evening sky.

Jaspre wandered in the vast room, windowless and lamplit, sipping from it, tasting of it. She had been nurtured and lessoned to gain much from the appearances of things, the sensations of their umbras, less from their functions. Hers was an intellect which dreamed and fantasized upon, rather than inquired into. So, she touched the statues, the telescope, gazed on the constellations, inhaled the sweet aroma of powders, and did not ask their natures, nor require to be informed.

Presently, the woman led her to a narrow alcove and drew aside a curtain of smoky samite, and then another behind it of black velvet. Beyond the curtains was a gate of horn scrolled by black iron, and with a gilded iron lock. This lock the woman negotiated without a key, using strange pressures of her hands. As the gate opened, a third curtain was disclosed, but this of a dull brazen chain mail.

Although she did not know, and had been told nothing of what lay in store, the suspenseful drawings of curtain upon curtain, the unlocking of the gate, the metallic mesh, the unsuspected depth of the alcove itself—all this had worked upon the young girl's imagination. That some pinnacle of importance was about to be attained, and revealed to her, was apparent.

The woman paused, her hand resting on the drapery of brazen mail.

"That I took you in," she said, "was for a purpose. I did not, as you have seen, bring you here to serve me. And yet, I did take you, raise you, keep you, in peerlessness and in innocence, that you might serve—another. And now you are fit to learn of him and to look upon his image."

Jaspre's heart beat quickly, instinctually, and she waited, her eyes fixed only on the curtain. Which, in another instant, the woman drew aside.

Jaspre had never seen a man before. Inside the alcove stood a man. Then, as the lamplight beat on him, she beheld he was made of stone, a pale stone finely planed, fantastically burnished, colored with all the most convincing nuances of life.

His long and thickly curling hair was black, and lay seemingly loosely against his forehead, cheeks and shoulders. His features were chisled, of a faintly Eastern cast, singularly handsome even to the point of beauty. His flesh was pale, but not with the dead pallor of the stone, rather a curious dark whiteness flushed through with somber tinctures, as if ichors flowed directly under the skin. In the eyes, which most of all might display lifelessness in a statue, there had been set dark jewels that glimmered, that seemed possessed of actual sight.

The image was represented as garbed in a black outer mantle of the ancient Parsua, diagonally cut and fringed with silver, with a broad belt that flashed with large bloody gems. Gems of blood and ink and blue water also crusted the shoes carved on his feet, and stared from his long fingers. One hand lay relaxedly at his side. The left hand was gracefully uplifted in an ambiguous gesture of offering or beckoning.

The statue's feet rested upon a low plinth, and in the plinth some words had long ago been cut, their letters softened now by time that had, in no other form, impaired the freshness of the work. After a while, as if impelled, Jaspre looked at them and next leaned close.

Deo Arimanio, they read. *Nox Invictus.*

The woman spoke quietly at Jaspre's side.

"You have deciphered the writing. Do you translate it?"

"He is," said the girl, "a god, and this is his name. And here it says that night—"

The woman broke in, softly as before:

"Unconquerable Night, is what it says. It is a good wish for his future victory, against the god of fires."

Jaspre's eyes fell. Her heart beat so fast now, the woman did not miss it.

"But that fight is far off. For now, he dwells in darkness and is at peace in his kingdom."

"Does he then," said Jaspre, "truly exist?"

"Yes. He is God. The King of the World, that is him. The Prince of Darkness, eternal adversary to the devil Lucifer, bringer of light and blinding. The Lord of Eternal Night. By some called Bel, and in the Roman tongue Arimanio, as it is carved here. But, as you shall worship him now, he is named Angemal. Angel, demon and god."

"And I am to serve him?"

"For this you were born."

Slowly, the young girl's cheeks stained red with blood. The lights in the eyes of the statue blazed and sang, as if he saw and smiled at it.

2

Into her world, then, of floral garden, of gracious room, of magical laboratory, a god had entered.

In miniature, a creation myth, Jaspre its feminine principle, her axis now fixed: A man who was also God. Who was also the Serpent.

She was thirteen, and everything spread before her, a glittering sea clothed in phantasmal mists, tossed by mystic gradual lights. On this her mind embarked, into the perpetual dawn of knowledge. And now knowledge was enhanced by that best accessory of all—desire.

Jaspre did not know that, in the person of the remarkable and lifelike statue, her desire and her love had come to reside, to put down tenacious roots, to burn into red blossom. But her feelings, senses, yearnings, these did the work for her. She did not need to think, to know, to reason. Her pulse and her spirit were now her guides.

The woman had been not only generous in the gifts of learning she had poured in on Jaspre's receptive intelligence; she had been also most selective. There from the first, always, was that which would enhance and increase this ultimate moment, the moments which succeeded it. Nothing to detract. Nothing to alarm, defame, erode.

Knowing nothing of this esoteric cult which now had been set shimmering before her, Jaspre knew no indecision and no doubt.

She had been born to magnify him. He had chosen her.

For a year then, she "served."

She brought her offerings, fruits and flowers from the walled garden, and laid them at his jeweled feet. She brought him wine, and music. She began to dream of him. Her dreams were lapped in fires, which were dark, heatless, sable, laval fires, such as burned in his kingdom, far, far beneath the earth.

Lord of Demons, Prince of Darkness. She began to hunger for him, for those things which were his. Less and less did she sleep by night. She slept by day, drawing her shutters and her curtains against the sun. At dusk, as if to blue morning, she woke. She sat among the closed night flowers, and played upon her guitars to the rising of the moon. She made her hymns to him then. And her skin grew moon-burned, she supposed, as was his.

For she too altered. Her hair hung long, to her waist, to the backs of her knees. She was taller, more slender. An ambient night-vision enabled her to perceive the silver apples on the tree, the nocturnal moths flying on their paper wings from the surface of the moon.

Angemal. Arimanio. Lord of winged things, lord of the panther and the black wolf, lord of quietude, lord of the silver caves a hundred miles beneath the ground.

Fruit and flowers she brought, her hymns she brought, and next her tears.

He lived. She worshiped. Should he never come to her? Would they never meet? Her mind, her spirit dreamed; her flesh spoke also—dreams were not enough.

"How old, Jaspre, are you now?"

"I am fourteen, my lady."

"I seldom see you in the garden, now, by day."

"I am there, after dark, my lady. I abhor the sun. I love only the night."

"And he that is the night. You love him."

Jaspre's face, lovely, savage, a storm.

"Yes! I would give him more than ever I gave."

"You shall."

The hidden door, the stair, the insularium.

There was a difference to the room.

At its every angle, aromatics burned, bittersweet, rose, terebinth, camfre, myrrh. The lamps were out. A single blue cloud burned high up on a massive chandelier of candles let down from the ceiling. On the floor there were marks: The Circle, the Star of the Five Points, the figures of an arcane zodiac—Fish, Serpent, Bull, Virgin. . . . At various stations stood the symbols, the Chalice, the Sword, the Crown, the Veil and others.

The girl knew little of any of this. But what if her baroque world grew still more unfamiliar and bizarre? She checked at nothing.

"Now," said the woman, "I will tell you what you must do."

She did so, and Jaspre obeyed her.

Jaspre removed her gown of icy satin, her undergarments and her shoes. Unaware that nakedness meant shame and vulnerability, she went to the Circle naked, and naked she lay down in it, her hands and her feet extended to conform with four points of the five-point Star, her head conforming with the fifth, and her hair like pale golden snow frayed out about her everywhere.

The scents of the smokes made Jaspre drowsy and sad. Her heart beat in her very womb, and she lay listening to it.

The woman said to her out of a blue fire-cloud in the air:

"You have brought many offerings to the Lord Angemal. Do you fear to give him of your blood?"

"No," said Jaspre.

She did not know what she had said. Yet her soul knew and beat its wings within her, attempting, like the caged bird it was, to fly.

How beautiful she was. The woman, bending above her with the silver knife, comprehended without human lust this beauty. After all, had she not trained it, complimented it, nourished it, setting all things to inspire the enchantment of physical perfection? A child of golden light.

"Fix your thoughts," the woman said, "upon him. Do you consent to be his?"

Jaspre breathed. "I do."

She felt a flicker of pain. It did not trouble her, she rejoiced in it. Her pain, too, she would render him. Was it sufficient? She almost entreated to be hurt again.

The dream began subtly, first with a vague awareness, then with a still certainty, of where she was, and the reason and the logic of it.

Far down under the house, beneath the very surface of the ground, the insularium was a cellar. Only the telescope craned, and that merely by the means of a stone funnel and twisted lenses, upward into the sky. Now, however, some portion of the chamber, that magian centre at which Jaspre lay—the pivot of the Star

—had become the head of a mighty tower.

The tower was stone. She could visualize it quite clearly, the roofed cup of its spire, which contained her, the perilous swooping descent of its sides. Slowly, Jaspre rose. She looked about. The room in the head of the tower was small, and, of course, pentagonal. In each of the five sides, a long window lacking glass framed an uncanny vaporous darkness, without form and void —indeed, as the first darkness of all, the dark of Chaos, had been described in the parchments of the Judaians.

Yet Jaspre was not afraid of the void darkness, nor of the height of the tower. She went to the window before her, toward which formerly her own skull had pointed, and looked out of it.

The scentless, moistureless yet somber mists, disturbed a little, seemingly by human warmth, swirled and floated. Nothing else was visible before her, and so she turned her eyes to gaze downward.

The spire plummeted below her, it seemed, forever. She grasped at once, as if she had always been cognizant of the fact, that the sub-earth cellar of the insularium could be also the top of a tower because such a place thrust on, by sorcerous means, keep into the core of the world, to those nether regions, those buried caverns that had been named Hell, or Hades, or Tellus Occultus in explanatory, analogous legend. It seemed to fall miles below her, growing ever more slender as it fell, becoming eventually nothing larger or stronger than a needle, and on this the upper masonry balanced, and she within it, so she seemed to experience all at once a gentle swaying in the cup of the tower, rhythmic as that of a pendulum, mild as that of a flower stalk in a breeze. And still she was not afraid, either to sense this motion, or to stare downward into the formless abyss.

There were carvings in the sides of the tower, the magic symbols from the chamber as it had been, the zodiac, the Crown, the Sword, the Chalice—she knew such seals must hold the spire safely.

And then she became aware of the little fluttering at her left wrist. She looked, and a scarlet butterfly flew away from her, away down the length of the tower, and then another, another, an unraveling scarf of butterflies like winged blood. Jaspre watched them descend, and as she leaned there, strands of her unbound hair came streaming over her shoulder and spilled away also, unfurling like a shining ribbon, down, down, down with the red ribbons of the butterflies, down, down into the dark below.

Jaspre was filled by wonder, but not by perplexity or questioning. The butterflies, which were born from her wrist, seemed spontaneous and natural. The way her hair trickled now from its fount, pouring over her, pouring down, a golden river, a silken robe, growing long and longer—as it had done in her life, but never so swiftly—this appeared also fitting, and right.

And then her very eyes, her very sight and spirit seemed to be freed of her body, and she herself, invisible, a thing of air, flowed down the tower.

She had no fear. She was exalted, glad.

Darkness before her, stone beside her, the falling of scarlet and gold. At length, she saw an ending to every descent: The base of the tower.

It was a doorless block of granite, high as the walls of the house had been. And cut in the stone in letters taller than Jaspre, when she had been in her body, the words NOX INVICTUS.

The butterflies played around these letters, blooming like garnets in the dullness. The golden hair touched them, and so the ground, and poured no more, a trembling fountain that ran away into a thread above, and thus into nothing. Up there, in that fresh, inverted abyss, Jaspre's body leaned from its window, no longer to be seen.

About the base of the tower, a plain of smooth and empty rock glided away and away, also into an inchoate nothingness that was its only horizon.

Jaspre knew only gladness. Incorporeal and weightless as the winged creatures in their dance, she danced with them. Caught in a spiral of heatless laval fire, she beheld another thing, and paused transfixed.

On the horizon of nothingness, many days' journey as it seemed from the tower, a flicker of blue luster had evolved. And, in a few seconds, drew nearer. And in a few seconds more, much nearer.

As the light began to swell, Jaspre saw that it was not light at all, but the essence of the dark given clarity, *unlight*, more sumptuous, more lambent than any luminence of the world's.

From the brilliancy, bringing it like great wings folded about him, a figure presently came.

He was like some picture from one of her books, animate, and imbued with all the qualities of life, and with some other thing which was not life at all, but more, perhaps, than life. He rode a horse blacker than the blackest material the earth was capable of, blacker than ebony, sable or jet. But its mane and tail were of an iridescent blueness, and it was accoutered in a blue and silver hail of sparkling stuffs, bells, gems. He, too, was garbed in the same black blackness as the flesh of the horse, as if he had stepped from some Avernal lake and its waters clung to him, becoming satin, and metal. His hair was the blackest thing of all. His face—but as he came closer, he turned his head. Some shadow then, the curling curtain of the hair, hid all his features from her. She did not need to see them. She knew they were the features of the statue in the insularium.

He had ridden now to the spot where the fountain of hair came down. The horse stopped at once. And he, the god-demon she was to call Angemal, stretched out one hand gloved in silvery mail and with one huge ring upon it, a fiery ring of an apricot color, the stone which was her name. He touched the golden rope of her hair with his fingers. And immediately Jaspre saw, without amazement, the hair twisted and refashioned itself. It became a ladder of silk—

She heard him laugh, then, a low sound, scarcely audible, musical as song and colder than frozen iron. Then he was gone. It was not that he vanished. He was; he was *not*.

Jaspre felt a desolation and an agony, as if her psychic fibers tore and frayed at their insubstantial roots. Her spiritual sight went out, and in that fading, she glimpsed the butterflies raining like blood on the plain, while above her the golden hair was burning, shriveling, blowing away; black butterflies where there had been red. Even her soul, witnessing this, seemed to shrivel also, and to die.

Jaspre opened her eyes. She lay on the floor of the insularium. The chandelier smoldered, the color of thunder, most of its candles extinguished, and the woman bent close. For the only time in all their acquaintance, Jaspre beheld a glaze of ghostly excitement on my lady's face, but it was almost instantly spent, or hidden.

"And what did you see?"

"I saw—a tower." Jaspre faltered. She was weak, and dazzled by the feeble light. Her left wrist, bound tightly with cloth, hurt her.

"Yes. A tower. What else?"

Jaspre's eyes closed of themselves. The woman leaned nearer and she whispered. "Speak, or I shall be angry. *What else*?"

"I saw—red butterflies, and my hair falling to the rock like a shower of gold. I never knew my hair would shine and blaze. . . . Oh, my lady, I am so weary."

"Speak. Or I shall strike you."

Jaspre's eyes opened wide. She was shocked and afraid. Never before had she been threatened—there had been no need.

"I—" Jaspre sought for words, found them, "I left my body and drifted down the tower to the plain beneath. There a man came, all in black, riding a black horse."

"And was it he?"

"I think that it was. But he turned aside. And when he touched the rope of hair, it became a silken ladder, and he laughed. Then my hair burnt and charred, and he was gone."

Jaspre, barely conscious that she did so, raised her hands, the left with pain and stiffness, and discovered her hair and that it was not charred, but whole, lying in a long swath all about her. Though it was not so long as it had been when she dreamed of it, and maybe not so golden.

The woman had gone away from her. In the darkest corner of the room she sat, rigid, silent. And then she said, "You have lain there enough. Dress. Go to your apartment." And her voice was like a frost.

Jaspre rose. Her sight clouded. She took up her clothes.

"Have I displeased you, my lady?"

"It is your master you have displeased, the princely lord Angemal. For he did not find you acceptable, it seems."

Jaspre wept as she clad herself in the gleaming garments which no longer gleamed.

"Why?" she murmured. "What have I done?"

"I do not know. You were reared to please him. A child of light consenting to the shadow. It should have delighted him, master of ironies that he is. But the emblem of the vision is blatant. He rejected you, and therefore the way into the world whereby he might have manifested."

Jaspre wept soundlessly, her heart, her spirit, breaking.

"*Go*," hissed the woman.

Jaspre ran soundlessly away.

After a while, the woman came to her feet. She returned across the chamber and regarded the opened Pentacle, the bowl of blood.

"Do you deny me still?" she asked. "Or do you only make a test of me? You shall have more. You shall have all of her, as I vowed, the supreme gift, the willing sacrifice of a human life. She will die for you with ecstasy and joy, in all her beauty, virgin, innocent, and wise. As I have caused her to be, a matchless unplucked flower set down upon your altar. Have I not devoted the sum of my energies to your service? You know I hunger for the power that only you can deliver. You *know*. But you will bargain, as in the days of the First Earth. Yes, you shall have more, much more."

3

The moon rose late upon the walled garden. It hollowed the sky above to a milky blueness, and touched the formal walks below with dainty traceries like lace, and in the wilder grottoes found out the pale limbs of nymphs and the mirrors of water. Passing the sundial, making of it a moon-dial, the moon let fall a long veil onto a lawn hedged by the briers of a savage shrubbery, and so found Jaspre, too. She sat upon the ground. Her hands, which had been dishes for her tears, now lay as if slain in her lap. Her eyes were dry, her heart a desert.

Her flight had brought her here, close to the outer wall, and she had glimpsed above it those claws of the blasted trees which were all she had ever seen of the outer world. A waste, wilderness must lie beyond the wall. And now, her life was such a wilderness. She could not mourn. She could no longer weep. Not grasping the essence of annihilation, she wished only to cease, to be no more, as if sunk in some profound sleep devoid of wakening.

It was unnecessary for her to search about herself. Even when the moon blushed through the garden, there was, for Jaspre's desolation, nothing to gaze on. And then some dormant nerve, rousing in spite of her, caused her to glance, to see the lawn, the dense shrubbery, and seated between the two, the still shape that was neither plant nor statue.

Jaspre's hands revived and sprang together. She started up, young enough to experience terror even in her misery. But the shape ascended with her, steeped in moonlight. So she saw—not image, not dream—but an actual man, and scarcely seven paces away. His unknown features were handsome, even in the mezzotint of the moon, though drained by the moon as if seen through a fine gauze. His hair looked dark,. his eyes brilliant. His clothes were quite alien to her, being classically functional—the wear of a woodsman or a hunter from one of her painted books.

She said nothing. Her sheer innocence did not provide for her the ready suspicion and the outcry of another. Yet she feared, feared till he spoke. And then his voice lulled her by its gentleness, by the curious words he offered.

"Sweet girl, your hair, which is like the sun by day, becomes the moon by night."

"How do you know me?" Jaspre asked, wonder easing her anxiety as anxiety had eased her despair.

"I do not know you. The witch's house is avoided. But once, I came through the wood and heard melody and singing. It was not she. A creeper robes the wall. I climbed it. I saw you. I see you now. But know you I do not."

Jaspre turned a little way, toward the distant house from which the wide length of the garden separated her. It was an intuitive response, to evade him. And yet it was the house she now wished to evade, and all remembered and familiar things, tainted by her failure, the harsh and hating phrases of the woman this man named "the witch." She had flown here, and could not fly back into such dismal shelter. Entrapped, she shuddered. She had been kept from her own kind. She guessed this was a crime—to converse with a man. She had been offered to a god. Who had refused her. A fresh dawn of pain broke on her, a fresh river of tears.

"Why do you weep?" the man murmured. He had drawn closer, and though she had turned from him, she did not move away. "Do you fear me so very greatly?"

"No," she said. Her tears were once more ceaseless.

"Is it then that hag who mistreats you?"

"I am worthless," said Jaspre. "I desire only to die."

"You are lovely," he said. "You must live."

"I was born for one purpose, and cannot hope for it."

"What strange purpose can that have been?"

Her tongue could not render all his titles, yet: "A lord," she sobbed, snared by the unique and final easement of confession, confiding. "A prince of a prince—and he does not want me. I am vile to him."

"He told you this?"

"My lady told me it was so."

His voice was already murmuring at her ear, and now his arm slid around her. In her grief and wretchedness she leaned against him, aware this was some further sin, yet unable to deny herself the comfort of it.

"Silver maiden," he said, and held her so she might rest, "say I am a prince. Will you take me as your lord instead?"

But Jaspre, truthful in her naïveté, answered quietly,

"You are not a prince."

"Yes," he said, and laughed. His laugh was like warm music, and she recalled that other laughter in her dream, so terrible, so cold, and the destructive icy flame that leapt from it. "These are merely the clothes I wander in. Trust me, I have finery, I have horses flowered in metal and jewels. I have a kingdom, and rule there."

"No," she said, but she laid her head against his shoulder.

He smiled. His lips found her hair, her forehead, eyelids, lashes, and her tears ended.

"Will you take me, then, for myself alone?"

"Take you for yourself?" she whispered.

"As love, as lord. Your prince, if no other's, gorgeous Jaspre?"

"How do you know my name?"

"I heard her call you, the hag in the house."

Jaspre raised her eyes. She beheld him again, more sufficiently now. Remotely, the darkness of his hair calmed her, a reminiscence. And it seemed to her that, although he was not the statue, nor a god, yet he was more wonderful than the phantom she had been given to, his eyes like stars, his face like an angel's—and though she had been allowed her life that she should serve one alone, and that the demon prince Angemal, yet it came to her all at once that to love him had been her error. Then the man who stood with her, holding her in his strong arms, warming and soothing her with his nearness and his own human beauty, kissed her mouth. The kiss was like no other touch, no other sensation ever before felt or looked for. It seemed to her indeed she slept and had passed thereby into some other world. Or that, for the very first, she had awakened.

From the depths of this extraordinary state, as if beneath water, she heard him say, "You are imprisoned here. Come with me, I will release you from your jail."

Metaphysically she struggled then, with everything, and with herself. And was brought at last to say: "No. I may not leave this place."

"Yes. You may, you shall."

Jaspre hung her head, the comprehension of the wrong she did now awesome, almost pleasing, yet dreadful and to be dreaded.

And in that moment flame burst like lightning from the far-off shadow of the house. A lamp had been kindled in Jaspre's apartment.

"She searches for you," he said. "Go in to her. Tomorrow, at moonrise, return to this spot. You will find me here."

"No, I shall not return."

"It is a charm I set on you."

"No. No."

"I will draw you back to me. You shall see. By a chain of stars."

"No."

A footstep clacked upon a path.

His arms let her free, and Jaspre moved toward the footstep like a clockwork thing. Deception was new to her, a sword which cut her hands. She did not look back, but beyond the clouded shrubbery, beyond a hedge, a walk, a tree with the moon like a white fruit in its branches, his voice stole once again to her ear, a moth of sound, no more, that replied only: *Yes.*

The woman stood, black on the lighted window, one foot on the paving which led into the garden, waiting. She spoke to Jaspre, toneless now, and cool, no longer harsh. There was in this mode a sort of forgiveness, a promise of leniency. Conjured before Jaspre's dazzled eyes, the image of Angemal in his black garments formed, and faded. The unknown lover's mortal kisses lingered on her skin.

The world was round and moved upon its axis, so the young girl knew quite well from her studies. The stars were fixed, it was the Earth which traveled, save for those wandering errants, the planets, which came and went on their own invisible roads across the dusks of morning and of evening and the enormous night of the outer spaces, which held everything. And yet, how contrary perception, which knew as well and better, that the sun, the moon, the stars arose and set. The earth was flat beneath a dome of ether which flooded with light or dark only as the fire of the sun illumined it or went out.

And so with Jaspre's world, which had become two things: The impossible, which was reality; the reality, which was impossible.

The witch's servant and doll, pressed now into rituals of fast and trance, into kneelings upon stone, crystals told like a rosary in her hands, incantations hymned, a pilgrimage along the inner path to him, the god of shadows, the prince of darknesses. Perfection to be made more perfect, fineness to be refined, until acceptable, until irresistible. This, the world as it was. And in the garden, the other earth, the landscape of truth growing every second more actual, making all else a ghost, and yet never to be realized. This, the deception, the mirage.

They walked under the black leaves, the silver branches. They leaned together on pillows of moss, only their hands linked, now and then their lips brushing, but as the leaves brushed overhead, like children. His patience in all seduction was inexhaustible, this stranger from beyond the wall. He spoke of the world's wonders, of seas and citadels, mountains, markets, the swarms of mankind, urging her to seek them with him. He mentioned a towered city and she knew he lied when he seemed to say that it was his. "I will not come away with you," she said. "Tomorrow, do not wait for me here." But always he returned, and Jaspre also. She came to gaze on him, to gaze and gaze, entranced by his features, the graceful gestures which he made. These trances were unlike the trances of the insularium. She fasted only in his absence. Like a certain flower, her love died in one area, sprang upward in another. To Jaspre now he was more handsome than the dream of Angemal. She worshiped at a human altar. The inspiration of the witch's god—Ahriman, Asmodeus, Bel, Satan—fell from her like charcoaled petals, and seemed done.

She felt no danger. Nor it seemed did her lover. His constant pleas, disciplined and never actually pleading, that she should escape with him at once, always *now* this night, this, or this, it had no slightest savor of panic. It seemed he thought time ever on his side, eternity before them in which he might persuade, in which she could decide.

And she, trained like a vine to the surface of her passions, heights but not depths, beheld all as it was, developing upon it her longings and her theme. She never checked at the sweep of a bird's wing over the moon, a shimmer of taloned briers, rustling among grasses. She had no guilt, no apprehension. She had a distant fear, but not of any subtle thing. She seemed to sense the abyss of the tower descending before her, and the great fall she must accomplish, and the ultimate rejection, no longer despair, but a terror past enduring. Yet it was to come. It was the earth-turning sunset, moon-set. A fact that all evidence perceptible assured her was not so.

"How old are you, Jaspre?" the woman asked.

"I am fifteen years of age, my lady."

"You are pale and sullen. Do you mean to be?"

"No, my lady."

"Give me your hand. Do you see this faint scar on your wrist? Do you remember how it came there?"

"I remember a binding. When the binding was taken away, I saw the mark."

"Tonight you may not wander in the garden. In an hour, when the twilight is finished, you will enter the insularium."

* * *

The woman sat brooding in her stone house, on fifteen years of power that had not yet come to her, on a statue with jeweled eyes, fingers, feet, until her servant advanced into the room, that tall man, the dark-skinned Eastern mute.

In his language of signs, which she had taught him and which only they knew, he spoke to her. He had watched the portico. It was ever the same. A young man would appear, slender, his movements catlike and elegant, his face in shadow, the moon at his back. And Jaspre would go to him. They would lie together, but not in carnality. She was a virgin yet, the pure child who was the price, the bargain, the golden rope into Hell the Underworld.

Demons had tempted maidens with apples. Peerless maidens, exquisite youths, these were the apples with which demons were tempted. Reared from birth to particular ways, definite forms, pliant, sweet, unblemished. Once bitten into, bruised, the spoiled fruit was useless and must be flung away.

Plucked, then, but untasted. Perhaps only readied the more certainly. . . .

But the woman saw suddenly with her inner eye, the scavenging father, the lustrous whore, mother to the child. And these devils of the mind, cringing before her also jeered. "Why," the man said, filthy and golden, "he is one step from enjoying her, one minute away from getting her, maybe, full of a pair of twins—a son, a daughter. A powder, then, a herb, to make the trouble go away—"

The woman dismissed him, this vision. Next, her flesh-and-blood servant was sent out. Only then was one darkened window opened upon the night-bloomed garden.

Black before moon-rise, it stretched its vistas out for her, a carpet, a maze. Nothing stirred, no white figure, the too-early moon of Jaspre. Not even the foliage of a forbidden tree rippled in the low wind.

Presently the woman passed from black night to a black lacquer door, and down into her sorcerous cellar.

4

Jaspre descended to the insularium, the first short prelude to that greater, abysmal descent. She knew, her very spirit guessed, that this night was the ending. And she was dull with terror, lax with it, walked like one almost asleep.

Within, her mind turned drearily about and about.

Her blond slippers on the stair, she thought of her lover, the moon's rising and his arrival in the garden to find, at last, she had not come to meet him. Her flaxen dress brushing over the occult threshold, she wondered how long he would linger before he went away. On each occasion of their parting she had said farewell to him as if forever, dimly acknowledging this last night would claim her finally, fold her away into its obscurity. From which, her instinct told her, she would not return. Her impulse was not to resist. Such seeds as resistance had never been planted in her character. She was just that creature her mentor had trained her to be—pliant, sweet—only he had left any imprint on her psyche, molding her gradually and mysteriously to other patterns. Yet he had been, it seemed, too gradual, too patient, too much an optimist. Seeing the shadow of the chamber spread like a deep well before her, Jaspre felt a moment's wilder fright, picturing how he might come to the house to seek her, batter on its doors, invite the wrath of the woman's cold and unstressed powers—but he, too, feared. *The witch* he had called her from the first. He had never gone close to the inner walls of the house. No, he would not risk himself in such a way. He would merely suppose the immaculate idyll ended, and so it was. He would hasten to safety. Jaspre mourned and she was glad it should be so.

She had never asked his name, even. In a year she, being herself, had not thought to ask it. Yet he had known her name, and might remember her a little while, grieve for her, perhaps. And she, adrift in endless, moonless, starless night, might sense that memory and tremulously burn like the palest spark, until he should utterly forget.

High in the vault of the chamber, the chandelier ignited into fire, not blue but purple. The witch stood waiting, straight and stony, her hands folded, each finger exactly fitted between two others.

"Come here, Jaspre. Disrobe."

Jaspre saw the marks upon the floor, the Circle, the Star of the Five Points, the figures of the zodiac—and other talismans, infinitely less clear and more inimical. The purple glare, while it showed all, seemed to give neither illumination nor dimension.

"Hurry," said the woman. "Why are you so reluctant? Have you mislaid who it is you serve? Yesterday, only then, you laid flowers at his feet and poured wine into the cup. You have been dutiful, but can you have omitted love?"

"No, my lady. Oh, no." If not to resist, she had learned somewhat to lie.

"For where else," mused the woman, "could you bestow your love? Not upon me, for sure. Not upon yourself, for yourself you do not know. Only Angemal is your motive and your lord. Remove your garments."

Jaspre shivered. Her hands hesitated over pearl buttons, satin lacings. Somehow she had also learned the vulnerability of nakedness.

But at length, naked, vulnerable, she lay down within the Circle, and it was closed upon her. Far away, then, she seemed to see her own luminous flesh, enmauvened by the ghastly candles, dashed with painted symbols, touched with oil and soot and water, and the unholy rosary of crystals pooled in chains between her breasts. The drugged resins uncurled their vapors. She floated in a syrupy sea of dread, her face beneath its surface, drowning.

The woman spoke aloud for a long while, but not at any time to her. It seemed the woman must be speaking to Angemal. And Jaspre felt his untrue beauty hover like a smoking star.

A knife slit the sea, the vapor, glittering.

"Kiss the blade."

Jaspre kissed the blade.

"Consent," said the woman. "Tell me so."

Jaspre shut her eyes. "I consent."

The pain licked out, her left wrist, her right wrist. Drums pounded in her veins. With abject horror, Jaspre felt herself commence to fall—

—And the dream began suddenly, and was appalling.

Jaspre hung from the fifth window of the great tower of stone, by her wrists. Two scarlet cords bound them, and she, depending from the cords, drew them tight. Her arms seared and throbbed so she moaned for their agony, while below, the endless drop of stone sheered down and down, and down and down. One other thing fell from the tower, a ladder of gold. Even as she looked at it, the ladder quivered. Its silken rungs sang out. Jaspre realized, even through her blinding hurt and fear, that something had sought the ladder's foot, something climbed toward her.

Angemal came to her, as he had been so ceaselessly invited to do. She recollected the black horse, the black-clad rider who turned away his face. His face was not beautiful, then, but hideous, so hideous it could blast with fire as his laughter had blasted the fountain of her hair. But how had such a notion claimed her? Pain and terror suggested it. The golden rope, enchanted from her hair and her soul, tingled, rang.

Jaspre writhed as she hung from the cords of her spilling

blood, and the incredible tower swayed like a granite stalk. Jaspre screamed—

And woke as if she had been flung upward through the floor, the witch's face above her, malevolent and intent, its eyes alive, its lips parted.

"Ah," said the witch. "Go back—" and struck Jaspre across the cheek.

Cast from fear into fear, Jaspre was flung down again.

She felt herself, weightless as a feather, spinning, tumbling.

She lay at the tower's foot, and before her the shaft of it ran up and up, becoming a slender pole, an awl, a needle, nothing. A black cloud clung to the side of the tower where it had thinned to an awl. The cloud moved stealthily upward, and she believed it was the thing which now Angemal had become. No ladder of gold, no cascade of golden hair remained to aid its journey. Jaspre lay fluttering on the rock plain beneath the tower, and found herself a white butterfly. Her body hung far away, out of her sight, screaming no longer, already dead.

Jaspre's wings flickered. She flew up into the air. She flew across the vacant rock, leaving the tower, the miasmic climbing cloud, the remembrance of her own self hung out for it, an empty vessel of flesh.

There was no more pain, and as she drew farther and farther from the immensity of the tower, very little sensation of any kind. She herself had already half forgotten herself. No longer did she have a name, or any care. Only love remained with her, though love was also nameless now, love and sorrow both, and both limitless and inexplicable. The void and its mists enveloped her. The tower was only a colossal specter at her back. The rocky plain ran on and on, barren of everything. And she, a shining flake of snow, sailed on her tiny tissue wings into the formless dark.

The woman stood, and experienced the enormous energy that seemed now to drive toward her. Its center was the girl who bled slowly to death in the heart of the Pentagram. But its source lay deeper down. The atmosphere of the insularium was charged and murmurous. Vials and vases shifted softly in their cabinets, the telescope rattled, the chandelier vibrated, splashing the floor and the inert body with wax, as if an earth tremor went on under the house.

The woman drew her breath thickly. Her dead eyes were quickened, her mask face almost galvanized to expression. Prepared and ready, her stance never altered as one by one the lights sank and bloodied to extinction.

A vast blackness, impenetrable and complete, brimmed upward through the chamber.

Seeing nothing, hearing no sound, still the woman knew some fabric of dimension gave way. A presence like a cool heat, invisible, untouchable, passed through, and was in that place with her.

The woman kneeled.

"Lord of lords," she said. "You are welcome, at last."

The voice which answered spoke within her head. It answered with one word, a word in a language obsolete and lost, a word no longer capable of any meaning. And yet the woman was granted a total understanding of that word, of all its myriad and profound convolutions, its nuances, its embryo.

She started instantly and involuntarily to her feet in a terror worse than any terror Jaspre had ever known.

And at once a hundred articles fell from their shelves and smashed all about, and the room was garishly lit by burning powders, so not a trace of darkness remained.

Darkness had failed, the desire of all one life had failed. Great fear stole in behind failure, shadow of a shadow.

Yet the woman walked from the insularium, straight as a rule, and in her cold unimpassioned voice, she called the mute servant to her. She instructed him on the cleansing and clearing of the chamber. One further item must be removed from it. The wrists of the girl were to be tightly bound, she was to be found some rag of clothing to put on. Then the servant should carry her outside the walls of the house, among the bone trees, and throw her down there. From her apartment, then, all the furnishings must be stripped, broken and burned. The bed, the chairs, the rich garments, the harpsichord. Even the jewels must be thrust into a fire, consumed.

The man gestured that he grasped what should be done, and went about it silently.

The woman proceeded through the house. As she moved beneath the many candelabra and the lamps, a silken thing glowed brightly in her hand. With one last stroke of her knife she had severed Jaspre's hair. She had stripped her of everything, her life, even her death—which now was purposeless.

Stiffly, the woman stepped into the avenues of the long garden, into darkness that was not darkness.

Among the pavilions of these trees, Jaspre had played as a

child, here she had wandered into her young womanhood, shut from the world. And here he, too, had come, the intruder, the ruiner of all, who should in turn be ruined.

The moon poised on the peak of an unseen mountain in the sky, as white as fear.

The woman reached the lawn ringed by its savage shrubbery, the spiked and twining briers, and there she saw him immediately, now seated, idle and dismayed, now springing up alarmed. The moon chalked in his pale face, the leaves rained black lights across it. The woman saw him as if he were some cipher only, the humble garb, wild hair, wide eyes. Here it was, that which had cheated her after all, had married the delicious fruit in some insidious manner the woman neither knew nor cared to know. He was the ultimate of all Jaspre's treasures that would be destroyed.

"Come seeking love?" the woman said. "Here it is then."

And she tossed to him the golden rope of hair like a spray of silver water over the night.

Then she spoke swiftly to the garden.

At once the shrubbery came alive, lifting on its stems to seize and tangle, and the long briers like spined serpents thrashed and fell down on him. She did not hear him shout or cry aloud. She did not even stay to witness what she had wrought on him, his body whipped, clawed, flayed, his eyes scratched out. She turned and retraced her way briskly toward the house and into it, not glancing back.

Directly returning to the insularium, she found the mess of misadventure already tidied; and the half-dead useless thing had been dragged from her sight. While perhaps only psychologically perceived, there swirled the smell of burning silk, the sharp cracks of splintering wood.

All that she must do, she had done. Yet she had importuned him, angered him, and now he had withheld at last what she had asked and schemed to get life-long—but still she must propitiate him, Angemal who was Arimanio, Prince of Darkness.

So, her rage in check, her anguish reined, she drew back the curtain of samite, the curtain of velvet, unlocked the door of horn and iron. Spat upon, degraded, his word of denial twisting in her brain, she would kneel and worship him, atoning all her days for ever once imploring him. And maybe he would be merciful. Then she pulled aside the curtain of mail and a brazen beast shrieked in her very soul, although the witch gazed in upon the alcove and therefore in upon herself as pitilessly as she gazed upon all other persons.

She never changed, although she felt, soft as a kiss, the curse he set on her, some future of blight, disease, or madness, felt it begin within her at that very instant she beheld the statue. There were marks of claws upon it, the precious tintings ripped away and the stone gouged to ugliness beneath. While from the blind bowls of its eyes, the sable jewels had been torn out.

And so she was made aware of the full measure of his jest, and his fastidious disdain, the one she had tempted with a rope of gold.

Jaspre had flown, a weightless butterfly in a waste of granite. Then there came a waste of coldness, where frost formed on her wings. They presently snapped off from her like broken shutters, and she smote the stony floor of Hell and crawled about there. But then there came the waste of a great and blazing light, and Jaspre opened her eyes upon a blanched sun with the face of a skull, and against this sun huge fleshless hands stretched out in supplication or in hate.

She had been cast out into the wood of dead trees, which seemed to her to be all the world there was for her now. Her hair had been sheared, coarse sacking covered her skin. Bracelets of agony held her wrists. Her hands were numb and flaccid, and there was no strength in her, not even the strength to lament. So she lay and watched the white sun creep across the fingertips of the trees. The earth was not as he had told her, her lover, yet she loved him only the more for his lies, which had been beautiful and kind. And if she must die here in the wilderness of the bone trees, she did not care, if he should only continue to live happily in some dream or magic place he had conjured.

"But I will take you there, my child," he said, his voice, for her, like music.

And she smiled with joy, supposing she imagined it, until he lifted her in his arms.

For a few moments she lay against him as the pain melted from her wrists and body and a warmth and strength flowed like wine through her limbs, her heart, her reverie, and then she raised her head and looked at him. She knew him immediately, no other but the wanderer who had found her in her garden, the young man she had loved. She knew him also as he truly was, since now he had set aside the screen of illusion. Tall and pale, his hair blacker than blackness, appareled in the dark of the moon and gemmed with its light, his eyes the oceans and the shores of night, his face no longer hidden, more wonderful than the face of any statue.

She was not afraid. Love cannot fear. She asked him nothing.

But as he held her now, the bandaging upon her healed wrists turned to jewels, the sacking robe to velvet. And as in her dream, her hair grew like a wind and poured over like a tide, a streaming silver that was gold, until it brushed the ground.

The bleached trees parted and darkness ran through. A black horse, flamed with a sapphire mane and tail, and hung with stars, stood against the sinking moon.

He mounted Jaspre before him.

"The soil, the roots of the trees, will open," he said. "My land lies there, beneath the earth. Whatever the woman told you of it you must unremember. The country is not as once it was, nor as you have seen it."

Then the horse danced on the ground and the ground gave way. Far off, Jaspre glimpsed—not darkness—but a glimmering multicolored luminescence, the flowering trees of an endless spring, the towers of a rainbow city, more beautiful than in any book, and winged with a gilded morning, there in the black pit of the world.

"And this is your kingdom," the young girl sighed.

"This is my kingdom," said the Prince of Darkness.

And to this they went.

Basileus

by

Robert Silverberg

In Christian lore, demons are literally "fallen angels," angels who have opted against God. The differences between demons and angels are thus purely doctrinal *differences . . . so that one might fairly say that a demon is just an angel with a Bad Attitude, one who has declared for evil rather than for good.*

Count them together or count them separately, though, one thing that is certain about demons and angels is that there are a lot of them. One rough count, by Kabbalists in the fourteenth century, estimated that there were 301,655,722 angels. Fallen or not, that's quite a few angels to keep tabs on, so many that perhaps the best way to keep track of them all would be to use a computer—

Or perhaps that would turn out to be a very bad idea indeed. . . .

One of the most prolific authors alive, Robert Silverberg can lay claim to more than 450 fiction and nonfiction books and over 3000 magazine pieces. Within SF, Silverberg rose to his greatest prominence during the late sixties and early seventies, winning four Nebula Awards and a Hugo Award, publishing dozens of major novels and anthologies—1973's Dying Inside, *in particular, is widely considered to be one of the best novels of the seventies—and editing* New Dimensions, *perhaps the most influential original anthology series of its time. In 1980, after four years of self-imposed "retirement," Silverberg started writing again, and the first of his new novels,* Lord Valentine's Castle, *became a nationwide best-seller. Silverberg's other books include* The Book of Skulls, Downward to the Earth, Tower of Glass, The World Inside, Born with the Dead, Shadrach in the Furnace,

Lord of Darkness (a historical novel), and Valentine Pontifex, the sequel to Lord Valentine's Castle. His collections include Unfamiliar Territory, Capricorn Games, Majipoor Chronicles, The Best of Robert Silverberg, and At the Conglomeroid Cocktail Party. His most recent book is Tom O'Bedlam's Song, a novel.

* * *

IN THE SHIMMERING LEMON-YELLOW OCTOBER LIGHT, CUNNINGHAM touches the keys of his terminal and summons angels. An instant to load the program, an instant to bring the file up, and there they are, ready to spout from the screen at his command: Apollyon, Anauel, Uriel, and all the rest. Uriel is the angel of thunder and terror; Apollyon is the Destroyer, the angel of the bottomless pit; Anauel is the angel of bankers and commission brokers. Cunningham is fascinated by the multifarious duties and tasks, both exalted and humble, that are assigned to the angels. "Every visible thing in the world is put under the charge of an angel," said St. Augustine in *The Eight Questions*.

Cunningham has 1,114 angels in his computer now. He adds a few more each night, though he knows that he has a long way to go before he has them all. In the fourteenth century the number of angels was reckoned by the Kabbalists, with some precision, at 301,655,722. Albertus Magnus had earlier calculated that each choir of angels held 6,666 legions, and each legion 6,666 angels; even without knowing the number of choirs, one can see that that produces rather a higher total. And in the Talmud, Rabbi Jochanan proposed that new angels are born "with every utterance that goes forth from the mouth of the Holy One, blessed be He."

If Rabbi Jochanan is correct, the number of angels is infinite. Cunningham's personal computer, though it has extraordinary add-on memory capacity and is capable, if he chooses, of tapping into the huge mainframe machines of the Defense Department, has no very practical way of handling an infinity. But he is doing his best. To have 1,114 angels on line already, after only eight months of part-time programming, is no small achievement.

One of his favorites of the moment is Harahel, the angel of archives, libraries, and rare cabinets. Cunningham has designated Harahel also the angel of computers: it seems appropriate. He invokes Harahel often, to discuss the evolving niceties of data processing with him. But he has many other favorites, and his tastes run somewhat to the sinister: Azrael, the angel of death, for example, and Arioch, the angel of vengeance, and Zebuleon, one of the nine angels who will govern at the end of the world. It is Cunningham's job, from eight to four every working day, to devise programs for the interception of incoming Soviet nuclear warheads, and that, perhaps, has inclined him toward the more apocalyptic members of the angelic host.

He invokes Harahel now. He has bad news for him. The invocation that he uses is a standard one that he found in Arthur Edward Waite's *The Lemegeton, or The Lesser Key of Solomon*, and he has dedicated one of his function keys to its text, so that a single keystroke suffices to load it. "I do invocate, conjure, and command thee, O thou Spirit N, to appear and to show thyself visibly unto me before this Circle in fair and comely shape," is the way it begins, and it proceeds to utilize various secret and potent names of God in the summoning of Spirit N—such names as Zabaoth and Elion and, of course, Adonai—and it concludes, "I do potently exorcise thee that thou appearest here to fulfill my will in all things which seem good unto me. Wherefore, come thou, visibly, peaceably, and affably, now, without delay to manifest that which I desire, speaking with a clear and perfect voice, intelligibly, and to mine understanding." All that takes but a microsecond, and another moment to read in the name of Harahel as Spirit N, and there the angel is on the screen.

"I am here at your summons," he announces expectantly.

Cunningham works with his angels from five to seven every evening. Then he has dinner. He lives alone, in a neat little flat a few blocks west of the Bayshore Freeway, and does not spend much of his time socializing. He thinks of himself as a pleasant man, a sociable man, and he may very well be right about that, but the pattern of his life has been a solitary one. He is thirty-seven years old, five feet eleven, with red hair, pale blue eyes, and a light dusting of freckles on his cheeks. He did his undergraduate work at Cal Tech, his postgraduate studies at Stanford, and for the last nine years he has been involved in ultrasensitive military-computer projects in northern California. He has never married. Sometimes he works with his angels again after dinner, from eight to ten, but hardly ever any later than that. At ten he goes to bed. He is a very methodical person.

He has given Harahel the physical form of his own first computer, a little Radio Shack TRS-80, with wings flanking the screen. He had thought originally to make the appearance of his angels more abstract—showing Harahel as a sheaf of kilobytes, for example—but like many of Cunningham's best and most austere ideas, it had turned out impractical in the execution, since abstract concepts did not translate well into graphics for him.

"I want to notify you," Cunningham says, "of a shift in jurisdiction." He speaks English with his angels. He has it on good, though apocryphal, authority that the primary language of the angels is Hebrew, but his computer's audio algorithms have no Hebrew capacity, nor does Cunningham. But they speak English readily enough with him: they have no choice. "From now on," Cunningham tells Harahel, "your domain is limited to hardware only."

Angry green lines rapidly cross and recross Harahel's screen, "By whose authority do you—"

"It isn't a question of authority," Cunningham replies smoothly. "It's a question of precision. I've just read Vretil into the data base, and I have to code his functions. He's the recording angel, after all. So, to some degree, then, he overlaps your territory."

"Ah," says Harahel, sounding melancholy. "I was hoping you wouldn't bother about him."

"How can I overlook such an important angel? 'Scribe of the knowledge of the Most High,' according to the Book of Enoch. 'Keeper of the heavenly books and records.' 'Quicker in wisdom than the other archangels.' "

"If he's so quick," says Harahel sullenly, "give *him* the hardware. That's what governs the response time, you know."

"I understand. But he maintains the lists. That's data base."

"And where does the data base live? The hardware!"

"Listen, this isn't easy for me," Cunningham says. "But I have to be fair. I know you'll agree that some division of responsibilities is in order. And I'm giving him all data bases and related software. You keep the rest."

"Screens. Terminals. CPUs. Big deal."

"But without you, he's nothing, Harahel. Anyway, you've always been in charge of cabinets, haven't you?"

"And archives and libraries," the angel says. "Don't forget that."

"I'm not. But what's a library? Is it the books and shelves and stacks, or the words on the pages? We have to distinguish the container from the thing contained."

"A grammarian," Harahel sighs. "A hairsplitter. A casuist."

"Look, Vretil wants the hardware, too. But he's willing to compromise. Are you?"

"You start to sound less and less like our programmer and

more and more like the Almighty every day," says Harahel.

"Don't blaspheme," Cunningham tells him. "Please. Is it agreed? Hardware only?"

"You win," says the angel. "But you always do, naturally."

Naturally. Cunningham is the one with his hands on the keyboard, controlling things. The angels, though they are eloquent enough and have distinct and passionate personalities, are mere magnetic impulses deep within. In any contest with Cunningham they don't stand a chance. Cunningham, though he tries always to play the game by the rules, knows that, and so do they.

It makes him uncomfortable to think about it, but the role he plays is definitely godlike in all essential ways. He puts the angels into the computer; he gives them their tasks, their personalities, and their physical appearances; he summons them or leaves them uncalled, as he wishes.

A godlike role, yes. But Cunningham resists confronting that notion. He does not believe he is trying to be God; he does not even want to think about God. His family had been on comfortable terms with God—Uncle Tim was a priest, there was an archbishop somewhere back a few generations, his parents and sisters moved cozily within the divine presence as within a warm bath—but he himself, unable to quantify the Godhead, preferred to sidestep any thought of it. There were other, more immediate matters to engage his concern. His mother had wanted him to go into the priesthood, of all things, but Cunningham had averted that by demonstrating so visible and virtuosic a skill at mathematics that even she could see he was destined for science. Then she had prayed for a Nobel Prize in physics for him; but he had preferred computer technology. "Well," she said, "a Nobel in computers. I ask the Virgin daily."

"There's no Nobel in computers, Mom," he told her. But he suspects she still offers novenas for it.

The angel project had begun as a lark, but had escalated swiftly into an obsession. He was reading Gustav Davidson's old *Dictionary of Angels*, and when he came upon the description of the angel Adramelech, who had rebelled with Satan and had been cast from heaven, Cunningham thought it might be amusing to build a computer simulation and talk with him. Davidson said that Adramelech was sometimes shown as a winged and bearded lion, and sometimes as a mule with feathers, and sometimes as a peacock, and that one poet had described him as "the enemy of God, greater in malice, guile, ambition, and mischief than Satan, a fiend more curst, a deeper hypocrite." That was appealing. Well, why not build him? The graphics were easy—Cunningham chose the winged-lion form—but getting the personality constructed involved a month of intense labor and some consultations with the artificial-intelligence people over at Kestrel Institute. But finally Adramelech was on line, suave and diabolical, talking amiably of his days as an Assyrian god and his conversations with Beelzebub, who had named him Chancellor of the Order of the Fly (Grand Cross).

Next, Cunningham did Asmodeus, another fallen angel, said to be the inventor of dancing, gambling, music, drama, French fashions, and other frivolities. Cunningham made him look like a very dashing Beverly Hills Iranian, with a pair of tiny wings at his collar. It was Asmodeus who suggested that Cunningham continue the project; so he brought Gabriel and Raphael on line to provide some balance between good and evil, and then Forcas, the angel who renders people invisible, restores lost property, and teaches logic and rhetoric in Hell; and by that time Cunningham was hooked.

He surrounded himself with arcane lore: M. R. James's editions of the Apocrypha, Waite's *Book of Ceremonial Magic* and *Holy Kabbalah*, the *Mystical Theology and Celestial Hierarchies* of Dionysius the Areopagite, and dozens of related works that he called up from the Stanford data base in a kind of manic fervor. As he codified his systems, he became able to put in five, eight, a dozen angels a night; one June evening, staying up well past his usual time, he managed thirty-seven. As the population grew, it took on weight and substance, for one angel cross-filed another, and they behaved now as though they held long conversations with one another even when Cunningham was occupied elsewhere.

The question of actual *belief* in angels, like that of belief in God Himself, never arose in him. His project was purely a technical challenge, not a theological exploration. Once, at lunch, he told a co-worker what he was doing, and got a chilly blank stare. "Angels? *Angels?* Flying around with big flapping wings, passing miracles? You aren't seriously telling me that you believe in angels, are you, Dan?"

To which Cunningham replied, "You don't have to believe in angels to make use of them. I'm not always sure I believe in electrons and protons. I know I've never seen any. But I make use of them."

"And what use do you make of angels?"

But Cunningham had lost interest in the discussion.

He divides his evenings between calling up his angels for conversations and programming additional ones into his pantheon. That requires continuous intensive research, for the literature of angels is extraordinarily large, and he is thorough in everything he does. The research is time-consuming, for he wants his angels to meet every scholarly test of authenticity. He pores constantly over such works as Ginzberg's seven-volume *Legends of the Jews,* Clement of Alexandria's *Prophetic Eclogues,* Blavatsky's *The Secret Doctrine.*

It is the early part of the evening. He brings up Hagith, ruler of the planet Venus and commander of 4,000 legions of spirits, and asks him details of the transmutation of metals, which is Hagith's specialty. He summons Hadranel, who in Kabbalistic lore is a porter at the second gate of Heaven, and whose voice, when he proclaims the will of the Lord, penetrates through 200,000 universes; he questions the angel about his meeting with Moses, who uttered the Supreme Name at him and made him tremble. And then Cunningham sends for Israfel the four-winged, whose feet are under the seventh earth and whose head reaches to the pillars of the divine throne. It will be Israfel's task to blow the trumpet that announces, the arrival of the Day of Judgment. Cunningham asks him to take a few trial riffs now—"just for practice," he says, but Israfel declines, saying he cannot touch his instrument until he receives the signal, and the command sequence for that, says the angel, is nowhere to be found in the software Cunningham has thus far constructed.

When he wearies of talking with the angels, Cunningham begins the evening's programming. By now the algorithms are second nature and he can enter angels into the computer in a matter of minutes; once he has done the research. This evening he inserts nine more. Then he opens a beer, sits back, and lets the day wind down to its close.

He thinks he understands why he has become so intensely involved with this enterprise. It is because he must contend each day in his daily work with matters of terrifying apocalyptic import: nothing less, indeed, than the impending destruction of the world. Cunningham works routinely with megadeath simulation. For six hours a day he sets up hypothetical situations in which Country A goes into alert mode, expecting an attack from Country B, which thereupon begins to suspect a preemptive strike and commences a defensive response, which leads Country A to escalate its own readiness, and so on until the bombs are in the air. He is aware, as are many thoughtful people both in Country A and Country B, that the possibility of computer-generated misinformation leading to a nuclear holocaust increases each year, as the time-window for correcting a malfunction diminishes. Cunningham also knows something that very few others do, or perhaps no one else at all: that it is now possible to send a signal to the giant computers—to Theirs or Ours, it makes no difference—that will be indistinguishable from the impulses that an actual flight of airborne warhead-bearing missiles would generate. If such a signal is permitted to enter the system, a minimum of eleven minutes, at the present time, will be needed to carry out fail-safe determination of its authenticity. That, at the present time, is too long to wait to decide whether the incoming missiles are real; a much swifter response is required.

Cunningham, when he designed his missile-simulating signal, thought at once of erasing his work. But he could not bring himself to do that: the program was too elegant, too perfect. On the other hand, he was afraid to tell anyone about it, for fear that it would be taken beyond his level of classification at once, and sealed away from him. He does not want that, for he dreams of finding an antidote for it, some sort of resonating inquiry mode that will distinguish all true alarms from false. When he has it, if he ever does, he will present both modes, in a single package, to Defense. Meanwhile, he bears the burden of suppressing a concept of overwhelming strategic importance. He has never done anything like that before. And he does not delude himself into thinking his mind is unique: if he could devise something like this, someone else probably could do it also, perhaps someone on the other side. True, it is a useless, suicidal program. But it would not be the first suicidal program to be devised in the interests of military security.

He knows he must take his simulator to his superiors before much more time goes by. And under the strain of that knowledge, he is beginning to show distinct signs of erosion. He mingles less and less with other people, he has unpleasant dreams and occasional periods of insomnia; he has lost his appetite and looks gaunt and haggard. The angel project is his only useful diversion, his chief distraction, his one avenue of escape.

For all his scrupulous scholarship, Cunningham has not hesitated to invent a few angels of his own. Uraniel is one of his: the angel of radioactive decay, with a face of whirling electron shells. And he has coined Dimitrion, too: the angel of Russian literature, whose wings are sleighs, and whose head is a snow-covered samovar. Cunningham feels no guilt over such whimsies. It is his computer, after all, and his program. And he knows he is not the first to concoct angels. Blake engendered platoons of them in his poems: Urizen and Orc and Enitharmon and more. Milton, he suspects, populated *Paradise Lost* with dozens of sprites of his own invention. Gurdjieff and Alastair Crowley and even Pope Gregory the Great had their turns at amplifying the angelic roster: why then not also Dan Cunningham of Palo Alto, California? So from time to time he works one up on his own. His most recent is the dread high lord Basileus, to whom Cunningham has given the title of Emperor of the Angels. Basileus is still incomplete: Cunningham has not arrived at his physical appearance, nor his specific functions, other than to make him the chief administrator of the angelic horde. But there is something unsatisfactory about imagining a new archangel, when Gabriel, Raphael, and Michael already constitute the high command. Basileus needs more work. Cunningham puts him aside, and begins to key in Duma, the angel of silence and of the stillness of death, thousand-eyed, armed with a fiery rod. His style in angels is getting darker and darker.

On a misty, rainy night in late October, a woman from San Francisco whom he knows in a distant, occasional way, phones to invite him to a party. Her name is Joanna; she is in her mid-thirties, a biologist working for one of the little gene-splicing outfits in Berkeley; Cunningham had had a brief and vague affair with her five or six years back, when she was at Stanford, and since then they have kept fitfully in touch, with long intervals elapsing between meetings. He has not seen her or heard from her in over a year. "It's going to be an interesting bunch," she tells him. "A futurologist from New York, Thomson the sociobiology man, a couple of video poets, and someone from the chimpanzee-language outfit, and I forget the rest, but they all sounded first rate."

Cunningham hates parties. They bore and jangle him. No matter how first rate the people are, he thinks, real interchange of ideas is impossible in a large random group, and the best one can hope for is some pleasant low-level chatter. He would rather be alone with his angels than waste an evening that way.

On the other hand, it has been so long since he has done anything of a social nature that he has trouble remembering what the last gathering was. As he had been telling himself all his life, he needs to get out more often. He likes Joanna and it's about time they got together, he thinks, and he fears that if he turns her down, she may not call again for years. And the gentle patter of the rain, coming on this mild evening after the long dry months of summer, has left him feeling uncharacteristically relaxed, open, accessible.

"All right," he says. "I'll be glad to go."

The party is in San Mateo, on Saturday night. He takes down the address. They arrange to meet there. Perhaps she'll come home with him afterward, he thinks: San Mateo is only fifteen minutes from his house, and she'll have a much longer drive back up to San Francisco. The thought surprises him. He had supposed he had lost all interest in her that way; he had supposed he had lost all interest in anyone that way, as a matter of fact.

Three days before the party, he decides to call Joanna and cancel. The idea of milling about in a roomful of strangers appalls him. He can't imagine, now, why he ever agreed to go. Better to stay home alone and pass a long rainy night designing angels and conversing with Uriel, Ithuriel, Raphael, Gabriel.

But as he goes toward the telephone, that renewed hunger for solitude vanishes as swiftly as it came. He *does* want to go to the party. He *does* want to see Joanna: very much, indeed. It startles him to realize that he positively yearns for some change in his rigid routine, some escape from his little apartment, its elaborate computer hookup, even its angels.

Cunningham imagines himself at the party, in some brightly lit room in a handsome redwood-and-glass house perched in the hills above San Mateo. He stands with his back to the vast-sparkling wraparound window, a drink in his hand and he is holding forth, dominating the conversation, sharing his rich stock of angel lore with a fascinated audience.

"Yes. 300 million of them," he is saying, "and each with his fixed-function. Angels don't have free will, you know. It's Church doctrine that they're created with it, but at the moment of their birth, they're given the choice of opting for God or against Him, and the choice is irrevocable. Once they've made it, they're unalterably fixed, for good or for evil. Oh, and angels are born circumcised, too. At least the Angels of Sanctification and the Angels of Glory are, and maybe the seventy Angels of the Presence."

"Does that mean that all angels are male?" asks a slender dark-haired woman.

"Strictly speaking, they're bodiless and therefore without sex," Cunningham tells her. "But in fact, the religions that believe in angels are mainly patriarchal ones, and when the angels are visualized, they tend to be portrayed as men. Although some of them, apparently, can change sex at will. Milton tells us that in *Paradise Lost*: 'Spirits when they please can either sex assume, or both; so soft and uncompounded is their essence pure.' And some angels seem to be envisioned as female in the first place. There's the Shekinah, for instance, 'the bride of God,' the manifestation of His glory indwelling in human beings. There's Sophia, the angel of wisdom. And Lilith, Adam's first wife, the demon of lust—"

"Are demons considered angels, then?" a tall professorial-looking man wants to know.

"Of course. They're the angels who opted away from God. But they're angels nevertheless, even if we mortals perceive their aspects as demonic or diabolical."

He goes on and on. They all listen as though he is God's own messenger. He speaks of the hierarchies of angels—the seraphim, cherubim, thrones, dominations, principalities, powers, virtues, archangels, and angels—and he tells them of the various lists of the seven great angels which differ so greatly once one gets beyond Michael, Gabriel, and Raphael, and he speaks of the 90,000 angels of destruction and the 300 angels of light; he conjures up the seven angels with seven trumpets from the Book of Revelation; he tells them which angels rule the seven days of the week and which the hours of the days and nights; he pours forth the wondrous angelic names, Zadkiel, Hashmal, Orphaniel, Jehudiel, Phaleg, Zagzagel. There is no end to it. He is in his glory. He is a fount of arcana. Then the manic mood passes. He is alone in his room; there is no eager audience. Once again he thinks he will skip the party. No. No. He will go. He wants to see Joanna.

He goes to his terminal and calls up two final angels before bedtime: Leviathan and Behemoth. Behemoth is the great hippopotamus-angel, the vast beast of darkness, the angel of chaos. Leviathan is his mate, the mighty she-whale, the splendid sea serpent. They dance for him on the screen. Behemoth's huge mouth yawns wide. Leviathan gapes even more awesomely. "We are getting hungry," they tell him. "When is feeding time?" In rabbinical lore, these two will swallow all the damned souls at the end of days. Cunningham tosses them some electronic sardines and sends them away. As he closes his eyes he invokes Poteh, the angel of oblivion, and falls into a black dreamless sleep.

At his desk the next morning, he is at work on a standard item, a glitch-clearing program for the third-quadrant surveillance satellites, when he finds himself unaccountably trembling. That has never happened to him before. His fingernails look almost white, his wrists are rigid, his hands are quivering. He feels chilled. It is as though he has not slept for days. In the washroom he clings to the sink and stares at his pallid, sweaty face. Someone comes up behind him and says, "You all right, Dan?"

"Yeah. Just a little attack of the damn queasies."

"All that wild living in the middle of the week wears a man down," the other says, and moves along. The social necessities have been observed: a question, a noncommittal answer, a quip, goodbye. He could have been having a stroke here and they would have played it the same way. Cunningham has no close friends at the office. He knows that they regard him as eccentric—eccentric in the wrong way, not lively and quirky but just a peculiar kind of hermit—and getting worse all the time. I could destroy the world, he thinks. I could go into the Big Room and type for fifteen seconds, and we'd be on all-out alert a minute later and the bombs would be coming down from orbit six minutes later. I could give that signal. I could really do it. I could do it right now.

Waves of nausea sweep him and he grips the edge of the sink until the last racking spasm is over. Then he cleans his face, and calmer now, returns to his desk to stare at the little green symbols on the screen.

That evening, still trying to find a function for Basileus, Cunningham discovers himself thinking of demons, and of one demon not in the classical demonology—Maxwell's Demon, the one that the physicist James Clerk Maxwell postulated to send fast-moving molecules in one direction and slow ones in another, thereby providing an ultra-efficient method for heating and refrigeration. Perhaps some sort of filtering role could be devised for Basileus. Last week a few of the loftier angels had been complaining about the proximity to them of certain fallen angels within the computer. "There's a smell of brimstone on this disk that I don't like," Gabriel had said. Cunningham wonders if he could make Basileus a kind of traffic manager within the program: let him sit in there and ship the celestial angels into one sector of a disk, the fallen ones to another.

The idea appeals to him for about thirty seconds. Then he sees how fundamentally trivial it is. He doesn't need an angel for a job like that; a little simple software could do it. Cunningham's corollary to Kant's categorical imperative: *Never use an angel as mere software.* He smiles, possibly for the first time all week. Why, he doesn't even need software. He can handle it himself, simply by assigning princes of Heaven to one file and demons to a different one. It hadn't seemed necessary to segregate his angels that way, or he would have done it from the start. But since now they were complaining—

He begins to flange up a sorting program to separate the files. It should have taken him a few minutes, but he finds himself working in a rambling, muddled way, doing an untypically sloppy job. With a quick swipe, he erases what he has done. Gabriel would have to put up with the reek of brimstone a little longer, he thinks.

There is a dull throbbing pain just behind his eyes. His throat is dry, his lips feel parched. Basileus would have to wait a little longer, too. Cunningham keys up another angel, allowing his fingers to choose for him, and finds himself looking at a blankfaced angel with a gleaming metal skin. One of the early ones, Cunningham realizes. "I don't remember your name," he says. "Who are you?"

"I am Anaphaxeton."

"And your function?"

"When my name is pronounced aloud, I will cause the angels to summon the entire universe before the bar of justice on Judgment Day."

"Oh, Jesus," Cunningham says. "I don't want you tonight."

He sends Anaphaxeton away and finds himself with the dark angel Apollyon, fish scales, dragon wings, bear feet, breathing fire and smoke, holding the key to the Abyss. "No," Cunningham says, and brings up Michael, standing with drawn sword over Jerusalem, and sends him away only to find on the screen an angel with 70,000 feet and 4,000 wings, who is Azrael, the angel of death. "No," says Cunningham again. "Not you. Oh, Christ!" A vengeful army crowds his computer. On his screen there passes a flurrying regiment of wings and eyes and beaks. He shivers and shuts the system down for the night. Jesus, he thinks. Jesus, Jesus, Jesus. All night long, suns explode in his brain.

On Friday his supervisor, Ned Harris, saunters to his desk in an unusually folksy way and asks if he's going to be doing anything interesting this weekend. Cunningham shrugs. "A party Saturday night, that's about all. Why?"

"Thought you might be going off on a fishing trip, or something. Looks like the last nice weekend before the rainy season sets in, wouldn't you say?"

"I'm not a fisherman, Ned."

"Take some kind of trip. Drive down to Monterey, maybe. Or up into the wine country."

"What are you getting at?"

"You look like you could use a little change of pace," Harris says amiably. "A couple of days off. You've been crunching numbers so hard, they're starting to crunch you, is my guess."

"It's that obvious?"

Harris nods. "You're tired, Dan. It shows. We're a little like air traffic controllers around here, you know, working so hard we start to dream about blips on the screen. That's no good. Get the hell out of town, fellow. The Defense Department can operate without you for a while. Okay? Take Monday off. Tuesday, even. I can't afford to have a fine mind like yours going goofy from fatigue, Dan."

"All right, Ned. Sure. Thanks."

His hands are shaking again. His fingernails are colorless.

"And get a good early start on the weekend, too. No need for you to hang around here today until four."

"If that's okay—"

"Go on. Shoo!"

Cunningham closes down his desk and makes his way uncertainly out of the building. The security guards wave at him. Everyone seems to know he's being sent home early. Is this what it's like to crack up on the job? He wanders about the parking lot for a little while, not sure where he has left his car. At last he finds it, and drives home at thirty miles an hour, with horns honking at him all the way as he wanders up the freeway.

He settles wearily in front of his computer and brings the system on line, calling for Harahel. Surely the angel of computers will not plague him with such apocalyptic matters.

Harahel says, "Well, we've worked out your Basileus problem for you."

"You have?"

"Uriel had the basic idea, building on your Maxwell's Demon notion. Israfel and Azrael developed it some. What's needed is an angel embodying God's justice and God's mercy. A kind of evaluator, a filtering angel. He weighs deeds in the balance, and arrives at a verdict."

"What's new about that?" Cunningham asks. "Something like that's built into every mythology from Sumer and Egypt on. There's always a mechanism for evaluating the souls of the dead —this one goes to Paradise, this one goes to Hell—"

"Wait," Harahel says. "I wasn't finished. I'm not talking about the evaluation of individual souls."

"What then?"

"Worlds," the angel replies. "Basileus will be the judge of worlds. He holds an entire planet up to scrutiny and decides whether it's time to call for the last trump."

"Part of the machinery of Judgment, you mean?"

"Exactly. He's the one who presents the evidence to God and helps Him make his decision. And then he's the one who tells Israfel to blow the trumpet, and he's the one who calls out the name of Anaphaxeton to bring everyone before the bar. He's the prime apocalyptic angel, the destroyer of worlds. And we thought you might make him look like—"

"Ah," Cunningham says. "Not now. Let's talk about that some other time."

He shuts the system down, pours himself a drink, sits staring out the window at the big eucalyptus tree in the front yard. After a while it begins to rain. Not such a good weekend for a drive into the country after all, he thinks. He does not turn the computer on again that evening.

Despite everything, Cunningham goes to the party. Joanna is not there. She has phoned to cancel, late Saturday afternoon, pleading a bad cold. He detects no sound of a cold in her voice, but perhaps she is telling the truth. Or possibly she has found something better to do on Saturday night. But he is already geared for party going, and he is so tired, so eroded, that it is more effort to change his internal program than it is to follow through on the original schedule. So about eight that evening he drives up to San Mateo, through a light drizzle.

The party turns out not to be in the glamorous hills west of town, but in a small cramped condominium, close to the heart of the city, furnished with what looks like somebody's college-era chairs and couches and bookshelves. A cheap stereo is playing the pop music of a dozen years ago, and a sputtering screen provides a crude computer-generated light show. The host is some sort of marketing exec for a large video-games company in San Jose, and most of the guests look vaguely corporate, too. The futurologist from New York has sent his regrets; the famous sociobiologist has also failed to arrive; the video poets are two San Francisco gays who will talk only to each other, and stray not very far from the bar; the expert on teaching chimpanzees to speak is in the red-faced-and-sweaty-stage of being drunk, and is working hard at seducing a plump woman festooned with astrological jewelry. Cunningham, numb, drifts through the party as though he is made of ectoplasm. He speaks to no one; no one speaks to him. Some jugs of red wine are open on a table by the window, and he pours himself a glassful. There he stands, immobile, imprisoned by inertia. He imagines himself suddenly making a speech about angels, telling everyone how Ithuriel touched Satan with his spear in the Garden of Eden as the Fiend crouched next to Eve, and how the hierarch Ataphiel keeps Heaven aloft by balancing it on three fingers. But he says nothing. After a time he finds himself approached by a lean, leathery-looking woman with glittering eyes, who says, "And what do you do?"

"I'm a programmer," Cunningham says. "Mainly I talk to angels. But I also do national security stuff."

"Angels?" she says, and laughs in a brittle, tinkling way. "You talk to angels? I've never heard anyone say that before." She pours herself a drink and moves quickly elsewhere.

"Angels?" says the astrological woman. "Did someone say angels?"

Cunningham smiles and shrugs and looks out the window. It is raining harder. I should go home, he thinks. There is absolutely no point in being here. He fills his glass again. The chimpanzee man is still working on the astrologer, but she seems to be trying to get free of him and come over to Cunningham. To discuss angels with him? She is heavy-breasted, a little walleyed, sloppy-looking. He does not want to discuss angels with her. He does not want to discuss angels with anyone. He holds his place at the window until it definitely does appear that the astrologer is heading his way; then he drifts toward the door. She says, "I heard you say you were interested in angels. Angels are a special field of mine, you know. I've studied with—"

"Angles," Cunningham says. "I play the angles. That's what I said. I'm a professional gambler."

"Wait," she says, but he moves past her and out into the night.

It takes him a long while to find his key and get his car unlocked, and the rain soaks him to the skin, but that does not bother him. He is home a little before midnight.

He brings Raphael on line. The great archangel radiates a beautiful golden glow.

"You will be Basileus," Raphael tells him. "We've decided it by a vote, hierarchy by hierarchy. Everyone agrees."

"I can't be an angel. I'm human," Cunningham replies.

"There's ample precedent. Enoch was carried off to Heaven and became an angel. So was Elijah. St. John the Baptist was actually an angel. You will become Basileus. We've already done the program for you. It's on the disk: just call him up and you'll see. Your own face, looking out at you."

"No," Cunningham says.

"How can you refuse?"

"Are you really Raphael? You sound like someone from the other side. A tempter. Asmodeus. Astaroth. Belphegor."

"I am Raphael. And you are Basileus."

Cunningham considers it. He is so very tired that he can barely think.

An angel. Why not? A rainy Saturday night, a lousy party, a splitting headache: come home and find out you've been made an angel, and given a high place in the hierarchy. Why not? Why the hell not?

"All right," he says. "I'm Basileus."

He puts his hands on the keys and taps out a simple formulation that goes straight down the pipe into the Defense Department's big northern California system. With an alteration of two keystrokes, he sends the same message to the Soviets. Why not? Redundancy is the soul of security. The world now has about six minutes left. Cunningham has always been good with computers. He knows their secret language as few people before him have.

Then he brings Raphael on the screen again.

"You should see yourself as Basileus while there's still time," the archangel says.

"Yes. Of course. What's the access key?"

Raphael tells him. Cunningham begins to set it up.

Come now, Basileus! We are one!

Cunningham stares at the screen with growing wonder and delight, while the clock continues to tick.

Twilla

by

Tom Reamy

The late Tom Reamy handled the milieu *of small-town America as well as anyone who ever worked in the genre. Here he introduces something monstrous, malefic, and strange into the dusty, sun-drenched Kansas landscape he loved so well, and treats us to an unlikely confrontation between a spinster schoolteacher and the forces of Hell itself . . . .*

Before his tragically early death, Tom Reamy had won both the Nebula and the World Fantasy Award for his short fiction, and was well on his way to becoming one of the most respected writers of the 1970s. His books include the acclaimed novel Blind Voices, *and* San Diego Lightfoot Sue and Other Stories, *a collection of his excellent short fiction.*

* * *

TWILLA GILBREATH BLEW INTO MISS MAHAN'S LIFE LIKE A pink butterfly wing that same day in early December the blue norther dropped the temperature forty degrees in two hours. Mr. Choate, the principal, ushered Twilla and her parents into Miss Mahan's ninth-grade homeroom shortly after the tardy bell rang. She had just checked the roll: all seventeen ninth graders were present except for Sammy Stocker, who was in the Liberal hospital having his appendix removed. She was telling the class how nice it would be if they sent a get-well card, when the door opened.

"Goooood morning, Miss Mahan," Mr. Choate smiled cheerfully. He always smiled cheerfully first thing in the morning, but soured as the day wore on. You could practically tell time by

Mr. Choate's mouth. "We have a new ninth grader for you this morning, Miss Mahan. This is Mr. and Mrs. Gilbreath and their daughter, Twilla."

Several things happened at once. Miss Mahan shook hands with the parents; she threw a severe glance at the class when she heard a snigger—but it was only Alice May Turner, who would probably giggle if she were being devoured by a bear; and she had to forcibly keep her eyebrows from rising when she got a good look at Twilla. Good Lord, she thought, and felt her smile falter.

Miss Mahan had never in her life, even when it was fashionable for a child to look like that, seen anyone so perfectly . . . pink and . . . doll-like. She wasn't sure why she got such an impression of pinkness, because the child was dressed in yellow, and had golden hair (*that's* the color they mean when they say golden hair, she thought with wonder) done in, of all things, drop curls, with a big yellow bow in back. Twilla looked up at her with a sweet, radiant, sunny smile and clear periwinkle-blue eyes.

Miss Mahan detested her on sight.

She thought she saw, when Alice May giggled, the smile freeze and the lovely eyes dart toward the class, but she wasn't sure. It all happened in an instant, and then Mr. Choate continued his Cheerful Charlie routine.

"Mr. Gilbreath has bought the old Peacock place."

"Really?" she said, tearing her eyes from Twilla. "I didn't know it was for sale."

Mr. Gilbreath chuckled. "Not the entire farm, of course. I'm no farmer. Only the house and grounds. Such a charming old place. The owner lives in Wichita and had no use for them."

"I would think the house is pretty run down," Miss Mahan said, glancing at Twilla, still radiating at the world. "No one's lived in it since Wash and Grace Elizabeth died ten years ago."

"It is a little," Mrs. Gilbreath said pleasantly.

"But structurally sound," interjected Mr. Gilbreath pleasantly.

"We'll enjoy fixing it up," Mrs. Gilbreath continued pleasantly.

"Miss Mahan teaches English to the four upper grades," said Mr. Choate, bringing them back to the subject, "as well as speech and drama. Miss Mahan has been with the Hawley school system for thirty-one years."

The Gilbreaths smiled pleasantly. "My . . . ah . . . Twilla seems very young to be in the ninth grade." That get-up made her look about eleven, Miss Mahan thought.

The Gilbreaths beamed at their daughter. "Twilla is only thirteen," Mrs. Gilbreath crooned, pride swelling in her like yeast. "She's such an intelligent child. She was able to skip the second grade."

"I see. From where have you moved?"

"Boston," replied Mr. Gilbreath.

"Boston. I hope . . . ah . . . Twilla doesn't find it difficult to adjust to a small-town school. I'm sure Hawley, Kansas, is quite unlike Boston."

Mr. Gilbreath touched Twilla lovingly on the shoulder. "I'm sure she'll have no trouble."

"Well." Mr. Choate rubbed his palms together. "Twilla is in good hands. Shall I show you around the rest of the school?"

"Of course," smiled Mrs. Gilbreath.

They departed with fond murmurings and goodbyes, leaving Twilla like a buttercup stranded in a cabbage patch. Miss Mahan mentally shook her head. She hadn't seen a family like that since Dick and Jane and Spot and Puff were sent the way of *McGuffey's Reader*. Mr. and Mrs. Gilbreath were in their middle thirties, good looking without being glamorous, their clothes nice, though as oddly wrong as Twilla's. They seemed cut with some outdated Ideal Family template. Surely there must be an older brother, a dog, and a cat somewhere.

"Well . . . ah, Twilla," Miss Mahan said, trying to reinforce the normal routine, "if you will take a seat; that one there, behind Alice May Turner. Alice May, will you wave a flag or something so Twilla will know which one?" Alice May giggled. "Thank you, dear." Twilla moved gracefully toward the empty desk. Miss Mahan felt as if she should say something to the child. "I hope you will . . . ah . . . enjoy going to school in Hawley, dear."

Twilla sat primly and glowed at her. "I'm sure I shall, Miss Mahan," she said, speaking for the first time. Her voice was like the tinkle of fairy bells—just as Miss Mahan was afraid it would be.

"Good," she said, and went back to the subject of a get-well card for Sammy Stocker. She had done this so often—there had been a great many sick children in thirty-one years—it had become almost a ritual needing only a small portion of her attention. The rest she devoted to the covert observation of Twilla Gilbreath.

Twilla sat at her desk, displaying excellent posture, with her hands folded neatly before her, seemingly paying attention to the

Great Greeting Card Debate, but actually giving the rest of the class careful scrutiny. Miss Mahan marveled at the surreptitious calculation in the girl's face. She realizes she's something of a green monkey, Miss Mahan thought, and I'll bet my pension she doesn't let the situation stand.

And the class surveyed Twilla, in their superior position of established territorial rights, with open curiosity—and with the posture of so many sacks of corn meal. Some of them looked at her, Miss Mahan was afraid, with rude amusement—especially the girls, and especially Wanda O'Dell, who had bloomed suddenly last summer like a plump rose. Oh, yes, Wanda was going to be a problem. Just like her five older sisters. Thank goodness, she sighed, Wanda was the last of them.

Children, Miss Mahan sighed again, but fondly.

Children?

They were children when she started teaching and certainly were when she was fifteen, but now she wasn't sure. Fifteen is such an awkward, indefinite age. Take Ronnie Dwyer: he looks like a prepubescent thirteen at most. And Carter Redwine, actually a couple of months younger than Ronnie, could pass for seventeen easily and was anything but prepubescent. Poor Carter, a child in a man's body. To make matters worse, he was the best-looking boy in town; and to make matters even worse, he was well aware of it.

And, she noticed, so was Twilla. Forget it, Little Pink Princess. Carter already has more than he can handle, Miss Mahan chuckled to herself. Can't you see those dark circles under his eyes? They didn't get there from studying. And then she blushed inwardly.

Oh, the poor children. They think they have so many secrets. If only they knew. Between the tattletales and the teachers' gossip, she doubted if the whole student body had three secrets among them.

Miss Mahan admonished herself for having such untidy thoughts. She didn't use to think about things like that, but then, fifteen-year-olds didn't lead such overtly sexual lives back then. She remembered reading somewhere that only thirty-five percent of the children in America were still virgins at fifteen. But those sounded like Big City statistics, not applicable to Hawley.

Then she sighed. It was all beyond her. The bell rang just as the get-well card situation was settled. The children rose reluctantly to go to their first class: algebra with Mr. Whittaker. She noticed that Twilla had cozied up to Alice May, though she still kept her eye on Carter Redwine. Carter was not unaware, and with deliberate, lordly indifference, sauntered from the room with his hand on Wanda O'Dell's shoulder. Miss Mahan thought the glint she observed in Twilla's eyes might lead to an interesting turn of events.

Children.

She cleared her mind of random speculation and geared it to *Macbeth* as the senior class filed in with everything on their minds but Shakespeare. Raynelle Franklin, Mr. Choate's secretary, lurked nervously among them, looking like a chicken who suddenly finds herself with a pack of coyotes. She edged her middle-aged body to Miss Mahan's desk, accepted the absentee report, and scuttled out. Miss Mahan looked forward to Raynelle's performance every morning.

During lunch period, Miss Mahan walked to the dime store for a get-well card which the ninth grade class would sign that afternoon when they returned for English. She glanced at the sky and unconsciously pulled her gray tweed coat tighter about her. The sky had turned a cobalt blue in the north. It wouldn't be long now. Though the temperature must be down to thirty-five already, it seemed colder. She guessed her blood was getting thin; she knew her flesh was. Old age, she thought, old age. Thin blood, thin flesh, and brittle bones. She sometimes felt as if she were turning into a bird.

She almost bumped into Twilla's parents emerging from the dry goods store, their arms loaded with packages. Their pleasant smiles turned on. Click, click. They chatted trivialities for a moment, adding new dimensions to Twilla's almost flawless character. Miss Mahan had certainly seen her share of blindly doting parents, but this was unbelievable. She had seen the cold calculation with which Twilla had studied the class, and that was hardly the attribute of an angel. Something didn't jibe somewhere. She speculated on the contents of the packages, but thought she knew. Then she couldn't resist; she asked if Twilla were an only child. She was. Well, there went that.

She looked at the clock on the high tower of the white rococo courthouse, and subtracting fourteen minutes, decided she'd better hurry if she wanted to eat lunch and have a rest before her one o'clock class.

The teachers' lounge was a reasonably comfortable room where students were forbidden to enter on pain of death—though it seemed to be a continuing game on their part to try. Miss Mahan hung her coat on a hanger and shivered. "Has anyone heard a weather forecast?" she asked the room in general.

Mrs. Latham (home economics) looked up from her needlepoint and shook her head vaguely. Poor old dear, thought Miss Mahan. Due to retire this year, I think. Seems like she's been here since Creation. She taught me when I was in school. Leo Whittaker (math) was reading a copy of *Playboy*. Probably took it from one of the children. "Supposed to be below twenty by five," he said, then grinned and held up the magazine. "Ronnie Dwyer."

Miss Mahan raised her eyebrows. Loretta McBride (history/civics) tsked, shook her head, and went back to her book. Miss Mahan retrieved her carton of orange juice from the small refrigerator and drank it with her fried egg sandwich. She put part of the sandwich back in the Baggie. She hardly had any appetite at all anymore. Guess what they say is true; the older you get . . .

She began to crochet on her interminable afghan. The little squares were swiftly becoming a pain in the neck, and she regretted ever starting it. She looked at Mrs. Latham and her needlepoint. She sighed. I guess it's expected of us old ladies. Anyway, it gave her something to hide behind when she didn't feel like joining the conversation. But today she felt like talking, though it didn't seem as if anyone else did.

She finished a square and snipped the yarn. "What do you think of the Shirley Temple doll who joined our merry group this morning?"

Mrs. Latham looked up and smiled, "Charming child."

"Yes," said Loretta, putting away her book, "absolutely charming. And smart as a whip. Really knows her American History. Joined in the discussion as if she'd been in the class all semester." Miss McBride was one of the few outsiders teaching in Hawley who gave every indication of remaining. Usually they came and went as soon as greener pastures opened up. Most were like Miss Mahan, Mrs. Latham, and Leo Whittaker, living their entire lives there.

It was practically incestuous, she thought. Mrs. Latham had taught her, she had taught Leo, and he was undoubtedly teaching part of the next crop. Miss Mahan had to admit that Leo had been something of a surprise. He was only twenty-five and had given no indication in high school that he was destined for anything better than a hanging. She wondered how long it would be before Leo connected his students' inability to keep secrets from the teachers with his own disreputable youth.

Now here he was. Two years in the army, four years in college, his second year of teaching, married to Lana Redwine (Carter's cousin and one of the nicest girls in town), with a baby due in a couple of months. You never can tell. You just never can tell.

"Well, Leo," Miss Mahan asked, bemused, "what did you think of Twilla Gilbreath?"

"Oh, I don't know. She seems very intelligent—at least in algebra. Quiet and well-behaved—unlike a few others. Dresses kinda funny. Seems to have set her sights on my cousin-in-law." He grinned. "Fat chance!" Miss Mahan wouldn't say Leo was handsome—not in the way Carter Redwine was—but that grin was the reason half the girls in school had a crush on him.

"Oh? You noticed that too? I imagine she may have a few surprises up her sleeve. I don't think our Twilla is the fairy-tale princess she's made out to be." She began another square.

"You must be mistaken, Miss Mahan," Loretta said, wide-eyed. "The child is an absolute darling. And the very idea: a baby like that running after Carter Redwine. I never heard of such a thing!"

"Really?" Miss Mahan smiled to herself and completed a shell stitch. "We shall see what we shall see."

The norther hit during the ninth-grade English class, bringing a merciful, if only temporary, halt to the sufferings of Silas Marner. The glass in the windows rattled and pinged. The wind played on the downspouts like a mad flautist. Sand ticked against the windows and the guard lights came on in the school yard. Outside had become a murky indigo, as if the world were underwater. Miss Mahan switched on the lights, making the windows seem even darker. Garbage cans rolled down the street, but you could hardly hear them above the howl of the wind. And the downtown Christmas decorations were whipping loose, as they always did at least once every year.

The sand was only temporary; a cloud of it blown along before the storm, but the wind could last all night or all week. Miss Mahan remembered when she was a girl during the great drought of the thirties, when the sand wasn't temporary, when it came like a mile-high, solid tidal wave of blown-away farmland, when you couldn't tell noon from midnight, when houses were half buried when the wind finally died down. She shuddered.

"All right, children. Settle down. You've all seen northers before."

Leo and Loretta were right about one thing: Twilla was intelligent. She was also perceptive, imaginative . . . and adaptable.

She had already dropped the Little Mary Sunshine routine, though Miss Mahan couldn't imagine why she had used it in the first place. It must have been a pose—as if the child had somehow confused the present and 1905.

The temperature had dropped to eighteen by the time school was out. The wind hit Miss Mahan like icy needles. Her gray tweed coat did about as much good as tissue paper. She grabbed at her scarf as it threatened to leave her head and almost lost her briefcase. She walked as fast as her aging legs would go and made it to her six-year-old Plymouth. The car started like a top, billowing a cloud of steam from the exhaust pipe to be whipped away by the wind.

She sat a moment, getting her breath back, letting the car warm up. She saw Twilla, huddled against the wind, dash to a new black Chrysler and get in with her parents. The car backed out and moved away. Miss Mahan wasn't the least surprised that little Miss Gilbreath wasn't riding the school bus. The old Peacock place was a mile off the highway at Miller's Corners, a once-upon-a-time town eight miles east of Hawley.

Well, I guess I'm not much better, she thought. I only live four blocks away—but I'll be darned if I'll walk it today. She always did walk except when the weather was bad, and oddly enough, the older she got, the worse the weather seemed to get.

She pulled into the old carriage house that served equally well with automobiles, and walked hurriedly across the yard into the big, rather ancient house that had belonged to her grandfather. She knew it was silly to live all alone in such a great pile—she had shut off the upstairs and hadn't been up in months—but it was equally silly not to live there. It was paid for, and her grandfather had set up a trust fund to pay the taxes. It was a very nice house, really; cool in the summer, but (she turned up the fire) a drafty old barn in the winter.

She turned on the television to see if there were any weather bulletins. While it warmed up, she closed off all the downstairs rooms except the kitchen, her bedroom, and the parlor, putting rolled-up towels along the bottoms of the doors to keep the cold air out. She returned to the parlor to see the television screen covered with snow and horizontal streaks of lightning.

She knew it. The aerial had blown down again. She turned off the set and put on a kettle of tea.

The wind had laid somewhat by the time Miss Mahan reached school the next morning, but still blew in fitful gusts. The air was the color of ice and so cold she expected to hear it crackle as she moved through it. The windows in her room were steamed over, and she was busily wiping them when Twilla arrived. Although Miss Mahan had expected something like this, she stared nevertheless.

Twilla's hair was still the color of spun elfin gold, but the drop curls were missing. Instead it fell in soft folds to below her shoulders in a style much too adult for a thirteen-year-old. But, then, this morning Twilla looked as much like thirteen as Mrs. Latham. All the physical things were there: the hair, just the right amount of makeup, a short, stylish skirt, a pale green jersey that displayed her small but adequate breasts, a lovely antique pendant on a gold chain nestling between them.

But it wasn't only the physical things—any thirteen-year-old would have appeared more mature with a similar overhaul—it was something in the face, in her bearing: an attitude of casual sophistication, a confidence usually attainable only by those secure in their power. Twilla smiled. Shirley Temple and Mary Pickford were gone; this was the smile of a conqueror.

Miss Mahan realized her face was hanging out, but before she was forced to say anything, several students, after a prelude of clanging locker doors, barged in. Twilla turned to look at them and the moment was electric. Their inane chatter stopped as if someone had thrown a switch. They gaped. Twilla gave them time for the full effect, then strolled to them and began chatting as if nothing were new.

Miss Mahan sat at her desk feeling a little weak in the knees. She waited for Carter Redwine to arrive as, obviously, was Twilla. When he did it, it was almost anticlimactic. His recently acquired worldliness and sexual sophistication melted away in one callow gawk. But he recovered quickly and his feelers popped up, testing the situation. Twilla moved to her desk, giving him a satisfied smile. Wanda O'Dell looked as if she'd eaten a bug.

Miss Mahan had to admit to the obvious. Twilla was a stunning beauty. But the whole thing was . . . curious . . . to say the least.

The conversation in the teachers' lounge was devoted almost exclusively to the transformation of Twilla Gilbreath. Mrs. Latham had noted it vaguely. Loretta McBride ceded reluctantly to Miss Mahan's observations of the previous day. Leo Whittaker expressed a masculine appreciation of the new Twilla, earning a fishy look from Loretta. "I never saw Carter act so goofy," he said, grinning.

But neither they nor any of the others noted the obvious strangeness of it all. At least, Miss Mahan thought, it seems obvious to me.

That day Miss Mahan set out on a campaign of Twilla watching. She even went upstairs to her grandfather's study and purloined one of the black journals from the bottom drawer of his desk. She curled up in the big chair, after building a fire in the parlor fireplace—the first one this year—and opened the journal to the first page ruled with pale blue lines. She wrote *Twilla,* after rejecting *The Twilla Gilbreath Affair, The Peculiar Case of Twilla Gilbreath,* and others in a similar vein.

She felt silly and conspiratorial and almost put the journal away, but instead wrote farther down the page: *Is my life so empty that I must fill it by spying on a student?*

She thought about what she had written and decided it was either unfair to Twilla or unfair to herself, but let it remain. She turned to the second page and wrote *Tuesday, the 5th* at the top. She filled that page and the next with her impressions of Twilla's first day. She headed the fourth page *Wednesday, the 6th* and noted the events of the day just ending.

On rereading, she thought perhaps she might have over emphasized the oddities, the incongruities, and the anachronisms, but after all, that was what it was about, wasn't it?

It began snowing during the night. Miss Mahan drove to school through a fantasy landscape. The wind was still blowing, and the steely flakes came down almost horizontally. She loved snow, always had, but she preferred the Christmas card variety when the big fluffy flakes floated down through still, crisp air like so many pillow fights.

She knew there had been developments as soon as Carter Redwine entered the room. His handsome face was glum and sullen and looked as if he hadn't slept. He sat at his desk with his head hunched between his shoulders and didn't look up until Twilla came in. Miss Mahan darted her eyes from one to the other. Carter looked away again, his neck and ears glowing red. Twilla ignored him; more than that—she consigned him to total nonexistence.

Miss Mahan was dumbfounded. What on earth . . .? Had Carter made advances and been rebuffed? That wouldn't explain it. Surely he had been turned down before. Hadn't he? Of course, she knew he had. Leo, who viewed his cousin-in-law's adventures with bemused affection, had been laughing about it in the teachers' lounge one day. "He'll settle down," Leo had said, "he just has a new toy." Which made her blush after she'd thought about it a while.

Surely, he hadn't tried to take Twilla . . . by force? She couldn't believe that. Despite everything, Carter was a very decent boy. He had just developed too early, was too handsome, and knew too many willing girls. What then? Was it the first pangs of love? That look on his face wasn't lovesickness. It was red, roaring mortification. Then she knew what must have happened. Carter had not been rebuffed, maybe even encouraged. But whatever she had expected, he had been inadequate.

Twilla had made another error. She had failed to realize that Carter, despite the way he looked, was only fifteen. Then the ugly enormity of it struck her. My God, she thought, Twilla is only thirteen. What had she wanted from Carter that he was too inexperienced or naive to give her?

Friday, the 8th

Billy Jermyn came in this morning with a black eye. It's all over school that Carter gave it to him in Gym yesterday when Billy teased him about Twilla. What did she do to humiliate him so? I've never known Carter to fight. I guess that's one secret that'll never penetrate the teachers' lounge.

Twilla is taking over the class. I've seen it coming since Wednesday. It's subtle but pretty obvious when you know what to look for. The others defer to her in lots of little ways. Twilla is being very gracious about it. Butter wouldn't melt in her mouth. (Wonder where that little saying came from—doesn't make much sense when you analyze it.)

I also wonder who Twilla's got her amorous sights on, now that Carter failed to make the grade. She hasn't shown an interest in anyone in particular that I've noticed. And there's been no gossip in the lounge. The flap created by Carter has probably shown her the wisdom of keeping her romances to herself. She's adaptable.

Sonny Bowen offered to put my TV aerial back up for me. I knew one of them would. Bless their conniving little hearts.

TGIF!

Miss Mahan closed the journal and sat watching a log in the fireplace that was about to fall. The whole Twilla affair was curious, but no more curious than her own attitude. She should have been scandalized (you didn't see too many thirteen-year-old combinations of Madame Bovary and the Dragon Lady—even these days), but she only felt fascination. Somehow it didn't seem quite real; more as if she were watching a movie. She smiled slightly. Wonder if it would be rated R or X, she thought. R, I guess. Haven't seen anyone with their clothes off yet.

The log fell, making her jump. She laughed in embarrassment, banked the fire, and went to bed.

The snow was still falling Monday morning, though the fierceness of the storm had passed. There was little wind, and the temperature had risen somewhat. That's more like it. Miss Mahan said to herself, watching the big soft flakes float down in random zigzags.

The bell rang and she turned away from the windows to watch the ninth-grade homeroom clatter out. The Gilbreaths must have been out of town over the weekend, she observed. Twilla didn't get that outfit in Hawley. But she was still wearing that lovely, rather barbaric pendant around her neck. She sighed. Two days away from Twilla had made her wonder if she weren't getting senile; if she weren't making a mystery out of a molehill; if she weren't imagining the whole thing. Twilla was certainly a picture of normalcy this morning.

Raynelle Franklin came for the absentee report, looking more like a frightened chicken than ever. She followed an evasive course to Miss Mahan's desk and took the report as if she were afraid of being struck. There were only two names on the report: Sammy Stocker and Yvonne Wilkins.

Raynelle glanced at the names and paled. "Haven't you heard?" she whispered.

"Heard what?"

Raynelle looked warily at the senior class shuffling in, and backed away, motioning for Miss Mahan to follow. Miss Mahan groaned and followed her into the hall. Students were milling about everywhere, chattering and banging locker doors. Raynelle grimaced in distress.

"Raynelle, will you stand still and tell me!" Miss Mahan commanded in exasperation.

"Someone will hear," she pleaded.

"Hear what?"

Raynelle fluttered her hands and blew air through her teeth. She looked quickly around and then huddled against Miss Mahan. "Yvonne Wilkins," she hissed.

"Well?"

"She's . . . she's . . . dead!"

Miss Mahan thought Raynelle was going to faint. She grabbed her arm. "How?" she asked in her no-nonsense voice.

"I don't know," Raynelle gasped. "No one will tell me."

Miss Mahan thought for a moment. "Go on with what you were doing." She released Raynelle and marched into Mr. Choate's office.

Mr. Choate looked up with a start. He was already wearing his three-o'clock face. "I see you've heard." He was resigned.

"Yes. What is going on? Raynelle was having a conniption fit." Miss Mahan looked at him over her glasses the same way she would a recalcitrant student.

"Miss Mahan," he sighed, "Sheriff Walker thought it best if the whole thing were kept quiet."

"Quiet? Why?"

"He didn't want a panic."

"Panic? What did she die of, bubonic plague?"

"No." He looked at her as if he wished she would vanish. "I guess I might as well tell you. It'll be all over town by ten o'clock anyway. Yvonne was murdered." He said the last word as if he'd never heard it before.

Miss Mahan felt her knees giving way, and quickly sat down. "This is unbelievable," she said weakly. Mr. Choate nodded. "Why does Robin Walker want to keep it quiet? What happened?"

"Miss Mahan, I've told you all I can tell you."

"Surely Robin knows secrecy will only make it worse? Making a mystery out of it is guaranteed to create a panic."

Mr. Choate shrugged. "I have my instructions. You're late for your class."

Miss Mahan went back to her room in a daze, her imagination ringing up possibilities like a cash register. She couldn't keep her mind on *Macbeth*, and the class was restless. They obviously didn't know yet, but their radar had picked up something they couldn't explain.

When the class was over, she went into the hall and saw the news moving through like a shock wave. She accomplished absolutely nothing the rest of the morning. The children were fidgety and kept whispering among themselves. She was as disturbed as they and made only half-hearted attempts to restore order.

At lunch time, she bundled and trounced through the snow to the courthouse. It was too hot inside and the heat only accentuated the courthouse smell. She didn't know what it was, but they all smelled the same. Maybe it was the state-issue disinfectant. The Hawley courthouse hadn't changed since she could remember. The same wooden benches lined the hall; the same ceiling fans encircled the round lights. No, she corrected herself, there was a change: the brass spittoons had been removed some twelve years ago. It seemed subtly wrong without the spittoons.

She was removing her coat when Rose Newcastle emerged in a huff from the sheriff's office, her heels popping on the marble floor, sending echoes ringing down the hall. Rose was the last of the three Willet girls, the daughters of old Judge Willet. People still called them the Willet girls, although Rose was considerably older than Miss Mahan. She was a widow now, her husband having finally died of insignificance.

"Hello, Rose," she said, feeling trapped. Rose puffed to a halt like a plump locomotive.

"Oh, Miss Mahan, isn't it awful!" she wailed. "And Robin Walker absolutely refuses to do anything! We could all be murdered in our beds!"

"I'm sure he's doing everything he can, Rose. What did he tell you?"

"Nothing! Absolutely nothing! If my father were still alive, I'd have that man's job. I told him he'd better watch his step come next election. I told him, as a civic leader in this town, I had a right to know what's going on. I told him I had a good mind to organize a Citizens Committee to investigate the whole affair."

"Give him a chance. Robin is a very conscientious man."

"He's a child."

"Come on, Rose. He's at least thirty. I taught him for four years and I have complete confidence in him. You'll have to excuse me. I'm here to see him myself."

"He won't tell you anything," Rose said, sounding slightly mollified.

"'Perhaps," Miss Mahan said. Rose echoed off down the hall. "He might have if you haven't put his tail over the dashboard," she muttered, and pushed open the door.

Loreen Whittaker, Leo's aunt by marriage, looked up and smiled. "Hello, Miss Mahan. What can I do for you?"

"Hello, Loreen. I'd like to see Robin, if I may."

Loreen chuckled. "He gave me strict orders to let no one in but the governor—right after Mrs. Newcastle left."

Miss Mahan grimaced. "I met her in the hall. Would you ask him? It's important."

Loreen arose from her desk and went into the sheriff's private office. Miss Mahan felt that she and Robin were good friends.

She had not only taught him, but his sister, Mary Ellen, and his little brother, Curtis, who was a senior this year. She liked all of them and thought they liked her. Robin's son was in the second grade and a little doll. She was looking forward to teaching him, too.

Loreen came out of his office, grinning. "He said you could come in but I was to frisk you first." Her smile wavered. "Try to cheer him up, Miss Mahan. It's the first . . . murder we've had since he's been in office, and it's getting to him."

Miss Mahan nodded and went in. The sheriff sat hunched over his desk. His hair was mussed where he had been running his hand through it. There was a harried look on his face but he dredged up a thin smile for her.

"You aren't gonna give me trouble, too, are you?" he asked warily.

"I ran into Rose in the hall." She smiled back at him.

He motioned her to a chair. "What's the penalty for punching a civic leader in the nose?"

"You should know that better than I."

He grunted. "Yeah." He leaned back in the chair and stretched his long legs. "I can't discuss Yvonne Wilkins, if that's what you're here for."

"That's why I'm here. Don't you think this secrecy is worse than the facts? People will be imagining all sorts of horrible things."

"I doubt if anything they could imagine would be worse than the actual facts, Miss Mahan. You'll have to trust me. I have to do it this way." He ran his fingers through his hair again. "I'm afraid I may be in over my head on this. There's just me and five deputies for the whole county. And we haven't anything to work on. Nothing."

"Where did they find her?"

"Okay," he sighed. "I'll tell you this much. Yvonne went out yesterday afternoon in her father's car to visit Linda Murray. When she didn't come home last night, Mr. Wilkins called the Murrays and they said Yvonne left about six-thirty. He was afraid she'd had an accident in the snow, so he called me. We found her about three this morning out on the dirt road nearly to the old Weatherly place. She was in the car . . . dead. It's been snowing for five days. There wasn't a track of any kind and no fingerprints that didn't belong. And that's all you're gonna worm out of me."

Miss Mahan had an idea. "Had she been . . . molested?"

Robin looked at her as if he'd been betrayed. "Yes," he said simply.

"But," she protested, "why the big mystery? I know it's horrible, but it's not likely to cause a . . . a panic."

He got up and paced around the office. "Miss Mahan, I can't tell you any more."

"Is there more? Is there more than rape and murder?" She felt something like panic rising in her.

Robin squatted in front of her, taking her hands in his. "If there's anyone in town I'd tell, it would be you. You know that. I've loved you ever since I was fourteen years old. If you keep after me, I'll tell you, so have a little pity on a friend and stop pushing."

She felt her eyes burning and motioned for him to get up. "Robin, you're not playing fair." She stood up and he held her coat for her. "You always were able to get around me. Okay, you win."

"Thank you, Miss Mahan," he said, genuinely relieved, and kissed her on the forehead. She stopped in the hall and dabbed at her eyes.

But I haven't given up yet, she thought as she huddled in her coat on the way to Paul Sullivan's office. The bell tinkled on the door and the nurse materialized from somewhere.

"Miss Mahan. What are you doing out in this weather?"

"I'd like to see the doctor, Elaine." She hung her coat on the rack.

"He's with the little Archer girl now. She slipped on the snow and twisted her ankle."

"I'll wait." She sat and picked up a magazine without looking at it. Elaine Holliday had been one of her students. Who in town hadn't? she wondered. Elaine wanted to talk about the murder, as did Louise Archer, when she emerged with her limping daughter, but Miss Mahan wasn't in the mood for gossip and speculation. She marched into Dr. Sullivan's sanctorium.

"Hello, Paul," she said before he could open his mouth. "I've just been to see Robin. He told me Yvonne had been raped, but he wouldn't tell me what the big mystery is. I know you're what passes for the County Medical Examiner, so you know as much as he does. I've known you for fifty years, and even thought at one time you might propose to me, but you didn't. So don't give me any kind of runaround. Tell me what happened to Yvonne." She plopped into a chair and glared at him.

He shook his head in dismay. "I thought I might propose to

you at one time, too, but right now is a good example of why I didn't. You were so independent and bull-headed, you scared me to death."

"Don't change the subject."

"You won't like it."

"I don't expect to."

"There's no way I can 'put it delicately,' as they say."

"You don't know high school kids. I doubt if you *know* anything indelicate that I haven't heard from them."

"Even if I tell you everything I know about it, it'll still be a mystery. It is to me."

"Quit stalling."

"Okay, you asked for it. And if you repeat this to anyone, I'll wring your scrawny old neck."

"I won't."

"All right. Yvonne was . . . how can I say it? She was sexually mutilated. She was split open. Not cut—torn, ripped. As if someone had forced a two by four into her—probably something larger than that."

"Had they?" Miss Mahan felt her throat beginning to burn from the bile rising in it.

"No. At least there was no evidence of it. No splinters, no soil, no foreign matter of any kind."

"My Lord," she moaned. "How she must have suffered."

"Yes," he said softly, "but only for a few seconds. She must have lost consciousness almost immediately. And she was dead long before they finished with her."

"They? What makes you think there was more than one?"

"Are you sure you want to hear the rest of it?"

"Yes," she said, but she didn't.

"I said we found no foreign matter, but we found semen."

"Wasn't that to be expected?"

"Yes, I suppose. But not in such an amount."

"What do you mean?"

"We found nearly a hundred and fifty cc's. There was probably even more. A lot of it had drained out onto the car seat." His voice was dull.

She shook her head in confusion. "A hundred and fifty cc's?"

"About a cup full."

She felt nauseous. "How much . . . how much . . . ?"

"The average male produces about two or three cc's. Maybe four."

"Does that mean she was . . . what? . . . fifty times?"

"And fifty different men."

"That's impossible."

"Yes. I know. One of the deputies took it to Wichita to be analyzed. To see if it's human."

"Human?"

"Yes. We thought someone might—"

She held up her hand. "You don't need to go . . . go any further." They sat for a while, not saying anything.

After a bit he said, "You can see why Robin wanted to keep it quiet?"

"Yes." She shivered, wishing she had her coat even though the office was warm. "Is there any more?"

He shook his head and slumped morosely deep in the chair. "No. Only that Robin is pretty sure she was . . . killed somewhere else and then taken out on the old road, because there was almost no blood in or around the car. How they ever drove so far out on that road in the snow is another mystery, although a minor one. The deputy was about to give up and turn around, and he had on snow chains."

Miss Mahan was late for her one o'clock class. The children hadn't become unruly as they usually did, but were subdued and talking in hushed voices. A discussion of *Silas Marner* proved futile, so she told them to sit quietly and read. She didn't feel any more like classwork than they did. She noticed that Twilla's eyes were bright with suppressed excitement. Well, she thought, I guess you can't expect her to react like the others. She hardly knew Yvonne.

It had stopped snowing by the time Mr. Choate circulated a memo that school would be closed Wednesday for the funeral. Apparently Robin had managed to keep a lid on knowledge of the rape. There was speculation on the subject, but she could tell it was only speculation.

When she got home, she saw the Twilla journal lying beside the big chair in front of the cold fireplace. Strange, Twilla had hardly crossed her mind all day. She guessed it only proved how silly and stupid her Twilla-watching really was. She put the journal away in the library table drawer and decided that was enough of that nonsense.

Tuesday, the 12th

This morning I saw Twilla jab Alice May Turner in the thigh with a large darning needle.

* * *

Miss Mahan stopped in the middle of a sentence and stared in disbelief. She walked slowly to Twilla's desk, feeling every eye in the class following her. "What's going on here?" she asked in a deathly quiet voice. Twilla looked up at her with such total incomprehension, she wondered if she had imagined the whole thing. But she looked at Alice May and saw her mouth tight and trembling and the tears being held in her eyes only by surface tension.

"What do you mean, Miss Mahan?" Twilla asked in a bewildered voice.

"Why did you stick Alice May with a needle?"

"Miss Mahan, I didn't!"

"I saw you."

"But I didn't!" Twilla's eyes were becoming damp, as if she were about to cry in injured innocence.

"Don't bother to cry," Miss Mahan said calmly. "I'm not impressed." Twilla's mouth tightened for the briefest instant. Miss Mahan turned to Alice May. "Did she jab you with a needle?"

Alice May blinked and a tear rolled down each cheek. "No, ma'am," she answered in a strained voice.

"Then why are you crying?" Miss Mahan demanded.

"I'm not crying," Alice May insisted, wiping her face.

"I think both of you had better come with me to Mr. Choate's office."

Mr. Choate wouldn't or, I guess, couldn't do anything. They both lied their heads off, insisting that nothing happened. Twilla even had the gall to accuse me of spying on her and persecuting her. I think Mr. Choate believed me. He could hardly help it when Alice May began rubbing her thigh in the midst of her denials.

Miss Mahan sent Twilla back to the room and kept Alice May in the hall. Alice May began to snuffle and wouldn't look at her. "Alice May, dear," she said patiently. "I saw what Twilla did. Why are you fibbing to me?"

"I'm not!" she wailed softly.

"Alice May, I don't want any more of this nonsense!" Why on earth did Twilla do it? she wondered. Alice May was such a silly, harmless girl. Why would anyone want to hurt her?

"Miss Mahan, I can't tell you," she sobbed.

"Here." Miss Mahan gave her a handkerchief. Alice May took it and rubbed at her red eyes. "Why can't you tell me? What's going on between you and Twilla?"

"Nothing," she sniffed.

"Alice May, I promise to drop the whole subject if you'll just tell me the truth."

Alice May finally looked at her. "Will you?"

"Yes," she groaned in exasperation.

"Well, my . . . my giggling gets on her nerves."

"What?"

"She told me if I didn't stop, I'd be sorry."

"Why didn't you pick up something and brain her with it?"

Alice May's eyes widened in disbelief. "Miss Mahan, I couldn't do that!"

"She didn't mind hurting you, did she?"

"I'm . . . I'm afraid of her. Everybody is."

"Why? What has she done?"

"I don't know. Nothing. I'm just afraid. You promise not to let her know I told you?"

"I promise. Now, go to the restroom and wash your face."

Twilla kept watching me the rest of the period. I imagine she suspects Alice May spilled the beans. The other children were very quiet and expectant, as if they thought Twilla and I would go at each other tooth and claw. I wonder who they would root for if we did?

I'll have to admit to a great deal of perverse pleasure in tarnishing Twilla's reputation in the teachers' lounge. I was a little surprised to find a few of the others had become somewhat disenchanted with her also. They didn't have such a concrete example of viciousness as I had, but she was making them uncomfortable.

I also discovered who Twilla's romantic (if you can call it that) interest is since Carter flunked out.

Leo Whittaker!

I was never so shocked and disappointed in my life. An affair between a teacher and student is bad enough but—Leo! No wonder she was being quiet about it. I thought he acted a bit peculiar when we discussed Twilla, so I said bold as brass: "I wonder who she's sleeping with?" He turned red and left the room, looking guilty as sin.

I don't know what to do about it. I've got to do something. But what? what? what? I can't do anything to hurt Leo, because it'll also hurt poor Lana.

How could Leo be so stupid?

Dark clouds hung oppressively low the morning of the funeral. They scudded across the sky so rapidly Miss Mahan got dizzy looking at them. She stood with the large group huddled against the cold outside the First Christian Church of Hawley, waiting for the formation of the procession to the County Line Cemetery. The services had drawn a capacity crowd, mostly from curiosity, she was afraid. The entire ninth grade was there, with the exception of Sammy Stocker, of course, and Twilla. Only two teachers were missing: Mrs. Bryson (first grade) who had the flu, and Leo Whittaker. Leo's absence was peculiar because Lana was there, looking pale and beautifully pregnant. She was with Carter Redwine and his parents. Carter seems to be recovering nicely from his little misadventure, she thought.

She spotted Paul Sullivan and crunched through the snow to his side. He saw her coming and frowned. "Hello, Paul. Did you get the report from Wichita?"

"Do you think this is the place to discuss it?"

"Why not? No one will overhear. Did you?"

He sighed. "Yes."

"Well?"

"It was human—although there were certain peculiarities."

"What peculiarities?"

He cocked his eyes at her. "If I told you, would it mean anything?"

She shrugged. "What else?"

"Well, it all came from the same person—as far as they could tell. At least, there was nothing to indicate that it didn't. Also, all the sperm was the same age."

"What does that mean?"

"The thought occurred to us that someone might be trying to create a grisly hoax. That someone might have . . . well . . . saved it up until they had that much."

"I get the picture." She grimaced. She thought a moment. "Can't they . . . ah . . . freeze it? Haven't I read something about that?"

"You can't do it in your Frigidaire. If the person who did it had the knowledge and the laboratory equipment to do that . . . well . . . it's as improbable as the other theories."

"Robin hasn't learned anything yet?"

"I don't know. Some of us aren't as nosy as others."

She smiled at him as she spotted Lana Whittaker moving toward the Redwine car. She began edging away. "Will you keep me posted?"

"No."

"Thank you, Paul." She caught up with Lana. "Hello, dear."

Lana started and turned, then smiled thinly. "Hello, Miss Mahan."

She exchanged greetings with Mr. and Mrs. Redwine and Carter as they entered their car. "Should you be out in this weather, Lana?"

Lana shrugged. She looked a little haggard and her eyes were puffy. "I'll be all right."

Miss Mahan took her arm. "Come on. My car is right here. Get in out of the cold and talk to me. We'll have plenty of time before they get this mess untangled." Lana went unprotesting, and sat in the car staring straight ahead. Miss Mahan started the car and switched on the heater although it was still fairly warm. She turned and looked at Lana.

"When you were in school," she said quietly, "you came to me with all your problems. It made me feel a little like I had a daughter of my own."

Lana turned and looked at her with love and pain in her eyes. "I'm not a little girl any more, Miss Mahan. I'm a married lady with a baby on the way. I should be able to handle my own problems."

"Where's Leo?"

Lana leaned back against the seat and put her fingers on the sides of her nose. "I don't know," she said simply, as if her tears had been used up. "He went out last night and I haven't seen him since. I told my aunt and uncle he went to Liberal to buy some things for the baby."

"Did you call Robin? Maybe he had an accident."

"No. There was no accident. I thought so the first time."

"When was that?"

"Last Friday night. He didn't come in until after midnight. The same thing Saturday. He didn't show up until dawn Monday and Tuesday. This time he didn't come back at all."

"What did he say?"

"Nothing. He wouldn't say anything. Miss Mahan, I know he still loves me; I can tell. He seems genuinely sorry and ashamed of what he's doing, but he keeps . . . keeps doing it. I've tried to think who she might be, but I can't imagine anyone. He's so tired and worn out when he comes home, it would be funny if it . . . if it were happening to someone else."

"Do you still love him?"

Lana smiled. "Oh, yes," she said softly. "More than anything. I love him so much it . . ." she blushed, ". . . it gives me goose bumps. I was crazy about Leo even when we were in high school, but he was so wild he scared me to death. I thought . . . I thought he had changed."

"I think he has." Miss Mahan took Lana's hand as she saw Robin get in his car and pull out with the pall bearers and the hearse directly behind him. "They're starting. You'd better go back to your car. I'm glad you told me. I'll do all I can to help."

Lana opened the car door. "I appreciate it, Miss Mahan, but I really don't see what you can do."

"We shall see what we shall see."

Miss Mahan managed to hang back until she was last in the funeral procession. The highway had been cleared of snow, and she hoped it wouldn't start again before they all got back to town. But she didn't know. The sky looked terrible. She turned off the highway at Miller's Corners, down the dirt road to the old Peacock place. There was nothing left of Miller's Corners now except a few scattered farm houses. The café had been moved into Hawley eight years ago and the Gulf station had closed when George Cuttsanger died last fall. The Gulf people had even taken down the signs.

If the Gilbreaths were fixing up the old Peacock farm, they must have started on the inside. It was still as gray and weary looking as it was ten years ago, if not more so. The black Chrysler was in the old carriage house, and smoke drifted this way and that from one of the chimneys, caught by small erratic gusts of air.

She parked and sat looking at the house a moment before getting out. The snow was clean and undisturbed on the front walk. She guessed they must use the back door; it was closer to the carriage house.

No one answered her knock, but she knew they were home. She waited and knocked again. Still no response. She took a deep breath and pushed open the door. "Mrs. Gilbreath?" she called. She listened carefully but there was not a sound. She could hear the melting snow dripping from the eaves and the little ticking sounds an old house makes. She went in and closed the door behind her. "Mrs. Gilbreath?" she called again, hearing nothing but a faint echo. The house was warm, but even more dilapidated than the last time she was in it.

She stepped into the parlor and saw them both sitting there. "Oh!" she gasped, startled, and then laughed in embarrassment. "I didn't mean to barge in, but no one answered my knock." Mr. and Mrs. Gilbreath sat in highback easy chairs facing away from her. She could only see the tops of their heads. They didn't move.

"Mrs. Gilbreath?" she said, beginning to feel queasy. She walked slowly around them, her eyes fixed so intently on the chairs she momentarily experienced an optical illusion that the chairs were turning slowly to face her. She blinked and took an involuntary step backward. They sat in the chairs dressed to go out, their eyes focussed on nothing. Neither of them moved, not even the slight movements of breathing, nor did their eyes blink. She stared at them in astonishment, fearing they were dead.

Miss Mahan approached them cautiously and touched Mrs. Gilbreath on the arm. The flesh was warm and soft. She quickly drew her hand back with a gasp. Then she reached again and shook the woman's shoulder. "Mrs. Gilbreath?" she whispered.

"She won't answer you." Miss Mahan gave a little shriek and looked up with a jerk. Twilla was strolling down the stairs, tying the sash of a rather barbaric looking floor-length fur robe. The antique pendant she always wore was around her neck. She stopped at the foot of the stairs and leaned against the newell post. She smiled. "They're only simulacra, you know."

"What?" Miss Mahan was bewildered. She hadn't expected Twilla to be here. She thought she would be with Leo.

Twilla indicated her parents. "Watch." Miss Mahan jerked her head back toward the people in the chairs. Suddenly, their heads twisted on their necks until the blank faces looked at each other. Then they grimaced and stuck out their tongues. The faces became expressionless again, and the heads swiveled back to stare at nothing.

Twilla's laugh trilled through the house. Miss Mahan jerked her eyes back to the beautiful child, feeling like a puppet herself. "They're rather clever, don't you think?" she cooed as she walked toward Miss Mahan, the fur robe making a soft sound against the floor. "I'm glad you came, Miss Mahan. It saves me the trouble of going to you."

"What?" Miss Mahan felt out of control. Her heart was beating like a hammer and she clutched the back of Mrs. Gilbreath's chair to keep from falling.

Twilla smiled at her panic. "I haven't been unaware of your interest in me, you know. I had decided it was time to get you out of the way before you became a problem."

"Get me out of the way?"

"Of course."

"What are you?" She felt her voice rising to a screech but she couldn't stop it. "What are these things pretending to be your parents?"

Twilla laughed. "A thirteen-year-old is quite limited in this society. I had to have parents to do the things I couldn't do myself." She shrugged. "There are other ways but this is the least bothersome."

"I won't let you get me out of the way," Miss Mahan hissed, dismissing the things she didn't understand and concentrating on that single threat, trying to pull her reeling senses together.

"Don't be difficult, Miss Mahan. There's nothing you can do to stop me." Twilla's face had become petulant, and then she smiled slyly. "Come with me. I want to show you something." Miss Mahan didn't budge. Twilla took a few steps and then turned back. "Come along, now. Don't you want all your questions answered?"

She started up the stairs. Miss Mahan followed her. Her legs felt mechanical. Halfway up she turned and looked back at the two figures sitting in the chairs like department store dummies. Twilla called to her and she continued to the top.

A hallway ran the length of the house upstairs, with bedroom doors on either side. Twilla opened one of them and motioned Miss Mahan in. The house wasn't as old as her own but it still had the fourteen-foot ceilings. But the ceilings, as well as the walls, had been removed. This side of the hall was one big area, opening into the attic, the roof at least twenty feet overhead, with what appeared to be some sort of trapdoor recently built into it. The area was empty except for a large gray mass hunched in one corner like a partially collapsed tent.

"He's asleep," Twilla said, and whistled. The mass stirred. The tent unfolded slowly, rustling like canvas sliding on canvas. Bony ribs spread gracefully, stretching the canvaslike flesh into vast bat wings which lifted out and up to bump against the roof. The wings trembled slightly as they stretched lazily and then settled, folding neatly behind the thing sitting on the floor.

It was a man, or almost a man. He would have been about sixteen feet tall had he been standing. His body was massively muscled and covered with purplish gray scales that shimmered metallically even in the dim light. His chest, shoulders, and back bulged with wing-controlling muscles. He stretched his arms and yawned, then rubbed at his eyes with horny fists. His head was hairless and scaled; his ears rose to points reaching above the crown of his skull. The face was angelically beautiful, but the large liquid eyes were dull and the mouth was slack like an idiot's. He scratched his hip with two-inch talons, making the sound of a rasp on metal. He was completely naked and emphatically male.

His massive sex lay along his heavy thigh like a great purple-headed snake.

"This is Dazreel," Twilla said pleasantly. The creature perked up at the sound of his name and looked toward them. "He's a djinn," Twilla continued. He turned his empty gaze away and began idly fondling himself. Twilla sighed. "I'm afraid Dazreel's pleasures are rather limited."

Miss Mahan ran.

She clattered down the stairs, clutching frantically at the banister to keep her balance. She lost her right shoe and stumbled on the bottom step, hitting her knees painfully on the floor. She reeled to her feet, unaware of her shins shining through her torn stockings. Twilla's crystal laughter, peeling down the stairs hardly penetrated the shimmering white layer of panic blanketing her mind.

She bruised her hands on the front door, clawing at it, trying to open it the wrong way. She careened across the porch, into the snow, not feeling the cold on her stockinged left foot. But her lopsided gait caused her to fall, sprawling on her face, burying her arms to the elbows in the snow. She crawled a few feet before gaining enough momentum to regain her feet. Her whole front was frosted with white but she didn't notice.

She locked the car doors, praying it would start. But she released the clutch too quickly, and it bucked and stalled. She ground the starter and turned her head to see Twilla standing on the porch, her arms hugging a pillar, her cheek caressing it, her smile mocking. The motor caught. Miss Mahan turned the car in a tight circle. The rear wheels lost traction and the car fishtailed.

Take it easy, she screamed to herself. You've made it. You've gotten away. Don't end up in the far ditch.

She was halfway to Miller's Corners when the loose snow began whipping in a cloud around her. She half heard the dull boom of air being compressed by vast wings. A shadow fell over her and Dazreel landed astraddle the hood of her car. The metal collapsed with a hollow *whump* as the djinn leaned down to peer curiously at her through the windshield. She began screaming, tearing her throat with short, hysterical, mindless shrieks that seemed to come from a great distance.

Her screams ended suddenly with a grunt as the front wheels struck the ditch, bringing the car to an abrupt halt. Dazreel lost his balance and flopped over backwards with a glitter of purplish gray and a tangle of canvas flesh into the snow drifts. Miss Mahan watched in paralyzed shock as he got to his feet, grinning an idiot grin, shaking the snow from his wings, and walked around the car. His wings kept opening and closing slightly to give him balance. Her head turned in quick jerks like a wooden doll, following his movements. He leaned over the car from behind and the glass of both side windows crumbled with a gravelly sound as his huge fingers poked through to grasp the tops of the doors.

The dim light became even dimmer as his wings spread in a mantle over the car. The snow swirled into the air, and she could see the tips of each wing as it made a downward stroke. The car shifted and groaned and rose from the ground.

She fainted.

A smiling angel face floated out of a golden mist. Soft, pink lips moved solicitously but no sound emerged. Miss Mahan felt a glass of water at her mouth and she drank greedily, soothing her raw throat. Sound returned.

"Are you feeling better, Miss Mahan? We don't want you to have a heart attack just yet, do we?" Twilla's eyes glittered with excitement.

Miss Mahan sucked oxygen, fighting the fog in her brain. Then raw, red fingers of anger tore away the silvery panic. She looked at the beautiful monstrous child kneeling before her, the extravagant robe parted enough at the top to reveal a small, perfect bare breast. The nipple looked as if it had been roughed. "I'm feeling quite myself again, thank you."

Twilla rose and moved to a facing chair. They were in the parlor. Miss Mahan looked around, but the djinn was absent. Only the parent dolls were there, in the same positions.

"Dazreel is back upstairs," Twilla assured her, watching her speculatively. "You have nothing to fear." She smiled slightly. "He will have only virgins."

Miss Mahan felt the blood draining from her face and she weaved in the chair, feeling the panic creeping back. Twilla threw her head back and her crystal laugh was harsh and strident, like a chandelier tumbling down marble stairs.

"Miss Mahan, you never cease to amaze me," she gasped. "Imagine! And at your age, too."

The anger returned in full control. "It's none of your business," she stated unequivocally.

"I'm ever so glad you decided to pay me a visit, Miss Mahan. It's, what do you say? Killing two birds with one stone?"

"What do you mean?"

"Dazreel has, as I said, limited, but strong appetites. If they aren't satisfied, he becomes quite unmanageable. And don't think he will reject you because you're a scrawny old crow. He has no taste at all, and only one criterion: virginity." Twilla was almost fidgety with anticipation.

"What possible difference could it make to that monster?"I must be losing my mind, Miss Mahan thought, I'm sitting here having a calm conversation with this wretched child who is going to kill me!

Twilla was thoughtful. "I really don't know. I never thought about it. That's just the way it's always been. It could be a personal idiosyncracy, or perhaps it's religious." She shrugged. "Something like *kosher*, do you think? Anyway, you can't fool him."

"I don't understand any of this," Miss Mahan said in confusion. "Did you say he was . . . a djinn?"

"Surely you've heard of them. King Solomon banished the entire race, if you remember." She smiled, pleased. "But I saved Dazreel."

"How old are you?" Miss Mahan breathed.

Twilla chuckled. "You wouldn't believe me if I told you. Don't let the body mislead you. It's relatively new. Dazreel has great power if you can control him. But he's crafty and very literal. One wrong move and . . ." She ran her forefinger across her throat.

"But . . ." Miss Mahan was completely confused. "If this is all true, why are you going to school in Hawley, Kansas, for heaven's sake?"

Twilla sighed. "Boredom is the curse of the immortal, Miss Mahan. I thought it might offer some diversion."

"If you're so bored with life, why don't you die?"

"Don't be absurd!"

"How could you be so inhuman? What you did to Yvonne . . . does life mean nothing to you?"

Twilla shifted in irritation. "Don't be tiresome. How could your brief, insignificant lives concern me?"

There was a restless sound from above. Twilla glanced at the stairs. "Dazreel is becoming impatient." She turned back to Miss Mahan with a smirk. "Are you ready to meet your lover, Miss Mahan?"

Miss Mahan sat frozen, the blood roaring in her ears. "You might as well go," Twilla continued. "It's inevitable. Think of your dignity, Miss Mahan. Do you really want to go kicking and screaming? Or perhaps you'd like another run in the snow?"

Miss Mahan stood up suddenly. "I won't give you the satisfaction," she said calmly. She walked to the stair, bobbing up and down with one shoe off. Twilla rose and ran after her, circling her in glee.

Twilla leaned against the newell post, blocking the stairs. She smiled wistfully. "I rather envy you, Miss Mahan. I've often wished . . . Dazreel knows the ancient Oriental arts, and sex *was* an art." She grimaced. "Now it's like two goats in heat!" Her smile returned. "I've often wished I had the capacity."

Miss Mahan ignored her and marched slowly up the stairs with lopsided dignity. Twilla clapped her hands and backed up ahead of her, taunting her, encouraging her, plucking at her gray tweed coat. Twilla danced around her, swirling the fur robe with graceful turns. Miss Mahan looked straight ahead, one hand on the banister for balance.

Then, at the third step from the top, she stumbled. She fell against the railing and then to her knees. She shifted and sat on the step, rubbing her shins.

"Don't lose heart now, Miss Mahan," Twilla sang. "We're almost there." Twilla tugged at her coat sleeve. Miss Mahan clutched Twilla's wrist as if she needed help in getting up. Then she heaved with all her might. Twilla's laughter became a gasp and then a shriek as she plummeted down the stairs with a series of very satisfying thumps and crashes. Miss Mahan hurried after her but the fall had done the job.

Twilla lay on her back a few feet from the bottom step, her body twisted at the wrong angle. She was absolutely motionless except for her face. It contorted in fury and her eyes were metallic with hate. Her rose-petal lips writhed and spewed the most vile obscenities Miss Mahan had ever imagined, some of them in languages she'd never heard.

"Dazreel!" Twilla keened. "Dazreel! Dazreel!" over and over. A howl reverberated through the house. It shook. Plaster crashed and wood splintered. Dazreel appeared at the top of the stairs, barely able to squeeze through the opening.

Twilla continued her call. Miss Mahan took a trembling step backward. Dazreel started down the steps. Miraculously, they didn't collapse. Only the banister splintered and swayed outward.

Miss Mahan commanded herself to think. What did she know about djinns? Very little, practically nothing. Wasn't there supposed to be a controlling device of some sort? A lamp? A bottle? A magic ring? A talisman? Something. She looked at Twilla and then at the djinn. She almost fainted. Dazreel approached the bottom of the stairs with an enormous erection.

She looked frantically at Twilla. She's not wearing rings. Then something caught her eye.

The pendant! Was it the pendant? It had slipped up and over her shoulder and beneath her neck. Miss Mahan scrambled for it. She pushed Twilla's head aside. The child screamed in horrible agony. She grasped the pendant and pulled. The chain cut into the soft flesh of Twilla's neck and then snapped, leaving a red line that oozed blood.

She looked at Dazreel. He had stopped and was looking at her tentatively. It *was* the pendant! "Give it back," Twilla groaned. "Give it back. Please. Please, give it back. It won't do you any good. You don't know how to use it."

Miss Mahan threw the pendant at him. Twilla screamed and the hair on the back of Miss Mahan's neck bristled. It was not a scream of pain or rage, but of the damned. Dazreel's huge hand darted out and caught the pendant. He held his fist to his face and opened his fingers, gazing at what he held. He looked at Miss Mahan and smiled an angelic smile. Then he rippled, like heat waves on the desert, and . . . vanished.

Miss Mahan sat on the bottom step, weak with relief, gulping air. She looked at Twilla, as motionless as the parent dolls in the chairs. Only her face moved, twisting in sobs of self-pity. Miss Mahan almost felt sorry for her . . . but not quite.

She stood up and walked through the kitchen and out the back door. She thought she knew where it would be. Everyone kept it there. She went to the shed behind the carriage house, floundering through the snow drift. She scooped away the snow to get the door open. She stepped in and looked around. There was almost no light. The scudding clouds seemed even lower and darker, and the single window in the shed was completely grimed over.

She spotted it behind some shovels, misted over with cobwebs. She pushed the shovels aside, grasped the handle and lifted the gasoline can. It was heavy. She shook it. There was a satisfying slosh. She smiled grimly and started back to the house, walking more lopsided than ever.

Then she stopped and gaped when she saw Leo Whittaker's car parked out of sight behind the house. She hurried on, letting the heavy can bounce against the ground with every other step. She opened the kitchen door and shrieked.

Mrs. Gilbreath stood in the doorway, smiling pleasantly at her, and holding a butcher knife. Without reasoning, without even thinking, Miss Mahan took the handle of the heavy gasoline can in both hands and swung it as hard as she could.

The sharp rim around the bottom caught Mrs. Gilbreath across the face, destroying one eye, shearing away her nose, and opening one cheek. Her expression didn't change. Blood flowed over her pleasant smile as she staggered drunkenly backward.

Miss Mahan lost her balance completely. The momentum of the gasoline can swung her around and she sat in the snow, flat on her skinny bottom. The can slipped from her fingers and bounced across the ground with a descending scale of clangs. She lurched to her feet and looked in the kitchen door. Mrs. Gilbreath had slammed against the wall and was sitting on the floor, still smiling her gory smile, her right arm twitching like a metronome.

Miss Mahan scrambled after the gasoline can and hid it in the pantry. She ducked up the kitchen stairs when she heard footsteps.

Mr. Gilbreath walked through the kitchen, ignoring Mrs. Gilbreath, and went out the back door. Miss Mahan hurried up the stairs. Oh Lord, she thought, I'll be so sore I can't move for a week.

She entered the upstairs hall from the opposite end. She stepped carefully over the debris from the wall shattered by the djinn. She looked in the bedrooms on the other side. The first one was empty with a layer of dust, but the second . . . She stared. It looked like a set from a Marla Montez movie. A fire burned in the fireplace and Leo Whittaker lay stark naked on the fur-covered bed.

"Leo Whittaker!" she bellowed. "Get up from there and put your clothes on this instant!" But he didn't move. He was alive; his chest moved gently as he breathed. She went to him, trying to keep from looking at his nakedness. Then she thought, what the dickens? There's no point in being a prude at this stage. Her eyes widened in admiration. Then she ceded him a few additional points for being able to satisfy Twilla. Why couldn't she have found a beautiful man like that when she was twenty-three? she wondered. She sighed. It wouldn't have made any difference, she guessed. It would have all turned out the same.

She put her hand on his shoulder and shook him. He moaned softly and shifted on the bed. "Leo! Wake up! What's the matter with you?" She shook him again. He acted drugged or something. She saw a long golden hair on his stomach and plucked it off, throwing it on the floor. She took a deep breath and slapped him in the face. He grunted. His head lifted slightly and then fell back. "Leo!" she shouted, and slapped him again. His body jerked and his eyes clicked open but didn't focus.

"Leo!" Slap!

"Owww," he said and looked at her. "Miss Mahan?"

"Leo, are you awake?"

"Miss Mahan? What are you doing here? Is Lana all right?" He sat up in the bed and saw the room. He grunted in bewilderment.

"Leo. Get up and get dressed. Hurry!" she commanded. She heard the starter of a car grinding. Leo looked at himself, turned red, and tried to move in every direction at once. Miss Mahan grinned and went to the window. She could hear Leo thumping and bumping as he tried to put his clothes on. The car motor caught and steam billowed from the carriage house. "Hurry, Leo!" The black Chrysler began slowly backing out, Mr. Gilbreath at the wheel. Then the motor stalled and died.

He's trying to get away, she thought. No, he's only a puppet. He's planning to take Twilla away! She turned back to Leo. He was dressed, sitting on the edge of the bed putting on his shoes. He looked at her shame-faced, like a little boy.

"Leo," she said in her sternest, most no-nonsense, unruly child voice. The car motor started again. "Don't ask any questions. Go down the kitchen stairs, and to your car. Hurry as fast as you can. Don't let Mr. Gilbreath see you. Bring your car around to the front and to the end of the lane. Block the lane so Mr. Gilbreath can't get out. Keep yourself locked in your car because he's dangerous. Do you understand?"

"No," he said, shaking his head.

"Never mind. Will you do what I said?"

He nodded.

"All right, then. Hurry!" They left the bedroom. Leo gave it one last bewildered glance. They ran down the kitchen stairs as fast as they could, Leo keeping her steady. She propelled him out the back door before he could see Mrs. Gilbreath still smiling and twitching. The black Chrysler was just pulling around to the front of the house.

She ran to the pantry, retrieved the gasoline can, and staggered into the entry hall. She could see Mr. Gilbreath getting out of the car. She locked the door and hobbled into the parlor. Twilla had been moved to the divan and covered with a quilt. He shouldn't have moved her, Miss Mahan thought, with an injury like that it could have killed her.

Twilla saw her enter and began screeching curses at her. Miss Mahan shook her head. She put the gasoline can down by the divan and tried to unscrew the cap on the spout. It wouldn't budge. It was rusted solid. Miss Mahan growled in frustration. The front door began to rattle and clatter.

Twilla's curses stopped suddenly, and Miss Mahan looked at her. Twilla was staring at her in round-eyed horror. Miss Mahan went to the fireplace and got the poker. Twilla's eyes followed her. She drew the poker back and swung it as hard as she could at the gasoline can. It made a very satisfactory hole. She swung the poker several more times and tossed it away. She picked up the can as Twilla began to scream and plead. She rested it on the back of the divan and stripped away the blanket. She tipped it over and pale pink streams of gasoline fell on Twilla.

Glass shattered in the front door. Miss Mahan left the can resting on the back of the divan, still gurgling out its contents, and went to the fireplace again. She picked up the box of matches as Mr. Gilbreath walked in. His expression didn't change as he hurried toward her. She took a handful of wooden matches. She struck them all on the side of the box and tossed them on Twilla.

Twilla's screams and the flames ballooned upward together. Mr. Gilbreath shifted directions and waded into the flames, reaching for Twilla. Miss Mahan ran out of the house as fast as she could.

She was past the black Chrysler, its motor still running, when the gasoline can exploded. Leo had parked his car where she told him. Now he jumped out and ran to her. They looked at the old Peacock house.

It was old and dry as dust. The flames engulfed it completely. The snow was melting in a widening circle around it. They had to back all the way to Leo's car because of the heat.

They heard a siren and turned to see Sheriff Walker's car hurrying down the lane, followed by some of the funeral procession on its way back to Hawley. The ones who hadn't turned down the road were stopped on the highway, looking.

"Leo, dear," she said. "Do you know what you're doing here?"

He rubbed his hand across his face, his eyes still a little bleary. "Yes, I think so. It all seems like a dream. Twilla . . . Miss Mahan," he said in pain. "I don't know why I did it."

"I do," she said soothingly, and put her arm around him. "And it wasn't your fault. You have to believe that. Don't tell Lana or anyone. Forget it ever happened. Do you understand?"

He nodded as Robin Walker got out of his car and ran toward them. He looks very handsome in his uniform, she thought. My, my, I've suddenly become very conscious of good-looking men. Too bad it's thirty years too late.

"Miss Mahan? Leo? What's going on here?" Robin asked in bewilderment. "Is anyone still in there?" He looked at her feet. "Miss Mahan, why are you running around in the snow with only one shoe on?"

She followed his gaze. "I'll declare," she said in astonishment. "I didn't know I'd lost it. Leo, Robin, let's get in your car. I have a lot to tell you both."

Miss Mahan sat before the fireplace in her comfortable old house, tearing the pages from her Twilla journal and feeding them one at a time to the fire. Paul Sullivan had doctored her cuts and bruises and she felt wonderful—stiff and sore, to be sure—but wonderful. Tomorrow the news would be all over town that, with brilliant detective work, Robin Walker, aided by Leo Whittaker, had discovered that Twilla Gilbreath's father was Yvonne's killer. In an attempt to arrest him, the house had burned and all three had perished.

She had told Robin and Leo everything that happened—well, almost everything. She had left out her own near encounter with Dazreel and a few other related items. She had also given the impression—sort of—that the house had burned by accident. Poor, sweet Robin hadn't believed a word of it. But after hearing Leo's account, taking a look at her demolished car, and seeing the footprints in the snow, he finally, grudgingly, agreed to go along with it. And it did explain all the mysteries of Yvonne's death.

She knew the *public* story was full of holes and loose ends, but she also knew the people in Hawley. They wanted to hear that an outsider had done it, and they wanted to hear that he had been discovered. Their own imaginations would fill in the gaps.

Lana Whittaker didn't really believe that Leo was working with Robin all those nights he was away, but they loved each other enough. They'd be all right.

She fed the last pages to the fire and looked around her parlor. She decided to put up a tree this year. She hadn't bothered with one in years. And a party. She'd have a party. There hadn't been more than three people in the house at one time in ages.

She hobbled creakily up the stairs, humming. "Deck the Halls with Boughs of Holly," considerably off key, heading for the attic to search for the box of Christmas tree ornaments.

The Purple Pterodactyls

by

L. Sprague de Camp

Although we are most familiar with them in the somewhat watered-down later-day role of genie-in-the-bottle (or lamp), jinn are really potent and fearsome supernatural creatures, the Moslem equivalent of demons. In the words of Jorge Luis Borges, "According to moslem tradition, Allah created three different species of intelligent beings: Angels, who are made of light; Jinn ('Jinnee' or 'Genie' in the singular), who are made of fire; and men, who are made of earth. The Jinn were created of a black, smokeless fire some thousands of years before Adam, and consist of five orders. Among those orders we find good Jinn and evil, male Jinn and female."

Like demons, jinn can be bound to servitude, and magically summoned to perform various tasks. Borges tells us that "certain scholars attribute to them the building of the pyramids or, under the orders of Solomon, the Great Temple of Jerusalem." Solomon, in fact, is said to have magically bound thousands of the jinn—which is how many of them ended up stuck in all those bottles and lamps beloved of cartoonists and moviemakers.

Jinn can be dangerous servants, though, and are likely to have their own ideas about how to handle even the simplist of tasks —as the wry story that follows amply demonstrates.

L. Sprague de Camp is a seminal figure, one whose career spans almost the entire development of modern fantasy and SF. For the fantasy magazine Unknown *in the late 1930s, he helped create a whole new modern style of fantasy writing—funny, whimsical, and irreverent—of which he is still the most prominent practitioner. His most famous books include* Lest Darkness Fall, The Incomplete Enchanter *(with Fletcher Pratt), and* Rogue

Queen. *His most recent book is* The Bones of Zora, *a novel written in collaboration with wife Catherine Crook de Camp.*

* * *

I AM AS ORDINARY, COMMONPLACE A GUY AS YOU CAN FIND: middle-sized, middle-class, middle-aged; engineer by training, banker by circumstance; with a nice wife, nice kids, nice house, and nice car. But the damndest things happen to me.

When the children were grown enough so that they could take care of themselves in summer, Denise and I spent a vacation by ourselves at the shore. My cousin Linda, who has a house there, had been raving about Ocean Bay. So we rented an apartment in a rambly wooden-frame building, a block from the beach. This was before the waterfront sprouted a host of huge condominiums, like a plague of concrete mushrooms. You could walk on the sand without stepping on somebody or getting hit in the eye with a Frisbee.

We swam, we sunned, and we walked the boardwalk. The second afternoon, Denise said: "Willy, my old, why do we walk not down to the park of amusement?"

She said it in French, since we speak it a lot *en famille.* It is her native tongue, and I try to keep mine up by practice. We tried to bring the children up bilingually, but it took with only one of them.

We walked a mile to the piers and concessions. There were the usual fun house, roller coaster, and shooting gallery. There was a fortuneteller who called himself Swami Krishna. There were concessions where you threw darts at rubber balloons, or threw baseballs at plywood cats, or tossed baseballs into baskets. These baskets were so set that, when you did get your ball in, it bounced right out again and did not count. If you succeeded in such endeavors, you won teddy bears, rubber pythons, and similar junk.

I am normally immune to the lure of such games. One, however, showed more originality.

You bought three rubber rings, four or five inches in diameter, for half a dollar. You tossed these rings over three little posts, a couple of feet high and a mere yard from the thrower. There were three sets of these posts, forming three sides of a square.

The upper part of each post was conical, and it was no trick to get the ring over the point of the cone. To win, however, the ring had to fall down the rest of the post, which was square in cross-section and barely small enough for the ring to go over it. Nearly always, the ring hung up on the corners at the top of the square section. You had to ring all three posts at once to win a prize.

The prizes were even more original: a flock of plush-and-wire pterodactyls. They came in several models and sizes, some with long tails and some with short, some with teeth and some with long, toothless beaks. The biggest were over a yard across the wings. They were made so that you could hang one from your ceiling as a mobile. If the wind was strong, you could lock the wings in place and fly the thing as a kite. They were all dyed in shades of purple.

"Purple pterodactyls!" I said. "Darling, I've got to have one of those."

"Oh, *mon Dieu!*" said Denise. "What on earth would you do with it?"

"Hang it in my study, I suppose."

"You had better not hang it where the people can see it. What do you like about these monsters?"

"I suppose it's the alliteration of the name. Only it's not a real alliteration, since you don't pronounce the *p* in 'pterodactyl.' That makes it just an eye-rhyme—I mean an eye-alliteration."

"In English, maybe. But in French we do pronounce the *p*: p'tero-dac-TEEL. That is what is wrong with the English; you never know when some letter at the beginning of a word is silent."

"Like 'knife,' you mean? Well, in French you never know when a letter at the *end* of a word is silent. Let me have a try at this."

The concessionaire was a short, tubby, bald man of about my age, with a big black mustache. The ends of the mustache were waxed and curled up, something like the *Schnurrbart* once worn by Kaiser Wilhelm II.

The man sold me a set of rings, and I threw. . . . Ten dollars and sixty rings later, I was no nearer to getting my purple pterodactyl.

"Will you sell me one of those?" I asked the proprietor. "How much?"

The man ducked a little bow. "I am so sorry, sir," he said with a slight accent, "but they are not for sale. Either you win them with the rings, or you do not get any."

A look from Denise told me I had better not throw any more of the Newbury fortune, such as it was, after Mesozoic reptiles just then. As we walked off, I growled something like: "I'll get one of those things if it's my last . . . "

"You say we can't afford a Mercedes," she said, "but you throw away money on those hideous . . . "

"Well, anyway," said I to change the subject, "if we go right back to the house, we can get another swim before dinner."

"Willy!" she said. "You have had one swim today. The waves are big, and you will get the sunburn. Do not kill yourself, trying to prove your manhood! You forget we are middle-aged."

"I may be middle-aged," said I with a leer, "but I can still do some of the things young men do."

"Yes, I know. You did it just this morning. Some day you will try to prove your manhood once too often, and you will have the stroke in the middle of it."

"I can't think of a better way to go."

"But think of your poor wife! Aside from the fact that I don't want to be a widow, consider how embarrassing it would be to explain to the policemen!"

Next morning, we went out for our sun-and-swim. There on the beach was our friend of the purple pterodactyls, also soaking up ultra-violet. In bathing trunks, with his pod and his jungle of graying chest hair, he was a walking argument against nudism. He had been swimming, for the water had dissolved the pomade out of his mustache, so the ends hung down in Fu-Manchurian style. He was spooning sand upon himself with a child's toy shovel.

"Hello," I said, since you never know when the unlikeliest people might want to do business with your bank. "How's the pterodactyl business?"

"Business is good," he said. "Three of my pterosaurs were won yesterday, so you see people do win sometimes. I regret that you did not. You must try again."

"I'll be back," I said. "Do you come out here every day before opening?"

"Yes. It is the only time I have, since I must be on duty from noon to midnight. It is not an easy business."

In answer to my questions, he told me something of the economics of boardwalk concessions. "Excuse me please," he said. "Permit me to introduce myself. I am Ion Maniu, at your service. I regret that I cannot give you my card."

"I'm Wilson Newbury," I said.

He repeated the name slowly, as if it really meant something to him. "Is there an initial?"

"Woodrow Wilson Newbury, if you want the whole thing," I

told him, "but I haven't used the 'Woodrow' in years. When I see you this afternoon, we can exchange cards." I thought Mr. Maniu's formality a little quaint but did not mean to let him outdo me.

In the afternoon, my cousin Linda wanted to take Denise on one of those endless female shopping trips, looking at hundreds of wares in dozens of stores but probably not buying anything. On these safaris, my knees give out after the first hour, like those of an old prizefighter.

I begged off and sneaked back to Maniu's concession. All that got me was another five dollars down the drain.

I was to meet the girls at a souvenir and notion shop, combined with a branch post office, on Atlantic Avenue. While waiting, I looked over a bin full of junk rings, offered for a quarter each. They were little brass things set with pieces of colored glass, for the pleasure of vacationers' children. Some were elaborate, with coiled serpents or skulls and crossbones.

I pawed over this stuff, not meaning to buy—our own children were much too grown-up—but to pass the time and muse on the costs, mark-ups, and profits of merchandising these things. Then I came upon one that did not seem to belong. I tried it on, and it fitted.

Although dull and dirty like the rest, this ring was more massive. It felt heavier than one would expect of a brass ring of that size. That proved nothing; it could be plated or painted lead. It seemed to have once been molded in a complex design, but the ridges and grooves were so worn down as to leave only traces.

The stone was a big green glassy lump, polished but unfaceted, with the original bumps and hollows preserved like those of a stream-worn pebble.

I gave the cashier a quarter, put the ring on my finger, and met the girls. Linda started to tell me about the women's club meeting, at which she had persuaded me, with some cousinly arm-twisting, to speak. Then Denise spotted the ring.

"Willy!" she said. "What have you done now?"

"Just a junk ring out of the bin there, but it appealed to me. For twenty-five cents, what did I have to lose?"

"Let me see," said Denise. "*Hein!* This does not look to me quite like what you call the junk. Look, we have just come from Mr. Hagopian the jeweller. Let us go back there and ask him what it is."

"Oh, girls," I said, "let's not be silly. You won't find a Hope diamond in a box of stuff like that."

"As you were saying," she persisted, "what have we to lose? Come along; it's only a block."

Hagopian screwed his loupe into his eye and examined the ring. "I won't guarantee anything," he said, "but it looks like real gold, and the stone like an uncut emerald. In that case, it could be worth thousands. It would of course take tests to be sure what this is. . . . Where did you get it?"

"An unlikely place," I said.

"This is pretty unlikely, too. For four or five hundred years, practically all gems used in jewelry have been faceted. Before that, they just smoothed them off and tried to cut out obvious defects, while keeping as much of the material as they could.

"This kind of mounting goes back much further than that—unless somebody is making a clever imitation of a real ancient ring. If you would leave it a few days for assaying . . . "

"I'll think about it," I said, taking the ring back. Hagopian might be perfectly honest (in fact, I think he was), but before I left anything with him I would check up on him.

Next morning was overcast. When we went for our swim, there was Maniu, half buried in the sand, with just his upper body, arms, and head sticking out. He was ladling more sand over his torso. I asked:

"Mr. Maniu, if you want the sun, why bury yourself? The sun can't get through the sand."

"I have a theory, Mr. Newbury," he said. "The vital vibrations will rejuvenate you. Shall I see you at my concession today?" He grinned at me in a peculiar way, which led me to wonder if he slept in a coffin full of earth from Transylvania.

"If it doesn't rain, maybe," I said.

It did rain, so we did not go boardwalking. Denise wrote letters in the sitting room, while I took off my shoes and lay down on one of the beds for a nap.

Then a rhythmic, squeaky sound kept waking me up. After I had jerked awake three times, I hunted down the source. It came from an aluminum-and-plastic rocking chair on the little terrace of our apartment. Chair and terrace were wet from the drizzle. Nobody was sitting in the chair, but it rocked anyway.

Thinking that the wind was moving this light little piece of furniture, I moved the chair to a more sheltered part of the terrace and went back to bed.

The sound awoke me again. I stamped out to the terrace. The

chair was rocking again, although there was no wind to speak of. The mate to this chair, in a more exposed place, stood still. I cast a few curses against the overcast heavens, turned both chairs upside down, and returned to the bed.

It seemed to me that I next woke up to find a strange man sitting on the other of the twin beds and looking at me.

He was a man of average size, very swarthy, with a close-cut black mustache. His clothes were up-to-date but what I should call "cheap and flashy": striped pants, loud tie, stickpin, and several rings. (But then, Denise is always after me to buy more colorful clothes. She says a banker doesn't *have* to dress like an undertaker.) I also noted that the man wore a big, floppy panama hat, which he kept on his head.

What makes me sure that this was a dream is that, instead of leaping up and demanding: "Who in hell are you and what are you doing here?" I just lay there with a weak smile and said: "Hello!"

"Ah, Mr. Newbury!" said the man. He, too, spoke with an accent, although one different from Maniu's. "Peace be with you. I am at your service."

I stammered: "B-but who—who are you?"

"Habib al-Lajashi at your service, sir."

"Huh? But who—how—what do you mean?"

"It is the ring, sir. That emerald ring from the Second Dynasty of Kish. I am the slave of that ring. When you are turning it round thrice on your finger, I appear to do your bidding."

I blinked. "You mean you—you're some sort of Arabian Nights genie?"

"Jinn, sir. Oh, I see. You were expecting me to appear in medieval garb, with turban and robe. I assure you, sir, we *jann* are keeping up with the times quite as well as mortals."

You might expect a suspicious, hard-headed fellow like me to scoff and order the man out. I have, however, come upon so many queer things that I did not dismiss Mr. al-Lajashi out of hand. I said:

"What does this service consist of?"

"I can do little favors for you. Like seeing that you are getting the choicest cuts of steak in a restaurant, or that you draw all aces and face cards in contract."

"Nothing like eternal youth for my wife and me?"

"Alas, no, sir. I am only a very minor jinn and so can do only small favors. The most powerful ones are all tied up with oil shaykhs and big corporations."

"Hm," I said. "If I knew which super-jinn served which corporation, it should affect the securities of that—"

"Ah, no sir, I am sorry; but that information is classified."

"How long does this service last? Is it one of those three-wishes-and-out deals?"

"No, sir. You remain my master as long as you keep the ring. When it passes to another, I pass with it."

"How do you like your job, Habib?"

Al-Lajashi made a face. "It depends on the master, like any other slavery. There is a jinn's liberation movement—but never mind that, sir."

"Is there any way you can end this servile status?"

"Yes, sir. If one of my masters is so grateful for services rendered that he is voluntarily giving me the ring, I am free. But that has not happened in three thousand years. You mortals know a good thing when you see it. You hang on to our service, even when you promise us liberty."

"Let's get down to cases," I said. "There's a concessionaire . . ." and I told Habib about the purple pterodactyls. "The next time I take a chance with Maniu's rings, I want to win one of those things."

Al-Lajashi took off his panama hat to scratch his scalp, disclosing a pair of small horns. "I think I can do it, sir. Leave it to me."

"Don't make it too obvious, or he'll get suspicious."

"I understand. Now, sir, pray lie down and resume your nap. I shall not disturb you again today."

I did as he said and woke up normally. I could see no dent in Denise's bed where the *soi-disant* jinn had sat. I did not think it wise to tell Denise about my experiences. Instead, I worked on my speech to Linda's clubwomen.

The next day was fair and breezy. Maniu was on the beach, all buried but his arms and head.

"Good morning, Mr. Maniu," I said. "If you'll pardon my saying so, you give a slightly macabre impression."

"How so, Mr. Newbury?"

"You look as if somebody had put your severed head on top of that pile of sand."

Maniu grinned. "Come to my concession this afternoon, and you shall see that my head is firmly affixed to the rest of me."

So I did. My first three rings stuck at the square sections of the posts. Of my second three, one slipped down all the way. Of my third, two scored. The fourth time, all three rings fell to the base of the posts.

Maniu stared. "My God, Mr. Newbury, you certainly have improved fast! Which pterosaur do you want?"

"That one, please," I said, indicating a long-beaked *Pteranodon.*

Maniu got down the prize, folded the wings, and showed me how to extend them again. "Come back tomorrow," he said. "You will never repeat this feat, ha-ha!"

"We shall see," I said. I bore my prize home, to the acute discomfort of Denise. She did not like the stares we got on the boardwalk, with that thing under my arm.

The next day, I was back, despite Denise's protest: "Willy, you big *pataud*, where would you put another of those monstrosities?"

"I'll find a place," I said. "This ganif has challenged me, and I'll show him."

And I did, coming away with a fanged *Dimetrodon.*

The following day, Maniu was not in his usual place on the beach. I took another nap after lunch and awoke to find al-Lajashi in the room.

"Mr. Newbury," he said, "shall you make another attempt on Mr. Maniu's prizes?"

"I thought of doing so. Why?"

"There may be difficulty, sir. Mr. Maniu is furious with you for winning two of his lizard-bats. He hardly ever gives one up."

"Stingy fellow! He told me three were won a few days ago."

"He lies. I doubt he has given out one all this season."

"So what?"

"He has rented the services of one of my fellow jann to protect him."

"Does that mean you won't be able to make the rings go over the posts?"

"Oh, I am thinking I can still do it, although not so easily. But this other fellow may make you trouble."

"What sort of trouble?"

"I do not know. But ibn-Musa can surely harass you."

"Why can't you protect me, as the other jinn does Maniu?"

"I cannot be everywhere at once, any more than you can. If he uses a phenomenon on the material plane over which I have no control, I cannot stop him."

"Where did Maniu get his spook? From another ring?"

"No, sir. He leased him from that astrologer on the boardwalk, Swami Krishna. The astrologer's name is really Carlos Jimenez, but no matter. He uses this jinn to make some of his little astrological predictions come true. Are you still determined to try your so-called luck again?"

"I am," I said.

When I bought rings from Maniu and began tossing, the rings did not fly so surely as before. They wobbled about in the air and hesitantly settled over the posts. I spent several dollars before I got my three rings over all three posts. When one ring started to fall to the base of the post, it fell partway, started to rise again, and bobbed up and down a couple of times before completing its descent.

Maniu watched it, chewing his lower lip. I could imagine two invisible entities struggling with the ring, one trying to push it down, and the other, to raise it off the post.

I walked off with a fine *Rhamphorynchus*, the one with a little rudder on the end of its tail. The waxy spikes of Maniu's whiskers quivered like those of a cat.

I wanted to sail. The day after I won my third prize, I found the boat I wanted. It was a sixteen-foot centerboard sloop, the *Psyche*, which the Ramoth Bay Sailing Club had for rent. Ocean Bay is built on a long spit of land, with the Atlantic on one side and shallow Ramoth Bay on the other.

That day, however, there was a flat calm. Since the boat had no motor, there was no point in taking it out. Instead, I went back to the boardwalk and won another pterodactyl. Maniu hopped up and down with excitement.

"It is unheard of!" he said. "You must have supernatural aid!"

"Don't you want me to play any more?" I asked innocently. He knew perfectly well that I had the help of my jinn—ibn-Musa would have told him—and I knew that he knew.

To tell the truth, I was losing enthusiasm for collecting these bulky objects. I suppose some childish spirit of rivalry kept me trying to put one more over on this con artist.

I surmised that, however much Maniu hated to lose his pterodactyls, neither did he wish to lose the money that my visits brought him, not to mention the publicity. The prizes probably cost him no more than I paid in throwing fees.

Red-faced, Maniu mastered his conflicting feelings. "No, no, nothing like that," he said. "Come as often as you like. I am a fair man."

That evening was the women's club meeting. We got dressed up and had dinner at Linda's house with her and her husband. They brought us up on the local gossip: how one of the councilmen had been caught with his hand in the municipal till, and about the motorcycle gang suspected of local depredations. Then we went to the little auditorium.

I am no public speaker. With a written text, I can give a fair rendition, remembering to look up from the paper now and then, and not to drone or mumble. But without a manuscript, rhetorically speaking, I fall over my own big feet. This time, I had my talk, written out, in the inside pocket of my jacket.

When the ladies assembled, there was the usual tedious hour while minutes were read, the treasurer's report was presented, delinquent members were dunned for their dues, committees presented reports, and so on.

At last the chairman (I absolutely refuse to say "chairperson") called me up and gave me a flowery introduction: ". . . and so Mr. Wilson Newbury, first vice president of the Harrison Trust Company, will speak to you on the importance of trusts to women."

I stepped up, put on my glasses, and spread out the sheets of my manuscript on the lectern.

The sheets were blank.

I may have goggled at them for only a few seconds, but it seemed an hour. I instantly thought: this is one of ibn-Musa's tricks.

Such reasoning, however, was of no help in getting me off the platform. There was nothing for it but to make the speech without this aid. I plunged in.

It was a pretty bad speech, even though I knew my subject. Even Denise, who is as loyal as can be, hinted at that later. But I got through my main points:

". . .Now—ah—let me tell you about it—uh—reversionary living trusts. Umm. Ah. They combine some of the—ah—features of revocable and—uh—irrevocable trusts. This is—umm—a—er—a temporary trust, often called the—ah—the 'Clifford trust,' after a taxpayer who um—ah—in—uh—1934, fought the IRS to a standstill. Such a—ah—trust . . . "

I finished at last, submitted to the insincere congratulations of the ladies, and went back to the apartment with Denise. When I looked again at my manuscript, all the writing was back in place.

Next day, I went to Maniu's for revenge. I got it, too. I came away with *two* purple pterodactyls, leaving Maniu practically frothing with ill-concealed rage.

The following day, since the weather looked suitable, I called the Ramoth Bay Sailing Club to confirm our reservation of the *Psyche*. On our way thither, Denise kidded me some more about the vagaries of English, which insisted on pronouncing the name SIKE-ee instead of the more logical French psee-SHAY.

"I'm sure Socrates wouldn't have known whom you were talking about in either case," I said.

"Willy, darling," said Denise, suddenly serious. "Are you sure you ought to take this boat out? The wind is pretty brisk."

"A mere ten to fifteen knots, and steady," I said. "You've sailed with me before, haven't you?"

"Yes, but—somehow I don't think this will turn out well."

I passed that off as women's intuition, which is wrong more often than not. People remember the times it works and forget those it fails.

We found the two young men in charge of the boats installing the sails, oars, life preservers, fire extinguisher, and other things called for by the maritime codes. In half an hour we were bowling along on Ramoth Bay under that brisk but soft, steady breeze abeam—a sailorman's ideal.

"Sun's over the yardarm," I said. "Let's break out the chow."

We had sandwiches, fruit, and enough whiskey to make the world look good but not enough to interfere with conning the boat. Denise unwrapped and sorted and poured. I raised my paper mug and said: "Here's to my one true love—"

Then, from an easy twelve-knot breeze, it hit us. A tornado or hurricane must be something like that. It came without warning, *wham!*, whipped the tops off the little waves, and hit our sails broadside.

I was a couple of seconds slow in starting the main sheet. Denise screamed, and over we went. Away went lunch, whiskey, and all, and away went Mr. and Mrs. Newbury into the water.

Luckily, we came down on top of the mainsail instead of under it. As soon as I got myself untangled from the lines and sail and coughed out the water I had inhaled, I grabbed for oars and life preservers, which were floating away to leeward.

The blast had died as quickly as it had risen. We thrashed

around, collected such gear as was still afloat, and held onto the hull, now lying peacefully on its side.

It occurred to me that all my sailing experience had been in keeled boats. Such boats cannot capsize, because the weight of the keel rights them again. A centerboard boat, however, easily overturns when a squall hits it, unless you are very spry at letting out the main sheet. And you cannot right the thing again while wallowing around in the sea.

All the Ramoth Bay sailboats are centerboard, because the bay is too shallow for keels. The place we had overturned, however, was too deep for us to stand on the bottom. There was nothing to do but hold on, wave, yell, and hope for rescue.

Soon the two young men at the club came out in a motorboat and hauled us aboard. They threw some tackle around the mast of the *Psyche* and had her right side up in a jiffy. One of them got aboard, struck the sails, and bailed out most of the water.

This took nearly an hour, while Denise and I huddled shivering in the motorboat. I do not think the young men had much sympathy for us. At last we returned to the pier, towing the *Psyche*.

It was still early afternoon by the time we were dried, changed, and fed. I took a nap and, as I more or less expected, had another visit from Habib al-Lajashi. The jinn looked grave.

"Mr. Newbury," he said, "I know of your troubles with the boat."

"Ibn-Musa's doing?

"Of course. Now I must tell you that Mr. Maniu has ordered ibn-Musa at all costs to destroy you."

"You mean to kill me? Murder me?"

"That is what is meaning by 'destroy.' "

"What for? If he wants me to quit his damned game, why doesn't he say so? I have all the purple pterodactyls I need."

"You are not understanding the psychology of Mr. Maniu. He has many ideas that would seem to you strange. I understand them better, because many mortals have ideas like that in my part of the world. With him it is a matter of what he calls his honor, never to let another get the better of him. You have wounded his—how do you say—your wife would know the French expression—"

"Amour-propre?"

"That is it. When someone does that to him, he never forgives them. It does no good to give him back his prizes, or to let him win them back, or to throw his rings for a month without scoring. He has a—what is that Italian word?"

"A vendetta?"

"Thank you, sir; a vendetta against you."

"I guess ibn-Musa really tried to drown us this morning. Luckily, we're both good swimmers. Well, Habib, what can you do for me?"

"Not much, I fear. Ibn-Musa can, by a slight adjustment of the material factors on this plane, bring all kinds of bad luck on you. You step into the street just once without noticing the speeding car; or you neglect a little cut and get the blood poisoning."

"It's up to you to get me out of this, old boy," I said. "After all, you got me into it, in a way."

Al-Lajashi shrugged. "I will do what I can, since you command. But I guarantee nothing."

"Look," I said, "suppose I promised to give you the ring, once I'm home free. Would that make a difference?"

Al-Lajashi pondered, lifting his hat to scratch between his horns. "If you will solemnly promise this thing, I do know one method that might work. It is risky, not only to you but also to me. But I am willing if you are."

"Don't see that I have much choice," I said. "Go ahead. I have to trust you, but you have impressed me as a pretty honest jinn."

Al-Lajashi smiled. "You are a shrewd judge of character, Mr. Newbury; but in your business you have to be. Very well, I am starting this project at once. I cannot explain the method, but do not be surprised at anything."

"I won't be," I said.

I was not, however, prepared for the frightful shriek that came from the beach, around three or four a.m. that night. It woke up Denise, too. We looked out but could see nothing.

We finally got back to sleep. I do not remember my dreams, save that they were much less pleasant than having cozy chats with Habib al-Lajashi.

Next morning, the night's events had receded into a vaguely-recalled bad dream. After breakfast, we put on our bathing suits for our morning's beaching.

There was Maniu, lying under a mound of sand with his head and arms sticking out. He seemed to be asleep. He had buried himself below high-tide mark, and the incoming tide would soon wash over his mound.

"Somebody ought to wake him up," I said, "before he gets a lungful of Atlantic Ocean."

"How pale he looks!" said Denise. "With all the sun he has been getting, one would think—"

She stopped with a terrible shriek. I had glanced away towards a couple of kids flying kites. When I looked back, Maniu's head was rolling gently down the slope of his mound.

The head had been set, like a macabre grave marker, on the mound, which covered the decapitated rest of him. A wave of the incoming tide had lapped up to it and set it rolling.

Just how this happened was never established. The police rounded up the motorcycle gang. The tracks of their vehicles were found on the beach, and there were other bits of circumstantial evidence, but not enough for conviction.

I did not see al-Lajashi for several days. When he paid another visit, I did not wait for him to ask for the ring. I tore it off and tossed it to him before he could speak.

"Take it away," I said, "and yourself with it."

"Oh, thank you, sir! *Kattar khayrak!* You are my liberator! In the name of the Prophet, on whom be peace, I love you! I—"

"I'm flattered and all that. But if you really want to express your gratitude, Habib, you will scram. I want nothing more to do with the jann."

Then I really woke up. There was no jinn; only my darling in the other bed. The ring, however, had gone.

I drew a long breath. Denise stirred. Well, I thought, this is as good a time as any to prove my manhood again. At my age, one should not pass up a chance.

Goslin Day

by

Avram Davidson

In Yiddish gozlin *means thief or swindler—a non-professional* gonif. *But what about goslins (with an* s*) that flicker-snicker and nimblesnitch and create havoc with pious people on hotsticky days, that swim in dusty mirrors and wait for propitious moments to escape through the cracks and swindle, thieve, and connive?*

Kabbalah is the mystical dark side of rationalistic Jewish thought, and in Kabbalistic lore, the manipulation of Hebrew words and numbers—numerology, gematria, noutricon, anagrams, acrostics—became magical tools to divine the secret names of angels and demons, and thus gain limited power over them. The Kabbalistic sorcerer has access to whole pantheons of angels and demons, to intervening worlds such as Yetzirah *—where the ten orders of angels can be found—and the dead, imperfect worlds that are the sources of evil. God created these imperfect worlds, so Kabbalists tell, and then destroyed them—but not completely, for God's works could not be totally destroyed, only changed.*

And if from one of those dead worlds come goslins, why then, naturally enough, it must be goslin day . . . .

For many years now Avram Davidson has been one of the most eloquent and individual voices in science fiction and fantasy, and there are few writers in any literary field who can hope to match his wit, his erudition, or the stylish elegance of his prose. His recent series of stories about bizarre exploits of Doctor Engelbert Esterhazy (collected in his World Fantasy Award-winning The Enquiries of Doctor Esterhazy*) and the strange adventures of Jack Limekiller (as yet uncollected, alas), for instance, are David-*

son at the very height of his considerable powers, and rank among the best work of the seventies. Davidson has won the Hugo, the Edgar, and the World Fantasy Award. His books include the renowned The Phoenix and the Mirror, Masters of the Maze, Rogue Dragon, Peregrine: Primus, Rork!, Clash of Star Kings, *and the collections* The Best of Avram Davidson, Or All the Seas With Oysters, *and* The Redward Edward Papers. *His most recent books are* Peregrine: Secundus, *a novel;* Collected Fantasies, *a collection; and, as editor, the anthology* Magic for Sale. *Upcoming is a new novel,* Vergil In Averno, *the sequel to* The Phoenix and the Mirror.

* * *

IT WAS A GOSLIN DAY, NO DOUBT ABOUT IT; OF COURSE IT can happen that goslin things can occur, say, once a day for many days. But *this* day was a *goslin* day. From the hour when, properly speaking, the ass brays in his stall, but here instead the kat kvells on the rooftop—to the hour when the cock crows on his roost, but here instead the garbageman bangs on his can—even that early, Faroly realized that it was going to be a goslin day (night? let be night: *It was* evening, *and* [after that] *it was morning: one day.* Yes or no?). In the warbled agony of the shriek-scream Faroly had recognized an element present which was more than the usual ketzelkat expression of its painpleasure syndrome. In the agglutinative obscenities which interrupted the bang-crashes of the yuckels emptying eggshells orangerinds coffeegrounds there was (this morning, different from all other mornings) something unlike their mere usual brute pleasure in waking the dead. Faroly sighed. His wife and child were still asleep. He saw the dimlight already creeping in, sat up, reached for the glass and saucer and poured water over his nails, began to whisper his preliminary prayers, already concentrating on his Intention in the name *Unity:* but aware, aware, aware, the hotsticky feeling in the air, the swimmy looks in the dusty corners of windows, mirrors; something a tension, here a twitch. Notgood notgood.

In short: a goslin day.

Faroly decided to seek an expert opinion, went to Crown Heights to consult the kabbalist. Kaplánovics.

Rabbaness Kaplánovics was at the store, schauming off the soup with an enormous spoon, gestured with a free elbow toward an inner room. There sat the sage, the sharp one, the teacher of our teachers, on his head his beaver hat neatly brushed, on his feet and legs his boots brightly polished, in between garments well and clean without a fleck or stain as befits a disciple of the wise. He and Faroly shook hands, greeted, blessed the Name. Kaplánovics pushed across several sheets of paper covered with an exquisitely neat calligraphy.

"Already there," the kabbalist said. "I have been through everything three times, twice. The *New York Times,* the *Morgen Dzshornal,* I.F. Stone, Dow-Jones, the *Daph-Yomi*, your name-Text, the weather report, Psalm of the Day. Everything is worked out, by numerology, analogy, gematria, noutricon, anagrams, allegory, procession and precession. So.

"Of course today as any everyday we must await the coming of the Messiah: 'await'—*expect?today?* not today. Today he wouldn't come. Considerations for atmospheric changes, or changes for atmospheric considerations, *not—bad. Not—bad*. Someone gives you an offer for a good air-conditioner, cheap, you could think about it. Read seven capitals of psalms between afternoon and evening prayers. One sequence is enough. The day is favorable for decisions on growth stocks, but avoid closed-end mutual funds. On the corner by the beygal store is an old woman with a pyshka, collecting dowries for orphan girls in Jerusalem: the money, she never sends, this is *her* sin, it's no concern of yours: give her eighteen cents, a very auspicious number: merit, cheaply bought (she has sugar diabetes and the daughter last week gave birth to a weak-headed child by a schwartzer), what else?" They examined the columns of characters.

"Ahah. Ohoh. If you get a chance to buy your house, don't buy it, the Regime will condemn it for a freeway, where are they all *going* so fast?—every man who has two legs thinks he needs three automobiles—besides—where did I write it? oh yes. There. The neighborhood is going to change very soon and if you stay you will be killed in three years and two months, or three months and two years, depending on which system of gematria is used in calculating. You have to warn your brother-in-law his sons should each commence bethinking a marriagematch. Otherwise they will be going to cinemas and watching televisions and putting arms around girls, won't have the proper intentions for their nighttime prayers, won't even read the protective psalms selected by the greatgrandson of the Baalshemtov: and with what results, my dear man? Nocturnal emissions and perhaps worse; is it for nothing that The Chapters of the Principles caution us, 'At age eighteen to the marriage canopy and the performance of good deeds,' hm?"

Faroly cleared this throat. "Something else is on your mind," said the kabbalist. "Speak. Speak." Faroly confessed his concern about goslins. Kaplánovics exclaimed, struck the table. "Goslins! You wanted to talk about goslins? It's already gone past the hour to say the Shema, and I certainly didn't have in mind when I said it to commence constructing a kaméa—" He clicked his tongue in annoyance. "Am I omniscient?" he demanded. "Why didn't you let me know you were coming? Man walks in off the street, expects to find—"

But it did not take long to soothe and smooth him—Who is strong? He who can control his own passion.

And now to first things first, or, in this case, last things first, for it was the most recent manifestation of goslinness which Faroly wished to talk about. The kabbalist listened politely but did not seem in agreement with nor impressed by his guest's recitation of the signs by which a goslin day might make itself known. " 'Show simônim,' " he murmured, with a polite nod. "This one loses an object, that one finds it, let the claimant come and 'show simônim,' let him cite the signs by which his knowledge is demonstrated, and, hence, his ownership . . ." But this was mere polite fumfutting, and Faroly knew that the other knew that both knew it.

On Lexington a blackavised goslin slipped out from a nexus of cracked mirrors reflecting dust at each other in a disused nightclub, snatched a purse from a young woman emerging from a ribs joint; in Bay Ridge another, palepink and blond, snatched a purse from an *old* woman right in front of Suomi Evangelical Lutheran. Both goslins flickersnickered and were sharply gone. In Tottenville, a third one materialized in the bedroom of an honest young woman still half asleep in bed just a second before her husband came back from the nightshift in Elizabeth, New Jersey; uttered a goslin cry and jumped out the window holding his shirt. Naturally the husband never believed her—would you? Two more slipped in and out of a crucial street corner on the troubled bordermarches of Italian Harlem, pausing only just long enough to exchange exclamations of *guineabastard! goddamnigger!* and goslin looks out of the corners of their goslin eyes. Goslin cabdrivers curseshouted at hotsticky pregnant women dumb enough to try and cross at pedestrian crossings. The foul air grew fouler, thicker, hotter, tenser, muggier, murkier: and the goslins, smelling it from afar, came leapsniffing through the vimveil to nimblesnitch, torment, buffet, burden, uglylook, poke, makestumble, maltreat, and quickshmiggy back again to gezzle guzzle goslinland.

The kabbalist had grown warm in discussion, eagerly inscribed circles in the air with downhooked thumb apart from fist " '. . . they have the forms of men and also they have the lusts of men,' " he quoted.

"You are telling me what every schoolchild knows," protested Faroly. "But from *which* of the other three of the four worlds of Emanation, Creation, Formation, and Effectation—from *which* do they come? And why more often, and more and more often, and more and more and more often, and—"

Face wrinkled to emphasize the gesture of waving these words away, Kaplánovics said, "If Yesod goes, how can Hod remain? If there is no Malchuth, how can there be Qether? Thus one throws away with the hand the entire configuration of Adam Qadmon, the Tree of Life, the Ancient of Days. Men tamper with the very vessels themselves, as if they don't know what happened with the Bursting of the Vessels before, as though the Husks, the Shards, even a single shattered Cortex, doesn't still plague and vex and afflict us to this day. They look down into the Abyss, and they say, "This is high,' and they look up to an Eminence and they say, "This is low'. . . And not thus alone! And not thus alone! Not just with complex deenim, as, for example, those concerning the fluxes of women—no! no! But the simplest of the simple of the Six Hundred and Thirteen Commandments: to place a parapet around a roof to keep someone from falling off and be killed. What can be simpler? What can be more obvious? What can be easier?

"—but do they do it? What, was it only three weeks ago, or four? a Puertorican boy didn't fall off the roof of an apartment house near dead? Dead, perished. Go talk to the wall. Men don't want to know. Talk to them *Ethics,* talk to them *Brotherhood*, talk to them *Ecumenical Dialogue*, talk to them any kind of nonsenseness: they'll listen. But talk to them: It's written, textually, in the Torah, to build a parapet around your rooftop to prevent blood being shed—no: to this they won't listen. They would neither hear nor understand. They don't know *Torah*, don't know *Text*, don't know *parapet; roof*—this they never heard of either—"

He paused. "Come tomorrow and I'll have prepared for you a kaméa against goslins." He seemed suddenly weary.

Faroly got up. Sighed. "And tomorrow will you also have prepared a kaméa against goslins for everyone else?"

Kaplánovics didn't raise his eyes. "Don't blame the rat," he said. "Blame the rat-hole."

Downstairs Faroly noticed a boy in a green and white skullcap, knotted crispadin coming up from inside under his shirt to dangle over his pants. "Let me try a sortilegy," he thought to himself. "Perhaps it will give me some remez, or hint. . . ." Aloud, he asked, "Youngling, tell me, what text did you learn today in school?"

The boy stopped twisting one of his stroobley earlocks, and turned up his phlegm-green eyes. " 'Three things take a man out of this world,' " he yawned. " 'Drinking in the morning, napping in the noon, and putting a girl on a winebarrel to find out if she's a virgin.' "

Faroly clicked his tongue, fumbled for a handkerchief to wipe his heatprickled face. "You are mixing up the texts," he said.

The boy raised his eyebrows, pursed his lips, struck out his lower jaw. "Oh indeed. You ask me a question, then you give me an answer. How do you know I'm mixing up the texts? Maybe I cited a text which you never heard before. What are you, the Vilna Gaon?"

"Brazen face—look, look, how you've gotten your crispadin all snarled," Faroly said, slightly amused, fingering the cinctures passed through one belt-loop—then, feeling his own horrified amazement and, somehow, *knowing . . . knowing* . . . as one *knows* the refrigerator is going to stop humming one-half second before it does stop, yet—"What is this? What is this? The cords of your crisadin are tied in *pairs?"*

The filthgreen eyes slid to their corners, still holding Faroly's. "Hear, O Israel," chanted the child: "the Lord our God, the Lord is Two."

The man's voice came out agonyshrill. "Dualist. Heresiarch. Sectary. Ah. Ah ah *ah—goslin!*"

"Take ya hands outa my pants!" shrieked the pseudo-child, and, with a cry of almost totally authentic fear, fled. Faroly, seeing people stop, faces changing, flung up his arms and ran for his life. The goslin-child, wailing and slobbering, trampled up steps into an empty hallway where the prismatic edge of a broken windowpane caught the sunlight and winkyflashed rainbow changes. The goslin stretched thin as a shadow and vanished into the bright edge of the shard.

Exhausted, all but prostrated by the heat, overcome with humiliation, shame, tormented with fear and confusion, Faroly stumbled through the door of his home. His wife stood there, looking at him. He held to the doorpost, too weary even to raise his hand to kiss his mazuzah, waiting for her to exclaim at his appearance. But she said nothing. He opened his mouth, heard his voice click in his throat. "Solomon," his wife said. He moved slowly into the room. "Solomon," she said.

"Listen—"

"Solomon, we were in the park, and at first it was so hot, then we sat under a tree and it was so *cool*—"

"Listen . . ."

". . . I think I must have fallen asleep . . . Solomon, you're so quiet . . . Now you're home, I can give the Heshy his bath. Look at him, Solomon! Look, look!"

Already things were beginning to get better. *"And the High Priest shall pray for the peace of himself and his house.* Tanya Rabbanan:—*and his house.* This means, his wife. He who has no wife, has no home." Small sighs, stifled sobs, little breaks of breath, Faroly moved forward into the apartment. Windows and mirrors were still, dark, quiet. The goslin day was almost over. She had the baby ready for the bath. Faroly moved his eyes, squinting against the last sunlight, to look at the flesh of his first born, unique son, his Kaddish. What child was this, sallow, squinting back, scrannel, preternaturally sly—? Faroly heard his own voice screaming screaming changeling! changeling!

—Goslin!

Nellthu

by

Anthony Boucher

There are basically two ways to deal with demons: You can go the witch's route, which involves going to Black Masses and chanting "Beelzebub, Beelzebub, Beelzebub" and praying to some horned-headed representative from Hell, or *you can make like a mage and* trick *the demons into giving you what you so richly deserve. Tricking demons is a time-honored tradition. You can learn the ins and outs by looking in any decent grimoire. It certainly* looks *easy . . .*

But you can't believe everything you read. Most of those grimoires are old and musty and out of date. Demons have smartened up these days. You've got to be creative *to trick them now, as the late Anthony Boucher points out in the very short, and very logical, story that follows.*

As a writer and reviewer Anthony Boucher had a considerable effect on science fiction, but it was as co-founder (with J. Francis McComas) and long-time editor of The Magazine of Fantasy & Science Fiction *that he really became a seminal influence on the field. Founded in 1949,* F&SF *soon became a showcase for the most literate and sophisticated work being done in the field, and Boucher earned himself a secure place in the pantheon of science fiction's greatest editors. Boucher wrote one science fiction novel—*Rocket to the Morgue, *under the pseudonym of H. H. Holmes—but as a writer he is best remembered for wry and ironic stories such as "The Quest for St. Aquin," "Barrier," "Snulbug," and "The Compleat Werewolf." His stories are collected in* Far and Away *and* The Compleat Werewolf and Other Stories of Fantasy and Science Fiction. *He had a separate and very successful career as a writer and critic in the mystery genre, and was* *a recipient of the prestigious Edgar Allen Poe Award of the Mystery Writers of America.*

* * *

AILSA HAD BEEN EASILY THE HOMELIEST AND THE LEAST TALented girl in the University, if also the most logical and levelheaded. Now, almost twenty-five years later, she was the most attractive woman Martin had ever seen and, to judge from their surroundings, by some lengths the richest.

". . . so lucky running into you again after all these years," she was saying, in that indescribably aphrodisiac voice. "You know about publishers, and you can advise me on this novel. I was getting so tired of the piano. . . ."

Martin had heard her piano recordings and knew they were superb—as the vocal recordings had been before them and the non-representational paintings before *them* and the fashion designs and that astonishing paper on prime numbers. He also knew that the income from all these together could hardly have furnished the Silver Room in which they dined or the Gold Room in which he later read the novel (which was of course superb) or the room whose color he never noticed because he did not sleep alone (and the word *superb* is inadequate).

There was only one answer, and Martin was gratified to observe that the coffee-bringing servant cast no shadow in the morning sun. While Ailsa still slept (superbly), Martin said, "So you're a demon."

"Naturally, sir," the unshadowed servant said, his eyes adoringly upon the sleeper. "Nellthu, at your service."

"But such service! I can imagine Ailsa-that-was working out a good spell and even wishing logically. But I thought you fellows were limited in what you could grant."

"We are, sir. Three wishes."

"But she has wealth, beauty, youth, fame, a remarkable variety of talents—all on three wishes?"

"On one, sir. Oh, I foxed her prettily on the first two." Nellthu smiled reminiscently. " *'Beauty'*—but she didn't specify, and I made her the most beautiful centenarian in the world. *'Wealth beyond the dreams of avarice'*—and of course nothing is beyond such dreams, and nothing she got. Ah, I was in form that day, sir! But the third wish . . ."

"Don't tell me she tried the old *'For my third wish I want three more wishes!'* I thought that was illegal."

"It is, sir. The paradoxes involved go beyond even our powers.

No, sir," said Nellthu, with a sort of rueful admiration, "her third wish was stronger than that. She said: *'I wish that you fall permanently and unselfishly in love with me.'* "

"She was always logical," Martin admitted. "So for your own sake you had to make her beautiful and . . . adept, and since then you have been compelled to gratify her every—" He broke off and looked from the bed to the demon. "How lucky for me that she included *unselfishly!*"

"Yes, sir," said Nellthu.

Snulbug

by

Anthony Boucher

And then again, sometimes you've got to use psychology *to get around a demon . . .*

* * *

"THAT'S A HELL OF A SPELL YOU'RE USING," SAID THE demon, "if I'm the best you can call up."

He wasn't much, Bill Hitchens had to admit. He looked lost in the center of that pentacle. His basic design was impressive enough—snakes for hair, curling tusks, a sharp-tipped tail, all the works—but he was something under an inch tall.

Bill had chanted the words and lit the powder with the highest hopes. Even after the feeble flickering flash and the damp fizzling *zzzt* which had replaced the expected thunder and lightning, he had still had hopes. He had stared up at the space above the pentacle waiting to be awe-struck, until he had heard that plaintive little voice from the floor wailing, "Here I am."

"Nobody's wasted time and power on a misfit like me for years," the demon went on. "Where'd you get the spell?"

"Just a little something I whipped up," said Bill modestly.

The demon grunted and muttered something about people that thought they were magicians.

"But I'm not a magician," Bill explained. "I'm a biochemist."

The demon shuddered. "I land the damnedest cases," he mourned. "Working for that psychiatrist wasn't bad enough, I should draw a biochemist. Whatever that is."

Bill couldn't check his curiosity. "And what did you do for a psychiatrist?"

"He showed me to people who were followed by little men and told them I'd chase the little men away." The demon pantomimed shooting motions.

"And did they go away?"

"Sure. Only then the people decided they'd sooner have little men than me. It didn't work so good. Nothing ever does," he added woefully. "Yours won't either."

Bill sat down and filled his pipe. Calling up demons wasn't so terrifying after all. Something quiet and homey about it. "Oh, yes it will," he said. "This is foolproof."

"That's what they all think. People—" The demon wistfully eyed the match as Bill lit his pipe. "But we might as well get it over with. What do you want?"

"I want a laboratory for my embolism experiments. If this method works, it's going to mean that a doctor can spot an embolus in the bloodstream long before it's dangerous and remove it safely. My ex-boss, that screwball old occultist Reuben Choatsby, said it wasn't practical—meaning there wasn't a fortune in it for him—and fired me. Everybody else thinks I'm wacky too, and I can't get any backing. So I need ten thousand dollars."

"There!" the demon sighed with satisfaction. "I told you it wouldn't work. That's out for me. They can't start fetching money on demand till three grades higher than me. I told you."

"But you don't," Bill insisted, "appreciate all my fiendish subtlety. Look—Say, what is your name?"

The demon hesitated. "You haven't got another of those things?"

"What things?"

"Matches."

"Sure."

"Light me one, please?"

Bill tossed the burning match into the center of the pentacle. The demon scrambled eagerly out of the now cold ashes of the powder and dived into the flame, rubbing himself with the brisk vigor of a man under a needle shower. "There!" he gasped joyously. "That's more like it."

"And now what's your name?"

The demon's face fell again. "My name? You really want to know?"

"I've got to call you something."

"Oh, no you don't. I'm going home. No money games for me."

"But I haven't explained yet what you are to do. What's your name?"

"Snulbug." The demon's voice dropped almost too low to be heard.

"Snulbug?" Bill laughed.

"Uh-huh. I've got a cavity in one tusk, my snakes are falling out, I haven't got enough troubles, I should be named Snulbug."

"All right. Now listen, Snulbug, can you travel into the future?"

"A little. I don't like it much, though. It makes you itch in the memory."

"Look, my fine snake-haired friend. It isn't a question of what you like. How would you like to be left there in that pentacle with nobody to throw matches at you?" Snulbug shuddered. "I thought so. Now, you can travel into the future?"

"I said a little."

"And," Bill leaned forward and puffed hard at his corncob as he asked the vital question, "can you bring back material objects?" If the answer was no, all the fine febrile fertility of his spell-making was useless. And if that was useless, heaven alone knew how the Hitchens Embolus Diagnosis would ever succeed in ringing down the halls of history, and incidentally saving a few thousand lives annually.

Snulbug seemed more interested in the warm clouds of pipe smoke than in the question. "Sure," he said. "Within reason I can—" He broke off and stared piteously. "You don't mean— You can't be going to pull that old gag again?"

"Look, baby. You do what I tell you and leave the worrying to me. You can bring back material objects?"

"Sure. But I warn you—"

Bill cut him off short. "Then as soon as I release you from that pentacle, you're to bring me tomorrow's paper."

Snulbug sat down on the burned match and tapped his forehead sorrowfully with his tail tip. "I knew it," he wailed. "I knew it. Three times already this happens to me. I've got limited powers, I'm a runt, I've got a funny name, so I should run foolish errands."

"Foolish errands?" Bill rose and began to pace about the bare attic. "Sir, if I may call you that, I resent such an imputation. I've spent weeks on this idea. Think of the limitless power in knowing the future. Think of what could be done with it: swaying the course of empire, dominating mankind. All I want is to take this stream of unlimited power, turn it into the simple channel of humanitarian research, and get me $10,000; and you call that a foolish errand!"

"That Spaniard," Snulbug moaned. "He was a nice guy, even if his spell was lousy. Had a solid, comfortable brazier where an imp could keep warm. Fine fellow. And he had to ask to see tomorrow's newspaper. I'm warning you—"

"I know," said Bill hastily. "I've been over in my mind all the things that can go wrong. And that's why I'm laying three conditions on you before you get out of that pentacle. I'm not falling for the easy snares."

"All right." Snulbug sounded almost resigned. "Let's hear 'em. Not that they'll do any good."

"First: This newspaper must not contain a notice of my own death or of any other disaster that would frustrate what I can do with it."

"But shucks," Snulbug protested. "I can't guarantee that. If you're slated to die between now and tomorrow, what can I do about it? Not that I guess you're important enough to crash the paper."

"Courtesy, Snulbug. Courtesy to your master. But I tell you what: When you go into the future, you'll know then if I'm going to die? Right. Well, if I am, come back and tell me and we'll work out other plans. This errand will be off."

"People," Snulbug observed, "make such an effort to make trouble for themselves. Go on."

"Second: The newspaper must be of this city and in English. I can just imagine you and your little friends presenting some dope with the Omsk and Tomsk *Daily Vuskutsukt.*"

"We should take so much trouble," said Snulbug.

"And third: The newspaper must belong to this space-time continuum, to this spiral of the serial universe, to this Wheel of If. However you want to put it. It must be a newspaper of the tomorrow that I myself shall experience, not of some other, to me hypothetical, tomorrow."

"Throw me another match," said Snulbug.

"Those three conditions should cover it, I think. There's not a loophole there, and the Hitchens Laboratory is guaranteed."

Snulbug grunted. "You'll find out."

Bill took a sharp blade and duly cut a line of the pentacle with cold steel. But Snulbug simply dived in and out of the flame of his second match, twitching his tail happily, and seemed not to give a rap that the way to freedom was now open.

"Come on!" Bill snapped impatiently. "Or I'll take the match away."

Snulbug got as far as the opening and hesitated. "Twenty-four hours is a long way."

"You can make it."

"I don't know. Look." He shook his head, and a microscopic dead snake fell to the floor. "I'm not at my best. I'm shot to pieces lately, I am. Tap my tail."

"Do what?"

"Go on. Tap it with your fingernail right there where it joins on."

Bill grinned and obeyed. "Nothing happens."

"Sure nothing happens. My reflexes are all haywire. I don't know as I can make twenty-four hours." He brooded, and his snakes curled up into a concentrated clump. "Look. All you want is tomorrow's newspaper, huh? Just tomorrow's, not the edition that'll be out exactly twenty-four hours from now?"

"It's noon now," Bill reflected. "Sure, I guess tomorrow morning's paper'll do."

"O.K. What's the date today?"

"August 21."

"Fine. I'll bring you a paper for August 22. Only I'm warning you: It won't do any good. But here goes nothing. Goodbye now. Hello again. Here you are." There was a string in Snulbug's horny hand, and on the end of the string was a newspaper.

"But hey!" Bill protested. "You haven't been gone."

"People," said Snulbug feelingly, "are dopes. Why should it take any time out of the present to go into the future? I leave this point, I come back to this point. I spent two hours hunting for this damned paper, but that doesn't mean two hours of your time here. People—" he snorted.

Bill scratched his head. "I guess it's all right. Let's see the paper. And I know: You're warning me." He turned quickly to the obituaries to check. No Hitchens. "And I wasn't dead in the time you were in?"

"No," Snulbug admitted. "Not *dead*," he added, with the most pessimistic implications possible.

"What was I, then? Was I—"

"I had salamander blood," Snulbug complained. "They thought I was an undine like my mother and they put me in the cold-water incubator when any dope knows salamandery is a dominant. So I'm a runt and good for nothing but to run errands, and now I should make prophecies! You read your paper and see how much good it does you."

Bill laid down his pipe and folded the paper back from the obituaries to the front page. He had not expected to find anything useful there—what advantage could he gain from knowing who won the next naval engagement or which cities were bombed—but he was scientifically methodical. And this time method was rewarded. There it was, streaming across the front page in vast black blocks:

MAYOR ASSASSINATED
FIFTH COLUMN KILLS CRUSADER

Bill snapped his fingers. This was it. This was his chance. He jammed his pipe in his mouth, hastily pulled a coat on his shoulders, crammed the priceless paper into a pocket, and started out of the attic. Then he paused and looked around. He'd forgotten Snulbug. Shouldn't there be some sort of formal discharge?

The dismal demon was nowhere in sight. Not in the pentacle or out of it. Not a sign or a trace of him. Bill frowned. This was definitely not methodical. He struck a match and held it over the bowl of his pipe.

A warm sigh of pleasure came from inside the corncob.

Bill took the pipe from his mouth and stared at it. "So that's where you are!" he said musingly.

"I told you salamandery was a dominant," said Snulbug, peering out of the bowl. "I want to go along. I want to see just what kind of a fool you make of yourself." He withdrew his head into the glowing tobacco, muttering about newspapers, spells, and, with a wealth of unhappy scorn, people.

The crusading mayor of Granton was a national figure of splendid proportions. Without hysteria, red baiting, or strike-breaking, he had launched a quietly purposeful and well-directed program against subversive elements which had rapidly converted Granton into the safest and most American city in the country. He was also a persistent advocate of national, state, and municipal subsidy of the arts and sciences—the ideal man to wangle an endowment for the Hitchens Laboratory, if he were not so surrounded by overly skeptical assistants that Bill had never been able to lay the program before him.

This would do it. Rescue him from assassination in the very nick of time—in itself an act worth calling up demons to perform—and then when he asks, "And how, Mr. Hitchens, can I possibly repay you?" come forth with the whole great plan of research. It couldn't miss.

No sound came from the pipe bowl, but Bill clearly heard the words, "Couldn't it just?" ringing in his mind.

He braked his car to a fast stop in the red zone before the city hall, jumped out without even slamming the door, and dashed up the marble steps so rapidly, so purposefully, that pure momentum carried him up three flights and through four suites of offices before anybody had the courage to stop him and say, "What goes?"

The man with the courage was a huge bull-necked plain clothes man, whose bulk made Bill feel relatively about the size of Snulbug. "All right, there," this hulk rumbled. "All right. Where's the fire?"

"In an assassin's gun," said Bill. "And it had better stay there."

Bullneck had not expected a literal answer. He hesitated long enough for Bill to push him to the door marked MAYOR—PRIVATE. But though the husky's brain might move slowly, his muscles made up for the lag. Just as Bill started to shove the door open, a five-pronged mound of flesh lit on his neck and jerked.

Bill crawled from under a desk, ducked Bullneck's left, reached the door, executed a second backward flip, climbed down from the table, ducked a right, reached the door, sailed back in reverse, and lowered himself nimbly from the chandelier.

Bullneck took up a stand in front of the door, spread his legs in ready balance, and drew a service automatic from its holster. "You ain't going in there," he said, to make the situation perfectly clear.

Bill spat out a tooth, wiped the blood from his eyes, picked up the shattered remains of his pipe, and said, "Look. It's now 12:30. At 12:32 a redheaded hunchback is going to come out on that balcony across the street and aim through the open window into the mayor's office. At 12:33 His Honor is going to be slumped over his desk, dead. Unless you help me get him out of range."

"Yeah?" said Bullneck. "And who says so?"

"It says so here. Look. In the paper."

Bullneck guffawed. "How can a paper say what ain't even happened yet? You're nuts, brother, if you ain't something worse. Now go on. Scram. Go peddle your paper."

Bill's glance darted out the window. There was the balcony facing the mayor's office. And there coming out on it—

"Look!" he cried. "If you won't believe me, look out the window. See on that balcony? The redheaded hunchback? Just like I told you. Quick!"

Bullneck stared despite himself. He saw the hunchback peer across into the office. He saw the sudden glint of metal in the hunchback's hand. "Brother," he said to Bill, "I'll tend to you later."

The hunchback had his rifle halfway to his shoulder when Bullneck's automatic spat and Bill braked his car in the red zone, jumped out, and dashed through four suites of offices before anybody had the courage to stop him.

The man with the courage was a huge bull-necked plain clothes man, who rumbled, "Where's the fire?"

"In an assassin's gun," said Bill, and took advantage of Bullneck's confusion to reach the door marked MAYOR—PRIVATE. But just as he started to push it open, a vast hand lit on his neck and jerked.

As Bill descended from the chandelier after his third try, Bullneck took up a stand in front of the door, with straddled legs and drawn gun. "You ain't going in," he said clarifyingly.

Bill spat out a tooth and outlined the situation. "—12:33," he ended. "His Honor is going to be slumped over the desk dead. Unless you help me get him out of range. See? It says so here. In the paper."

"How can it? Gwan. Go peddle your paper."

Bill's glance darted to the balcony. "Look, if you won't believe me. See the redheaded hunchback? Just like I told you. Quick! We've got to—"

Bullneck stared. He saw the sudden glint of metal in the hunchback's hand. "Brother," he said, "I'll tend to you later."

The hunchback had his rifle halfway to his shoulder when Bullneck's automatic spat and Bill braked his car in the red zone, jumped out, and dashed through four suites before anybody stopped him.

The man who did was a bull-necked plainclothes man, who rumbled—

"Don't you think," said Snulbug, "you've had about enough of this?"

Bill agreed mentally, and there he was sitting in his roadster in front of the city hall. His clothes were unrumpled, his eyes were bloodless, his teeth were all there, and his corncob was still intact. "And just what," he demanded of his pipe bowl, "has been going on?"

Snulbug popped his snaky head out. "Light this again, will you? It's getting cold. Thanks."

"What happened?" Bill insisted.

"People!" Snulbug moaned. "No sense. Don't you see? So long as the newspaper was in the future, it was only a possibility. If you'd had, say, a hunch that the mayor was in danger, maybe you could have saved him. But when I brought it into now, it became a fact. You can't possibly make it untrue."

"But how about man's free will? Can't I do whatever I want to do?"

"Sure. It was your precious free will that brought the paper into now. You can't undo your own will. And anyway, your will's still free. You're free to go getting thrown around chandeliers as often as you want. You probably like it. You can do anything up to the point where it would change what's in that paper. Then you have to start in again and again and again until you make up your mind to be sensible."

"But that—" Bill fumbled for words, "that's just as bad as . . . as fate or predestination. If my soul wills to—"

"Newspapers aren't enough. Time theory isn't enough. So I should tell him about his soul! People—" and Snulbug withdrew into the bowl.

Bill looked up at the city hall regretfully and shrugged his resignation. Then he folded his paper to the sports page and studied it carefully.

Snulbug thrust his head out again as they stopped in the many-acred parking lot. "Where is it this time?" he wanted to know. "Not that it matters."

"The racetrack."

"Oh—" Snulbug groaned. "I might have known it. You're all alike. No sense in the whole caboodle. I suppose you found a long shot?"

"Darned tooting I did. Alhazred at twenty to one in the fourth. I've got $500, the only money I've got left on earth: Plunk on Alhazred's nose it goes, and there's our $10,000."

Snulbug grunted. "I hear his lousy spell, I watch him get caught on a merry-go-round, it isn't enough, I should see him lay a bet on a long shot."

"But there isn't a loophole in this. I'm not interfering with the uture; I'm just taking advantage of it. Alhazred'll win this race vhether I bet on him or not. Five pretty hundred-dollar parimuuel tickets, and behold: The Hitchens Laboratory!" Bill jumped pryly out of his car and strutted along joyously. Suddenly he aused and addressed his pipe: "Hey! Why do I feel so good?"

Snulbug sighed dismally. "Why should anybody?"

"No, but I mean: I took a hell of a shellacking from that plug-gly in the office. And I haven't got a pain or an ache."

"Of course not. It never happened."

"But I felt it then."

"Sure. In a future that never was. You changed your mind, idn't you? You decided not to go up there?"

"O.K., but that was after I'd already been beaten up."

"Uh-uh," said Snulbug firmly. "It was before you hadn't een." And he withdrew again into the pipe.

There was a band somewhere in the distance and the raucous urble of an announcer's voice. Crowds clustered around the $2 vindows, and the $5 weren't doing bad business. But the $100 vindow, where the five beautiful pasteboards lived that were to reate an embolism laboratory, was almost deserted.

Bill buttonholed a stranger with a purple nose. "What's the ext race?"

"Sccond, Mac."

Swell, Bill thought. Lots of time. And from now on— He astened to the $100 window and shoved across the five bills that e had drawn from the bank that morning. "Alhazred, on the ose," he said.

The clerk frowned with surprise, but took the money and urned to get the tickets.

Bill buttonholed a stranger with a purple nose. "What's the ext race?"

"Second, Mac."

Swell, Bill thought. And then he yelled, "Hey!"

A stranger with a purple nose paused and said, " 'Smatter, Iac?"

"Nothing," Bill groaned. "Just everything."

The stranger hesitated. "Ain't I seen you someplace before?"

"No," said Bill hurriedly. "You were going to, but you aven't. I changed my mind."

The stranger walked away shaking his head and muttering how e ponies could get a guy.

Not till Bill was back in his roadster did he take the corncob om his mouth and glare at it. "All right!" he barked. "What was wrong this time? Why did I get on a merry-go-round again? I didn't try to change the future!"

Snulbug popped his head out and yawned a tuskful yawn. "I warn him, I explain it, I warn him again, now he wants I should explain it all over."

"But what did I do?"

"What did he do? You changed the odds, you dope. That much folding money on a long shot at a parimutuel track, and the odds change. It wouldn't have paid off at twenty to one, the way it said in the paper."

"Nuts," Bill muttered. "And I suppose that applies to anything? If I study the stock market in this paper and try to invest my $500 according to tomorrow's market—"

"Same thing. The quotations wouldn't be quite the same if you started in playing. I warned you. You're stuck," said Snulbug. "You're stymied. It's no use." He sounded almost cheerful.

"Isn't it?" Bill mused. "Now look, Snulbug. Me, I'm a great believer in Man. This universe doesn't hold a problem that Man can't eventually solve. And I'm no dumber than the average."

"That's saying a lot, that is," Snulbug sneered. "People—"

"I've got a responsibility now. It's more than just my $10,000. I've got to redeem the honor of Man. You say this is the insoluble problem. I say there *is* no insoluble problem."

"I say you talk a lot."

Bill's mind was racing furiously. How can a man take advantage of the future without in any smallest way altering that future? There must be an answer somewhere, and a man who devised the Hitchens Embolus Diagnosis could certainly crack a little nut like this. Man cannot refuse a challenge.

Unthinking, he reached for his tobacco pouch and tapped out his pipe on the sole of his foot. There was a microscopic thud as Snulbug crashed onto the floor of the car.

Bill looked down, half smiling. The tiny demon's tail was lashing madly, and every separate snake stood on end. "This is too much!" Snulbug screamed. "Dumb gags aren't enough, insults aren't enough, I should get thrown around like a damned soul. This is the last straw. Give me my dismissal!"

Bill snapped his fingers gleefully. "Dismissal!" he cried. "I've got it, Snully. We're all set."

Snulbug looked up, puzzled, and slowly let his snakes droop more amicably. "It won't work," he said with an omnisciently sad shake of his serpentine head.

* * *

It was the dashing act again that carried Bill through the Choatsby Laboratories, where he had been employed so recently, and on up to the very anteroom of old R.C.'s office.

But where you can do battle with a bull-necked guard, there is not a thing you can oppose against the brisk competence of a young lady who says, "I shall find out if Mr. Choatsby will see you." There was nothing to do but wait.

"And what's the brilliant idea this time?" Snulbug obviously feared the worst.

"R.C.'s nuts," said Bill. "He's an astrologer and a pyramidologist and a British Israelite—American Branch Reformed—and Heaven knows what else. He . . . why, he'll even believe in you."

"That's more than I do," said Snulbug. "It's a waste of energy."

"He'll buy this paper. He'll pay anything for it. There's nothing he loves more than futzing around with the occult. He'll never be able to resist a good solid slice of the future, with illusions of a fortune thrown in."

"You better hurry, then."

"Why such a rush? It's only 2:30 now. Lots of time. And while that girl's gone there's nothing for us to do but cool our heels."

"You might at least," said Snulbug, "warm the heel of your pipe."

The girl returned at last. "Mr. Choatsby will see you."

Reuben Choatsby overflowed the outsize chair behind his desk. His little face, like a baby's head balanced on a giant suet pudding, beamed as Bill entered. "Changed your mind, eh?" His words came in sudden soft blobs, like the abrupt glugs of pouring syrup. "Good. Need you in K-39. Lab's not the same since you left."

Bill groped for the exactly right words. "That's not it, R.C. I'm on my own now and I'm doing all right."

The baby face soured. "Damned cheek. Competitor of mine, eh? What you want now? Waste my time?"

"Not at all." With a pretty shaky assumption of confidence, Bill perched on the edge of the desk. "R.C.," he said, slowly and impressively, "what would you give for a glimpse into the future?"

Mr. Choatsby glugged vigorously. "Ribbing me? Get out of here! Have you thrown out— Hold on! You're the one— Used to read queer books. Had a grimoire here once." The baby face grew earnest. "What d'you mean?"

"Just what I said, R.C. What would you give for a glimpse into the future?"

Mr. Choatsby hesitated. "How? Time travel? Pyramid? You figured out the King's Chamber?"

"Much simpler than that. I have here"—he took it out of his pocket and folded it so that only the name and the date line were visible—"tomorrow's newspaper."

Mr. Choatsby grabbed. "Let me see."

"Uh-uh. Naughty. You'll see after we discuss terms. But there it is."

"Trick. Had some printer fake it. Don't believe it."

"All right. I never expected you, R.C., to descend to such unenlightened skepticism. But if that's all the faith you have—" Bill stuffed the paper back in his pocket and started for the door.

"Wait!" Mr. Choatsby lowered his voice. "How'd you do it? Sell your soul?"

"That wasn't necessary."

"How? Spells? Cantrips? Incantations? Prove it to me. Show me it's real. Then we'll talk terms."

Bill walked casually to the desk and emptied his pipe into the ash tray.

"I'm underdeveloped. I run errands. I'm named Snulbug. It isn't enough—now I should be a testimonial!"

Mr. Choatsby stared rapt at the furious little demon raging in his ashtray. He watched reverently as Bill held out the pipe for its inmate, filled it with tobacco, and lit it. He listened awestruck as Snulbug moaned with delight at the flame.

"No more questions," he said. "What terms?"

"Fifteen thousand dollars." Bill was ready for bargaining.

"Don't put it too high," Snulbug warned. "You better hurry."

But Mr. Choatsby had pulled out his checkbook and was scribbling hastily. He blotted the check and handed it over. "It's a deal." He grabbed up the paper. "You're a fool, young man. Fifteen thousand! *Hmf*!" He had it open already at the financial page. "With what I make on the market tomorrow, never notice $15,000. Pennies."

"Hurry up," Snulbug urged.

"Goodbye, sir," Bill began politely, "and thank you for—" But Reuben Choatsby wasn't even listening.

* * *

"What's all this hurry?" Bill demanded as he reached the elevator.

"People!" Snulbug sighed. "Never you mind what's the hurry. You get to your bank and deposit that check."

So Bill, with Snulbug's incessant prodding, made a dash to the bank worthy of his descents on the city hall and on the Choatsby Laboratories. He just made it, by stopwatch fractions of a second. The door was already closing as he shoved his way through at three o'clock sharp.

He made his deposit, watched the teller's eyes bug out at the size of the check, and delayed long enough to enjoy the incomparable thrill of changing the account from William Hitchens to The Hitchens Research Laboratory.

Then he climbed once more into his car, where he could talk with his pipe in peace. "Now," he asked as he drove home, "what was the rush?"

"He'd stop payment."

"You mean when he found out about the merry-go-round? But I didn't promise him anything. I just sold him tomorrow's paper. I didn't guarantee he'd make a fortune off it."

"That's all right. But—"

"Sure, you warned me. But where's the hitch? R.C.'s a bandit, but he's honest. He wouldn't stop payment."

"Wouldn't he?"

The car was waiting for a stop signal. The newsboy in the intersection was yelling "Uxtruh!" Bill glanced casually at the headline, did a double take, and instantly thrust out a nickel and seized a paper.

He turned into a side street, stopped the car, and went through this paper. Front page: MAYOR ASSASSINATED. Sports page: Alhazred at twenty to one. Obituaries: The same list he'd read at noon. He turned back to the date line. August 22. Tomorrow.

"I warned you," Snulbug was explaining. "I told you I wasn't strong enough to go far into the future. I'm not a well demon, I'm not. And an itch in the memory is something fierce. I just went far enough ahead to get a paper with tomorrow's date on it. And any dope knows that a Tuesday paper comes out Monday afternoon."

For a moment Bill was dazed. His magic paper, his fifteen-thousand-dollar paper, was being hawked by newsies on every corner. Small wonder R.C. might have stopped payment! And then he saw the other side. He started to laugh. He couldn't stop.

"Look out!" Snulbug shrilled. "You'll drop my pipe. And what's so funny?"

Bill wiped tears from his eyes. "I was right. Don't you see, Snulbug? Man can't be licked. My magic was lousy. All it could call up was you. You brought me what was practically a fake, and I got caught on the merry-go-round of time trying to use it. You were right enough there; no good could come of that magic.

"But without the magic, just using human psychology, knowing a man's weaknesses, playing on them, I made a syrup-voiced old bandit endow the very research he'd tabooed, and do more good for humanity than he's done in all the rest of his life. I was right, Snulbug. You can't lick Man."

Snulbug's snakes writhed into knots of scorn. "People!" he snorted. "You'll find out." And he shook his head with dismal satisfaction.

One Other

by

Manly Wade Wellman

Manly Wade Wellman, who was born in Angola and raised in Portuguese West Africa, has been writing dark fantasy or supernatural horror tales for some fifty-eight years, and is considered to be one of the genre's finest practioners. He is probably best known for his vivid and evocative series of regionalist stories and novels about John the Minstrel or "Silver John," who wanders through the remote mountain country of Southern Appalachia, combating the dark forces of magic and encountering the ancient creatures of legend and folklore. The Silver John stories have been collected in Who Fears the Devil?, *Wellman's most influential—and probably his best—book. His Silver John novels include* The Old Gods Waken, After Dark, The Lost and the Lurking, The Hanging Stones, *and* The Voice of the Mountain. *His non-Silver John stories have been assembled in the mammoth collection* Worse Things Waiting, *which won the World Fantasy Award as the Best Anthology/Collection of 1975. Wellman himself won another World Fantasy Award, the prestigious Life Achievement Award. His nonfiction has been nominated for a Pulitzer prize.*

In the chilling story that follows, Wellman shows us that if you try to conjure up a demon, you'd better really really *want it to arrive. . . .*

* * *

UP ON HARK MOUNTAIN I CLIMBED ALL ALONE, BY A TRAIL AS steep as a ladder and no way near as easy to hold to. Under my old army shoes was sometimes mud, sometimes rock, sometimes rolling gravel. I laid hold on laurel and oak scrub and sourwood and dogwood to help me get up the steepiest places. Sweat soaked the back of my hickory shirt through and hung under the band of my old hat. Even my silver-strung guitar, bouncing on its sling cord behind me, felt as weighty as an anvil. Hark Mountain's not the highest I ever went up, but it's sure enough one of the steepiest.

I reckoned I was getting close to the top when I heard a murmuring voice up there, a young-sounding woman's voice. All at once she yelled out a name, and the name was mine.

"JOHN!" she said, and murmured lower again, and then, "JOHN . . ."

Gentlemen, you can wager I purely sailed up the last stretch of that trail, on my hands and knees, to the very top.

On top of Hark Mountain's tipmost top was a pool.

Hush, gentlemen, without ary stream or draw or branch to feed it, where no pool should ought by nature to be expected, there was a clear blue pool, bright-looking but not just exactly sweet-looking. The highest place on Hark Mountain wasn't any much bigger than a well-sized farmyard, and it had room for hardly the pool and its rim of tight-set rocks. And the trees that grew betwixt those tight rocks at the rim looked leafless and gnarly, but alive. Their branch-twigs crimped and crooked, like claw-nails ready to seize on something.

Almost in reach of me, by the edge of the pool, burnt a fire, and to tend it kneeled down a girl.

She was a tall girl, but not strong built like country girls. She was built slim, like town girls, and she wore town clothes—a white blouse-shirt, and dark pants tight to her long legs all the way up and down, and soft shoes like slippers on her feet. Her arms and neck were as brown as nut meat, the way fashiony women seek to be brown. Around her head was tied a blue silk handkerchief.

Kneeling, she put a tweak of stuff on the fire, and I saw her long, sharp, red fingernails. She spoke again, singing almost, and my name rose out of what she said:

"It is the bones of *John* that I trouble. I for *John* burn this laurel."

On the fire she put some laurel leaves and they sent up steam.

"Even as it crackles and burns, even thus may the flesh of *John* burn for me."

In went something else.

"Even as I melt this wax, with *One Other* to aid me, so speedily may *John* for love of me be melted."

She took up a little clay pot and dripped something. *Drip,* the fire danced. *Drip,* it danced again, jumping up. *Drip,* a third jump-up dancing flame.

"Thrice I pour libation," she said. "Thrice, by *One Other,* I say the spell. Be it with a friend he tarries, with a woman he lingers, may *John* utterly forget and forsake them."

Then she stood up, slim and tall, and held out something red and wavy that I knew.

"This from *John* I took, and now I cast it into—"

But quick and quiet I was close beside her, and I snatched that red scarf away.

"It's been wondering me where I might could have lost that," I said, and she turned and faced me.

Just some slight bit I felt I knew her from somewhere. She was yellow-haired, blue-eyed, brown faced. She had a little bitty nose, and a mouth as red as red wine. Her blue eyes widened out almost as wide as the blue pool itself, and she smiled. Her teeth were big and white and even in her smile.

"John," she said my name softer, halfway singing it to me. "I was saying the spell for the third time, and you came here to my call." She licked those red lips of hers, and they shone. "Just the way Mr. Howsen promised you'd come."

I never let on to know who Mr. Howsen might possibly be. I wadded up the red scarf into the hip pocket of my blue jeans pants.

"Why were you witch-spelling me?" I inquired her. "What did I ever do to you? I even disremember where it was I met you."

"You don't remember me?" she said, smiling. "But do you remember Enderby Lodge, John?"

"Why, sure."

A month back I'd strolled through those parts with my guitar. Old Major Enderby had bade me rest my hat a while. He was having a dance, and to pleasure him and his guests I'd picked and sung for them.

"You must have been there," I said. "But what was it I did to you?"

Her lips tightened, and now they looked as red and hard and sharp as her painted nails. "Nothing at all, John," she told me. "Not a thing. You did nothing. You ignored me. Doesn't it make you furious to be ignored?"

"Ignored? No, ma'am, it never makes me furious, or I'd be furious a big part of the time."

"It makes me furious. I don't often look at a man twice, and usually they look at me at least once. I don't forgive being ignored." Again she licked her mouth, like a cat over a basin of milk. "I'd been told my charm can be said three times, beside the Bottomless Pool on Hark Mountain, to burn a man's soul with love. And here you came when I called you. Don't shake your head like that, John. You're in love with me."

"I'm sorry, ma'am, I ask your pardon humbly. I'm not in love with you any such thing."

She smiled in pride and scorn, the smile you'd give to a liar. "But you climbed up Hark Mountain to me."

"I reckoned I'd like to have a look at the Bottomless Pool."

"People don't know Bottomless Pool is up here. Only Mr. Howsen and his sort come here. When you talk about bottomless pools, you mean the ones near Lake Lure, on Highway 74."

"Those aren't rightly bottomless," I said. "Anyway, this one, the real one, is sung about in a country song."

Pulling my guitar around, I picked chords and sang:

"Way up on Hark Mountain
I climb all alone,
Where the trail is untravelled,
The top is unknown.

"Way up on Hark Mountain
Is the Bottomless Pool.
You look in its water
And it shows you a fool."

"You're making that up," she charged me.

"No, ma'am, it was made up long before my daddy's daddy was born. Most country songs have got truth in them. It was the song fetched me here, not your witch-spell."

She laughed, short and sharp; she almost yelped her laugh. "Call it the long arm of coincidence, John. You're here, anyway. Go look in the water and see whether it shows you a fool."

Plainly she didn't know the next verse, so I sang that, too:

"You can boast of your knowledge
And brag of your sense,
It won't make no difference
A hundred years hence."

* * *

Stepping one foot on a rock of the rim, I looked down.

The water didn't show me a fool nor either a wise man. I could see down forever and forever, and I recollected all I'd ever heard tell about the Bottomless Pool. How it was as blue as the blue sky, but it had a special light of its own; how no water ever ran into it, excusing some rain, but it always stayed full; how you couldn't measure its bottom, if you let down a sinker on a line it would go down till the line broke of its own weight.

Though I couldn't spy out the bottom, it wasn't rightly dark down there. Like a man looking up into the blue sky, I looked down into the blue water, and in the blue, far away down, was a many-colored shine, like lights deeper than I could tell you.

"I didn't need to use that stolen scarf," she said at my elbow. "You're lying about why you came here. My spell brought you."

"I'm sorry to say, ma'am," I replied, "I can't even call your name to my mind."

"Do names make a difference if you love me? Call me Annalinda. I'm rich. I've been loved for that alone, and for myself alone."

"Well, I'm plain and poor," I told her. "I was raised hard and put up wet. I don't have ary cent of money in these old clothes of mine. It sure enough wonders me, Miss Annalinda, why you think you need to bother yourself about me."

"I'm just not used to being ignored," she said again.

Down there in the Bottomless Pool's blueness wasn't a fish or a weed of grass. Only that deep-away sparkly flash of lights, changing as you see changes on a bubble of soap blown by a little baby child.

Somebody cleared his throat and said, "I see the spell I gave you worked, ma'am."

I knew Mr. Howsen as he came up the trail to the top of Hark Mountain.

He was purely ugly. I'd been knowing him ten years, and he looked as ugly that minute as the first time I'd seen him, with his mean face and his great big hungry nose and the black patch over one eye. When he'd had his two eyes, they were put so close together in his head you'd be sworn he could look through a keyhole with the two of them at once.

"Yes," said Miss Annalinda. "I want to pay you what I owe you."

"No, ma'am, you pay One Other," said Mr. Howsen, and put

his hands in the pockets of the long black coat he wore summer and winter. "For value received, ma'am. I only passed along his word to you."

He tighted his lips at me, in what wasn't anything like a smile. "John," he said, "you relish journeying. You've relished it ever since you was just a chap, going what way you felt like going. You've seen a right much of this world. But she toled you to her, and now you'll stay with her, and for that you can be obliged to One Other."

"One other what?" I inquired him.

Though that was just a defy at him. Of course, a-hearing of Hark Mountain and the Bottomless Pool, I'd sure enough heard of One Other. How mountain folks swear he's got the one arm and the one leg only, that he runs fast on the one leg and grabs hold with the one arm, and whatever he grabs goes with him into the Bottomless Pool. And that it's One Other's power and knowledge that lets witches do their spells up there by the Bottomless Pool.

"Be here with the lady when One Other asks payment," said Mr. Howsen. "That there spell was good a many years before Theocritus written it down in old Greek. It'll still be good when English writing is as old as Greek writing. It toled you here."

But for the life of me I couldn't recollect seeing Miss Annalinda at Major Enderby's. "My own wish and will brought me here, not hers," I said. "I wanted to see the Bottomless Pool. I wonder at that soap-bubble color in it."

"Ain't any soap in there, John," said Mr. Howsen. "Soap bubbles don't never get so big as to have all that much color."

"You rightly sure about how big soap bubbles get, Mr. Howsen?" I asked. "Once I heard a science doctor say how this whole life of ours, the heaven and the earth, the sun and moon and stars and all, may be holding a shape like a big soap bubble. He said it stretched and spread like a soap bubble, with all the suns and stars and worlds getting farther off apart as time passes."

"Both of you stay here where you are," Mr. Howsen bade us. "One Other's going to want to find the both of you here."

"But—" Miss Annalinda made out to begin.

"Both of you stay," Mr. Howsen said again, and with his shoe toe he scuffed a mark across the head of the trail. Then he hawked, and spit on the mark. "Don't cross that line. It would be worse for you than if fire burnt you behind and before, inside and out."

Like a lizard he bobbed over the edge and away down the trail.

"Let's us go too," I said to Miss Annalinda, but she stared at the mark made by Mr. Howsen's shoe, and the healthy blood had paled out from under the tan on her face.

"Pay him no mind," I said. "Let's start, it's coming on to sunset."

"He said not to cross the mark," she reminded me, scared.

"I don't care a shuck for aught he said. Come on, Miss Annalinda," and I took her by the arm.

That quick I had her to fight. Holding to her arm was like holding the spoke of a runaway wheel. Her other hand came up and her sharp red nails racked hide and blood off my cheek, and she tried to bite. I couldn't hold her without hitting her, so I turned her loose, and she sat down on a rock by the poolside and cried into her hands.

"Then I'll have to go alone," I said, and took a step.

"John!" she called, loud and shaky as a horse's whinny. "If you step across that mark, I'll throw myself into this Bottomless Pool!"

Sometimes you can tell when a woman means the thing she says. This was one of the times. So I walked back to her, and she was a-looking to where the down-sinking sun made the edge of the sky turn red and fiery. It would be cold and dark when that sun was gone. With trembling hands she smoothed the tight pants tighter to her legs.

"I'll just build up the fire," I said, and tried to break off a branch from a claw-looking tree.

But it was tough and had thorny stickers. So I went to the edge of the open place, off from where Mr. Howsen had drawn his mark on us, and gathered up an armful of dead-fallen wood. I brought it back and freshened the fire she'd made for her witching. It blazed up red, the color of the sun that sank down. High in the sky, that turned pale before it would turn dark, slid a great big old buzzard. Its wings flopped, slow and heavy, spreading out their feathers like long fingers.

"You don't believe all this, John," said Miss Annalinda, in a voice that sounded as if she was just before freezing from the cold. "But the spell was true. The rest of it's true, too, about One Other. He must have been here since the beginning of time."

"No, that's one thing peculiar enough to be the truth," I answered her. "There's not much been told about One Other till this last year or so. About his being here at the Bottomless Pool, or about folks being able to do witch things with his help, or how he aids the witches and takes payment for his aid. It's no old country tale, it's right new and recent."

"Payment," she said after me. "What kind of payment?"

I poked up the fire. "That all depends. Sometimes one thing, sometimes another. You notice how Mr. Howsen goes around with only the one eye. I've heard it said that One Other took an eye from him. Maybe he won't want an eye from you, but he'll want something. Something for nothing."

"What do you mean?" and she frowned her brows at me.

"You put a witch-spell on me to make me love you, but you don't love me. You did it for spite, not love."

"Why—why—"

Nothing devils a woman like being caught in the truth. She laid hold on a poolside rock next to her.

"That will smash my head or either my guitar," I gave her quick word. "Smash my head, and you're up here on the mountain, all alone with a dead corpse. Smash my guitar, and I'll go right down the trail."

"And I'll jump in the pool."

"All right, you can jump. I won't stay where folks fling rocks at me. Fair warning's as good as a promise."

She let go the rock again. She was ready to start crying. I came and set my foot at the edge of the pool and looked down into the water.

By now the sky was a-getting purely dark, but low down and away was that soap-bubble shiny light. I brought back to mind an old tale they say came from the Indians who owned the mountains back before the first white folks came. It was about people living above the sky and thinking their world was the only one, till somebody pulled up a great long root, and through the hole they could see down to another world below, where people lived. Then Miss Annalinda began to talk.

She was talking for the company of her own voice, and she talked about herself. About her rich father and her rich mother, and all her rich aunts and uncles and rich friends, the money and automobiles and land and horses they owned, and the big chance of men who wanted to marry her. One was the son of folks as rich as her folks. One was the governor of the state, who was ready to put away his wife if Miss Annalinda said the word she'd have him. And one was a noble-born man from a foreign country.

"And you'd marry me, too, John," she said.

"I'm just sorry to death," I said. "But I wouldn't."

"Now you're lying, John."

"I never lie, Miss Annalinda."

"Everybody lies. Well, talk to me, anyway. This isn't any sort of place to keep quiet in."

So I talked in my turn, about myself. How I'd been born next to Drowning Creek and baptized in its waters. How my folks had died in two days of each other, how an old teacher lady had taught me to read and write, and I'd taught myself how to play the guitar. How I'd roamed and rambled. How I'd fought in the war, and a thousand had fallen at my side and ten thousand at my right hand, but it hadn't come nigh me. I left out some things, like meeting up with the Ugly Bird, because she was nervous enough. I said that though I'd never had aught and never rightly expected to have aught, yet I'd always made out for bread to eat and sometimes butter on it.

"How about pretty girls, John?" she asked me. "You must have had regiments of them."

"None to mention," I said, for it wouldn't have been proper to mention them. "Miss Annalinda, it's a-getting full dark."

"And the moon's up."

"No, ma'am, that's the soap-bubble light from down there in the Bottomless Pool."

"You make me shiver!" she scolded at me, and drew up her shoulders. "What do you mean with all this talk about soap bubbles?"

"Only just what I was telling Mr. Howsen. That science man said our whole life, what he called our universe, was swelling and stretching out, so that suns and moons and stars pull farther apart all the time. He said our world and all the other worlds are inside that stretching skin of suds that makes the bubble. We can't study out what's outside the bubble, or either inside, only just what's in the suds part. It sounds crazyish, but when he talked it sounded true."

"That's not a new idea, John. James Jeans wrote a book about it, *The Expanding Universe.* But where does the soap bubble come from?"

"I reckon that Whoever made all things must have blown it, from a bubble pipe too big for us to study out."

She snickered, so she must have been feeling better. "You believe in a God who blows soap bubbles." Then she didn't snicker. "How long do we have to go on waiting here?"

"No time at all. We can go whenever you're ready."

"No," she said, "we have to stay."

"Then we'll stay till One Other come. He'll come. Mr. Howsen's a despicable man, but he knows about One Other."

"Oh!" she cried out. "I only wish he'd come and get it over with."

And her wish came true.

The firelight had risen high, and as she spoke, something hiked up behind the rocks on the pool's edge. It hiked up like a wet black leech, but much bigger by about a thousand times. It slid and oozed to the top of a rock, and as it waited a second, wet and shiny in the firelight, it looked as if somebody had flung down a wet coat. Then it hunched and swelled, and its edges came apart.

It was a wet hand, as broad in the back as a shovel, and with fingers as long as the tines of a hayfork.

"Get up and start down trail," I said to Miss Annalinda, as quiet and calm as I could make out to be. "Don't argue, just start."

"Why should I?" she snapped out, without moving, and by then she saw, too, and any chance for her to get away was gone.

The hayfork fingers grabbed hold of the rock, and a head and shoulder heaved up to where we could see them.

The shoulder was like a cypress root humping out of the water, and the head was like a dark pumpkin, round and smooth and bald, with no face, only two eyes. They were green, but not bright green like cat-eyes or dog-eyes in the night. They were stale rotten green, like something spoiled.

Miss Annalinda's shriek was like a train blowing for a crossing. She jumped up, but she didn't run. Maybe she couldn't. Then a big black knee lifted into sight, and all of One Other came up out of the Bottomless Pool and rose straight up before us.

One Other was twice as tall as a tall man, and it was sure enough true that he had just the one arm and the one leg. The arm would be his left arm, and the leg his right leg. Maybe that's why the mountain folks had named him One Other. But his stale green eyes were two, and both of them looked down at us. He made a sure hop on his big single foot, big and flat as the top of a table, and he put out his hand to touch or to grab.

I dragged Miss Annalinda clear back around the fire. I reckon she'd fainted, or near to. Her feet didn't work under her, she only moaned, and she was double heavy in my arms, the way a limp weight can be. My strength was under tax to pull her toward where I'd flung down my guitar. I wanted to get my hands on the guitar. It might could be a weapon—its music or its silver strings might be a distaste to an unchancy thing like One Other.

But One Other had circled the fire the other way around, so

that we came almost in touch again. He stood on his one big foot, between me and my guitar. It might be ill or well to him, but I couldn't get it and find out.

Even then, the thought of running across Mr. Howsen's mark and down the mountain in the night never entered my head. I stood still, holding Miss Annalinda on her feet that were gone so limp her shoes were near about to drop off, and looked up twice my height into what wasn't a face save for those two green eyes.

"What have you got in mind?" I inquired One Other, as if he could understand my talk; and the words, almost in Miss Annalinda's ear, brought back her strength and wits. She stood alone still shoving herself close against me. She looked up at One Other, and she said a couple of holy names.

One Other bent his big lumpy knee and sank his bladdery dark body down and put out that big splay paw of his. The firelight showed his open palm, slate gray, and things dribbling out from it in a clinking, jangling little strew at our feet. He straightened up again.

"Oh, John!" And Miss Annalinda dropped down to grab. "Look, he's giving us—"

Tugging my eyes away from One Other's, I looked at what she held out to me. It shone and lighted up, like a hailstone by lantern light. It was the size of a hen egg, and it had a many little edges and flat faces, all full of fire, pale and blue outside and innerly many-colored like the soap-bubble light in the Bottomless Pool. She shoved it into my hand, and it felt slippery and sticky, like soap. I flung it on the ground again.

"You fool, that's a diamond!" she squeaked at me. "It's bigger than the Orloff, bigger than the Koh-i-noor!"

She scrabbled with both hands for more of the shiny things, that lighted up with every color you could call for. "Here's an emerald," she yipped, "and here's a ruby. John he's our friend, he's giving us things worth more money than—"

Down on her knees before One Other, she clawed up two fistfuls of those things he'd flung for her to get down and gather. But I had my eyes back on him. He was looking at me—not at her, he was sure of her. Well he knew humankind's greed for shiny stones. About me, he wasn't sure yet. He studied me as I've seen folks to study an animal, to see whether to hit it with a stock or slice it with a knife. The shiny stones didn't fetch me. He reckoned to find something that would.

Oh, I know how like a crazy tale to scare young ones all this sounds. But there and then, One Other was so plain to see and make out, the way you could see him if I was to make a clay image of him and stand it up on one leg in your sight, and it grew till it was twice as tall as you, with stale green eyes and one hay-fork paw and one tabletop foot. In a moment there was no sound, he and I looked at one another. Miss Annalinda, down on the ground between us, gopped and goggled at the stones she scooped up in her hands. Then the silence broke. A drop of water fell. Another. *Drip, drip, drip,* like what Miss Annalinda had dripped into the fire—water from the Bottomless Pool, dripping off at One Other's body and head and his one arm and his one leg.

Then he turned his eyes and mind back to Miss Annalinda, for long enough to spare me for a big jump past him to where my guitar was.

He turned quick and swung down at me with his paw, like a man swatting a bug; but I had the guitar and I was running backward out of his reach. I got the guitar across me, my left hand on the frets, and my right hand a-clawing the silver strings. They sang out, and One Other teetered on the broad sole of that foot, cocked his head to hark.

I started the *Last Judgment Song,* the one old Uncle T. P. Hinnard had told me long ago was good against evil things:

"Three holy kings, four holy saints,
At heaven's high gate that stand,
Speak out to bid all evil wait
And stir no foot or hand. . . ."

But he came at me anyway. The charm wasn't serving against One Other, as I'd been vowed to it would serve against any evil in this world. One Other wasn't of this world, though just now he was in it. He was from the Bottomless Pool, and from whatever was beyond, below, behind where its bottom had ought to be.

I ran around the fire and around Miss Annalinda, still crouched down among all those jewels. After me he hopped, like the almightiest big one-legged rabbit in song or tale. He had me almost headed off, coming alongside me, and I ran right through the fire that was less fear to me than he was. My shoes kicked its coals as I ran through. On the far side I made myself stop and turn again. Because I had to face him somehow. I couldn't just run off from him and leave Miss Annalinda to pay, all alone, for her foolishness.

He'd stopped, too, in his one track. The fire, scattered by my feet, blazed up in scattered chunks, and he was sort of pulling himself together and back from it. *Drip, drip,* the water fell off him. I felt there couldn't be any standing that dripping noise, so I sang out loud with another verse of the *Last Judgment Song:*

"The fire from heaven will fall at last
On wealth and pride and power—
We will not know the minute, and
We will not know the hour. . . ."

One Other hopped a long hop back, away from the fire and away from me and away from the song.

Something whispered me what I'd needed to know.

From out the water he'd come. If I didn't want him to get me, to hold me at a price I'd never redeem—the way jewels beyond all reckoning could buy Miss Annalinda—I'd have to fight him like any water thing.

Fight fire with water, wise folks say. Fire and water are sworn enemies. Fight water with fire . . .

He circled around again, and that time I didn't flee from before him. I grabbed down toward the scattering of the fire. One Other's big flat hand slapped me spinning away, but my own hand had snatched up a burning chunk. When I staggered back onto my feet, I still held my guitar in one fist, the chunk in the other.

I whipped that fire in a whirl around my head, and it blazed up like pure lightwood. As One Other came bending down for me again, I rushed to meet him and I shoved the fire at him.

He couldn't face it. He broke back from it. I jumped sidewise my own self, so that he was between me and the fire, and sashayed that burning stick at him again. He jumped back, and his foot slammed right down among the coals.

Gentlemen, I hope none of you all ever hear such a sound as he made, with no mouth to make it. Not a yell or a roar or a scream, but the whole top of Hark Mountain hummed and danced to it. He flung himself clear of the fire again, hurting and shaking every ounce of him, and then I stabbed my torch like a spear for where his face ought to be, and made a direct hit.

I tell you, he couldn't front up to fire, he couldn't stand it. He just spun around and jumped, and then he dived into the water from which he'd come to us, into the Bottomless Pool, and the splash he made was like a wagon falling from a bridge. Running to the rocks, I saw him cleave down below there, into the deep clearness, like a diving one-legged frog—all among the soap-bubble colors, getting small while I watched, so small he looked a hand's size. A finger's size. A bean's size. And then the light gulped him. And he was gone from my sight.

I stepped back to the scattered fire, and dropped my burning chunk.

Miss Annalinda still huddled on the ground. I question whether she'd paid aught of mind to what had gone on, that scrambling fight. Her hands were grabbed full of jewels shining green, red, blue, white, all colors.

I said nothing, but took her by the arm and pulled her to her feet. She looked at me and waved her both full fists in joy.

"Give them here," I said.

Her eyes stabbed at me like fish gigs. She couldn't believe I'd spoken such words. I put down my guitar and took her right wrist and pried open her right hand. I tried not to hurt her as I took the jewels. Into the Bottomless Pool I plunged them, one by one. They splashed and sank down like pebbles.

"Don't, John!" she screamed, but I took her other hand and pried away the rest of them. *Plop,* I flung one after the first bunch. *Plop,* I flung another. *Plop, plop, plop,* more.

"They're a fortune," she gabbled, dragging at my arm. "The greatest fortune ever dreamed of—"

"No, ma'am," I said. "A misfortune. The greatest misfortune ever dreamed of."

"But no!"

Plop, plop, I flung them in, the last of the jewels. "What were you ready to pay for them?" I inquired her.

"Anything," she said as if she was tired out. "Anything."

"You mean everything. If he paid high for us, he meant to have his worth from us. He needs folks of this world to serve him, more folks than just Mr. Howsen." I pointed into the Bottomless Pool, for her to look down there. "I hope and pray he stays now, where things are more comfortable than what taste I gave him."

She looked, down to where the Bottomless Pool had no bottom.

"John, you're right," she said, as if she talked out of a dream. "Those colors do look like the tints of a soap bubble—stretched out, with nothing beyond its film of suds that we can imagine. A great big unthinkable soap bubble, like the one you say God blew."

"Might could be so," I said. "Might could be there's more

than the one soap bubble we're in. A right many soap bubbles. Each one a life and a universe strange to this one we're in."

The pain of that new thought went into her like a knife and made her silent. I talked on:

"Might could be there's two soap bubbles touching. And the spot where they come together is where something can leave the one and come into the other."

She sat down. The new thought was weight as well as pain. "Oh," she moaned in herself.

"Some born venturer dares try to move into the new bubble," I said, "through whatever matches the Bottomless Pool on that far side, in that other life and universe. Maybe, I say. There's God's great plenty of maybes about it."

"No maybes," she said, all of a sudden. "You saw him, no such creature was ever born into our world. Anything looking like that must be—"

"You still don't understand," and I shook my head. "I don't truly reckon he'd look like that in his own soap bubble. He makes himself look thataway, to be as possibly much like our kind he meets in our world. We can't guess what he'd naturally look like."

"I don't want to guess," and she sounded near about to cry.

"Such a stranger needs friends and helpers in the strange new world. Some things he knows from his own home are like power here, power we think is witch stuff. He'll pay high for helpers like Mr. Howsen. He'd have paid high for us."

"Will he come back?" she asked.

"Not right off." I picked up my guitar. "Let's grope down trail in the dark, so if he does come back he won't find us. Somewhere below we'll build a fire and in the morning get all the way down."

"John," said Miss Annalinda, talking fast, "you were right about me. My spell was to get you up here for spite. But now, if you don't have anywhere to go—"

"I've got everywhere to go," I said. "Soon as I get you down safe, I'll go everywhere."

"It's not spite anymore, John, it's love." She said that word as if she'd never said it before. "It's love, I love you, John."

She maybe didn't know that she was lying and I wanted to stop her.

"You know," I changed the subject, "there's one more thing about this soap-bubble idea. The bubble we live in keeps on a-stretching and a-swelling. But a soap bubble can't last forever. Some time or other, it stretches and swells so tight, it just bursts."

That did what I was after, it stopped her flood of words. She stared up and off and all around. I saw the whites of her eyes glitter in the last glow of the fire.

"Bursts?" she said slowly. "Then what?"

"Then nothing. When a soap bubble bursts, it's gone."

And we had silence to start our climb down Hark Mountain.

An Ornament to His Profession

by

Charles L. Harness

The nineteenth-century French sorcerer Eliphas Levi wrote that "He who affirms the Devil, creates or makes the Devil." And what better way is there to affirm the Devil than to sell him your eternal soul . . .? We can trace the idea of forming a pact with the powers of darkness back to the Bible (Isaiah 28:5), but the idea of legally binding contract *can probably be credited to St. Augustine, who roundly condemned "the pestiferous association of men with demons, as if formed by a pact of faithless and dishonorable friendship." But it's the legend of Faust—a supposed sixteenth-century sorcerer who has been credited with being the equal of Virgil, Bacon, the Count de St. Germain, Agrippa, and Crowley—that has set fire to our imaginations for the last four hundred years. Embellished by such literary giants as Marlow, Lessing, and Goethe, the Faust legend has become one of our most compelling and potent archetypes. Faust is the great symbol of civilized man at his most base* and *his most noble, for it was in return for knowledge that he sold his soul to the Devil. In the preface to the sixteenth-century* Fausti Hollenzwang *(Faust's Harrowing of Hell), Faust himself is credited with writing: "He who wishes to practice my art, let him love the spirits of hell and those who reign in the air; for these alone are they who can make us happy in this life; and he who would have wisdom must seek it from the devil."*

The elegant and subtle story that follows is in the very best sense a modern Faust, *a tale of the commitments and potential betrayals that live in every heart.*

For, after all, aren't we all committed to something . . . or someone?

Charles L. Harness was born in 1915 in Colorado City, Texas.

He received a B.S. in chemistry from George Washington University, and subsequently worked as a patent attorney for a firm in Stamford, Connecticut. An often underrated writer, Harness produced some of the best work being done in science-fiction in the 1950s and early 1960s, specializing in what James Blish has called the "extensively recomplicated plot"—which meant that he threw everything but the kitchen sink into his stories . . . and then for good measure tossed in the sink as well. This baroque and pyrotechnic style produced stories like "The New Reality," which were years ahead of their times, as well as classic novels such as Flight Into Yesterday, *and* The Rose. *After a long absence Harness has been writing again in recent years, and his recent novels have included* The Catalyst, Firebird, *and* The Venetian Count. *His most recent book is* The Paradox Men, *a revised version of* Flight Into Yesterday. *Upcoming is a new novel,* Redworld.

* * *

> *The world has different owners at sunrise . . .Even your own garden does not belong to you.*
>
> Anne Lindbergh

CONRAD PATRICK REACHED OVER AND SHUT OFF THE ALARM. The dream of soft flesh and dark hair faded into six o'clock on a Friday morning. Patrick lay there a moment, pushing Lilas out of his thoughts, keeping his mind dark with the room, his body numb.

To move was to accept wakefulness, and this was unthinkable, for wakefulness must lead to knowledge, and then the problem barbs would begin to do their ulcerous work in his brain. They would begin, one by one, until all were in hideous clamor. None of them seemed ever to get really solved, and getting rid of one didn't necessarily mean he had solved it. More often, getting rid of it just meant he had found some sort of neutralizing paralysis, or that he had once more increased his pain threshold.

Patrick got up heavily, found his robe and slippers, and stumbled into the bathroom, where he turned on the light and surveyed his face with overt distaste. It was a heavy, fleshy face, and the red hair and mustache were awry. He was not exactly thin, but not really fat, either. His cheeks and stomach showed the effects of myriad beers in convivial company. He considered these beers, these cheerful hours, one by one, going back, in a mirrored moment of wonder and gratitude. He considered what life would have been like without them, and as the realization hit, his forehead creased uneasily. He scowled, dashed water over his eyes, and reached for a towel.

"Patrick," he muttered to himself in the mirror, "it's Friday. Another day has begun, and still the Company hasn't found you out."

Patrick no longer knew exactly what he meant by this routine, which he had started some years before, when he was the newest chemical patent attorney with Hope Chemicals. He had first been a chemist, but not a very good one, and then, after he and Lilas had got married, he had gone to law school at night. After he got his LLB he had discovered, with more fatalism than dismay, that he was not a very good lawyer, either. Yet all was by no means lost. He was accepted by Hope's Patent Department. And not just barely accepted; he was accepted as an excellent chemical patent attorney. He found this incredible, but he did not fight it. And finally, he deliberately masked his supposed deficiencies; when he was in the company of chemists, he spoke as a lawyer, and when with lawyers, he didn't mind being just a fifty-fifty chemist-lawyer. They had his problem, too. It was like group therapy. Patent lawyers had a profound sympathy for each other.

From the beginning he had thrown himself into his work with zest. And now, with Lilas and the baby gone, his work was not just an opiate; it was a dire necessity.

He got the kettle boiling in the kitchen. There was now a pink glow in the east. He looked out the kitchen window and almost smiled. It was going to be a beautiful morning. He made the coffee quickly, four spoons of coffee powder in his pint mug, took the first bitter, exhilarating sip, tightened his robe about him, stepped out the kitchen door, and padded off down the garden path, holding his coffee mug carefully.

This, again, was all part of his morning routine. Today, of course, there was a special reason. Theoretically the house and grounds were ready and waiting for a little party tonight, but it would do no harm to take a look around, down by the pool.

The flagstone path lay down a grassy slope, and was lined with azaleas. He and Lilas had put them in together. At the foot of the slope was a tiny stream, fed mostly by a spring half a mile away, on his neighbor's property. In this little stream Patrick had contrived a series of pools by dint of fieldstone and mortar, slapped together with such indolence into the stream side that the result was a pleasing but entirely accidental naturalness. These little pools were bordered with watercress, cat-o'-nine-tails, arrowhead, water iris, and lovely things with names he could no longer remember. He and Lilas had splurged one summer and bought all manner of water plants by mail. They had got very muddy planting them, and they had sorrowed over those that had died the next spring or that the baby had happily yanked. And then suddenly everything had begun to grow like weeds, and in a wild way, it was all very pretty.

The path along the stream led toward a grassy sward. Patrick stopped on the path a moment, and listened. Yes, there it was, very faint, like a tinkling of tiny bells. He held his breath. Around the turn of the path, and so far invisible, was the bench. He and Lilas used to sit here, overlooking the lily pond. Only then, of course, it wasn't the lily pond, but the baby's wading pool. It was . . . how long ago? . . . that she had splashed in the pool and her baby delight had shattered the garden peace. And that was what he heard now. And he could hear Lilas' answering laughter. This had happened to him on many past mornings. To him, it was not a conjured thing; it was faint, very far away, but it was real.

He began to walk again, and rounded the bend in the path. But as soon as the pool and the bench came in view, the sounds stopped abruptly. He had tried to deal with the phenomenon logically. This led him to various alternative conclusions, neither of which he completely disbelieved: (a) he was subject to hallucinations; (b) Lilas and the baby were really there.

Patrick sighed and looked about him. Here, all within a few steps of each other, were the lily pool, the benches, the outdoor grill, and the arbor. The arbor was a simple structure, framed with two-by-fours, bordered with lilacs that had never bloomed and which enclosed his "worktable." This was a stone-stepped table with a drawer, which contained writing materials and a few scribbled pages.

He looked into the arbor. From somewhere up in the ceiling of honeysuckle there was a flutter of wings. Sparrows. The "room" seemed to concentrate the odor of grass clippings, fresh from yesterday's mowing. Patrick glanced over at the stone table and permitted himself the habitual morning question: Would he have a few moments to work on his article? This was followed by a prompt companion thought. He was being stupid even to think about it. In three years he had not even finished the first chapter. And already the Court of Customs and Patent Appeals had wrought far-reaching revisions in the law of prior printed publication. Maybe he should pick another subject. An article he could do quickly, get into print quickly, before the court could hand down a modifying decision. Somehow, there must be a way to get this thing off dead center. A top-flight professional in any field ought to publish. Not that he was really that good. Still, as Francis Bacon had said, a man owed a debt to his profession.

He opened the drawer and pulled out the sheaf of papers. But he knew that he wasn't going to work on it this morning. A breeze fluttered the sheets. His eye cast about for a paperweight and found the candle bottle; a stub of candle sticking in the neck of a wine bottle, used when he sat here at night and did not want to use the floodlights. He put the bottle on the papers.

Glumly he accepted his first inadequacy of the day. No use trying to hold the others back. The line forms to the right. The magic was gone from the morning; so be it. Let them come. He finished off his coffee. In his own garden he was a match for all of them. He felt girded and armored.

They came.

One. His department was about to lose a secretary—Sullivan's Miss Willow. He hadn't told Sullivan. But maybe Sullivan knew already. Maybe even Miss Willow knew. These things always seemed to get around. He didn't mind interdepartmental promotions for the girls. He'd used it himself on occasion. But he didn't like the way Harvey Jayne was using company personnel policy to pressure him. And right now was a bad time to lose a secretary, with all those Neol cases to get out. As an army travels on its stomach, so his Patent Department traveled on its typewriters, or more exactly, on the flying fingers of its stenographers as applied to the keys of those typewriters, "thereby to produce," as they say in patentese, a daily avalanche of specifications, amendments, appeals, contracts, and opinions.

He halfway saw an angle here. Maybe he could boomerang the whole thing back on Harvey Jayne. Have to be careful, though. Jayne was a vice-president.

Two, and getting worse. Jayne wanted publication clearance for the "Neol Technical Manual," and he wanted it today. It had to be cleared for legal form, proofread, and back to the printers tonight, because bright and early Monday morning twenty-five crisp and shining copies, smelling beautifully of printer's ink, had to be on that big table in the Directors' Room. Monday, the Board was going to vote on whether the company would build a six-million-dollar Neol plant.

Three, and still worse. John Fast, Neol pilot plant manager, wanted the Patent Department to write a very special contract. Consideration, soul of the party of the first part, in return for, inter alia, guarantee of success with Neol. It was impossible, and there was something horrid and sick in it, and yet Patrick was having the contract written by Sullivan, his contract expert, and in fact the first draft should be ready this morning. He was *not* going to refer Fast to the company psychiatrist. At least not yet. Maybe in two or three weeks, after Fast was through helping Sullivan get those new Neol cases on file in the Patent Office, he might casually mention this situation to the psychiatrist. Why did it always happen this way? Nobody could just go quietly insane without involving him. Forever and ever people like John Fast sought him out, involved him, and laid their madness upon him, like a becoming mantle.

Fourth, and absolutely and unendurably the worst. The patent structure for the whole Neol process was in jeopardy. The basic patent application, bought by the company from an "outside" inventor two years before, was now known to Patrick, and to several of the senior attorneys in his department, to be a phony, a hoax, a thing discovered to have been created in ghastly jest—by a man in his own department. This was the thing that really got him. He could think of nothing, no way to deal with it. The jester, Paul Bleeker, was the son of Andy Bleeker, his old boss and good friend. (Did anybody have any real friends at this crazy place anymore?) And that was really why he had come up with an answer. It would kill Andy if this got out. Certainly, he and both Bleekers would probably have to resign. After that there would come the slow, crushing hearings of the Committee on Disbarment.

Problems.

Was this why he couldn't write, why he couldn't even get started? He blinked, shook his head. Only then did he realize that he was still staring, unseeing at the handwritten notes in front of him.

He leafed slowly through the scribblings. How long ago had he started the article? Months? Nearly three years ago, in fact. He had wanted to do something comprehensive, to attain some small measure of fame. This was the real reason lawyers wrote. Or was it? Some time soon, he'd have to reexamine this thing, lay bare his real motives. It was just barely conceivable it would be something quite unpleasant. He gave a last morose look at the title page. "The College Thesis as Prior Art in Chemical Patent Interferences" and put the papers back in the envelope. He just didn't know how to put this thing back on the rails. Fundamentally he must be just plain lazy.

But time was wasting. He looked at his wristwatch, put the papers back, closed the drawer, and walked out to the lily pond again.

It was in the same wet sparkle of sunlight that he remembered his baby daughter, splashing in naked glee that warm summer day so many months ago. Lilas had stood there and called the baby out of the pool to get dressed, for that fatal Saturday afternoon trip to the shopping center. And his daughter had climbed out of the pool, ignored the tiny terry-cloth robe, and dashed dripping wet into her father's arms. At least her front got dried as he held her writhing wetness against his shirt, patting her dancing little bottom with the palm of his hand.

Slowly he sat down again. It must have been that sunbeam on the pool. It was going to be bad. He began to shudder. He wanted to scream. He bent over and buried his face in his hands. For a time he breathed in noisy rasps. Finally he stood up again, wiped his gray face on the sleeve of his robe, and started back up the garden path to the house. He would have to be on his way to the office. As soon as he got to the office, he would be all right.

> 'Tis all a Chequer-board of
> Nights and Days
> Where Destiny with Men for
> Pieces plays . . .
> OMAR KHAYYAM

Patrick sometimes had the impression that he was just a pawn on Alec Cord's chessboard. Cord was always looking seven moves deep, and into a dozen alternate sequences. Patrick sighed. He had long suspected that they were all smarter than he was, certainly each doing his job better than Patrick could do it. It was only the trainees that he could really teach anything anymore, and even here he had to fight to find the time. Nothing about it made sense. The higher you rose in the company, the less you knew about anything, and the more you had to rely on the facts and appraisals developed by people under you. They could make a better patent search than he; they could write a better patent specification, and do it faster; they could draft better and more comprehensive infringement opinions. In a gloomy moment he had wondered whether it was the same way throughout the company, and if so, why had the company nevertheless grown into the Big Ten of the American chemical industry. But he never figured it out.

He looked up at his lieutenant. "I understand it was the crucial game, in the last round. If you beat Gadsen, you won the tournament, and if he beats you, he won."

"Didn't realize you followed the sports page, Con," said Alec Cord.

"Gadsen had white, and opened up with the Ruy Lopez. You defended with Marshall's Counter Gambit. They gave the score in the paper. Somebody said it was identical, move for move, with a game between Marshall and Capablanca in 1918, when Marshall first pulled his gambit on Capablanca."

"I wouldn't know."

"That's a surprise. They say you even had an article in *Chess Review* last year on the Marshall Counter Gambit."

Cord was silent. Patrick took a new tack. "Gadsen's that Examiner in Group 170, the one handling your Neol cases?"

"That's right."

"Including the basic case, the one we know now is the phony? The one our whole Neol plant depends on?"

"The very one."

"The one you would have given just about anything, even the Annual D.C. Chess Tournament, for Gadsen to allow?"

"All right, Con. But it's not what you think. I didn't throw the tournament. And Gadsen didn't throw the allowance. We didn't discuss it at all. I admit I let him win that game, but there wasn't any deal. It would have to occur to him, with no help from me, that there was something he owed me. He could have done it either way, and I'd have had no kick. Maybe he'd have given the allowance anyhow. In fact, for all you know, maybe he allowed the case despite the game, and not because of it."

"I won't argue the point, Alec. We may never know. Anyhow, the thing I came to see you about is this." He handed the other a legal-sized sheet.

Cord's eyes widened. "An interference!"

"So maybe Gadsen allowed the claims just to set you up for an interference."

"Maybe. But not likely. If he were going to do that, he would have just sent the interference notice, this thing, without the allowance."

"Any ideas who the other party is?"

"Probably Du Santo. We've been picking up their foreign patents in the quick-issue countries, like Belgium. We'll know for sure after the inventors file their preliminary statements. Which brings me to the next question: How can we file a preliminary statement sworn to by a phony inventor who doesn't even exist?"

"I don't know. I want you to figure out something after we talk to Paul Bleeker."

"Take it from the beginning, Paul" said Patrick.

Paul Bleeker's face rippled with misery.

Cord said: "Maybe I'd better go."

"Stay put," said Patrick shortly. "Paul, you understand why we have to have Alec in on this. You're emotionally involved. You might not be able to do what has to be done. Alec has to listen to everything, so he and I together can plan what to do. You trust him, don't you?"

The young man nodded.

"It began as sort of a joke . . .?" prompted Patrick.

"Yes, a joke," said Paul. "When I was a freshman in law school. Harvey Jayne and those others were teasing Dad. That was when Dad was still Director of the Research Division, before they promoted him."

The light was dawning. Patrick sat up. "They were teasing him about the Research Division?"

"Yes, then Mr. Jayne said Dad's Research Division was essential, but only to verify outside inventions he bought."

"So you decided to booby trap Mr. Jayne?"

"Yes."

"You then wrote those patent attorneys in Washington?"

"Yes, I mailed them the examples for the patent application. They took them and changed them around a little bit, the same way we do here in the Patent Department. They added the standard gobbledygook at the front, and eight or ten claims at the back. They sent the final draft back to me for execution. The standard procedure. They sent me a bill for three hundred dollars. I paid that out of the money Mr. Jayne sent them, when he bought the invention. I still have the rest—four thousand and seven hundred dollars. I haven't spent any of it." He looked uncertainly at Patrick. "You won't tell Dad about this, will you?"

"Certainly not." Patrick looked at him with genuine curiosity.

"But how were you able to make the oath? What notary would notarize the signature of 'Percy B. Shelley'?"

"Absolutely any, Con. They all just assume you are who you say you are, so long as you pay the fee."

Patrick was momentarily shaken. "But that's the whole idea of notarizing to make the inventor swear he's truly the inventor, the person named in the oath."

Cord smiled faintly. "Not all notaries waive identification, Con."

"Well," said Patrick, "now we've committed perjury, sworn falsely to the United States Patent Office. So far, all they can do to you, Paul, besides disbarring you, followed by imprisonment in the federal penitentiary, is to strike your Shelley case from the files in the Patent Office."

The young man was silent.

Cord said: "Harvey Jayne bought the patent application only after he knew it worked. The whole thing depended on whether John Fast could reproduce it in the lab. Paul, how could you be so sure it would work?"

"If John did it right, it couldn't *not* work. I copied the examples right out of something in the library. Somebody's college thesis."

Patrick brightened. "Alec?"

Cord shook his head. "Nothing like that ever turned up in our literature searches. We hit the Dissertation Abstracts, all the way back to the beginning."

Patrick turned back to Paul Bleeker. "You'll have to tell us more about this thesis. What was the name of the student? We'd also like the name of the university, and the year. In fact, anything and everything you can remember."

"All I can remember is these runs, tucked away in the back pages. They didn't really seem pertinent to the main body of the thesis. Other than that, I can't remember anything."

"You must have seen the title page," pressed Patrick.

"I guess so."

"You could identify it if you saw the thesis again?"

"Sure, but it's gone."

"Gone?"

"The library just had it on loan. They have hundreds come in this way. Our people keep them a while, then send them back. You know the procedure."

"There must be some record."

Cord shook his head. "We've checked all the inter-library loans for the past five years. We found nothing. If Paul's memory is correct on the facts, that it *was* within the last five years, and the library *did* have it on loan, we are led to the conclusion that the thesis was done by somebody here at Hope, and lent on a personal basis to the library, without any formal record."

Patrick groaned. "Our own inventor, here all the time? That's all we need. He'll scream. He'll take it to court. We've got to find him first, before he finds us." He turned to Cord. "Alec, add it all up for us, will you?"

"It admits of precise calculation," said Cord, "in the manner of a chess combination. There are two primary variations. Each of these has several main subvariations. None of them is really difficult. The only problem is to recognize that our tactics are absolutely controlled, move by move, by events as they develop."

Patrick raised his hand. "Not so fast. Let's take the main angles. The primary variations.

"First primary. We do nothing. If we're senior party in the interference, this means we take no testimony, but rely purely on our filing date. Chances: better than even. If we're junior party, we lose hands down.

"Second primary. We fight. Firstly, this gives subvariant A. With Paul's help we find the real inventor. We buy this invention from him, and if he hasn't already published, we file good and true application for him. We enter a motion to substitute a new case for Paul's case, and then we expressly abandon Paul's case. If this inventor actually has published in the way Paul remembers, this gives subvariant B. We find that thesis, then we move to dissolve the interference, contending that the sole count is unpatentable over the disclosures in the thesis."

Patrick twisted his mustache nervously. "However you state it, we wind up with no chance of a patent. Maybe we can live with that. Perhaps we can forego a patent-based monopoly. But there's one thing we *must* have—and that's the right to build the plant, free and clear from interference or infringement of anybody else's patent. Can we tell the board we have that right? The board wants to know. They're going to vote on it Monday. And I don't think we can tell them anything . . . not yet. The economics and market are there. Everything hangs on the patent situation. Bleeker says the vote will be to build, if the patent picture is clear. We're holding the whole thing up in our shop right here." He turned back to Cord. "Alec, take it from the college thesis. Run the variations off from that."

"Variation One," said Cord, "the thesis is a good reference. This means it adequately describes the invention, that it was at least typewritten, that it was placed on the shelves at the university library, available to all who might ask for it, and that all of this was done more than one year before either Paul or his opponent filed their respective cases. This would support the motion to dissolve. Both parties would lose, and neither would get a patent, fraudulent or otherwise. With no basic patent to be infringed, it follows that anybody could build a Neol plant. Paul's application would be given a prompt final rejection and would be transferred to the abandoned files in the Patent Office. Then it would lie buried until destroyed under the twenty-year rule. Nobody would ever learn about it.

"Variation Two. The thesis for some reason is not citable as a good, sufficient and competent reference under the Patent Office rules. For example, we might not find it in time, or if we do find it, it might really present substantial differences from Paul's disclosure. Even if we are senior party, we will not be able to negotiate a settlement of the interference without grave danger of discovery of what Paul did. If we turn out to be junior party, it's even more certain we can't settle the interference, but there's actually less risk of being found out, if only because the opposition won't talk to us."

Patrick's mouth dropped. "All right. We always come back to the thesis. We've got to find it. If we find it, we can build a Neol plant. If we can't find it, we can't build a Neol plant, and even worse things will probably happen to a number of people in this company." He turned to Cord. "Have you and Paul exhausted every possibility, every lead?"

Cord nodded glumly. Paul Bleeker bent over and put his face in his hands.

Patrick sighed. He thought, I'll have to do it the hard way. Tonight. He said, "Paul, you'll be over tonight, won't you?"

"Yes, Con."

"Thanks, fellows. Paul, would you ask Sullivan to come in?"

He must needes goe whom the devill doth drive.
JOHN HEYWOOD

Patrick smiled at Sullivan. "Good morning, Mike. How are those Neol cases coming?"

"We're in good shape. John Fast and I will need a couple of more weeks, though. It's a whole series of cases. Covers the catalysts, the whole pilot-plant set up, the vapor phase job, everything. John and I get together every morning and dictate this stuff to Willow. She types her notes in the afternoon. Except that as of now she's about a week behind in transcription. If she left right now, the Neol patent cases would be in quite a hole."

Patrick met Sullivan's studied gaze noncommittally. He knows, he thought. They all know about Willow. He said easily, "I guess you're right. How about John? Will he stick with your program?"

Sullivan shrugged his shoulders. "He'd better. We need him. But like I said, he needs us, too. And he insisted that you approve the contract. Do you want to see it?"

Patrick shifted uncomfortably. "It's nearly ten o'clock. He'll be here in a minute. You can read it to both of us, then."

Sullivan smiled. "You're getting off easy."

Patrick said, "I know what you're thinking, Mike. And you're right. We *are* going to turn him over to the psychiatrist. But not just yet. Not until you get these last three Neol disclosures written up. Another couple of weeks won't hurt him."

Sullivan's smile deepened.

Patrick said, "Medically, it certainly can't hurt to humor him."

Sullivan laughed. "Con, you're a sham, a fraud, and a hypocrite. Preserve him long enough for him to file his cases, then let him drop dead."

Patrick bridled. "That's putting it a little strong. If I thought for a moment—"

"Oh, come off it, Con. We're all on edge with this thing. Anyhow, you can take comfort in the thought that the Patent Department has simply ground out one more contract, one out of a hundred a year, doing their daily hacking, what they are paid to do, and therefore what they rejoice in doing. If you look at it that way, you have served your client to the very best of your ability, and at night you can sleep with sound conscience."

Patrick growled, "If I didn't need you—"

Sullivan held up his hand. "Speak of the devil—"

"Come in," called Patrick.

John Fast entered the room. He was an average-looking man, average size, of an average grayness. His face was almost without expression, perhaps a little sad. There was something unnerving in his eyes. They were acquainted with—

Horror? thought Patrick, wondering. No. That was too simple. John Fast was acquainted with the sub-elements of horror, with the building stones of terror, and with the unrest of darkness. And this was the man whom he would need tonight. "Hello, John," he said, genially. "I hear your Neol cases are going a mile a minute."

"Going nicely, Con, thanks." Fast looked at Sullivan, then back at Patrick. "Is my contract ready?"

"Contract? Yes, of course, the contract. Mike and I have been going over it. Before we read it to you, though, we'd like to make sure we've covered everything. Now Mike here has heard your story, but I haven't. I'd like to hear it from you, straight, exactly the way it happened."

"It's a long story, Con."

"We've got lots of time."

"All right, then." Fast took a deep breath; his eyes grew distant. "I think it began with a ozonator. You know what ozone smells like? It's sharp, electric. In certain concentrations it's hard to distinguish from chlorine or sulfur dioxide. You know how the Bible talks about brimstone? Brimstone is sulfur, but there wasn't any sulfur in Palestine. The old prophets were just trying to identify an odor that was there long before they learned about sulfur. This creature moves in an atmosphere of ozone. He moves around in time and space, and to do this he applies an electrical field on the space-time continuum. Ozone is sort of a by-product, the same as when you run an electric motor. So this thing moves around in a fog of ozone. Not only that, ozone seems to attract him, the way nectar attracts bees.

"For a long time I didn't really realize he was around. And then last week I met him. It might have been an accident. But with all this Freudian theory, maybe there's no such thing as an accident. Maybe, on a subconscious level, I did it deliberately. Anyhow, you know we have a big structural formula of pentacyclopropane drawn in white paint on the floor of the pilot plant. This makes a star, with the methylene groups as the five points. It is also a pentagram—a starlike geometric design used in certain . . . rituals. Within the history of the United States, people have been burnt for making a pentagram. The stage was set. Just one more thing was needed: the Lord's Prayer recited backwards. This was provided. I'm a steady church-goer. Bible class on Sunday mornings. Last Sunday I took my office tape recorder to

Bible class. Yes, we said the Lord's Prayer. It was still on the tape when I was going to dictate my monthly progress report. I rewound the tape, so there it was, everything going backwards on audio. I was inside the pentagram. And suddenly, there—it—was, on the other side. I was so scared I was petrified. I wasn't surprised. Just scared. Maybe that means I knew what I was doing. So we stared at each other. Except I wasn't sure what I was staring at. But it was definitely a shape, with arms, head, eyes. . . ."

"You were tired," said Patrick. "You know how fatigue can induce hallucinations."

"It's not that simple, Con. There—*was*—there *is*—something there, some kind of elemental force. It's a being, an intelligent being. And powerful, in strange ways. It can . . . alter the laws of chemistry and physics. I got it to increase the yield of terpineol—'Neol.' At first, by about ten percent. Then another ten percent. It was easy. And then last night we started up the pilot plant. We ran the C-10 through first, cold, just to flush the lines and check the flow meters. We got the ozonator tied in about midnight. Now you understand the ozone won't start reacting with the C-10 until you hit about one sixty F., and we'd planned to turn steam into the jacket after the ozone concentration had built up to about five percent. But the reactor began to warm up. It hit one sixty in a matter of seconds. The two technicians on shift were scared. They ran over behind the explosion mat. I stayed put. I knew what was going on. *He* was doing it. I wanted to know how far he could push it. I shunted the C-10 through the flow meter. I switched in the product receiver. It took about thirty minutes to feed one pound mole of C-10 . . . exactly one hundred and thirty pounds. I shut everything off. I had been watching the product scales all along, so I knew what it was going to be. It was one hundred fifty-four pounds, one pound mole of Neol, exactly. Yield: one hundred percent of theory.

"They came out from behind the mats, then. They looked at the graphs. Nobody believed the graphs. They looked for a weighing error. They knew it couldn't happen. So I told them to check the meters. The meters were all right. I knew there was nothing wrong with the meters. Then we started another run. The reaction didn't start cold this time. So we turned the steam into the jacket. That was supposed to start the reaction. We usually start getting terpineol in the receiver at about one sixty. We watched it for a good hour. Not a drop of product. Just C-10 going in, C-10 coming out. We couldn't explain it. We were making ozone. The ozonator was O.K. We had the right concentration of C-10, the right temperature, mole ratio, space velocity, everything was right. But not a gram of terpineol was coming out. *He* wanted to *show* me, you understand, that he could control it either way. But he was going to leave it up to me which way it went. I didn't want to decide right then. I didn't know what to do. Just then I didn't even know how I could tell him, if I did decide. So we simply shut down and knocked off.

"I went home, but I couldn't sleep. I tried to think it through. And I guess I did think it through. This *being* can put me through. With him on my side I can do anything. There's no position in this corporation I couldn't have. And *that* would just be a starter. I don't know where the end would be. So I want to make the deal. I know exactly what I want. And what *he* wants. He wants, well, he wants *me*. Not my body, really, or anything like that. It's more like something mental. He wants to take it from me a little at a time, like a parasitical drain. But it wouldn't affect me physically or mentally. In fact, I'd get sharper all the time. And whatever it is, it would go slowly, day by day, that I wouldn't notice it. This goes on for years. I'll even have a normal life expectancy. When he's got all of it, I'll die. And that's the deal. The next thing is to get it down on paper. Something he and I can both sign. A binding contract. It doesn't matter whether you believe he exists. Call him the Devil if you like. And call the thing I'm giving him, my soul. A lot of people who believe in God don't believe the Devil exists. And some of them don't believe in souls, either. Although, as I said, it isn't really that simple."

There was a long silence.

"The contract?" prompted Fast.

Patrick nodded, as in a dream, to Sullivan.

Sullivan began: "This Agreement, made as of this blank day of blank, in the year of our Lord—"

"Not 'of our Lord,' " said Fast.

"Quite so," said Sullivan. "I'll fix that." He continued: ". . . By and between John Fast, hereinafter sometimes referred to as 'Fast', and His Satanic Majesty, hereinafter sometimes referred to as 'The Devil,' Witnesseth: Whereas Fast is desirous of certain improvements in his present circumstances; and Whereas The Devil is able to cause and bring about said improvements; now therefore, in consideration of the mutual promises herein contained, and for other good and valuable consideration, the receipt of which is hereby acknowledged, the parties agree as follows: Article One. The Devil shall promptly cause the Hope Chemical Company to erect a plant for the production of terpineol, hereinafter referred to as 'Neol,' and to make Fast the manager thereof. The Devil shall, with all deliberate speed, cause Fast to become a world-famous chemist, rich, respected, and to win at least two Nobel prizes. Without limiting the generality of the foregoing, The Devil will immediately enter upon the performance, and will continue same, for the full term of this Agreement, of every obligation set forth on Exhibit A, annexed hereto, and incorporated by reference herein."

Sullivan looked up at Fast. "You wrote out the list?"

"Right here."

"Mark it 'Exhibit A,' " said Sullivan. He continued. "Article Two. Fast hereby assigns, grants, conveys, sets over, and transfers all his right, title, and interest in and to his soul, to the said Devil, on the death of Fast; provided, however, that Fast shall live until the age of seventy, and that during said period The Devil shall have met faithfully, and in a good and workmanlike manner, all his obligations, both general and specific, as above set forth."

Patrick nodded. "That's fine."

"We had to change some of our 'boiler-plate' clauses," said Sullivan. "Others we had to leave out altogether. For example, we thought it best to omit completely the 'Force Majeure' clause, whereby the Devil is relieved from his obligation to perform, if prevented by an Act of God, but can nevertheless require you to perform, that is, give up your soul!"

"Logical," agreed Fast.

"And we had to change the 'construction and validity' clause. Ordinarily we provide that our contracts shall be construed, and their validity determined, under the laws of the State of New York. However, we think that under New York law the contract might be held invalid, as having an immoral object, and hence unenforceable by either side. So we changed it to Hawaiian law."

"Yes," said Fast. "It's all ready to sign, then?"

"Right there, there're lines for the signatures of both, ah, parties," said Sullivan. "Are we to understand, John, that the Devil will actually affix his signature to this document, in real pen and ink?"

"I sign in blood," said Fast calmly. "How *he* signs, I'm not really sure. All I know is, he'll do something, maybe make a special appearance, to let me know that he accepts."

"I see," said Patrick. (He saw nothing.) He asked curiously, "But why do you think you need the Devil? An energetic man with a solid technical background and a high I.Q. in a big, growing chemical company doesn't need assistance such as this."

Fast looked at him in surprise. "Coming from you, Con, that's a very strange question."

"How is that?"

"I accept aid from any source, because I am totally committed. But so are you, and therefore, you, too, will accept assistance without asking the cost, or to whom the payment will be made."

Patrick felt a flurry of confusion. "And to what am I totally committed?"

"To your patents. Did you not know?"

Patrick had to think about this. Finally, he shook his head, not in denial, but to admit incomprehension. "Well," he defended. "It's my job."

Fast's mouth, immobile and cryptic as the Mona Lisa's, seemed almost to smile. "Yes, but only because you have contracted for it. So you see, what I have done is not a particularly strange thing. You . . . everyone . . . has entered into his own private contract, with something. My only difference is that I have put mine in writing. This does not necessarily mean that I am more honest than you. Perhaps I am merely more perceptive.

"True, my deal is with the Devil. But is that immoral? Morality is relative. *My* action, *my* way of life, has to be evaluated against the background of *your* action, and *your* way of life. You think me immoral, if not insane. Yet you wrote this contract for me. Why? Because you want to keep me happy. And why do you want to keep me happy? So that I'll keep your patents coming. Therefore you've made your own contract—with your patents. You resolve all questions of sin, virtue, and morality in light of the effect on your patents. With you, nothing can be sinful—even an assignment to hell—if it helps your terpineol patents. Before you judge my contract, take a look at your own."

Patrick stared at the gray man. Finally he smiled uneasily. "Whatever you say, John."

"And now I'll do *you* a favor, Con. Change the name."

"Change what name?"

"Neol. It's wrong."

"What's wrong with it?"

"The sound; wrong altogether. If you should ever have to . . . call . . . anyone with it, it wouldn't do it. Also, you ought to have five letters, exactly, one letter for each point of the pentagram. Correct symbology is essential."

"Whom would I be calling?" said Patrick. "And why?"

"You know . . . for your patents."

Patrick looked blank, then frowned, then finally he smiled. "All right, John. Whether or not you're a mystic, I'll give you 'x-plus,' for mystification."

After Fast had gone, Patrick and Sullivan stared at each other.

"Do *you* believe any of that?" said Patrick.

"I believe he *thinks* he saw something. A kind of self-hypnosis."

"How about the yield. You know one hundred percent of theory is impossible."

"No, Con, I don't know that. And neither do you. Within experimental errors, he may well have got one hundred percent. And even if he didn't, he really might have got fairly close to it. A pilot plant always does much better than a bench-scale unit. You just naturally expect the yield to be high. All the variables are optimized, easily controlled."

"So you think he just hypnotized himself into seeing the devil?"

"Why not? Actually, he's an accomplished amateur hypnotist. I'm told he is quite a parlor performer, if you can catch him."

"I know. He'll be at the party tonight, for something like that. But he's wrong about me. I'm *not* totally committed to my patents. It's my job, the same as it's your job. John Fast doesn't know what he's saying."

Sullivan's eyes twinkled wickedly. "You're absolutely right, Con. There are *some* things you would not resort to, even to save the Neol patent position. You would *not* sell your own grandmother into white slavery even if it would win the interference and solve the whole problem." He paused, then added maliciously, "Would you, Con?"

Patrick snorted. "Don't tempt me!"

"Are you going to change the name?" asked Sullivan.

" 'Neol'?"

"You know what I mean."

"Well, maybe. There's nothing really wrong with 'Neol.' "

"Except that John Fast thinks it's wrong."

". . . Without saying how to make it right," added Patrick. "I want to think about it. And I might change it, just to be ornery."

* * *

That which we call a rose
By any other name would smell as sweet.
SHAKESPEARE

Patrick sat in his office, looking at the proofs of the "Neol Technical Manual," and thinking hard. This was Harvey Jayne's manual, and Jayne was trying to steal Miss Willow. But Jayne needed Patent Department clearance for his manual. Right away, this suggested possibilities. This morning, he had it nearly figured. And then John Fast had decided the name was wrong. And what difference did it make to John Fast? He wasn't even going to ask, because tonight he was going to need the man.

But *could* he change the name? How sacred was this manual to Jayne?

Patrick considered the matter.

He knew, certainly, that a technical manual prepared and published by an American chemical giant was like nothing else in the world of books. It was the strange child of the mating of the laboratory with Madison Avenue, midwifed by the corporate public relations committee. It told all. It was rich in history, process descriptions, flow sheets, rotogravures, chemical equations, and nomographs. It was comprehensive, and its back pages were filled with thousands of arrogant footnotes. The stockholders of Hope Chemical were given the impression that the sole function of the "Neol Technical Manual" was to incite an unendurable craving for Neol in the hearts of purchasing agents throughout the country. But Patrick knew that the compiler privately harbored other motives. For that man, Harvey Jayne, it represented an opportunity for creativity that comes only when the company builds a new plant; it could not happen to Jayne twice in one lifetime.

In this manual, Harvey Jayne would have a ready-made solace for whatever disasters might lie ahead. His wife might on occasion fail to recognize his greatness; his son might fail in school; he might, alas, even be laterally transferred within the company. Yet withal, his faith in himself would be restored, and the blood brought back into his cheeks, when he gets out his old Technical Manual, to read a little in it, to fondle its worn covers, and to look at the pictures. So doing, Harvey Jayne might murmur, with tears in his eyes, as did Jonathan Swift, re-reading *Gulliver's Travels*, "God, what genius!"

So, thought Patrick, this volume will be cherished forever by Harvey Jayne. He will keep it in his office bookcase, with a spare in his den at home. When he transfers, it will be carefully packed. Years later, for presentation at his retirement dinner, his lieutenants will borrow his last copy from his wife, or perhaps steal one from the company library. They will have it bound in the company colors, blue and gold; and the chairman of the board, the president, and numerous fellow vice-presidents will autograph its pages.

Now, brooded Patrick, the whole of this immense and immemorial undertaking, this monster, this manual, centers around the product trademark, which is as essential to it as the proton to the atom, the protoplasmic nucleus to the growing cell. The manual is known by this name. Once thus baptized, the name is sacred. And to deny this book its name, to suggest that its name is wrong, that it should have another name, is to invite the visitation of the Furies, for this is desecration, a charge so sinister that it must rank with defamation of motherhood, or with being against J. Edgar Hoover.

Yes, there were possibilities. For personal disaster. He could not change the name of the manual. And yet he was going to. Why? he wondered. Why am I going to do this? I am as crocked as John Fast. His mind floundered, searching. I have to fight Harvey Jayne, that's why. No. That's not why. It's something else. John Fast said the name was wrong. The new name should have five letters. He tugged briefly at his mustache, then leaned over to the intercom.

Books cannot always please.
GEORGE CRABBE

"Con," said Cord, "it's not really bad. A few editorial changes should do the job."

Patrick's face was a blank. "How about 'Neol'?"

"It's clear. The closest thing is 'Neolan,' registered for textiles."

Patrick brightened. "Clear? It's a clear case of infringement!"

Cord stared at him. "What . . . what did you say?"

"I said it infringes. And I hasten to add, Cord, my boy, that you look quite strange with your mouth open." He reached for the phone and dialed Jayne.

"Oh, hi there, Harvey . . . No, I didn't call to protest about

Miss Willow. We're really grateful you can do something for her, Harvey. Her place is with you, Harvey. On one condition . . . It's this, Harvey, that you double her raise. She's worth every bit of it. Good, Harvey, splendid you see it our way . . . Tech Manual, Harvey? Yes, we're looking at it right now. No, Harvey, I'm afraid we can't do that. There's a very close prior registration that will probably kill Neol as a trademark. No, Harvey, please get that out of your head. Miss Willow has nothing to do with it. She will transfer with our very best wishes . . . That is indeed your privilege, Harvey. If you want to present the manual to the board on Monday morning without Patent Department clearance, go right ahead. It would, of course, be my duty to give Andrew Bleeker a memo itemizing my objections, absolving the Patent Department of all responsibility for the content of the manual. There will be carbons, of course, to . . . You will? Why that's fine, Harvey." He hung up. "He's coming over."

"I'm amazed," said Cord dryly.

"Keep your fingers crossed on Willow."

"But you said the louse could have her, with a double raise," said Cord.

"Alec, you wouldn't believe me if I told you what is about to happen. So I won't waste time. We have only a few minutes before Harvey is due to show. So—*Cord*."

"Yes, Con?"

"I didn't address you. I merely stated your name. It turns crisply from the tongue, like honest bacon in the griddle. A fine name. Cord, Cord, Cord. A good word to say. Here, I'll write it, too. Flows easily on paper. Cord looks good. Listens good. Charming. A man's name is the best thing about him. Like Narcissus. Hello there, you beautiful name!"

Cord flushed red. "Con, for goodness' sake. It isn't at all remarkable!"

"Yes, my boy, it is . . . to you." He leered at his lieutenant. "A man's name is his most enchanting possession. For you, for me, for Harvey Jayne, for anybody."

"So?"

"That's how we find a substitute for Neol. We will derive us a new word, from 'Jayne.' Harvey will find it irresistible. And it will be a good trademark. Think of the trouble American Cyanamid had, trying to find a trademark for their acrylic fiber. They finally named it after the project leader, Arthur Cresswell. They called it 'Creslan.' And Cluett-Peabody, naming their 'Sanforize' process for pre-shrunk fabric after the inventor, Sanford.

And think of how many of Willard Dow's products are 'Dow' something or other, 'Dowicide,' for example. And look at Monsanto's 'Santowax'; 'Santowhite,' 'Santomerse.' And Du Pont's 'Duponol,' and W. R. Grace's 'Grex' polyethylene. So we'll name our terpineol after Harvey Jayne. 'Jayne-ol.' Of course not exactly 'Jayne-ol.' We'll have to fix it so he won't recognize it. Some phonetic equivalent."

"He'll recognize it, Con. It'll just make him madder."

"No, I don't think he will. A man has a selfish complex on his own name. He loves it, and he doesn't want other people to have it. He has trouble remembering people who have similar names. So if we do this right, he won't recognize it when he hears it. It'll fascinate him, but he won't understand why. He'll approve it on the spot. But first, we'll have to work him over, soften him up a little. So listen carefully as to what you have to do."

"Harvey," said Patrick, "you're making us revise our company leaflet on trademarks."

"I didn't know you had one," said Harvey Jayne suspiciously.

"It lists everything that shouldn't be done—all possible error. At least it *did*. Now, you've added a few more. We'll have to revise."

"This brochure. You wouldn't happen to have a copy—"

Patrick handed him the leaflet. "Brand-new edition, just off the press this afternoon."

Jayne read slowly. " 'The trademark should be capitalized, and preferably set in distinctive type. If the trademark is registered in the United States Patent Office, follow it with the registration symbol, ®. If no application for registration has been filed, or, if filed, not yet granted, then use an asterisk after the trademark, with footnote identification. Hope Chemical Company's trademark for . . .' " I don't care whether it's capitalized or not. And I didn't say 'trademark' every time I said 'neol.' I just said plain old neol. I want it to become so familiar to our customers that they'll think of it as a household word."

Patrick shook his head sadly. "Harvey, I understand your viewpoint, and I deeply sympathize. Such charity and philanthropy are all too infrequent in this hatchet-hearted corporation."

"Charity? Philanthropy?"

"Yes. Really touching. Gets me, *here*." Patrick struck his fist to his chest. "You want to give the trademark to the general public, including our competitors. Come one, come all, anybody can use this name, which isn't a trademark any more, because Harvey doesn't want it spelled with a capital."

"I don't see how spelling it lowercase prevents it from being a trademark."

"It converts it into the *thing itself*. Remember 'cellophane'? It used to be Du Pont's trademark for transparent wrappings, and it was spelled with a capital C. And then it became so well known that the newspapers and magazines began spelling it lowercase, and they never mentioned it was Du Pont's brand of anything, because everybody by that time thought of cellophane only as the transparent wrapping itself. It had become the common name of the thing itself: it had become *generic*. Now anybody can sell his own transparent wrapping and call it 'cellophane.' Cellophane has now joined the list of irresistible trademarks that are wide open to the public: shredded wheat, mineral oil, linoleum, escalator, aspirin, milk-of-magnesia."

"Anything else wrong?"

"Several other points. On the title page, you ought to say 'Copyright, Hope Chemical Company.' "

"But how can I say 'Copyright' before we publish? I thought you just said you couldn't do that. You said we couldn't say Neol was registered."

"I won't try to explain it, Harvey. That's the way it has worked out historically."

"Anything else?"

"We don't like your trademark, 'Neol,' " said Patrick. "We think it infringes at least one mark already registered. Besides which, it's a weak mark, made up of weak syllables."

"What . . . what are you saying?" sputtered Jayne. "There's nothing wrong with 'Neol.' How can it be weak?"

"Look at it this way," said Patrick smoothly. "Fashions in trademarks come and go, like women's hats. At the moment, the ad people are conditioned to think in terms of certain well-worn prefixes and suffixes. The suffix is supposed to classify the product as a liquid, a solid, a plastic, a synthetic fiber, a flooring compound, soap, deodorant, toothpaste, and so on. True, they have their differences, but these are minuscule. The pack of them are so much alike you'd take them for a children's a capella choir."

"That's probably true for most trademarks," said Harvey Jayne smugly, "but not for 'Neol.' 'Neol' was selected by our computer, which was programmed to synthesize words from certain mellifluous-sounding syllables, and to discard everything harsh. And not only that, but to present a final list of one hundred names graded according to final audial acceptance. 'Neol' headed the list."

Patrick shook his head pityingly. "Look, Harvey, when you use a computer, you've got two-and-a-half strikes against you from the start. In the first place, the only marks the computer can grind out will be made up of these forbidden syllables we've already ruled out. And secondly, no computer can zero in on the gray area between the legally acceptable 'suggestive' marks and the legally unacceptable 'descriptive' marks. Even the courts have a hard time with this concept. To demonstrate this, we are going to decomputerize 'Neol' for you."

"De . . . computerize . . . ?"

"Yes, our decomputer takes a computerized trademark and tells us whether it's too close to known marks or names to be registrable."

"May I see it, this decomputer?"

"You could, but that won't be necessary. It's so simple, I'll just describe it to you briefly. It consists of two cylinders, rotating on the same shaft, one next to the other. On the left cylinder we have prefixes, on the right, suffixes. All our syllables were compiled from trademarks in the chemical and plastics fields. When a new trademark comes in, we break it down into syllables and see if it's in our decomputer. If it's not here, we search it in the Trademark Division of the Patent Office, in Washington."

"What syllables do you have on your, ah, decomputer?" said Jayne uneasily.

"Really only the extremely common ones. For prefixes, things like 'ray, hy, no, ko, kor, di, so, ro,' the 'par-per-pro' set, 'vel, val,' and of course, 'neo.' "

"Neo, you said?"

"Yes, 'neo,' which is simply the Greek variant of 'new,' which again frequently comes out as 'nu,' or in the Latin form, 'novo.' "

"And I presume 'ol' is among your proscribed suffixes?" demanded Jayne bitterly.

"Yes, that's 'ol,' from Latin, 'oleum,' oil. So that gives us 'Neol,' or 'new oil.' "

Jayne frowned and looked at his notes. "Well, how about 'Neolan'? Or do you have 'lan' in your suffixes, too?"

"Yes, indeed. But there again, we consider 'lan' as a species of the 'on' family, from 'rayon,' of course. Between vowels, 'on' takes a consonant, so you would come out with 'lin, lan, lon,' and so you have 'neolan.' "

Jayne threw up his hands. "Well, then, you fellows just do whatever you have to do, to fix this. Say the right words over it. Do your legal mumbo jumbo."

Patrick studied Jayne quietly for a moment. "Harvey. I'm going to do something I shouldn't. I'll clear a trademark—no, not Neol. Some other mark."

Jayne looked dubious. "*We* would have to originate it. Our ad people have to screen these things. All kinds of image and audio requirements."

"Impossible, Harvey. This is not a job for the agency. All they can do is put together syllables to skirt along the fringes of what they think your customers will almost but not quite recognize. The way they draw up those lists, they practically guarantee their mark will be weak. Leave them out of this. I'll give you a mark I will guarantee *you* will like and that will not infringe any existing mark."

"But if it isn't on my list, how can you be so sure I'll like it?"

Patrick smiled. "We've never lost a customer."

"Probably it will be very similar to a trademark on my list."

Patrick picked up the list and scanned it briefly. "No, I think not. But we're wasting time. Let's move on to the next item."

"Next item?"

"Payment."

"Charge my department."

"You don't quite understand, Harvey. Let's go over it again. I'm promising you a clean, desirable trademark. I'm giving you a guarantee—on something that as yet doesn't even exist. I don't have to do it. This is above and beyond the call of duty. A big favor to you."

"So?"

"If the company gets sued, you're in the clear, but it's a black eye for me. They'll say Hope needs a younger man in their Patent Department. Patrick is slipping. And then the next time it happens, I'm out on my ear. So I'm taking a chance, and I want payment."

Jayne was suspicious. "Like what?"

"We need not be crass. You could offer a prize for a suitable mark."

"And *you* would win it?"

"The Patent Department would win it."

"Go on," said Jayne acidly.

"The prize couldn't be money."

"I can see that. As you say, crass. How about wall-to-wall carpeting?"

"No."

"A conference room . . ."

"Not that, either."

"Electric typewriters . . ."

"Not exactly what I had in mind."

"Then what *do* you want?"

Patrick leaned over and murmured, "Willow."

Jayne was silent for a moment. Finally he said, "I don't know what to say. It's cheap, shoddy, not in character with you, Con. Furthermore, I don't make the rules. This promotion program is a company policy. It's not anything you or I have anything to do with. I need a secretary. I have a vacancy. I either fill it by promoting a girl from the lab, or I go outside. I think it's a good policy."

"So do I," said Patrick morosely. "I hate to do this."

"You don't have to do it. In fact, you're being absolutely unreasonable. If you insist on doing this to me, I'll have to take it up with Andrew Bleeker."

"If you do that, you could get me in trouble."

"As you say, I would hate to have to do it."

"At the same time, you will also have to mention to Bleeker that you couldn't get the Manual out in time for the Board. You won't have to tell him why, though. He'll be first on my list of carbons of my trademark infringement report to you. He will not be happy."

The room became very quiet. The pale drift of typewriters ebbed and flowed in the outer bays.

Jayne's restraint was massive. "You win."

"Thank you, Harvey. And now, just so we won't have any misunderstandings, when Miss Willow comes back to us from having been your secretary, she'll keep her double raise?"

"I thought that she was never leaving you. How can she come back to you?"

"It's all over the place, Harvey, that she's being transferred to you. If we kept her here, she'd be entitled to think that we cheated her out of a raise. So we have to get her transferred to you on the books, get her double raise, and then transferred back to us on the books. Physically, of course, there would seem to be no reason for her to transfer . . . that is, clean out her desk, or anything like that."

"So that not only I don't get a secretary, Willow gets two raises."

"But you get a clean bill of health for your manual."

"And a good trademark?"

"Absolutely." Patrick was solemn. "We can pick one here and now. We guarantee we can get the trademark application on file this afternoon. All we need is a more exotic name—one not made out of these garden variety building units. A really *beautiful* name."

Cord picked up the cue. "How about some foreign words that mean beautiful?"

"Well, there's a thought. Harvey, what do you think?"

Jayne shrugged his shoulders. "Like what?"

"*Pulchra*—Latin for 'pretty,' " said Cord.

"Hard to do anything with it," said Patrick. "What else?"

"*Kallos*—'beautiful' in Greek."

Patrick looked doubtful.

"Bel?" said Cord.

"That's a little better. What is it in Italian?"

"Bella."

"Still not quite right," said Patrick.

"You could take a big jump. 'Beautiful' in German is *schoen*. You'd have to Anglicize the accent a little, give it a long *a*."

"Ah yes. 'Shane.' *Shane*!" Patrick's eyes lit up. "I really like that. Harvey?"

"Not bad. 'Shane.' Hm-m-m. Yes, I must admit, there's something about it. Something tantalizing."

"I hear it, too, Harvey."

Cord's eyes rolled upward briefly.

"How long will it take to search it out in the Washington trademarks?" demanded Jayne.

"We can do it this afternoon. My man will call in, any minute now, and we'll tell him to go ahead."

"I'll take it," said Jayne.

"Good enough. If it's clear in the Trademark Division, we'll get the application on file this afternoon."

Jayne looked surprised. "You'll have to have labels made up. Then you'll have to make a bona fide sale in interstate commerce.

And then have the trademark application executed by Andy Bleeker. I don't think you can do all that in three hours. And I won't pay off on a phony."

"Of course not." Patrick smiled angelically as the other left.

In the early afternoon Patrick walked across the court to the terpineol pilot plant and into the cramped dusty office of John Fast. As he stepped inside, his eyes were drawn immediately across the cubicle, beyond Fast's desk, to a large painting, in black and white, hanging on the wall behind Fast. He poised at the doorway, slack-jawed, staring at this . . . thing.

Within the plain black frame were two figures, one large, and, in front, a smaller. The outlines of the larger figure seemed initially luminous, hazy, then, even as he squinted, perplexed and uneasy; the lines seemed to crystallize, and suddenly a face took form, with eyes, a mouth, and arms. The arms were reaching out, enfolding the figure in front, a man wearing a medieval velvet robe and feathered beret.

Unaccountably, Patrick shivered. His eyes dropped, and found themselves locked with those of John Fast, unquestioning, waiting.

Fast murmured, "It is an oversize reproduction of Harry Clarke's pen-and-ink drawing, the end-piece of Bayard Taylor's translation of Goethe."

"What is it?" blurted Patrick.

"Mephistopheles, taking Faust," said John Fast.

Patrick took a deep breath and got his voice under control. "Very effective." He paused. "John, I'm here to ask a favor."

Fast was silent.

"I understand you have a certain skill in the art of hypnosis."

Fast's great dark eyes washed like tides at Patrick. "That's not quite the right word. But perhaps the result is similar."

"I'll come to the point. All this is highly confidential. Our basic terpineol patent application is in interference in the Patent Office. We intend to dissolve the interference by a motion contending that the interference count is unpatentable over the prior art. This prior art is a college thesis. The problem is, Paul Bleeker is the only one who has seen the thesis, and he can't remember anything about it. Is it possible for him to remember, under hypnosis?"

"It's possible," said Fast, "but by no means a certainty."

"But isn't it true that everyone records, somewhere on his

cerebrum, everything he has ever experienced?"

"Possibly. But that doesn't necessarily mean we can remember it all. Recall is a complicated process. The theory in fashion today is the 'see-all-forget-nearly-all!' theory. In this one, every bit of incoming sensation is recorded and filed away in your subconscious. But to bring it up again, you not only have to call for it, you also have to walk it out, holding it by the hand, chopping along with a mental machete to clear away all the subconscious blocks along its path. Persistence will turn up many a forgotten item in this way. But if it's quite old, there may be so many blocks that it will never be able to penetrate the conscious mind. In this case you have to get down there with it, in your far subconscious —take a good look at it, and then holler out to somebody what you see. Hypnosis is the accepted procedure. In the hands of an expert, all kinds of oddities can be turned up in this way: stimuli the subject barely had time to receive; or things, which, if recalled on a conscious level, would be intolerable."

"I want you to try it on Paul Bleeker tonight."

Fast hesitated a moment. "I gather you renamed Neol?"

Patrick's eyebrows arched. "Yes. How did you know?"

"It was best for your patents, and you always do what's best for your patents."

" 'Neol' was a poor trademark," said Patrick doggedly. "That was the only reason we changed."

"What is the new name?" asked Fast.

And now Patrick hesitated. He found himself unwilling to answer this question. Suddenly, he almost disliked John Fast. He shook himself. "Shane," he said curtly.

Tiny iridescent lights seemed to sparkle from somewhere deep in the eyes of the other.

"Well?" demanded Patrick.

"Exquisite," murmured Fast. "I will do this thing for you. It may involve something more than hypnotism. You understand that, don't you?"

"Of course."

"No, you don't. You can't, at least not yet. But no matter. If Paul is willing, I will do it for you anyway. Since you are totally committed, it cannot be otherwise."

Those who have lost an infant are never, as it were, without an infant child. They are the only persons who, in one sense, retain it always.

LEIGH HUNT

* * *

Andrew Bleeker swung his swivel chair slowly back and forth as he motioned to the two chairs nearest his desk.

Patrick said cheerfully, "Good afternoon, Andy."

Harvey Jayne grunted. He was not cheerful.

Bleeker's eyes flickered broodingly at Patrick's face. He had a horror of these nasty internecine arguments. Patrick beamed back, and Bleeker sighed. "I'll come to the point, Con. There seems to be some question about the way you handled Harvey's Neol manual."

"Really? I realize I wasn't able to satisfy him completely, but I didn't think he felt strongly enough about it to take it to the head office."

"What was the problem, Con?"

Harvey rose out of his chair. "Andy, let *me* state—"

"Con?" said Bleeker quietly.

"I sort of blackmailed him, Andy. I pressured him into giving one of our secretaries a double raise, out of *his* budget. In return I got him a good trademark, made an infringement search on it, and got the trademark application on file in the Patent Office, all within four hours. He still has time to get his brochure proofs corrected and back to the printers tonight. But it isn't the Neol manual anymore. We changed the trademark to Shane."

"Shane?"

"Harvey picked it out, all by himself."

"You don't say," murmured Bleeker.

"The name is all right," grumbled Jayne. "It's the trademark *application* I'm protesting. It's a fraud, a phony. Andy, you perjured yourself when you made oath that the company had used the trademark in commerce. The mark didn't even exist until a few hours ago, and I know for a fact our shipping department hasn't mailed out anything labeled 'Shane' across a state line. It has to be interstate commerce, you know. But there hasn't been any shipment at all. Not one of the packages has left the Patent Department. I just checked."

Bleeker hunched his shoulders and began to swing his chair in slow oscillations. "Con?"

"He has the facts very nearly straight, Andy, but his inference is wrong. There was no fraud. When you signed the declaration, you did not commit perjury."

"But doesn't the form say that the goods have been shipped in interstate commerce? Didn't I sign something to that effect?"

"The trademark application simply asks for the date of first use in commerce. The statute defines commerce as that commerce regulated by Congress. *That's* been settled for over a hundred and fifty years. Congress controls commerce between the states and territories, commerce between the United States and foreign countries, and commerce with the Indian tribes."

"But we didn't ship in interstate commerce," said Jayne.

"That's right," said Patrick.

"Nor in foreign commerce?" asked Bleeker.

"No, Andy."

"That leaves—"

"The Indians," said Patrick.

"Apaches," said Jayne acidly, "disguised as patent attorneys."

"Not exactly Apaches, Harvey," said Patrick. "But we do have a lawful representative of the Sioux tribe, duly accredited to the Bureau of Indian Affairs in Washington. Commerce is with the Sioux, through their representative. A sale to her is a sale to the tribe. If you checked on the packages, you probably noticed that one was on her desk."

"*Her* desk," rasped Jayne. "This . . . Indian . . . *you mean—*"

"Miss Green Willow, late of the Sioux reservation? Of course. Drives a hard bargain. We finally settled on fifteen cents for the gallon jug of terpineol. Her people back in Wyoming will make it into soap for the tourists."

Bleeker seemed suddenly to have problems with his face, and this was detectable largely by the efforts he was making to freeze his mouth in an expression of polite inquiry. Then his cheeks turned crimson, his stomach jumped, and he hastily swiveled his chair away from his visitors.

There was a long silence. Jayne looked from Bleeker's back to Patrick's earnest innocence. He was bewildered.

Finally Bleeker's chair swung around again. His eyes looked watery, but his voice was under control. "Harvey, can't we be satisfied to leave it this way?"

Jayne stood up. "Whatever you say, Andy." He refused to look at Patrick.

Bleeker smiled. "Well, gentlemen."

Jayne walked stiffly out the door. Patrick started to follow.

"Just a minute, Con," said Bleeker. He motioned Patrick back inside. "Close the door."

"Yes, Andy?"

Bleeker grinned. "One day, Con, they'll get you. They'll nail you to the wall. They'll hang you up by the thumbs. You have got to stop this. Is Willow really an Indian?"

"Certainly she is." Patrick was plaintive. "Doesn't *any*body trust me? The arrangement is legal."

"Of course, of course," soothed Bleeker. "I was just thinking, how convenient to have your own Indian when you need a quick trademark registration. It's like having a notary public in your office."

"All our secretaries are notaries," said Patrick, puzzled.

Bleeker sighed. "Of course. They would be. I stepped into that one, didn't I?"

"What?"

"Never mind." Bleeker's chair began its slow rhythm again. "How's that chess player getting along? Alec Cord?"

"He made second place in the D.C. Annual."

"He's still not in your league, though, Con. Nobody, absolutely nobody, can equal your brand of chess."

Patrick squirmed. "I don't even know the moves, Andy."

"And your contract man, Sullivan? Can he write as good a contract as you?"

"Much better," said Patrick.

"Did he write the contract that bound you to the Hope Patent Department?"

"What do you mean, Andy?"

"Oh, never mind. I don't know what I mean. I don't think I'll ever understand you patent fellows. Take Paul. Chemists become lawyers; lawyers never become chemists. Paul can't—or won't—explain it. There's probably something profound in this, but I've never been able to unravel it. Does it mean chemists have the intellect and energy to rise to advocacy, but that lawyers could never rise further into the realm of science? Or does it mean that the law is the best of all professions, that once in the law, other disciplines are attainted?"

Bleeker's chair began to swivel slowly again. Patrick knew what was coming. He got everything under control.

"How *is* Paul the patent lawyer?" asked Bleeker.

"A competent man," said Patrick carefully. "We're glad you sent him around to us."

Bleeker was almost defensive. "You know why I did it, Con. There's nobody else in the company I could trust to make him toe the mark. Really make him. You know what I mean."

"Sure, Andy, I know. He's a bright kid. I would have hired him anyway. Quit worrying about him. Just let him do a good job, day by day. Same as I did when I worked for you."

"I worked you hard, Con. Make Paul work hard."

"He works hard, Andy."

"And there's one more thing, Con. You switched trademarks. Neol to . . . Shane, you said?"

"That's right. Neol is a poor trademark. Shane is better."

"That's another thing Jayne is going to hold against you, Con. Switching marks on his cherished manual."

"It isn't really that bad, Andy." Patrick marveled at the older man's technique. At no time during the conversation had Bleeker asked Patrick whether the Patent Department was going to approve the terpineol plant, nor in fact had he asked him anything at all about the terpineol patent situation, even though they both knew this was vital to Bleeker's future in the company. And yet the questions and the pressure were there, all the same, and the questions were being asked by their very obvious omission. Patrick decided to meet the matter with directness. He said simply: "We haven't completely resolved the patent problem, Andy. But we certainly hope to have the answer for you well before the board meeting Monday morning. With luck, we may even have it tonight."

Bleeker murmured absently, "That's fine, Con."

Patrick started to get up, but Bleeker stopped him with a gesture.

"Shane," said Bleeker thoughtfully. "Very curious." His eyes became contemplative. "Perhaps you never realized it, Con, but we regarded your wife as an outstanding scientist. *You* were wise, however, to take up law in night school."

Patrick nodded, wondering.

"We got interested in her," continued Bleeker, "when she was just finishing up her master's degree at State. I think we still have her thesis around somewhere. Old Rohberg made a special trip to drive her up for her interview. She was so pretty, I made her an offer on the spot. My only error was in turning her over to you for the standard lab tour. You louse."

Patrick smiled, his face warmly reminiscent.

Bleeker studied the other man carefully. "What was the name of your little girl?"

"Shan."

"Odd name."

"Lilas picked it. It's short for *chandelle*, French for 'candle.' Lilas was French, you know. Lilas Blanc. White lilac. And Shan was our little candle. The wallpaper in the nursery was designed with a candle print. The lights above her crib were artificial candles. We painted fluorescent candles inside her crib. She would pat them every night before I tucked her in."

Bleeker cleared his throat. "Con, sooner or later somebody's going to tell Harvey Jayne that you renamed Neol after your baby daughter."

Patrick didn't get it. He stared back, stupidly. "After . . . Shan?"

"Well, didn't you? Shan . . . Shane . . . ?"

Patrick felt his insides collapsing. "But I didn't . . ." he blurted. "It didn't occur to me." Then his mouth twisted into a lopsided smile. "At least, consciously. But there it is, isn't it? So maybe you're right, Andy. I really walked into that one. There I was, telling Cord that Jayne's mental blocks wouldn't let him see why he liked Shane. The same rule applied to me, although I don't want my daughter's name on terpineol, plastered on tank cars, warehouses, stationery, magazine ads. Too late now. Botched the whole thing."

Bleeker regarded him gravely. "Con, how long has it been now, since the . . . accident?"

"Three years."

"You're still a young man, Con. Relatively speaking. Our young ladies think it's about time you got back into circulation."

"You might be right, Andy."

Bleeker coughed. "You're just being agreeable to avoid an argument. Believe me, Con, it's one thing to remember the dead. It's an altogether different thing to have your every waking thought controlled by your memories. You ought to get away from that place."

Patrick was shocked. "Move? From the garden? The house? It has our bedroom. Shan's room. How about Lilas? How about Shan? They're *buried* there. Their ashes—"

"Ashes?"

"They were cremated. Lilas wanted it that way. I spread the ashes in the lilacs."

The older man looked at him with compassion. "Then release *them*, Con. *Let them go!*"

"I *can't,* Andy." Patrick's face twisted. "They're all I have. Can't you understand?"

"I guess I do, Con. I guess I do. I'm sorry. None of my business, really."

> *On this night of all nights in the year,*
> *Ah, what demon has tempted me here?*
> EDGAR ALLAN POE, *Ulalume*

The evening was warm, and along about ten o'clock the party drifted down into the garden.

Patrick, as usual drinking only beer, was for all practical purposes cold sober, a condition that enhanced rather than alleviated an unexplainable and growing sense of anxiety. The nearness of the lilacs, usually a thing of nostalgic pleasure, somehow contributed to his edginess. He was startled to note that several clusters were on the verge of opening. He started to call Cord's attention to this, then thought better of it. And then he wondered, Why didn't I? What's the matter with me? What's going on?

The group was in the arbor now. He would have to get on with it, the reason why they were all here. Paul Bleeker and John Fast knew what they were supposed to do. All he had to do was to ask them to start. Paul was already seated at the stone table. As he watched, Paul pulled the table drawer out in an idle exploratory gesture.

"My notes for a patent law article I started . . . a couple of years ago," said Patrick wryly. "I just can't seem to get back to it."

"Then perhaps you should be thankful," said Fast.

"What do you mean?"

"A professional man writes for a variety of reasons," said Fast. "I'm working now on my Encyclopedia of Oxidative Reactions. I know why I'm writing it. And I know why you're not writing, Con. It's because life has been kind to you. Let it stay that way."

Paul Bleeker broke in. "You say a professional man writes for a variety of reasons, John. Name one. Why do you write?"

Fast's dark eyes turned on Paul Bleeker. "You have heard it said, a man owes a debt to his profession. This may be true. But no professional man pays his debt by writing for the profession. If he is an independent, say a consulting engineer, or a partner in a law firm, or a history professor in a big university, he publishes because it's part of his job to advertise himself and his establishment. There's very little money in it per se. If he's a rising young man in a corporate research or corporate law department, he writes for the reputation. It helps him move up. If his own company doesn't recognize him, their competitors will. But if he's already at the top of his department in his company, he has none of these incentives. But he doesn't need them. If such a man writes, he has behind him the strongest force known to the human mind."

"And what might that be?"

"Guilt," said Fast quietly. "He writes to hide from the things he has done in the name of his profession. It gives him a protective cocoon to burrow into. A smoke screen to hide behind."

"In the name of the patent system," said Patrick firmly, "I've committed every crime known to man. And still I can't get started."

"You've done very little, really," said Fast in his nearly inaudible monotone. "But when you really have done something, you'll know it. You won't have to wonder or conjecture. Then, you'll begin to write. It'll come instantly. No floundering. No lost motion. You'll leap to it. The words, pages, and chapters will pour out in a torrent. It will be your salvation, your sure escape."

They stared at him. Cord laughed nervously. "So why do *you* write, John? What is your unspeakable crime?"

Fast turned his great black eyes on the other, almost unseeing. "I cannot tell you, my friend. And you wouldn't believe me if I did tell you. Anyhow, it can never happen to you." He looked away to Patrick. "But to you, Con, it could happen. And it could happen soon. Tonight. In this place."

Patrick laughed shakily. "Well, now, John. You know how careful I am. Nothing is going to happen to me. It's spare time I need to start writing, not penitence."

Fast looked at him gravely. "You do not weep. You smile. Before the Nazarene called Lazarus up, He wept." His toneless eyes seemed almost sad. "How can I explain this to you. Then let it be done. I have placed the Shane manual at the five angles of the pentagram. I think they are waiting."

"They?" stammered Patrick. "Oh yes, of course. The fellows. Perhaps we should begin."

"What's that smell?" called Sullivan.

"It's a terpineol," said Fast, sniffing a moment. "Like Shane. Maybe a mixture of alpha and gamma terpineols." He snapped his fingers. "Of course!"

"Of course . . . *what?*" said Patrick. His voice was under control, but he felt his armpits sweating copiously.

"The mixture . . . very correctly balanced, I'd say. Just right for synthetic oil of lilac."

Patrick was struck dumb.

"That's very odd," said Sullivan. "Con's lilacs are not open yet."

"The odor must be coming from somewhere."

"Maybe we're all tired," said Cord. "Breeds hallucinations, you know."

Patrick looked at him in wonder.

"It's hard to convince anybody that odor can have a suprachemical source," said Fast.

Cord laughed incredulously. "You mean there's something out there that is synthesizing oil of lilac . . . or Shane . . . or whatever it is?"

"We are so accustomed to thinking of the impact of odors *on* people that we don't think too much about the creation of odors *by* people. Actually, of course, everyone has his characteristic scent, and it's generally not unpleasant, at least under conditions of reasonable cleanliness. In this, man is not really basically different from the other animals. But man—or rather, a certain few extraordinary people—seems to have the ability, quite possibly involuntary, of evoking odors that could not possibly have come from the human sweat gland."

"Evoking?" said Sullivan.

"No other word seems to describe the phenomenon. Chemically speaking, in the sense of detectable airborne molecules dissolving in the olfactory mucosa, the presence of odor is indeed arguable. On the other hand, in the strictly neuropsychic sense, that an 'odor' response has been received in the cerebrum, there can be no real doubt. The phenomenon has been reported and corroborated by entire groups. The 'odor of sanctity' of certain saints and mystics seems to fall in this category. Thomas Aquinas radiated the scent of male frankincense. Saint John of the Cross had a strong odor of lilies. When the tomb of Saint Theresa of Avila—the 'great' Theresa—was opened in 1583, the scent of violets gushed out. And more recently, the odor of roses has been associated with Saint Theresa of Lisieux—the 'little' Theresa." He looked at Patrick. "I think everyone is ready."

Patrick wiped his face with his handkerchief. "Go ahead," he said hoarsely.

* * *

Ma chandelle est morte . . .

FRENCH NURSERY RHYME

Paul Bleeker was seated in the iron chair at the stone table. John Fast faced him, from one side. The others stood behind Paul.

"You are in a long dark tunnel," said John Fast quietly. "Just now everything is pitch black. But your eyes are beginning to adjust."

There was absolute silence. Then Fast's voice droned on. "In a little while, far ahead of you, you will be able to see the tunnel opening. It will be a tiny disk of light. When you see this little light, I want you to nod your head gently."

From far downstream drifted the plaintive call of a whippoorwill.

Paul Bleeker's eyes were heavy, glazed. His stony slump in the iron chair was broken only by his slow, rhythmic breathing.

"You now see the little light the mouth of the tunnel," monotoned Fast. "Nod your head."

"Candle," whispered Paul.

Patrick started, then recovered himself instantly.

Fast picked it up smoothly. "Watch the candle," he said. "Soon it will start to move toward you. It is beginning to move."

"Closer," murmured Paul.

In a flash of feverish ingenuity Patrick stepped forward, seized the wine bottle and its stub of candle from the stone table, struck his lighter, then lit the candle. He replaced the bottle on the table front. The flame wavered a moment, then flickered up. Patrick stole a glance at Paul's face. It was frozen, impassive.

Fast continued gravely: "Soon you will have enough light to see that you are sitting at your desk in the library. In a moment you will see the piles of books on the tables near by. There are several books on your desk. There's a big book just in front of you. Now the candle is close enough."

"Close," murmured Paul.

The hair on Patrick's scalp was rising. The odor of lilacs was stifling. And he then noticed that the lilacs were opening, all around him. He somehow realized that lilacs do not bloom in minutes. It was a botanical impossibility. He could almost hear the tender calyxes folding back.

Fast continued. "You are opening the front cover. You are

looking at the title page. It is typewritten. It is a thesis. You are able to read everything. You can see the name clearly. The name of the student is—"

Patrick heard gasps behind him, and his eyes suddenly came into focus. Beyond Paul, on the far edge of the stone table, beyond the candle, he saw the two figures. They were wavering, silent, indistinct, but they were there. The larger one would just about reach his chin. The eyes of the small one came barely to the table edge.

He wanted to scream, but nothing would come out of his throat.

The taller figure was leaning over the table towards Paul, and she was holding something . . . an open book. But neither figure was looking at Paul. Both of them were looking at him. He knew them.

In this frozen moment his nose twitched. The scent of lilacs wavered, then was suddenly smothered by something sharp, acrid. Patrick recognized it, without thinking. It was ozone. And as if in confirmation of its olfactory trademark, a luminous . . . thing . . . was taking shape behind the two figures. Suddenly it acquired a face, then eyes. Then arms, reaching out, encircling.

Patrick had a horrid, instantaneous flash of recognition. The portrait in John Fast's office. Mephistopheles taking Faust.

"The name of the student is Lilas Blanc," said Paul Bleeker metallically. "State U—"

"Oh, God, *NO!*" screamed Patrick.

The candle blew out instantly. Paul struggled in his chair. "Hey, what . . . where?" He knocked the chair over getting up.

The voices rose up around Patrick in the darkness.

He dropped in a groaning heap on the grass. "Lilas, Shan, forgive me. I didn't know." But he must have known. All along.

And now his mind began to swing like a pendulum, faster and faster, finally oscillating in a weird rhythm of patterns so bewildering and contradictory that he could hardly follow them. His mind said to him, They escaped. It said to him, They did not escape. It said to him, They were there. It said, Nothing was there. And then it started again. His throat constricted, his teeth bit the turf, and by brazen command his thoughts slowed their wounded flailing. He ceased to ask, to wonder. And finally he refused to think at all.

He heard Cord's firm voice. Somebody found the light switch. There were querulous whispers. And then there was something on his back. Some of them had dropped their jackets on him. A man's hand lingered briefly on his shoulder. It was a gentle, even affectionate gesture, and he recognized the touch as that of a man accustomed to tucking small children into their beds at night. He had used the same touch, many times, and long ago.

And now the sound of footsteps fading. And then, motors starting. And finally nothing, just the splash of the little falls, the crickets, and far away, the whippoorwill.

He did not want to move. He wanted only never to have been born.

He closed his eyes, and sleep locked him in.

> *I hold every man a debtor to his profession; from the which, as men, of course do seek to receive countenance and profit, so ought they of duty to endeavor themselves by way of amends to be a help and ornament thereunto.*
>
> FRANCIS BACON,
> Preface to Maxims of the Law

It was early morning, and with the pink of dawn on his cheek, waking was instantaneous. His mind was clear and serene as he threw the jackets aside and got to his feet. He rubbed his eyes, stretched with enormous gusto, and walked over to the lily pond. A green frog was sitting on a pad of the yellow lotus but jumped in as Patrick bent over to splash water on his face. He dried his face on his shirttail, which was flopping out over his belt.

The sun was now barely over the little hill, and a shaft of light was slicing into the pond. Patrick considered this phenomenon briefly, then peered into the bottom of the pool for the refracted beam. There was some kind of rule of optics—law of sines. Somebody's law. Check into it. Meanwhile, there was work to be done. Important work.

He walked into the arbor, picked up the overturned iron chair, sat down at the stone table and pulled a pencil and paper pad out of the drawer. After a moment, he began to write; slowly, at first.

"Ex parte Gulliksen revisited. The typewritten college thesis as a prior printed publication. This decision from the Patent Office Board of Appeals in . . ."

Then faster and faster. ". . . essential, of course, that the thesis be available to the public. This requirement is satisfied by . . ."

Now he was writing furiously, and the pages were accumulating.

He was going to make it. Just a question of staying with it now, and it would give him complete protection. No need to worry about what to work on *after* this article, either. He knew he could turn out a text. No trouble at all. Or even an encyclopedia. Patrick, *Chemical Patent Practice,* four volumes. He could see it now. Red vinyl covers, gilt lettering.

The stack of sheets torn from his pad was now quite bulky. He pushed the pile to the table corner, and in so doing knocked the bottle and candle unheeding to the ground and into the withering lilacs. Already he could visualize his "Preface to the First Edition." It should be something special, based perhaps on a precisely apt quotation. What was that thing from Bacon? He frowned, puzzled. No. There was something not quite right about *that.* But never mind. Plenty of others. Somehow, somewhere, there would be a word for him.

FURTHER READING

Fiction

Anderson, Poul. "The Tale of Hauk," *Swords Against Darkness.*
Asimov, Isaac. "One Night of Song," *The Winds of Change and Other Stories.*
Attanasio, A.A. "One Night of Song," *Nameless Places.*
Balzac, Honore de. "The Succubus," *Once Against the Law.*
Beekman, Allan. "Dog Spirit," *Hawaiian Tales.*
Benson, A.C. "The Slype House," *Return From the Grave.*
Bester, Alfred. "Hell is Forever," *The Unknown Five.*
Bierce, Ambrose. "Eyes of the Panther," *The Complete Stories of Ambrose Bierce.*
Blish, James. "Wolf in the Fold," *The Star Trek Reader I.*
Bloch, Robert. "The Dark Demon."
Bloch, Robert. "Enoch," *The Best of Robert Bloch.*
Bloch, Robert. "Return to the Sabbath" (under Tarleton Fiske), *The Hollywood Nightmare.*
Bloch, Robert. "Sweet Sixteen," *Pleasant Dreams–Nightmares.*
Bowles, Paul. "The Circular Valley," *Collected Stories, 1939–1976.*
Bretnor, Reginald. "All the Tea in China," *SF 7th Annual.*
Brown, Fredric. "Nasty," *Great Black Magic Stories.*
Brown, Fredric. "The New One," *Unknown*, October 1942.
Campbell, Ramsey. "The Chimney," *Whispers I.*
Campbell, Ramsey. "Jack's Little Friend," *The Height of a Scream.*
Campbell, Ramsey. "Out of Copyright," *Whispers IV.*
Carter, Lin. "Out of the Ages," *Nameless Places.*
Cartmill, Cleve. "Hell Hath Fury," *Unknown*, August 1943.
Cave, Hugh B. "The Door Below," *Whispers III.*
Chetwynd-Haynes, R. "The Elemental," *Uncanny Tales of Un-*

earthly and Unexpected Horrors.

Chittum, Ida. "The Cruel Girl," *Tales of Terror.*

Collier, John. "Possession of Angela Bradshaw," *The John Collier Reader.*

Cowles, Frederick. "Eyes for the Blind," *The Thrill of Horror.*

Cuddon, J.A. "Isabo," *Splinters.*

Dann, Jack. "The Dybbuk Dolls," *Timetipping.*

Dann, Jack. "Fairy Tale," *The Berkley Showcase.*

Davidson, Avram. "The Ape."

Davidson, Avram. "A Bottle Full of Kismet," *Strange Seas and Shores.*

Davidson, Avram. "Church of St. Satan," *The Notebooks of Dr. Esterhazy.*

De La Mare, Walter. "A Mote," *Eight Tales.*

DeBill, Walter C. "In Ygiroth," *Nameless Places.*

Defoe, Daniel. "The Friendly Demon," *Best From F&SF, 1st Series.*

Derleth, August. "The Dweller in Darkness," *Tales of the Cthulhu Mythos.*

Derleth, August. "Here, Daemos!," *Alfred Hitchcock Presents: The Master's Choice.*

Derleth, August. "A Room in a House," *Lonesome Places.*

Diop, Birago. "Sarzan," *African Short Stories.*

Dish, Thomas M. "The Foetus," *The Berkley Showcase*

Drake, David. "The Red Leer," *Whispers II.*

Gilchrist, Murray R. "The Basilisk," *Terror by Gaslight.*

Goulart, Ron. "The Return of Max Kearny," *Alfred Hitchcock's Fatal Attractions.*

Guernsey, Clara Florida. "The Silver Bullet," *Sisters of Sorcery.*

"Han Wu-niang Sells Her Charms at the New Bridge Market," *Traditional Chinese Stories.*

Heald, Hazel. "The Man of Stone," *The Horror in the Museum and Other Revisions.*

Hogg, James. "The Brownie of the Black Haggs," *Scottish Short Stories.*

Howard, Robert E. "The Black Stone," *Tales of the Cthulhu Mythos.*

Hubbard, L. Ron. "The Ethnologist," *Lives You Wished to Lead but Never Dared.*

Irwin, Margaret. "Monsieur Seeks a Wife," *The Black Magic Omnibus.*

Jagendorf, M.A. "The Demon and the Rabbi," *Devils, Devils, Devils.*

John, Jasper. "The Spirit of Stonehenge," *The Supernatural Omnibus.*

Kay, Marvin and Brother Theodore. "The Possession of Immanuel Wolfe," *The Possession of Immanuel Wolfe and Other Improbable Tales.*

Keller, David H. "Finger in the Sky," *The Folsom Flint and Other Curious Tales.*

King, Stephen. "I Am the Doorway," *Night Shift.*

King, Stephen. "Suffer the Little Children," *The Evil Image.*

Klein, T.E.D. "The Events at Poroth Farm," *The First World Fantasy Awards.*

Kuttner, Henry. "Call Him Demon."

Kuttner, Henry. "The Devil We Know," *Unknown*, August 1941.

Kuttner, Henry. "Threshold," *Unknown*, December 1940.

Leeman, Bob. "Skirmish on Vestable Street," *Best Fantasy #8.*

Leiber, Fritz. "Dark Wings," *Superhorror.*

Leiber, Fritz. "The Oldest Soldier," *Another World.*

Leiber, Fritz. "Smoke Ghost."

Lem, Stanislaw. "The Sixth Sally . . . ," *The Cyberiad.*

Leroux, Gaston. "In Letters of Fire," *The Black Magic Omnibus.*

Leroux, Gaston. "Phantom of the Opera," *The Ghouls.*

London, Jack. "Who Believes in Ghosts," *Curious Fragments.*

Long, Frank Belknap. "Diploma Time," *Whispers IV.*

Long, Frank Belknap. "The Space-Eaters," *The Early Long.*

Lovecraft, H.P. "The Call of Cthulhu," *Dying of Fright.*

Lovecraft, H.P. "The Thing on the Doorstep."

MacCreagh, Gordon. "Dr. Muncing, Exorcist," *The Black Magic Omnibus.*

Machiavelli, Niccolo. "Belphagor," *A Renaissance Storybook.*

MacKiewicz, Josef. "Adventures of an Imp," *10 Contemporary Polish Stories.*

Malzberg, Barry N. "As in a Vision Apprehended," *The Best of Barry N. Malzberg.*

Masterton, Graham. "The Root of All Evil," *Modern Masters of Horror.*

Maupassant, Guy de. "The Horla," *Nighttouch.*

Miller, Walter M., Jr. "Trifflin Man," *Off the Beaten Orbit.*

Mitchell, Edward Page. "The Cave of the Splurgles," *The Crystal Man.*

Mowat, Farley. "The Blinding of Andre Maloche," *Bodies and Spirits.*

Mrabet, Mohammed. "The Spring," *The Boy Who Set the Fire and Other Stories.*

Mrabet, Mohammed. "The Well," *The Boy Who Set the Fire and Other Stories.*

Musaus, John Karl August. "The Bottle Imp," *Gothic Tales of Terror.*

Pain, Barry. "The Moon-Slave," *The Phoenix Tree.*

Pater, Roger. "A Porta Inferi," *The Devil's Children.*

Petaja, Emil. "Dark Balcony," *Stardrift, and Other Fantastic Flotsam.*

Prest, Thomas Peckett. "The Demon of the Hartz . . . ," *Gothic Tales of Terror.*

Priestley, J.B. "The Demon King," *Haunting Tales.*

Pushkin, Alexander (supposed author). "The Lonely Cottage on Vasilev Island," *Alexander Pushkin: Complete Prose Fiction.*

Richie, Donald. "The Holy Demon," *Zen Inklings.*

Riddell, Charlotte. "The Banshee's Warning," *Wild Night Co.*

Roberts, Keith. "Boulter's Canaries," *New Writings in SF3.*

Russ, Joanna. "The Man Who Could Not See Devils," *Alchemy and Academe.*

Scott, Sir Walter. "A Night in the Grave; or The Devil's Receipt," *The Clans of Darkness.*

Serling, Rod. "The Man in the Bottle," *Rod Serling's Twilight Zone Revisited.*

Shelley, Mary. "Transformation," *The Evil Image.*

Silverberg, Robert. "The Dybbuk of Mazel Tov IV," *Wandering Stars.*

Singer, Isaac Bashevis. "The Black Wedding, *An Isaac Bashevis Singer Reader.*

Singer, Isaac Bashevis. "The Dead Fiddler," *The Collected Stories of Isaac Bashevis Singer.*

Singer, Isaac Bashevis. "The Lantuch," *A Crown of Feathers and Other Stories.*

Singer, Isaac Bashevis. "Lost," *A Crown of Feathers and Other Stories.*

Singer, Isaac Bashevis. "A Night in the Poorhouse," *The Collected Stories of Isaac Bashevis Singer.*

Sky, Kathleen. "Motherbeast," *Cassandra Rising.*

Sologub, Fedor. "The Invoker of the Beast," *The Black Magic Omnibus.*

Stevenson, Robert Louis. "Bottle Imp," *Famous Mysteries.*

Stevenson, Robert Louis. "Thrawn Janet," *Oxford Book of Short Stories.*

Summers, Montague. "The Grimoire," *The Nightmare Reader.*
Talman, Wilfred Blanch. "Two Black Bottles," *The Horror in the Museum and Other Revisions."*
Tsalka, Dan. "The Terrible Tale of Josef de la Reina," *New Writing in Israel.*
Uyeda, Akinari. "Demon," *Tales of Moonlight and Rain.*
Vance, Jack. "Guyal of Sfere," *The Ends of Time.*
Vance, Jack. "The Miracle Workers," *Eight Fantasms and Magics.*
Walton, Evangeline. "The Mistress of Kaer-Mor," *The Phoenix Tree.*
Webb, Sharon. "A Demon In Rosewood," *Shadows 8.*
Wilde, Lady. "The Demon Cat," *Spine-Chillers.*
Wilson, F. Paul. "Demonsong," *Heroic Fantasy.*
Woolrich, Cornell. "I'm Dangerous Tonight," *The Fantastic Stories of Cornell Woolrich.*
Yarbro, Chelsea Quinn. "Lammas Night," *Cautionary Tales.*

Nonfiction

Adler, Mortimer J. *The Angels and Us.*
Borges, Jorge Luis. *The Book of Imaginary Beings.*
Briggs, Katherine. *An Encyclopedia of Faeries, Hobgoblins, Brownies, Bogies, and Other Supernatural Creatures.*
Carroll, David. *The Magic Makers: Magic and Sorcery Through the Ages.*
Cavendish, Richard. *The Black Arts.*
Cohn, Norman. *Europe's Inner Demons.*
Frazer, Sir James G. *The Golden Bough.*
Goldenson, Robert M. *The Encyclopedia of Human Behavior: Psychology, Psychiatry, and Mental Health.*
Gonzalez-Whippler, Megene. *A Kabbalah for the Modern World.*
La Vey, Anton Szandor. *The Satanic Bible.*
Robbins, Russell Hope. *Encyclopedia of Witchcraft and Demonology.*
Spence, Lewis. *Encyclopedia of Occultism.*

ABOUT THE EDITORS

GARDNER DOZOIS was born and raised in Salem, Massachusetts, and now lives in Philadelphia. He is the author or editor of twenty books, including the novel *Strangers* and the collection *The Visible Man.* He is the editor of *Isaac Asimov's Science Fiction Magazine*; he also edits the annual series *The Year's Best Science Fiction.* His short fiction has appeared in *Playboy*, *Penthouse*, *Omni*, and most of the leading SF magazines and anthologies. His story "The Peacemaker" won the Nebula Award for Best Short Story in 1984, and his short story "Morning Child" also won the Nebula in 1985. He has been a finalist many times for other Hugo and Nebula Awards. His critical work has appeared in *Writer's Digest*, *Starship*, *The Washington Post*, *Thrust*, *The Writer's Handbook*, *Science Fiction Chronicle*, and elsewhere, and he is the author of the critical chapbook *The Fiction of James Tiptree, Jr.* His most recent books are *Sorcerers*!, an anthology edited in collaboration with Jack Dann, *Jack the Ripper*, an anthology edited with Susan Casper, and *The Year's Best Science Fiction, Third Annual Collection.* He is currently at work on another novel, tentatively entitled *Flash Point.*

JACK DANN is the author or editor of twenty-one books, including the novels *Junction*, *Starhiker*, and *The Man Who Melted*, which *The Washington Post Book World* compared to Ingmar Bergman's classic film *The Seventh Seal.* He is the editor of the anthology *Wandering Stars*, one of the most acclaimed anthologies of the 1970s, and several other well-known anthologies such as *More Wandering Stars.* His short stories have appeared in *Playboy*, *Penthouse*, *Omni*, and many major SF magazines and anthologies. He has frequently been a finalist for the Nebula Award, and has also been a finalist for the World Fantasy Award and the British Science Fiction Award. Some of his stories can be found in his collection *Timetipping.* His critical work has appeared in *The Washington Post*, *Starship*, *Nickelodeon*, *The*

Bulletin of the Science Fiction Writers of America, *Empire*, *The Fiction Writer's Handbook*, and other magazines and newspapers. His most recent anthologies are *Sorcerers!*, edited in collaboration with Gardner Dozois, and *In the Field of Fire*, edited with Jeanne Van Buren Dann. Forthcoming is the mainstream novel *Counting Coup* and two more anthologies in the fantasy series edited with Gardner Dozois. He is currently working on a historical fantasy novel about Leonardo da Vinci, tentatively entitled *Da Vinci Rising*, and several other novel and anthology projects. In progress is a bibliography and guide to his work, edited by Jeffrey M. Elliot, entitled *The Work of Jack Dann*. Dann lives with his family in Binghamton, New York.